THE THUCYDIDES TRAP

by
Melinda M. Snodgrass

Credits
Cover Design: by Fakel Barros

Thucydides Trap: A point when one great power threatens to displace another, and war is unavoidable

Thracius "Tracy" Belmanor has struggled to do his patriotic duty after losing the love of his life: Empress Mercedes de Arango. Embroiled in a desperate war, the Solar League has no pity for his grief and he cannot afford the distraction of longing for a woman he can never have.

For duty alone—as a soldier and as a father—Tracy enters into a marriage of state. Now a member of the royal family that once shunned him for being a commoner, he fights to stabilize the throne threatened by civil war. That the throne belongs to Mercedes, and he's forced to see her every day, is fresh salt in an old wound.

Tracy and Mercedes face an even greater danger than their unrequited love, however. A mysterious force is destroying all in its path and will lead to extinction on a galactic scale unless it's stopped.

DEDICATION

New and old friendships have immeasurably improved my life. So, this one is for Elijah Byrnes and Sage Walker. Sage listened to me wail when I hit a plotting problem and let me talk out loud to solve it. And El has restored my joy in reading with his beautiful prose and deeply emotionally affecting stories. Thank you both for being in my life, for being my friends and counselors.

ACKNOWLEDGMENTS

It's been a long time since I met with Daniel Abraham, Ty Frank, and Walter Jon Williams at Daniel's house and they helped me plot out all five books in the *Imperials Saga*. Their brilliance, help and support meant I knew where I was going from the first word written on book one, *The High Ground*, all the way through to the final conclusion that you now hold in your hands. Thank you, guys, for everything.

THE THUCYDIDES TRAP

THE IMPERIALS SAGA • BOOK 5

NEW YORK TIMES BESTSELLING AUTHOR

MELINDA M. SNODGRASS

1

FEARS & FURY

Mercedes Adalina Saturnina Inez de Arango, Empress of the Solar League and First Star Lord of the *Estrella de Orden,* should have been feeling well satisfied with the current state of the galaxy. She had just led her military to a massive and stunning victory over an alien threat that had killed and injured several million of her citizens and resulted in billions of dollars of damage to the infrastructure on five worlds.

She should have been reunited with her child, back on the capital world and beginning to rebuild the palace and the League, but instead she was on Hellfire because Admiral Marqués Ernesto Chapman-Owiti, head of the military's R&D division, had requested an urgent meeting. The planet held the bulk of the Solar League's military command structure, and the couple currently inhabited a secure conference room deep in the bowels of the *Ministerio de Guerra* known more colloquially as the Octagon.

She and Ernesto had been classmates at the imperial military academy, and Ernesto had always been the personification of *cool,* so when his message had contained words like *urgent* and *critically important,* Mercedes had changed her plans and taken her dreadnaught straight to Hellfire rather than home to Ouranos.

Mercedes studied the threads of grey that were now woven through Chapman-Owiti's dark curls and reflected that it had been a damn long time since they had all been in school together. Of course, the same silver wove through her hair as well. Inwardly she still might feel like that eighteen-year-old who had gone off to military school in order to win a throne, but the truth was etched in the lines on her face, the grey in her hair and the ache in her bones.

Ernesto usually had a blazing smile, but not today. Today his expression was both grim and exhausted. She braced herself for terrible news, but it had to wait until a soft footed alien servant finished setting up the tea service and pastries, bowed and withdrew. Neither she nor Ernesto moved to avail themselves of the refreshments. She finally said,

"Ernesto, you asked for this meeting, which is delaying my return to Ouranos, and I have another damn military campaign to plan, so this had better be important."

A rebellious noble had led a mutiny among her troops, stolen large numbers of starships, and declared their system and associated planets to be the Nephilim Confederacy. Mercedes didn't think much of Baron Jasper Talion's branding strategy. "Confederate" as the root word was probably not the best choice given the divisive human history surrounding it, but then subtlety had never been Talion's strong suit.

Ernesto shook himself out of his reverie, which set the single gold earring glinting against his ebony skin. "Wouldn't this be a better place to plan the campaign to pacify Nephilim than the capital?" he asked.

"Undoubtably, but they are bringing my son back to Hisselek; since I haven't seen him for over two years, I am damn well going to be there to meet him. Talion and his little Confederacy can wait."

Finish one war, start another, she thought wearily and then added more as a prayer than a hope; *One more battle and then I can rest.* At Ernesto's expression she quickly amended, *or not.*

"So, spill it. I doubt your news will get any sweeter over time," Mercedes said.

Ernesto touched the controls, activating full security measures on the office. Dread crept down her spine and took up residence in the pit of Mercedes stomach.

He exhaled and said, "The *necrófagos* were a Potemkin people."

Dread turned into confusion. "I beg your pardon?" Potemkin sounded vaguely familiar, but Mercedes couldn't place it, and what the hell it had to do with their recently defeated enemies she could not fathom. She raised a questioning eyebrow.

"Prince Grigory Aleksandrovich Potemkin-Tavricheski, a courtier in the court of Catherine the Great of Russia. Famous for—"

"Yes, yes, now I remember. Didn't he built fake villages to fool his queen?"

"Exactly," Ernesto said.

"And this is relevant how?" Mercedes asked.

Chapman-Owiti opened up several holo windows on his TapPad and arranged them in the air all around them. "Since the mass suicide…or maybe die off, hard to tell which it was, I've had teams crawling through every aspect of the *necrófagos* worlds and culture. My doubts and concerns began with the language. Remember how I told you it more resembled Esperanto or some other created language then a real one?"

"Yes, so?"

"Well, it goes deeper than that. We've been studying their religions—all two of them."

"Again…I should care…why?"

"No planetary culture has only two religions. Even us, with a state religion, still have Muslims, Buddists, Jews, Hindus, Sikhs, Wiccans and so forth. And within those religions there are branches and variants—Mormons, Presbyterians, Sunni, Shia. Even the BEMS have a plethora of pagan creeds."

"I don't need a lesson in comparative religion, Ernesto," Mercedes said sharply. "Get to the point."

"Forgive me, Highness, the curse of suffering from OCD." The smile briefly flickered on his lips, but it never reached his eyes. "What I'm saying is that this so unbelievable as to be impossible. Then there is the history and archeology…or lack thereof. Cultures and societies are messy things. They develop in fits-and-starts dark ages followed by a renaissance. The *necrófagos* history indicates a triumphant march from primitivism to space. It's simply not credible."

"So, what are you saying? And don't talk to me about ancient Russia again," Mercedes warned.

"I think the *necrófagos* were created and thrown against us. And whoever did it wasn't trying all that hard to hide their tracks."

He fell silent and they measured gazes across the table. What neither of them wanted to say hung between them like the rumble of distant thunder. Mercedes shivered gripped by that sense of something hiding in the shadows unseen but still threatening.

"They're gone. They've been gone for decades," Mercedes said softly.

"Gone doesn't mean dead, ma'am. The Cara'ot were master geneticists." Ernesto by naming them turned her inchoate fear into grim reality. "They could have been using those missing years to grow these creatures and then launch a war against us."

Mercedes surged out of her chair and began to pace. "But why? For what possible purpose?"

Ernesto gave a bedeviled head shake. "Damned if I know. Remember what Westfield used to say in our xeno biology class—*they're fucking aliens, who knows why they do anything,* and the Cara'ot were the most alien of all of the civilized species."

"Not very civilized if they did create a race specifically designed to kill humans," Mercedes countered.

"The necrófagos killed a lot of Isanjo, Hajin, Sidone and Flutes too," Ernesto reminded her.

"And if they wanted to destroy us why not fight us themselves? They almost beat us three centuries ago."

"Maybe that defeat made them decide that using proxies was a better choice? Why not use others as cannon fodder? The Egyptians and Romans had their auxiliaries—"

"Didn't work out all that well for the Romans," Mercedes

said. Resting her hands on the table Mercedes leaned in on him. "Ernesto, think about what you are suggesting. It would mean that the Cara'ot had…have the resources to engineer an entire race, make sure the *necrófagos* had the resources to launch a massive space fleet—"

"And then throw the tool away once it had served its purpose," he concluded quietly.

"Which was…" The import of what he was suggesting penetrated. "What?"

"I'm not sure the mass death of the *necrófagos* was a choice on their part."

Ice seemed to edge down her spine as she absorbed the full horror of what he was saying. "That would be monstrous."

"I know, and right now all of this is mere speculation based on a knowledge of history and a mass die off I can't explain."

"What do you want me to do?" Mercedes asked.

"Right now, nothing. We don't want to go public or even talk to parliament about my inchoate fears. At least not yet. And you've got a rebellion to suppress. I just wanted you to be aware of my…suspicions, misgivings, the thing that's giving me night terrors. And I may be completely wrong, and this is just paranoid fantasy on my part."

They stared at each other for a long moment, Mercedes hoping such was the case. Unfortunately, she didn't think it was.

+ + +

Jahan bet Ahara stood braced in front of her former captain (and perhaps soon to be former friend) blocking his way to the corridor that led off from the galley aboard the small trading starship. Her arms were akimbo, fists on hips, tail twitching, and she could feel her fur trying stand up along the length of her spine.

Several decks below a military shuttle craft waited to carry Thracius Ransom Belmanor, Admiral of the Green, back to his frigate. What had precipitated the stand-off was her determination that a certain little boy would *not* be aboard that shuttle when it left. A certain little boy who just happened to be the son of the Empress and heir to the Solar League.

The problem was that Prince Cyprian Marcus Sinclair Amadeo de Arango hadn't been sired by the royal Consort. Instead, the man who stood bristling with fury in front of her was Cyprian's father, and he'd just found out he had a son. It was an unfortunate fact that information like that tended to do odd things to male brains.

"You all *lied* to me," Tracy said, and his face twisted into a snarl.

"*I* didn't fucking lie to you. *I* didn't know about this until I laid eyes on the kid when we picked him up to take him to Freehold. Go yell at Dalea if you want to yell at somebody."

"Oh, believe me, she's next on my list. After. I. Take. My. Son."

She had ordered the human boy, Hayden McKenzie, to take the younger human child out of the galley and back to her cabin.

"You are *not* keeping that child from his mother," she

said, and she realized she was baring her rather vicious incisors.

"Did I ever say I was? But that child is *mine* and I have rights!" the human yelled. By League standards he was quite fair skinned so she could see the angry color surging in his cheeks and the grey eyes looked like flint.

Jahan gave a mental sigh. Males, no matter their species, were a royal pain in the rear end.

"Yeah, he is, but your rights are just a tad limited in this situation given how his mom is the *Empress of the fucking Solar League.* Which is why you can't take him on your ship. Anyone with eyes and half a brain will see the resemblance."

"Good."

"Not good. Can you imagine what it'll do to the government?" Jahan gestured wildly. "We've got thousands of people homeless and desperate after the war. The economy's in shambles. There's a fucking civil war brewing. You create a scandal, and it could bring down the government—"

"I don't care," he gritted.

"Bullshit. You've always been a goddam altar boy. You were still using the O-Trell toast despite having been dishonorably discharged. When the military came calling, wanting to reinstate you, you immediately saluted and reported for duty. And finally, what do you think the Consort will do to *Mercedes* if he figures this out?"

That got through to him. However angry and hurt he might be his love for Mercedes had endured for decades. Jahan pushed her advantage.

"Tracy," she said gently. "Cyprian is six years old. He's been away from his mama for almost two years, been kidnapped, watched his nanny get killed in front of him, nearly died escaping, and he's going to need a fucking lifetime of therapy to deal with all this. Right now, he does *not* need to be confused about who his daddy actually is." She paused and gathered the human's hands in her own. "Please, think about that little boy. He needs his mama and…and the only man he's ever known as his father."

A look of bitter grief swept across Tracy's face. He spun away and began to pace. "How much more do I have to endure, to sacrifice for crown and empire? I gave her up seven years ago for the sake of the League. Never knowing…shit, I should have killed Cullen when I had the chance."

"'Cause that always makes things better," Jahan snapped.

Shoulders slumping, he reached out a hand to support himself against the bulkhead. Jahan hurried to his side, slipped an arm around his waist and gave him a hug. His arm dropped across her shoulders, and he hugged her back. The kind of deep breath that marked a man preparing to face battle and inevitable loss shook his frame. He looked down at Jahan.

"Okay, I'll leave him with you, and leave Cipriana aboard as well. But we'll be your escort back to the capital."

"Really, you don't have to. We'll be fine."

"They got off a message before I blew them to Hell. If I know Talion, and I do, he'll be looking for payback."

"Oh, Christ on a crutch. You humans. Okay, but please just get us into orbit at Ouranos and then *go back to your fleet.*"

"You can't ask that of me. I need to see her. Hear directly

from her *why*. Also, I and my crew deserve some of the credit for rescuing the boy." He gave a sharp, bitter laugh. "Who knows, maybe this time I'll finally get a title."

She gazed up at him trying to fathom this complicated man. In all the years she had known him he had displayed a deep contempt for the FFH, yet he still desperately craved a title of nobility.

He cleared his throat. "May I see him once more…before I go?"

The naked longing in the grey eyes almost broke her resolve. This was a man who craved family so deeply he had built one within the hull of this ship that he had once commanded. It had been a strange and awkward family that had included more aliens than humans, but then wasn't every family strange and awkward in their own unique ways?

"Of course. Hayden was taking him to bed. Why don't you go tell him goodnight?"

He didn't reply just nodded and headed down the corridor toward the cabins.

✦ ✦ ✦

CIPRIANA'S SON LOOKED up as the cabin door slid open. He was sitting on the gimbaled bunk stroking Cyprian's dark amber hair. The little boy was crying softly.

Memory draped in grief took Tracy. It was in this room and on that narrow bunk he and Mercedes had first made love. Perhaps their son had even been conceived there.

"Hey, Cypri, look. Here is an admiral come to pay his respects. You don't want him to see you crying, do you?"

Hayden said.

A barely audible "no" emerged from where the child's face was buried in a pillow. Hayden rose, he had the same almost boneless grace of his mother and gave Tracy a nod. He then slipped out of the cabin.

Tracy taking his cue from the teenager stepped up to the bunk and gave Cyprian a smart salute. "Your Highness," he said.

Cyprian might have been barely six, but he knew his duty. He scrubbed at his tear-stained face and left a swipe of snot on his sleeve. Tracy hid a smile. Cyprian looked up at him and inclined his head.

"Thank you," he said. "Haydi says you blew up the bad men."

"I did, sir." Tracy indicated the edge of the bunk. "May I sit down?"

"Uh huh." Then realizing that probably wasn't proper he added with odd dignity, "You may."

"I know your mother very well."

The veneer of royal protocol was swept away. "You do? Is she coming? Will she come soon? Where is she?"

"She fought a great battle and won, and now she's coming home. We're going to take you to her."

Tracy stiffened as Cyprian threw himself into his arms then folded the child in an embrace. If a dwarf star had taken up residence in his chest Tracy couldn't have felt more pressure as he held his son for the first time.

"Won't be the last. I swear it can't be the last time," he murmured softly into the boy's curls.

A plump hand wound into the lapel of Tracy's jacket. "I

was scared," Cyprian whispered. "Are you ever scared?"

"Lots of times. It's okay to be scared. Sometimes things are just scary."

"Lizzie fell down. There was red all over her chest." He raised his eyes to meet Tracy's. "Is she dead?"

He had no experience with children, but Tracy had a sense that lying to them wasn't the best option. Especially not to a child who would lead an empire.

"Yes," Tracy said softly. Cyprian gave a little hiccupping sob. "But she's in heaven with *el Santo Padre* and all the angels," Tracy added.

"Will you hear my bedtime prayers?" the little boy sniffed.

"Of course."

Cyprian slipped out of his arms and knelt at the side of the bunk. Tracy knelt beside him. Cyprian folded his hands and closed his eyes. "*Querido Dios* pleases bless mama and papa and Haydi and Snowball—that's my cat," he explained. "And Bouncy—" Another aside. "That's my pony. And—" The child broke off and looked up at Tracy. "I should pray for you too. What's your name?"

"My friends call me Tracy…and I hope we'll be friends…Highness."

"We will. You killed the bad men." The golden eyes were once more lifted toward heaven. "And *Dios bendiga*, Tracy too."

Cyprian stood up. Tracy thought the boy tall for his age. *Thank God he has his mother's beauty,* he thought, *and doesn't take after me.*

"Haydi said I had to go to bed. I don't want to."

"Aren't you tired?" Tracy asked.

"Uh huh, but when I close my eyes I...I... see things." Cyprian's voice caught on another small sob.

"Why don't I sing you a song that my father used to sing for me when I went to bed," Tracy suggested.

"Can you sing?" Cyprian asked. The suspicious look Tracy received had him disguising a chuckle as a cough. "My *niñera* before Lizzie said she could sing too, and she was *horrible*."

"Well why don't you listen, and you can tell me if I'm horrible or not, and if I am, I'll stop."

"*Bueno*. That is acceptable." Cyprian scrambled back into the bunk and pulled up the covers.

Tracy sat on the edge of the bunk and let the words and lyrics of the song *La Nanita Nana* came back to him. He hadn't sung in a long time. He wanted to be good for his son. Taking a deep breath, he began.

"*A la nanita nana nanita ella, nanita ella. Mi niño tine sueño benito sea, bandit sea. Fuentecita que corre clara y sonora. Ruiseñor que en la selva Cantando y llora.*"

Nightingale that in the forest sings and weeps. Haunting words that almost broke Tracy's heart. Cyprian's long eyelashes trembled on his cheeks, a small sigh. He was asleep.

Tracy leaned down and softly kissed the child's cheek, then slipped out of the cabin. Stood panting in the corridor for a moment before he drove his fist hard into the wall. Felt the bones break. Welcomed the pain.

2

STRATAGEMS

THE AIR WAS filled with the rumble of the engines on the giant earth movers; their growl periodically punctuated by sharp warning beeps when they reversed. The rubble of what had once been the imperial palace on Ouranos was being cleared away. Occasionally as dirt and debris dribbled from the voracious maws of the machines there would be a sparkle, a flash of color and a worker would run over to inspect whatever treasure might have been unearthed.

"So, what's next, sir? Nephilim?" Anselmo Moran, yelling over the din, asked his boss.

There was no doubt about Beauregard Honorius Sinclair Cullen, Knight of the Shells, Shareholder General of the Grand Cartel, Duque de Argento y Pepco and royal Consort's, reaction to Anselmo's statement. The prince's glance was both horrified and incredulous.

"Christ, we just finished one war. You want to send me off to another already? *Gracias*, but no."

Anselmo could understand Boho's reluctance. You could get killed in a war. Like every boy of his social station Anselmo had been sent to The High Ground, the empire's elite military academy only to wash out at the end of the first year. There was no shame in it. Most of the FFH youth forced to attend failed to pass the *prueba*, and since Anselmo was the sixth son of a mere *caballero* his family didn't lay any guilt on him.

No, it had been his decision to pursue journalism that had left his father grumbling about *slumming in careers better suited to an intitulado*, but the old man wasn't grumbling now. Not after Anselmo's work in the palace press office had led him first to be the Consort's personal spokesman and now Boho's chief of staff.

"So, the Empress will handle Talion?" Anselmo asked.

"You don't think she's capable?"

Boho cocked an eyebrow at Anselmo who immediately back pedaled. Anselmo knew his boss's moods very well. Boho might have spent the nearly thirty years of marriage shagging his way through the wives and daughters of the Fortune Five Hundred with a side dish of pretty commoners thrown in for good measure, but he wouldn't tolerate any questioning of his wife's abilities.

"By no means, *la Emperatriz* is fully capable," Anselmo soothed. "I'm just looking at the advantage of having you both once more working in concert to bring about a brilliant military victory." He brought up the latest poll numbers on his pad. "Approval of the royals is at an extraordinary ninety-three percent right now, sir."

That stopped Boho in his tracks. "Really? That high?"

"Yes, sir."

An odd, distant expression crossed the Consort's still handsome face and he seemed to be looking through him. Anselmo wondered what scheme was being concocted in that cunning mind? No matter, whatever it might be the prince would share it with loyal henchman soon enough.

Whatever thought had gripped Boho was shaken off and the Consort walked toward the excavation crews, hand upraised. Engines went to idle, and the workers gathered around him. Within moments they were laughing, nodding, talking eagerly with Cullen.

Anselmo shook his head. The man was a bloody miracle. Now if only there was a way to infuse even a quarter of her husband's charm into the wife.

+ + +

EVEN AS BOHO shook hands and asked the automatic questions about wives, children, relatives in the military, and made the proper responses all while displaying the appropriate emotional reaction Boho's mind kept turning back to that stunning ninety-three percent.

But what it triggered was the image of a girl with long golden-brown hair, cocoa skin, and pansy brown eyes—*Paloma*. Boho believed she had loved him, discovered she was merely spying on him on behalf of the imperial intelligence service, but despite the betrayal he could not shake the hold she had over him.

During the war he had approached her, and they had begun speaking again. *So, what? What are you hoping for*, he asked himself *That this level of popularity might mean the public would tolerate you having a public mistress.*

And Mercedes? Well, why wouldn't she agree? She had tolerated his many liaisons over the years and hadn't set him aside. Now that she was too old to bear another child and he had done his duty and provided the League with an heir would she really care? As long as he and Paloma promised not to have a child…for some reason that hurt, the idea that that beautiful *mariposa* would never hold an infant to her breast. And what a child they would produce given their respective good looks.

His daydream shuddered to a halt. Paloma would never agree. She thought him feckless, narcissistic and vain. Well, she was right about the vain, but hadn't the past few years of war and his efforts to protect the League proved his worth?

A worker ran up brushing the dirt off a diamond tiara. It was twisted and the heat had darkened some of the gems, but he recognized it. Mercedes had worn it at their wedding.

Boho cast his eyes toward the sky and murmured. "All right, all right, *Santo Padre*. I get it. No need to be quite so obvious."

"Sir?" the worker said.

"Nothing. Thank you so much for finding this. You must have unearthed the royal treasury. Let's hope more of our history can be recovered." He raked them all with an approving look. "And on behalf of the Empress and myself, thank you all for everything you're doing."

"God bless the prince and our Empress," the foreman called, and the assembled workers cheered.

Boho gave them all a smile and a wave and walked back to Anselmo.

"They love you, sir," the younger man said.

"If only it weren't so…abstract," Boho said as he pocketed the tiara.

"Would you like me to arrange for some discreet…ah…company, sir?"

"No." He smiled at Anselmo's expression. "No, I'm not horny…well, actually I'm always horny, but I want…" He searched but couldn't find the words for what he was feeling.

"I expect you're missing your son," Anselmo said diplomatically.

Boho noticed Anselmo didn't include Mercedes in the statement. "That I am." He clapped Moran on the shoulder. "Where to next?"

"A meeting with the cabinet. Rafe wants to discuss converting the war bonds into treasury bonds."

"Sounds riveting," Boho drawled.

+ + +

THE PALACE WASN'T the only building that had been reduced to rubble in the alien attack. The parliament building had also been destroyed. Right now, the government of the Solar League was temporarily housed in various office buildings that had survived the attacked. Many were damaged, but they could at least keep out the weather.

Mercedes had barely returned to the capital only to be immediately summoned to meet with the Prime Minister. They now sat in his office, a corner suite with windows for walls. One section of glass had a spiderweb of small cracks occluding the view, but through the other Mercedes could see the silhouettes of enormous cranes like metal monsters scratching at the sky. She hoped that Kronos, and Paradise Lost, Yggdrasil and Nueva Terra were equally rich with construction equipment and not just the capital world. Another thing she had to check on, probably in person. *But not until Cypri was back and in her arms.*

The Prime Minister himself filled and overflowed the leather chair behind the desk. Rohan Danilo Marcus Aubrey, Condé de Vargas was well into his eighties now and the red in the sparse wisps of hair that covered his skull had been completely replaced with white. While the hair might have retreated his paunch had grown into a massive swollen belly, and his eyes peered out from pouches of flesh. Still her godfather's smile was warm and familiar.

"You look tired, my dear."

"I am. But no time to rest. Once Cypri is home I must get back to Hellfire and set in motion plans for subduing Talion and his breakaway planets."

"Is that the best use of your time and our resources?" Rohan asked.

That made her sit up. "I beg your pardon? You want me to allow a member of the FFH to just flout the authority of the crown and set himself up as a tinpot dictator?"

"I'm just thinking that the war against the *necrófagos* took a toll on our armed forces and our worlds. Better perhaps to recuperate, rebuild our forces before plunging into another fight."

"If I do that what's to stop some royal governor on Belán or Cuandru or Yggdrasil decides to do the same?" She shook her head. "No, I have to make an example of him."

"As you think best, Highness" he murmured and inclined his head, but she sensed the argument wasn't finished. And right on cue he said, "Perhaps it is possible to have both…"

"Go on."

"Try diplomacy first. See if a compromise can be reached. Talion's no doubt thinking that as an independent confederacy he can sell the lithium from Nephilim at an elevated price back to the League. This may be nothing more than economics. He also probably wants to keep these new worlds they discovered exclusively for his population, so there might be room to put limits on the number of settlers from other League planets that could also sweeten the deal."

"He abandoned us during the final and most desperate battle of the war. I'm not inclined to be diplomatic...or sweet."

"I understand, Majesty but while the parties would be talking, we could be rebuilding our fleets and replacing the lost troops." The old man's expression reminded Mercedes forcefully of when one of her cats was caught stealing food from her plate.

"And he'll be doing the same," Mercedes objected.

"But he's starting at a disadvantage," Rohan continued. "Nephilim doesn't have a shipyard and these newly discovered planets certainly don't. Those will have to be constructed. Again, buying us time"

"So, you're suggesting I negotiate in bad faith," Mercedes said.

Rohan gave a moue but didn't demur. "Wasn't it Clausewitz who said peace is that state which exists before nations know who they want to invade, or the time during which they are preparing to do so?"

"He also said war is the continuation of diplomacy by other means," Mercedes countered. "And I fear that is where, sooner or later, we will ultimately end up."

"But later would be better, Highness."

Mercedes gripped the arms of her chair and pushed to her feet. "All right. I'll have Jaakon draft a proposal. And yes, I'll have you weigh in on it, Señor Prime Minister, *Sir!*" She gave him a mock salute.

+ + +

TRACY HAD CALLED for the senior officers to assemble in the frigate's conference room. Some he knew he could trust—Luis who had served with him aboard the trading vessel, the young lieutenant Flintoff who was a foster child from a Hidden World. The others he couldn't be sure of, hence the need for this meeting.

To stress the seriousness, he had dispensed with having batBEMs provide refreshments. That was one of the cues among the FFH that he had learned in this stratified society; no treats meant serious business. Right now, Tracy was waiting in the corridor some distance from the conference room.

His Hajin batBEM Kallapus emerged from the room and joined him. The alien turned that long, bony head so he could give Tracy a sideways eye. His white mane set a contrast against the blue of his jacket. "They're all assembled and ready for you, sir."

Tracy checked the chronometer set into the sleeve of his coat. "Let's give it another minute or two."

"You really do want them sweating," the alien said.

Tracy didn't answer. He waited, counting down the seconds, then walked down the ship's corridor to the door of the conference room.

Every pair of eyes focused on him as he strode in, noting his dress uniform and the *Distinguido Servicio Cruzar*, one of the highest military honors that could be bestowed, glittering on the left breast of his jacket. Like the lack of refreshments those too sent a message. There was rustle as the assembled officers came to their feet, braced, and saluted.

He reached the head of the table, returned the salute then said, "Be seated." Silence held the room. Tracy waited until their anxiety was like an over tightened piano wire then he said,

"The treaty our Empress negotiated with the Hidden Worlds was that no League military vessel would ever enter a solar system held by a Hidden World. In exchange those planets agreed to house our children and kept them safe from the war as long as they were brought only by trusted civilian vessels. We have obviously violated that agreement. Emissaries have explained to the government of this particular world the reason for this intrusion, and our explanation has been accepted. However—"

He paused and raked them all with a cold glance.

"I must have your solemn word that you will never reveal the location of this particular planet."

"Sir, it is the established policy of the League that Hidden Worlds are to be reported and assimilated." It was Acevedo the weapons officer who voiced the first objection.

"I would argue that a recently negotiated treaty between our sovereign lord would take precedence over that particular policy," Tracy countered.

"Wouldn't that be for Parliament to decide?" It was the commander of the *fusilerios*.

"We're not under the command of parliament. We swear an oath to the crown," Tracy shot back.

"One could argue that means the government as a whole," said another officer.

Tracy clung to his rapidly vanishing patience. "The Empress is the supreme commander of all military forces. In this matter I think we defer to her. And she agreed to this arrangement." He rested his palms on the table and leaned forward. "And a number of these worlds *still have our children.* They find out we betrayed one of their fellows and I'd say they have some very powerful leverage to use against us. So, what say we *not* be the ship and crew that fucks this up?"

That penetrated. It was a military truism that nobody wanted to be first. Far better to see the way the wind was blowing and then be the first to be second.

One by one they gave their word of honor.

✦　✦　✦

TEN DAYS IN Fold. Ten days during which they would have no communication with the people and planets inhabiting normal space nor with the warship that she had to presume was somewhere nearby in this Not Space place through which they were currently traveling.

After which they would pop back into reality, and Jahan would have the three days of their transit from the outer solar system to Ouranos to warn Mercedes what was coming.

She still had the Empress's private contact number. Jahan sighed and smoothed the fur around her eyes. She was just a simple little Isanjo trader, mother, and wife, how the hell had she ended up in such rarified company? *Blame Thracius Random Belmanor, the chaos maker.* That had become the crew's mantra over the years, and it showed no sign of abating.

Her tail was stiffly upright. She ran a hand down the length of it and tried to relax. The cup of coffee still steaming in front of her probably hadn't been the best move. It was deep into the ship's night cycle.

The Tiponi Flute Jax was in the corner of the galley standing in his pool of water with his blue tinged resting lights shining on his fronds.

Ernie, as was his wont, was sleeping in the engine room.

Jahan had her nephew standing watch on the bridge. It really wasn't necessary to have someone in the command center when they were in Fold, but she thought it was good discipline for Kielli.

Dalea was asleep in the med bay, and the prince was in the captain's cabin while Commander Lady Cipriana McKenzie and her son shared one of the others.

There was the click of boot heels on the composite decking and as if Jahan's thoughts had summoned her, Cipriana entered the galley. Apparently, Jahan wasn't the only person who couldn't sleep. Cipriana McKenzie was a Janus figure. One side of her face was a mass of twisted burn scars and she had lost her eye on that side. The artificial eye was a dull grey with a red dot like a burning cinder in the center. There was no hair on the right side of her skull. The left side of her face was unblemished and revealed that the woman had been an incredible beauty and even now at fifty the elegant bone structure and ebony skin were exquisite. The long braids inset with beads chimed softly as she crossed to the table.

"Couldn't sleep either?" the human woman asked.

Jahan shook her head. "Trying to prepare myself to call the Empress and tell her that Tracy…uh, Admiral Belmanor—"

Cipriana raised a hand. "Relax. It's clear you're all intimately acquainted. You don't have to feign the appropriate obsequious demeanor with me. But you were saying?"

"Just that I need to warn Mer—the Empress—that Tracy is on his way that that he knows—Oh shit."

"*Cálmese*, it's not like it isn't as obvious as the fur on your face."

"So, we put Cyprian—shit—the prince in a sack and you hustle him off the *Selkie* and back to his mama while Tracy takes a bow?"

"And you and your crew. You should take a bow too."

"Oh, hell no. Folks like *us* do better when folks like *you* don't notice us."

Cipriana shook her head setting the beads to again chiming. "When I knew Tracy at school and that brief time we served together he tried so very, very hard to fit in, to ape all of us in the FFH, lose his lower-class accent, learn to fence and dance. What I don't underst—"

"And it did fuck all to save him," Jahan interrupted. "Your lot cashiered him anyway because apparently he was dumb enough to believe all that bilge about honor and duty."

Cipriana cocked her eyebrow at Jahan. "If it makes you

feel any better, I was going to be a character witness for him. I never could believe that Tracy would steal."

"He didn't," Jahan said shortly. "But that's all ancient history now, and I interrupted you. You were saying."

"That I don't understand what's still driving him. He's had a meteoric rise. He's an admiral."

"And he's still a simple *señor*," Jahan replied.

"He knows the worst of us. How entitled and feckless we all are. Why would he care when he has the love and respect of people like you and his soldiers and crews who think he practically hung the moons?"

"Because he's a man in love and people in love do stupid, crazy shit even when they know it's crazy and stupid. If he had a title, he thinks…well, you know what he thinks."

"But that's mad. Even if he was made a *duque* he doesn't have the pedigree to ever be considered as a royal Consort."

"Yeah, like I said love makes you nuts."

Cipriana reached out and nervously spun Jahan's mug. "What I wonder is how they ever—" She broke off and cast a glance over at the Tiponi Flute.

Jahan waved it off. "Oh, don't worry about Jax. He's in his fugue state. It takes a klaxon to get his attention."

"All right then. How did they ever get together?"

"It was a fucking fairy tale rescue with a horror story at the end," Jahan said, and she told the human woman about coming into orbit around a Hidden World to find a destroyed fleet and a single survivor, the Empress. About the mass suicide of the planet's residents, Mercedes' emotional devastation, the romantic two-week interlude that followed.

"And at the end Tracy gave her up because he does believe in all that bilge about duty and honor, and mostly because he was protecting us. No one would have believed she had stayed with us willingly. We would all have been executed."

"And he didn't know—

"No. That's why his shorts are in a twist. This has hit him hard."

Cipriana laid a hand over Jahan's six figured hand. "Tell you what, let's talk to Mercedes together. And maybe the three of us can come up with a plan that gives everybody at least a bit of what they want."

"Yeah, okay."

"You sound dubious."

"Because most of our plans have always gone pear shaped."

3

LOVE HAS NO PLACE IN THE HALLS OF POWER

EACH HOOFBEAT RAISED a puff of dust as Boho and Mercedes cantered side by side. Mercedes latest mount was the complete opposite of her beloved Utopia. Vento da Broha was an iridescently white stallion with a whimsical sense of equine humor. Utopia had been jet-black and had taken himself far more seriously. Boho's newest horse was a big buckskin with the smoothest gaits of any horse he'd ever owned or ridden.

They were alone on the chaparral—apart from the twenty-person security detail mounted on horses or in flitters, the drones circling overhead to seek and kill any press drones, and all of them carefully scanning for more lethal dangers. *Not that the unblinking eye of the media couldn't be almost as deadly,* Boho thought.

Boho studied his wife's profile, noted the tension in her jaw, the narrowed eyes shaded by the brim of her helmet. He reached out and laid a hand on the right rein and pulled her stallion to a walk.

"You've been grim ever since you got back from seeing Rohan. What's wrong?" he asked.

She sighed and twisted in the saddle to face him. The sunlight kissed her face deepening the angles of her cheekbones and intensifying the warmth of her dark skin.

"I need you to lead a diplomatic mission to Nephilim."

It was the last thing he had expected, and he clenched his hands on the reins bringing Donhador to a sudden halt. "What? Are you insane? Put me in the hands of that traitor?" He broke off and calmed his breathing. "Oh, I see, this is Rohan's doing."

She circled her horse back to him and stopped. "He's not wrong. Entering into another war when we haven't recovered from the last one is madness."

"And Nephilim never suffered any damage," Boho said bitterly.

"Exactly. We need time to recover in case we *do* have to fight. You can buy us that time—"

"By becoming a potential hostage?"

"And that risk is why it has to be *you* and not *me*," Mercedes said. She reacted to his expression. "If this is going to seem legitimate, I have to send someone of real stature. Also, you're far better suited for this type of mission than I could ever be. You play politics like a virtuoso. I'm awkward and it feels like I always say the wrong thing." He could feel his frown deepening, and she added brightly, "And who knows, you might succeed."

If her intent was to mollify it was a spectacular failure. Boho tried to breathe through a growing panic settling into this chest. "But you don't really expect me to succeed. I'm just chum being thrown into the water to buy us time!" he snapped.

"No." She looked distressed at the accusation. "I want you to honestly try. Humans shouldn't be killing each other. Who knows what other threats might be out there." She waved vaguely at the sky. Even in full daylight the nebulae overhead was faintly visible. "There's something odd going on with the *necrófagos*. Ernesto is on it, but we don't know anything for certain yet," she broke off and then added, "And there also sector 470 to consider."

It was the boogey man. A portion of space where ships and the men who crewed them vanished. During the reigns of Mercedes' grandfather and father it had been used as a convenient place to remove troublesome individuals. Mercedes had used it only once; sending the men with whom Boho had conspired to sell promotions into oblivion so they could never reveal his involvement in the corruption. Since then, it had been studiously avoided.

"Fair enough," he acknowledged.

"You and Talion always got along. You were in the same fencing society. You recommended him for Admiral of the Gold."

"Blaming me for that?"

"No. It was the right call at the time. No one could have predicted he would turn against us." She looked thoughtful. "And I suppose by his lights it made sense. His system was unscathed. There was no guarantee we were going to win that final battle against the *necrófagos*. By deserting when he did, he preserved a large number of his ships."

"Just his bad luck that we *did* win," Boho grunted.

"With more than a little help from the aliens themselves," Mercedes added. "That's what Ernesto is on about. He thinks it's more than just ritual seppuku."

"I sincerely hope he's wrong," Boho said.

"Amen."

"All right. I'll go. But may I wait until Cypri comes home? I want to see my son."

"Of course. I know he'll want to see you too. I wonder how much he's grown. I've missed so much…" Her voice trailed away, and he reached over and gripped her hand. Mercedes shook off her mood and returned to business. "The diplomats will have to do their dance, set out all the terms for the meeting. That will take some time. I messaged the captain of the trading vessel that I wanted them to pick up Cyprian and Hayden. I should hear back from her soon."

+ + +

THE CALL CAME in on her private account. As the hologram stabilized Mercedes found herself looking at Cipriana, her oldest and closest friend in the world. Mercedes pleased smile slipped however when the little alien, Jahan thrust her way into the image. Mercedes was able to make out a bit of the background and realized they were in the galley of the trading ship. A frown wrinkled her brow. Cipriana was assigned to the flagship *Sutāburezā* commanded by Tracy. So why was Cipri aboard the *Selkie*?

Her thoughts were interrupted by Cipriana apparently reading her mind.

"No, I'm not aboard the *Sutāburezā*. I'm on the *Selkie* with your son and my son." Mercedes opened her mouth to respond, but Cipriana rushed on. "No, I'm not going to give you the entire backstory right now. Suffice it to say it involves Talion, Nephilim and all kinds of chicanery, shenanigans, and skullduggery. But that's not our biggest problem—"

"It's Tracy, Highness," the Isanjo interrupted.

"He commandeered a frigate and rode to the rescue," Cipriana said. "Which was good. Otherwise, our sons would be hostages on Nephilim by now—"

"What? How? How did Talion find out about Cyprian's whereabouts?"

The little alien looked uncomfortable. "Again, long story. The problem is Tracy. He knows, ma'am" Jahan said.

There was no mystery to the meaning of Mercedes' appalled expression and the two females, one human and one alien, understood instantly.

"Is Boho on Ouranos?" Cipriana asked. Mercedes could only nod. She couldn't force words past the terror that was closing her throat. "Don't suppose you can send him away?" Cipriana suggested.

Mercedes cleared her throat and managed to croak out, "How long do I have?"

"We just dropped back into normal space and are three days out from Ouranos," said Jahan.

"That may give me enough time. He's supposed to head a delegation to Nephilim. I'll just up the timeline."

"We just have to make sure nobody gets a look at Tracy and the prince together," Jahan said.

"How obvious is it?" Mercedes asked.

"My fifteen-year-old son saw it instantly," Cipriana said. Mercedes gave a moan of despair.

"And Tracy intends to see you, ma'am, and he is *really* pissed," Jahan added.

Mercedes anger flared. "Well, what did he expect? *He's* the one who said we couldn't be together."

"Yeah, but he didn't know you were pregnant back then, and you know what he's like when he's angry. Personally, I'd advise you not to see him," Jahan said. "Tell him to get his butt back to his fleet." She gave a little cough. "Not that I should be telling you what to do, ma'am…Highness."

"Among our class it's not such a big thing to have a cuckoo in the family nest, it's just part of the culture of the FFH," Cipriana mused. "Though to be fair it's usually *not* the first born."

"Yeah, but Tracy isn't a member of your exclusive club. I doubt he's going to be that open minded," Jahan countered.

"Nor will Boho," Mercedes said. "Especially given how he feels about Tracy."

"You should have planned this better, Mer," Cipriana complained. "Why couldn't you arrange to get knocked up by Davin, God rest his soul, or somebody else in our circle?"

Mercedes sat silent for a moment then said quietly, "Because I didn't love him."

The look of devastation on her friend's scarred face was ample evidence that Cipriana shared Mercedes grief, but her words were stripped of any such sentiment.

"You are who you are, Mer, and love has no place in the halls of power."

+ + +

ANSELMO WAS HAPPILY married, but even he felt a tingle of desire as he looked down at Paloma. The girl was breathtakingly beautiful, though the eyes that looked out from that piquant face were older than her years and carried the wisdom and cynicism of a much older soul.

The hallway in the orphanage smelled of dirty diapers, baking bread, talcum powder and the stringent cleaner a mop wielding Hajin was swabbing across the tiled floor. There was the sound of children's laughter and children's tears, and the murmur of women's voices teaching, soothing, playing and reading to the orphans. The war might be over, but they were going to be dealing with the wreckage for decades to come.

"Is there an elegant title for Imperial Pimp?" Paloma asked.

Such ugly words to be delivered in such bell-like tones, Anselmo thought. He felt the heat rising in his cheeks, but he firmly put aside his first impulse, however justified, to snap back. His master usually had his way with any women he wanted, so sooner or later this one would be back in Boho's arms and in his bed and it wouldn't do to have made an enemy of her. He forced himself to smile.

"I actually prefer Palace Procurer, sounds more official. But believe me, the prince has no unworthy intentions toward you. He's going to be undertaking a delicate and dangerous mission and he wanted to see you."

"Why?"

Anselmo decided on candor. "Truthfully, I have no idea, but it feels less like seduction and more like he just wants to talk to you. That being said the prince has had a lot of women over the years, but you're the only one he can't forget."

"Am I supposed to be flattered by that? And is his wife in the *can't forget* category too?" she asked with sweet sarcasm.

"*Dios* you are tough," Anselmo said and decided that he would rather take a cobra to bed then mess with this girl no matter how beautiful she might be.

Still his employer was obsessed, and it wasn't going to be Anselmo's dick that was in jeopardy of going through a wringer if this reunion went badly. Right now, his only task was to satisfy his employer's desire and get this girl to accompany him. Anselmo decided to try an appeal to pity.

"Look, I think he's lonely and frankly he's scared. I think he fears he won't come back, and he wants to try and mend things with you."

She stood very still, a thoughtful expression on her face. "So, he's heading to Nephilim," the girl mused.

Anselmo stared at her in shock. How she had deduced that from his remarks he had no idea. He knew Boho and Paloma had had an affair that seemed to have ended badly so he wasn't entirely sure why his boss was so set on this meeting, but his was not to question why. His was but to do or—Studying Paloma's cold eyes Anselmo once again found himself thinking about snakes and wringers and felt his balls trying to pull up into his scrotum.

Anselmo took a quick look around, leaned in closer and said softly, "Yes, but not with troops. At least not yet. The Empress is sending a delegation to try and negotiate a peaceful settlement."

"Interesting. And smart. All right, now I'm intrigued. But

make it clear to the Consort that this meeting better take place in an office or preferably a public setting. And if there is a hint of a couch, bed, rollaway, cot, futon, sleeping bag, air mattress, *anything*, I will walk out."

"I will relay your conditions."

+ + +

IT WAS THE second day Tracy had spent aboard the *Selkie* and now as the five hours he allowed himself to spend with his son drew toward an end he tried once again to convince himself not to return tomorrow. But it would be his final opportunity. They would enter Ouranos orbit around seven in the evening Hisselek time. Tomorrow morning, he had to contact the Empress's office and request a discreet security detail meet them. He had to arrange for the Selkie to be allowed to land in the area of the *Cristóbal Colón* spaceport reserved for military vessels. He had to request—no, *demand* a private audience with Mercedes.

And if she refused? What then?

His hand tightened on one of the plastic Lego block he'd had his fabricators aboard the SwiftSure make for Cypri. The corners pressed sharply into Tracy's palm almost hard enough to draw blood.

Cyprian gave him a frowning look. "I *need* that one."

Tracy hid a smile at the imperious little voice. "Your pardon, Highness." He handed over the piece and watched Cyprian, tongue sticking out of the corner of his mouth, fit it into place on the edifice he was constructing.

Tracy had nothing to measure against and was also undoubtably biased, but he thought Cyprian displayed an abundance of intelligence and creativity.

"When am I going to see mommy and daddy?" Cyprian asked as he rocked back on his heels and critically surveyed his creation.

"Tomorrow evening."

"Why is it taking so long?" He drew out the vowel on the last word making it into a petulant whine.

Tracy smiled at him. "Because space is big."

"That's not an answer."

"You're going to get that answer a lot. Even when you go off to The High Ground."

"Do I have to? Go."

"Everyone does. Your mother went. Your…Prince Cullen went. I went. Don't you want to?" Tracy asked.

An almost imperceptible head shake. "War is why mommy sent me away. Why Lizzie is dead. I don't like war."

Tracy slipped an arm around the boy's shoulders and hugged him close. "Neither do I, but sometimes we don't have a choice."

✦ ✦ ✦

"PUBLIC ENOUGH FOR you?" Boho hoped it didn't sound petulant.

He was seated at a rickety table at an ad hoc open-air cafe that had sprung up in the aftermath of the war. Behind the large portable grill, a pair of enterprising chefs were preparing tacos and fajitas. Even in the midst of devastation humans would always find a way to make a Real, he mused.

The smell of grilling chicken, beef and vegetables and the sharp tang of salsa fought for primacy over the dust being kicked up by earth movers clearing debris at the end of the street.

"Well done," Paloma said as she took the chair opposite him. "Clever too, the noise from the machinery will cover our conversation and your security will keep any eavesdroppers well away while you get to smile and wave," she said as he was doing just that to a pair of women who stood across the street beaming and simpering at him. "And makes the people feel like their government cares."

"So cynical for one so young," Boho said turning back to her and away from the matrons who went on their giggling way. Paloma merely gave a shrug in response.

"So, why am I here?" Paloma asked.

"I'd like you to accompany me to Nephilim," Boho said. He held up a hand to forestall the objection he saw rising to her lips. "And no, not as my mistress. As part of my staff."

"They're still going to assume we boinking again, and that I'm just a bed warmer," Paloma said.

"Which is fine. Add to that your youth and beauty and no one will take you seriously. You'll be completely overlooked."

"My, you're making this seem *so* attractive," she drawled.

Boho gave a sigh of exasperation. "Point being you can move about more freely, talk to more people, learn far more than I ever could locked away in meetings. You're a trained SEGU agent, but I doubt that Talion or anyone on his staff knows that."

She cocked her head in that bird-like motion that he

found so adorable. "Okay, beginning to sound more attractive. When would we leave?" she asked.

"Well, I thought it would be several weeks if not months, but Mercedes has pushed up the timeline. She wants me to leave tomorrow.

"I could probably pack a few ball gowns by then," Paloma said. She glanced up at him from beneath her lashes and gave him that enchanting little smile. "All right. I'm in, but I best have my own cabin on the ship, and I've taken to sleeping with a knife under my pillow. If you take my meaning."

"Your message has been received…loudly and clearly."

She stood. "By the way. What ship are we taking? Probably wouldn't do to arrive in a dreadnaught."

"We'll be taking the Imperial pinnace and have a frigate for escort."

"Let's hope Talion plays fair," Paloma said.

"I've never known him to," Boho responded.

That gave her a moment's pause, but then she smiled. "Well, you certainly know how to show a girl an interesting time."

+ + +

"SIR, DO YOU know why Admiral Belmanor is arriving on Ouranos this evening?" Iris Nabiyev asked. "He also requested a private audience with the Empress according to Jaakon."

Anselmo waved away the various holographs floating over his desk and peered at his assistant over the top of his glasses. He was bucking tradition in that he had hired a woman and not only a woman but an *intitulado* for the position. There had been more than a few grumbles from the old guard who felt that a woman's place was in the home trying to out-breed the aliens, but Anselmo didn't give a rat's ass for their disapproval. Iris was whip smart, and never hesitated to tell Anselmo when she thought he had his head up his ass.

To avoid the inevitable gossip and innuendo Iris was in her mid-fifties. She was a large woman but carried the weight with neither embarrassment nor defiance. She dressed elegantly but made no effort to disguise her belly or hips. This was a woman who was entirely comfortable with herself.

"Now how would you know that Iris? A nun in a celibate order is less protective of her virtue than Jaakon is with the Empress's calendar."

"Because I made friends with his file clerk who keeps his cloud storage in order. Gave her some of my new eye shadow."

Anselmo gave her a nod of approval. The company Iris had founded after the death of her *intitulado* husband was proving to be very useful. It had brought her to Anselmo's attention because his wife wore her products, and Julia had recommended Iris for the job.

Iris had been intrigued by the offer and since she had groomed her eldest daughter to run the company, she had accepted saying she'd wanted to see how the sausage got made.

"The Green fleet has returned?" Anselmo asked pulling his thoughts back to the moment.

"No, the Orbital Port Master reports only two arriving

ships. A fire lance frigate, the Swiftsure, and a trading vessel, the *Selkie*. A landing request for the trading vessel and a shuttle from the frigate have been sent to the military side of the spaceport."

The Swiftsure didn't ring any bells, but the *Selkie* sure as hell did. It was the private vessel that had carried the crown prince to safety on a Hidden World. And Belmanor rang a fucking *alarm* bell for Anselmo. Belmanor was the man Anselmo's boss had ordered Anselmo to have killed. Fortunately, Anselmo had managed to talk the Consort out of that rash move.

"I don't like this," Anselmo said.

"Maybe he's looking to segue into politics now that the war is over, and he wants to play up his fame? He was the man who captured that alien ship. Gave us our first real victory," Iris suggested.

Anselmo shook his head. "I don't think so. Man is not known for his diplomatic skills. Brash and brilliant is more his reputation. Neither work well in politics." Anselmo tugged at his upper lip and considered. "Do we have a manifest of who's aboard?"

"I thought you might want that." She looked down at her tap pad. "Aboard the *Selkie*, the crew, mostly aliens oddly enough, but what's interesting is Commander Lady McKenzie is aboard along with her son, Hayden, and an unidentified minor. Aboard the military shuttle is the admiral and a full security team."

It all snapped into place. "They're bringing back the crown prince. That has to be it. That's why there are MP's aboard the shuttle."

"Do you want me to be down at the spaceport when he lands? I can let you know—"

"We've got to do more than that. This is a golden opportunity. We need press. Lots of press. *Hero returns bringing the beloved heir back to the arms of his doting mother.*" Anselmo bracketed the final sentence with his hands picturing the banner headline. His hands dropped like deflating balloons. "Damn shame Boho left earlier today. Wonder why they didn't delay his departure?"

"Maybe they didn't know," Iris suggested.

"That doesn't make any sense. You don't just drop in on royalty with a *oh by the way I have your son and heir with me.*"

"Or perhaps the Empress wanted a private reunion with her son."

"That leaves out her husband and the boy's father? That doesn't make any sense. Damn the woman—understand I say that with respect—but I wish she could grasp the importance of controlling the news cycle. This kind of moment—heroic mother, warrior and ruler greets her only child—could push that approval number to a level never before seen. It's publicity gold. Would be fucking platinum if Boho were here too."

"Anselmo, not everything needs to be a moment to drive the narrative. Sometimes you have to let people just be normal people. Even royal people," Iris said.

Anselmo stood, came around the desk and dropped an arm over her shoulders. "First, they're not normal people. And sometimes, Iris, we know better than our employers what's in their best interests."

4

WHAT A FINE MESS

THEY HAD TO wait for the heat of the landing to dissipate before they could open the bay door and lower the ramp. The entire crew had gathered to say farewell to their unexpected guests. The time Jahan had spent with Cipriana gave her an appreciation of the woman's brains and grit. And of course, they all adored Hayden. The little prince was trying to be proper, but he was alternating between excitement and tears as the reunion with his parents drew near.

Hayden was brushing shoulders with Kielli. The pair had grown close during the time Hayden had been a crew member, and now it was coming to an end. It was unlikely this grandson of a *duque* would ever again be permitted to crew on a simple trading vessel filled with aliens.

Jahan had finally confessed to Cipriana about how the boy had blackmailed his way into becoming a crew member, and how his heroic actions had allowed them to escape Nephilim and bring the warning of Talion's impending treachery back to the League.

"I have no idea where it comes from. His father was a dreamy history professor, and I'm a social drone," Cipriana had said.

Jahan had rolled her eyes. "Oh please." They had then looked over at the two human boys and the one Isanjo. "I wonder what their futures will hold?" Jahan had asked softly.

"I expect that Hayden will always be at the side of his friend and future emperor as will your nephew," Cipriana said.

Jahan had shivered. "It's never wise to get too close to royalty."

"Doesn't seem to have done you any harm."

"But what about Tracy? I think his love for Mercedes has blighted his life," Jahan had countered. Cipriana hadn't had an answer to that.

And now they were moments from returning a child to his mother. Jahan hoped at some point she would have the opportunity to point out to Mercedes all the heroic actions on the part of the *Selkie* and her crew. They needed to replace the damaged Wasp and they had burned fuel in order to ride to the rescue *and* return the prince. Another big royal payday wouldn't be amiss.

The light on the console switched to green indicating it was safe to exit. Ernie keyed the controls and the ramp lowered with a whine. And blazing lights filled the hold. Instead of Mercedes and some discreet security there was a mob…of reporters and camerabots.

At the front of it all was Mercedes. Jahan could read the Empress's expression of frozen fury, and Jahan's stomach tried to exit through her spine. *She can't think* we *alerted the press*, Jahan thought.

Cyprian gave a cry of joy. "Mama!" He ripped his hand out of Cipriana's, ran down the ramp and threw himself into his mother's arms.

Well, at least that much went as planned, Jahan thought.

Only to have the hopeful thought die into ashes as some of the surging crowd turned their cameras away from the mother and child and pointed them at the shuttle off the Swiftsure.

Tracy peering around the side of the shuttle doors was pinned like a bug by the lights from the cameras.

+ + +

AFTER BEING MOMENTARILY blinded by the lights Tracy blinked his eyes clear and was able to fully appreciate what seemed like a hundred reptilian lenses focused on him. He spun back into cover behind the walls of the shuttle mentally cursing himself for his stupidity and damning to hell whoever had alerted the press to their arrival.

He had only wanted to see Mercedes and take one final look at Cyprian, and now the hoard of press was rushing him. Panicked he turned on his chief of security and rapped out,

"Get those doors shut!"

"Sir, is that the best idea—"

"It's an order! Not a discussion!"

"Yes, sir!"

The ramp began to slide back into place, but one younger, fleeter journalist managed to jump aboard before the doors could iris shut. His camerabot floated at his shoulder.

"Admiral Belmanor, did you know you were escorting the prince? How did you learn the prince's location? The treaty required the coordinates of Hidden Worlds be kept out of the hands of the military. Have you violated the terms of the treaty?"

The questions pecked at him like verbal hail. Tracy wanted to punch the reporter. Instead, he grabbed the camerabot and slammed it onto the deck of the shuttle shattering the lens. It died with a sad sizzle of electricity.

"Hey! What the fuck? You're going to pay for that!"

Luis who had piloted the shuttle came rushing out of the cockpit and said,

"Sergeant, arrest this man and turn him over to the port authorities," Luis snapped.

"On what grounds? I'm the press!"

"Unauthorized entry onto a military vessel in a time of war," Luis said promptly.

The smooth response had Tracy looking at the younger man in surprise. Clearly the three years back in uniform and going through officer training had burnished the rough edges off the boy who had once crewed with Tracy aboard the *Selkie*.

"The war is over," the young man bawled as he was hustled away to the back of the shuttle.

"And a new one is starting," Tracy replied.

"If you mean the one you've just started with the press, yeah, I gotta agree," Luis murmured to him.

"What was I supposed to do?" Tracy muttered back.

"Not lose your shit, Admiral, sir."

Tracy sighed. The Luis he knew was back. On the other hand, he couldn't disagree. "I'm making a mess of everything," he whispered.

✦   ✦   ✦

"WELL, YOU'VE MADE a fine mess of this," Iris said laconically.

Anselmo couldn't disagree. The look the Empress bestowed on him as she carried her son to the royal flitter froze the blood in his veins. She had been trailed by Commander Lady Cipriana McKenzie and her stunningly handsome son. The boy had been a fixture around the palace after the star base his mother commanded had become the first casualty in the *necrófago* war. A boy had been sent off with the prince. A young man was returning.

"Well, it's over now."

"Uh…maybe hold off on your celebration," Iris said.

"Why?"

"Did you get a look at Admiral Belmanor?"

"Yeah. So?"

She grabbed him by the shoulders and turned him around to where the prince was climbing into the backseat of the royal flitter. "*Look!*"

"At what?"

She sighed and rolled her eyes. "I'm going to let the morning news feeds explain it to you. *Men,*" she muttered as she walked toward their flitter.

✦   ✦   ✦

CYPRIAN WAS ASLEEP sprawled across her lap. He had refused to nap in the bedroom that had been set up for him. Understandable since it wasn't really his room. His old bedroom in the main palace had been reduced to rubble. They had tried to find replacements for his toys, but he instantly knew the difference which led to an explosion of tears. A full-blown tantrum was only averted when Mercedes had rushed him out to the stables to visit his pony.

She looked down and gently stroked the hair off her son's forehead. "It's like he's reverted to a two-year-old," she whispered.

"He's been through a lot," Hayden said quietly.

"Tell me," Mercedes said.

He didn't look at her, kept his head averted. She studied his profile as he began to softly speak. "The Keim's were really kind, but it wasn't the same as having your real family."

Mercedes noted that Cipriana winced at that because she had in fact abandoned her son after the death of her husband and daughter, and her own disfigurement. Thankfully they seemed to have reconciled.

"It was what happened on the racing yacht." The muscles in the boy's jaw tightened. "I had overheard Admiral Belmanor issue his ultimatum to Lord Bellard."

Mercedes didn't have to rifle through the memorized list of FFH families to place the man. He had been in command of one of the frigates that had abandoned her in the middle of the final, desperate battle against the *necrófagos*, and thrown in with Talion.

"And I knew we had to get off the yacht before the fight started. Since the admiral had arrived, I figured that Jahan had gotten my message and was also near-by. At least I hoped so."

"And you were right," Cipriana said and rested a hand on the back of his neck.

"Yeah. Anyway, they had brought Elizabeth along to care for Cy. The three of us had made it to suit storage when one of Bellard's men found us. I was in my suit then I was going to help Elizabeth and tuck Cy in with her. But the guy shot Elizabeth. A bunch of times. There was a lot of blood." The boy's changing voice skipped a few octaves before settling once more. "Cy saw it all." Hayden fell silent.

"How did you manage to get away?" Mercedes asked.

"I killed him." Flat, emotionless but Mercedes could see the lingering horror in his dark eyes.

Mercedes was ready to leave it at that, but Cipriana was not as gentle.

"How?" she demanded.

Mercedes inwardly flinched, but then decided that Hayden's mother was probably right. Keeping such a traumatic event bottled up inside could not be healthy.

"The wrist-rocket. I fired the maneuvering propellant into his eyes. He was screaming, clawing at his eyes. Loosened his grip on the gun. I got it away from him." A deep shuddering breath. "I used it." Hayden paused for a long moment. "Then I grabbed Cy and jammed him in the suit with me. Released all the escape pods except for the one we were going to use. Jahan found us…that's all."

Cipriana wrapped her arms around her son and kissed the top of his head. He gave a hoarse sob and buried his face against his mother's breast. Mercedes stood, and carrying Cyprian she quietly left the room.

An hour slipped past as Mercedes sat by her child's bed.

She knew she should have returned to work, there was still so much to be done, but couldn't bring herself to leave Cyprian's side. Eventually, she checked the messages on her ring. Jaakon had asked her again if he should grant Admiral Belmanor the audience he was requesting. Clearly Tracy had no intention of letting this go despite the debacle at the spaceport.

The door opened and Cipriana slipped in. "You should get some dinner," she whispered. "Fingell's had the kitchen holding it for us, but your chef is about to have apoplexy, and I have a feeling Hayden is about to perish from hunger. Teenage boys seem to be a bottomless pit."

"All right." Mercedes bestowed a final kiss on Cyprian's forehead. He stirred briefly and murmured something then clutched at the Teddy bear and sank back into a deep sleep.

"I need your advice," Mercedes said as they walked down the hall toward the dining room.

"Sure. I can't guarantee it will be *good* advice. I'm not known for that."

Mercedes rolled her eyes. "Oh please…"

"Everybody keeps giving me that *oh please* thing, like I'm more than I actually am."

Mercedes pulled her friend into a tight hug. "You are that and more. So, here's my dilemma, Tracy has asked to meet with me. Should I do it?"

"Yes." At Mercedes wince Cipriana added, "I rather think you owe it to him."

"Damn it, Cipri, how could I have told him? He would have raised holy hell. You know what he's like."

"Whether you should have told him six years ago is not

the issue. He found out. That's the reality and I think he deserves to hear your reasoning."

"He won't accept it," Mercedes said.

"Probably not, but he's not stupid, he'll at least understand it."

"All right. I'll see him. But not tonight. I have no emotional surplus left right now."

✦   ✦   ✦

YOUNG LIEUTENANT LADY Flintoff had made a search through the displaced persons rolls and located Tracy's father. Alexander was at a shelter on the outskirts of one of the alien quarters of Hissilek contemptuously known to the ruling humans as Pony Town. The other alien ghettos had similarly dismissive and insulting names—Stick Town and Squirrel Town. Since the Sidone, who looked like five-foot tall tarantulas, didn't tend to leave their home world there wasn't a Spider Town. Which was good. Given most humans reactions to large arachnids they would not have had an easy time of it.

Even without the presence of big spiders these areas of the city were poorer, more run down, and more diverse in terms of businesses, cuisine and population than the human quadrants. They had also largely escaped the bombardment that had leveled entire sections of the capital city.

So now displaced humans found themselves living cheek to jowl with their second-class alien citizens. In truth the less affluent humans did have more interactions with aliens outside of the role of servant, but what was different now was that the broad middle class was learning a lot about the creatures that lived, served, and toiled among them.

Not the FFH of course. Their mansions and palaces might have been damaged or destroyed but they had the means to retire to second, third or fourth homes on this or other planets, or take up residence in a five-star hotel.

As Tracy walked down the streets, he had a moment of dislocation where the past overlaid the present. He was walking past an Isanjo restaurant where all through junior high and high school he had met his father on Fridays after class to dine. There was a line of people outside and more in the open-air eatery, but no credit spikes were in evidence. Instead, Isanjo staff raced up the wooden poles and flew along the webbing of ropes delivering packaged meals to people who then filed out another entrance. While there were aliens in the line it was mostly humans.

People noticed his uniform, and a few seemed to recognize him. An older woman nodded to him and said, "Thank you for your service, sir."

Then one of the Isanjo whose fur was tipped with grey swarmed down a rope and landing on the pavement in front of Tracy looked up at him. "I remember you. You used to come in with your father."

"Yes. I did. Loved your food. So, what's going on here?"

"City is trying to get back to normal, but a lot of grocery stores are empty and deliveries to restaurants are pretty sporadic. The military's been distributing MRE's, but folks need real food, hot food. Something comforting in their bellies. We're trying to do that but all the media talks about are the reconstruction in the financial district. They forget we need more than having the stock market open again."

"I'll mention it to central command."

"Thanks. You're that human who used Isanjo workers to help capture those *pendjo* motherfucker's ship. I guess you liked more than just our food. Good on you. Gotta get back to it. Nice seeing you again."

"And you," Tracy called as the alien scampered back up the pillars and ropes. Tracy made a mental note to tell Jahan about the food shortages. It might be an opportunity for the *Selkie*.

As he walked, he checked his ScoopRing again. It was stupid. If he had a message from Mercedes, his ring would have alerted him. Checking wasn't going to get her to reply any faster. He toyed with the idea of just going up to the palace and banging on the gates until he was either arrested, shot, or she came out to see him. He shook off the foolish notion. It was nine-thirty at night. She had just been reunited with her child. At some point she would see him. Mercedes was many things, but coward was not among them.

He reached the shelter and once again his uniform and rank opened all doors. He caught a young nun hurrying past with a stack of towels. "I'm looking for Alexander Belman-or."

"He's in the recreation room. You must be his son." At his expression she added with a smile. "You look a lot like him. Down this hall, up the stairs. It's the big room on the left."

"Thank you, sister."

"*De nada.*"

His footfalls seemed loud on the tile floor. As Tracy

climbed the stairs, he heard a woman's muffled sobs, a child's voice wailing in fear and a soothing answer from a father. The shelter smelled of disinfectant, spaghetti sauce and people who weren't getting regular showers or a chance to do laundry.

Tracy reached the doorway and stood studying his father. Alexander was hunched in a shabby armchair with a bright work light shining over his left shoulder. On the floor next to him was a pile of clothing, all in various states of disrepair. Alexander was wielding a needle making repairs to a child's torn jacket. He held it with his withered right arm legacy of a stroke he'd suffered. Tracy admired the way the needle darted through the material. Having to learn to use his left hand hadn't slowed down his father at all.

"Dad," he called softly.

"Tracy!" The jacket went flying and his father surged out of the chair. They embraced and Tracy grieved over the boney shoulders he felt beneath the material of his father's jacket and shirt.

"I didn't know you were coming," Alexander said as Tracy helped him get settled back into the armchair. Tracy picked up the discarded jacket, pulled over a chair and settled in front of his father. He began to finish stitching up the torn pocket.

"It was sudden."

Alexander snagged a dress with a ripped hem from the pile and began sewing. "How long can you stay?"

"Not as long as I'd like. I left my fleet orbiting the *necrófago* home world."

His father looked alarmed. "Won't that get you into

trouble."

Tracy gave a rueful smile. "It would have except I was rescuing the prince, so I think I'll get a pass on this one."

He had expected excitement and eager interest from his father. All through Tracy's childhood his father had taken immense pride in the fact he "made" for the emperor and for other FFH figures who preferred the understated but elegant drape of his suits.

Instead, Alexander looked worried and upset. "Oh, I wish it hadn't been you," he murmured, and his hands clenched on the dress.

Tracy reached out and laid his hand over his father's. "Dad, what's wrong?"

"Your involvement with…them has brought you nothing but sorrow."

"Dad, you sound like grandfather, and you always said his bitterness wasn't healthy," Tracy said softly. "I've become an admiral. Won honors. Helped win a war. Isn't this what you wanted when you made sure I'd attend The High Ground?"

"Yes…no. I wanted you to have a happy and successful life. A wife. Children. A career that could offer you more than life in a tailor shop. But it's never good when people like us rise too high. We end up crushed." His eyes filled with tears. "And now I don't even have the shop to leave to you."

Tracy dropped to his knees and hugged the older man. "Don't worry about that, dad. I have money. Lots of money. In fact, there is no reason for you to be living in a shelter and sewing at night. I can set you up in a hotel. In the best hotel that's still standing."

Alexander smiled at that and laid a hand on Tracy's head. "I sew because I want to. I'm helping. Most of the people staying here fled with only the clothes on their backs. I volunteer by altering donated clothing to fit. I'm teaching some of the older children how to tailor, so they'll have a skill going forward. What would I do with myself in one of those fancy places? I would be so out of place."

"Nonsense. You made for the emperor. You made Merc—the Empress's wedding gown. You're the equal of any of the FFH bastards."

"Trace, my boy, listen to yourself. You have the accent, the bearing," he flicked at the ribbons and medals on Tracy's jacket. "The honors. If a visitor from another galaxy were to show up, he'd think you *were* a member of the FFH. But you're not and in their eyes you *never will be*. The war is over. Get out. Get away from them. People like us shouldn't meddle in the affairs of royalty."

Tracy couldn't control it. He gave a snort. His father looked at him in alarm. "What? Why are you looking like that?"

"Dad, it's a little fucking late for that."

5

CRAFTING THE NARRATIVE

A BUBBLE FLOATED up from the tub and landed on Mercedes nose. With her hands in the bath water her only recourse was to blow it away. Cyprian laughed and caught the errant bubble. She was kneeling at the side of the deep tub helping her son take this late bath.

He had awakened, screaming, from a nightmare. Mercedes, sleeping on the settee in his bedroom, had rushed to his side as he had clung to her shivering and sobbing. She had decided that a warm bath might help soothe and calm him.

Her Hajin maid, Venia, had offered to handle the task, but Mercedes had declined. She wanted time with her little boy, time to marvel at how much he had grown.

"I can scrub most of my bits now, mama," he said. "But Lizzie helped me with my hair. I get soap in my eyes if I do it all by myself."

"Lean back and I'll do that," Mercedes said. She wet his brown curls with the hand sprayer and worked shampoo into his hair.

He wrinkled his nose. "That smells kinda girly."

"Probably because I'm a girl and this is my bathroom."

"When is daddy coming?" he asked.

"Daddy had to go on a very important mission," Mercedes said as she rinsed away the lather. "He'll be back soon, and we can talk to him once he's out of Fold. Okay, out you come. Let's get you dry and back into bed."

"I'm not tired," he said, those his lids were dropping over his tawny eyes.

"Well then we'll just curl up on the bed and read and Sapphire will keep us company."

"Whose Sapphire?"

"My new kitty."

"What happened to Misty?" he asked as she helped him climb out of the tub and wrapped him in a large towel that Venia had heated for her. She rubbed him energetically trying to decide what to say and how to say it. He took the decision from her when he said in a voice too old for his years, "Is she dead? Like Lizzie?" Tears welled in his eyes.

She stroked his hair. "Sometimes bad things happen in war," Mercedes said softly.

"I don't like war."

She hugged him close and kissed the top of his head. "Neither do I."

As Venia helped her get Cyprian back into his pajamas and settled into the big fourposter bed Mercedes reflected that she really did need to find her little boy a counselor. Like clockwork the elegant blue point Siamese came stalking into the bedroom, hopped on the bed, inspected Cyprian and decided he met with the feline's exacting standards and settled down purring next to him.

The little boy's hand stroked at the cat's fur and Mercedes opened a story book. She had read barely a page before the child's deep, regular breaths told her he was sleeping.

Mercedes took pictures of Cypi as he slept and sent them to Boho's ScoopRing. He would see them when the day cycle began on the royal yacht, but at least she had done that much after denying him the chance to see his son.

Except he's not his son, is he? Hateful little internal voice.

Turning her ScoopRing to mute and being careful not to wake Cyprian, Mercedes laid down next to her son, her arm protectively across his body. She ought to contact Jaakon and tell him to set a time for her to meet with Tracy. She dreaded the upcoming confrontation but knew it could not be avoided. Cipriana was right, she owed him that much. Tracy's expression as he looked out from the doors of the shuttle haunted her.

She felt guilty that she had sent Boho away before he got to see Cyprian, but she couldn't risk having the two men in the same vicinity. *You're only postponing the inevitable,* she thought. She had seen it herself, the resemblance was obvious, so it wouldn't be long before Boho realized the truth, and….

And what?

His pride might keep him from making a scene that could only result in his being made the butt of cruel and crude jokes, but the whispers would drive him mad. And how would the FFH and citizens across the League react?

But wasn't the only blood that mattered *hers*? She was the Empress. The true Arango. On the other hand, the idea the heir to the Solar League had been sired by an *intitulado* would not sit well with her class. Would it even among the ordinary citizenry? They could sometimes be even more traditional than their betters and they were often far more judgmental of moral lapses. If the worst came to pass, she would need to find a way to make Tracy acceptable.

What was clear was that however the upper and lower classes of the League might react she needed to confess all to Boho; before he found out from other sources. She owned him that much. It seemed she owed a lot of men....

The urgent emergency override from her ScoopRing awoke her from a sleep she hadn't intended to take. Pushing up onto an elbow Mercedes looked at the clock. *Two forty-five a.m.*

Climbing carefully out of bed she padded into the small sitting room off her bedroom. She hesitated, but Jaakon had used the emergency override, so she called him.

It was clear he hadn't been asleep, and the tension etched on his face had her tensing in response.

Before she could speak, he said, "Check the newsfeeds and then call Ian," and he ended the call. Such a display of outright rudeness was so unlike her staid assistant that she didn't even think about calling him back an delivering a reprimand. Instead, she pulled up a selection of media sites ranging from the staid LBC and the Times. She wasn't seeing what had Jaakon's hair on fire. There were single articles about the return of the heir to Hisselek. It wasn't until she hit the more sensational and sleazy outlets that the full scope of the disaster which was about to crash over her became clear.

✦   ✦   ✦

TRACY COULDN'T SLEEP. He had tried one of the bunks at the shelter, in the same room as Alexander and six other men, but it reminded him too much of his first posting when his bunk mates had all been first lieutenants, while he himself had been denied that rank because of his low birth. He had endured being ordered about and tormented for months. The snorts, snores, farts, and general man scent had him grabbing his boots and slipping out of the crowded room. He had spent too many years with a cabin of his own to endure this.

Outside he enjoyed the fresh air. The nebula threw its gaudy colors across the night sky while two of the moons like ugly stepsisters struggled to be seen against that flamboyant display. Brilliant lights illuminated the top of the *Palacio Colina,* and the muted growl of heavy equipment was like a giant's snores. Clearly, they were running around the clock shifts to try and get the palace and the homes of the titled, wealthy, and powerful rebuilt.

There were cranes in the financial district to the east and north, but those were silent. It seemed the FFH took precedence even over commerce. What didn't take precedence were the common citizens homes and businesses and as for the alien neighborhoods…well, perhaps someday the reconstruction would reach them.

Tracy thought about going to the *Selkie* and begging a bunk. Maybe one of the crew was out and about. Ernie the grizzled engineer might be at a brothel or a bar. But if he wasn't Tracy would look a perfect fool. The other option was to roust his shuttle crew and security detail out of whatever beds they had found and return to the *Swiftsure.* Since most of those beds were likely being shared with *damas* or *caballeros de la noche* it seemed like a truly dickish thing to do. Tracy gave a little laugh at his own feeble humor.

An unlikely pair joined him on his perambulation. The dog was a lanky mutt with a smooth red coat, and its companion was a calico cat whose fluffy fur was matted and tangled. They both looked at him with a mixture of hope and suspicion.

Tracy squatted down and held out his hand. As expected, the dog came wriggling toward him, ears flat, tail wagging. The mongrel began to lave his hand with his tongue. The cat gave them both a superior look and held back to watch.

"You're hungry, aren't you, buddy? Well, it's a little late…or a little early for a restaurant. Maybe I can find something in a trashcan for you and your friend." Tracy paused and considered. "Although, the Royal Mark might do room service. Shall we find out?"

He straightened and headed off toward the posh hotel. It was crazy and he had no idea why he was doing this flanked by his mangy escort. Maybe because Mercedes had not responded to his request…no, his *demand* for an audience. Because his father thought the best the Belmanor father and son deserved was a crowded room in a refugee center. Because he needed someone to acknowledge who he was. That he had captured an enemy dreadnaught. Rescued a prince. *Fathered* a prince. By arriving with strays, he would test if he had become somebody or if he and his ragtag companions would be thrown back into the street.

And maybe Mercedes would call.

✦   ✦   ✦

SLIPPING OUT OF the bedroom Mercedes hurried to her office, set the security protocols, and keyed her ScoopRing. Her call was to the head of the intelligence service, Lord Ian Rogers. Rogers had led her palace security detail until the retirement of old Kemel DeLonge who had lead SEGU for over forty years.

Boho was rather contemptuous of Rogers thinking he wasn't tough enough for the job, but Mercedes knew Ian to be a man of integrity (perhaps not the best quality in a spymaster, but no matter), and that he was also in love with her so he would keep her confidences and do his damndest to protect her.

Unlike Jaakon who had never married and continued to pine after her, Rogers had done his duty to his class and the League. He had married, sired five children, and lost one to the war. So, Mercedes wasn't surprised when Ian's wife, Natalie answered.

The younger woman nodded and said, "Ma'am, he'll be on his way to you in ten minutes. He's dressing."

"Jaakon called him then."

"Yes, ma'am."

"Sorry to have disturbed you at this ungodly hour."

"It is our honor and our pleasure to serve."

Mercedes thanked her and broke the connection. She was finding all the formality and obsequiousness wearing and wondered if the other woman did it as a subtle rebuke for her husband's divided affections.

Whatever, it was time to face the horrid reality. She brought up the news feeds again, so the most offensive headlines were displayed in all their holographic glory. The worst of them had a picture of Boho with the horns of a cuckold placed on his head.

Thirty minutes later the Hajin butler informed her that Lord Rogers had arrived. Mercedes dropped the locks and security devices and had him escorted in. Fingell was his usual efficient self and was carrying a tray with a coffee carafe, cups, cream and sugar and an assortment of small sandwiches and cookies. Once the alien had left, Mercedes keyed back on the security measures while Ian filled two cups with coffee, but his focus seemed to be more on the ugly headlines then his task.

Mercedes followed his gaze as she accepted the cup. "Yes, it's true. Yes, it's bad."

"So, what can I do?" Rogers asked.

He was still a fit and dapper fifty-nine, and his dark curls were hardly touched with grey. There was a grey tinge to his dark skin, and Mercedes felt a flash of guilt, as the head of the *Seguridad Imperial* he probably didn't get much sleep on a *normal* day, and now she'd kept him from what little he might manage.

"It's still twenty-eight hours until the yacht reaches the heliopause and can make a safe translation into Fold. I need to make sure Boho doesn't receive any transmissions from Ouranos until he's safely in Fold. After that it's seventeen days to Nephilim which gives me…" Her voice trailed away, and she shook her head.

"Time to deal with this…er…delicate situation," Ian

suggested.

"Exactly." Mercedes sighed. "And figure out how to phrase my confession and apology."

"So, do you have a plan about how to resolve this?" Rogers asked and gave an uncomfortable cough.

"Yes, but the ultimate plan doesn't require your agency's particular skills. What I need from you right now is to ensure radio silence aboard the royal yacht until they have entered Fold. I know you have an agent aboard. Can they disable the Foldstream and not make it look like sabotage?"

"Actually, I have two agents aboard, and yes, either one of them can handle it. I'll get a message to them right away."

She held out her hand and he bowed over it. "Thank you, Ian. I don't know what I would do without you. And thank you for not..." She cast about for the appropriate word. *Castigating? Rebuking? Reproaching?* "For not judging me."

"You are my Empress. I would never contemplate such a thing." He gave her a final look, his heart in his eyes, turned smartly on his heel and headed for the door.

Mercedes steeled herself for the next and most difficult call. Dealing with family was always the most challenging.

✦   ✦   ✦

BOHO HELD OUT his coffee cup for a refill and glowered at the silver topped chaffing dishes on the elaborate carved buffet.

"There is no reason for a buffet style breakfast. There are only nine of us aboard," he groused to Paloma. She was serenely slicing a banana onto her cereal.

"Actually, there are forty-six of us aboard," she said. The

contradiction irked him, and he shot her an icy look. Which intimidated her not at all. "The nine of us. Our personal attendants, that's another nine, five crew and their attendants, two chefs, two dishwashers, four waiters, five maids, and the seven-man security team plus their seven batBEMS.

"I wasn't counting all the alien servitors."

"I know, but they have to eat, sleep and excrete too. So, what really has you so cranky this morning." Her intonation put quotes around the word morning since it was an arbitrary choice given the fact, they were in the third and final day of their journey to a safe translation point.

He gave her a rueful smile. "You're right, I'm being a surly bear. I wanted to talk with my son before we left the system. It's seventeen days to Nephilim and I haven't seen Cyprian for almost two years. And I would like to have said farewell to Mercedes and my boy before we enter Fold. I don't understand why they're having so much trouble locating and correcting this communication glitch."

"I'm sure they will have it fixed by the time we reach Nephilim."

"I don't handle waiting well," he huffed.

"Really? I never noticed."

"Sarcasm is particularly unbecoming in a lady," Boho said, frowning at her.

At that point the other seven people who counted as real people in Boho's mind entered the dining room. The *Servicio Diplomático* had sent along five individuals who thus far had seemed interchangeable in their dull bureaucratic affect. All men, of course. Paloma was the only human female aboard the ship.

Boho had added a bright young man from the Exchequer, Michael Oldziej, with the intent of seeing if improved trade and financial agreements between the distant world and the more prosperous inner League planets, might be an incentive to bring Talion and Nephilim back into the fold.

The final individual to enter was, like Paloma, a SEGU agent. Boho had thought of Constantine Ragsdale as an older fellow, but when he had perused the man's file Boho had discovered to his dismay that Ragsdale was actually six years younger than himself. When had he gotten old? And how did Paloma view him? As a randy old *macho cabrío* spraying and bleating as he pranced about?

Not a good thought. Still, they would have seventeen days of isolation in which he might be able to make an assault against the girl's…woman's current embrace of celibacy.

Boho looked up to find Paloma gazing at him with a very knowing expression, and a sardonic smile as if she knew *exactly* what he had been thinking. The coffee soured in his stomach, and Boho decided he really wasn't hungry. Throwing his napkin on the table he left the dining room while everyone tried to juggle plates and bow without depositing their breakfasts onto the exquisite Sidone silk carpet.

6

BRAZEN IT THROUGH

THE IMAGES OF two of her sisters wavered above her desk. Carisa and Beatrisa were both affecting the hair style (or lack of) adopted by Beatrisa when she had begun her military career. Meaning they were both sporting a half inch fuzz on their skulls. Beatrisa was in her early forties. With the sharp angles of her face and taut body she reminded Mercedes of a greyhound. Carisa, the acknowledged beauty of the family, was in her early thirties. The only analogy Mercedes could think of for the youngest of the Arango daughters was a swan.

"Mer, you look tired and worried. Don't tell me you're letting that bastard Talion cost you any sleep," Beatrisa said.

"No. It's Trac—Admiral Belmanor who's the problem."

Carisa's eyebrows swept up and Beatrisa frowned. "How so? During my time serving with him I found him to be a man of honor and genius," Beatrisa said stiffly.

"Oh, please don't have some terrible information about him. I can't take any more disappointments about people's character," Carisa said lightly. "I do rather owe him for keeping me out of Talion's hands." She gave a pout. "And may I say, I am getting *very* tired of being viewed as nothing more than a bridal trading card in other people's plots and intrigues."

Mercedes winced. "Well, actually…" She paused cleared her throat and started again. "I have a confession to make." Despite being on separate ships several thousand kilometers from each other the younger sisters managed to use the holographs to exchange glances.

"Okay," Beatrisa said slowly.

"After the debacle at Kusatsu-Shirane I was picked up by a trading vessel," Mercedes began.

"And we know all this." Beatrisa was being prickly. Mercedes pushed down her annoyance.

"What you don't know is that Tracy…Belmanor was the captain of that ship but living under an assumed name."

"Oh," Carisa said hollowly.

"Okay, starting to understand some of his more cryptic remarks about his checkered past," Beatrisa said slowly.

"We had an affair. I got pregnant. Cyprian is Tracy's child." It all emerged in a breathless rush.

"Oh my."

"Oh shit."

Mercedes drew in a settling breath. "It's becoming obvious, and the press has noticed."

"And Boho?" Beatrisa asked.

"He doesn't know. At least not yet. I sent him to Nephilim for a summit."

"Well…I expect he won't be in the most diplomatic of moods when he gets *this* news," Carisa said. Mercedes wondered when the baby of the family had learned to be so dry and ironic.

"He'll be angry, but he'll understand how we have to play this," Mercedes said with more hope than belief.

"Sublime and majestic indifference," Beatrisa said.

"But Parliament will never accept a…a…*bastardo* on the throne," Carisa argued.

"Well, first, Cyprian's not a bastard. I'm not some unwed mother. Second, *I'm* the sovereign not Boho. And third he's my son with my blood."

"But Tracy is…is…" Words failed Carisa.

"A hero. An admiral. Rescuer of the heir to the throne," Mercedes snapped.

"And an *intitulado*," Beatrisa said flatly.

"Yes. Until I ennoble him." Mercedes sucked in a deep breath, briefly closed her eyes. "And make him part of the family." Carisa's expression said it all. "Look, I understand how you feel, but Cari you've always known that your marriage would be in service of the crown. And it must be you. Everyone else is either married or a nun—"

"Or a big *lesbiana*," Beatrisa said cheerfully. "And Tanis would probably cut off his dick," she added. She cocked her head thoughtfully. "Or maybe not. She sure did love popping out babies for that bastard priest, Jose."

"She's also functionally in prison in that convent after her part in the coup," Mercedes said.

Carisa had remained silent. Mercedes gave her holographic image a pleading look. "So, will you do it, Cari? For the sake of the crown? For my sake? For Cyprian's?"

"*Jesucristo.*" Carisa released a pent-up breath. "Well, at least he's not *too* old. Not exactly an Adonis, pretty eyes though, and he's smart and he seems kind. Could be worse.

Still, it's just going to be just swell to have a husband who you know is in love with your older sister," Carisa concluded a touch bitterly.

"Thank you. You won't regret it. He's…he's really rather wonderful," Mercedes said.

"Scratch what I said before. It's just going to be just swell having my sister in love with my husband. So, what do you want me to do?"

"Get back to Hisselek as quickly as you can, and we'll start the process of crafting your romantic story."

+ + +

ANSELMO SETTLED INTO his chair at the head of the table and beamed at his four children. Deidre in her high-chair, young Andrew, Josephine, and his eldest Ansel who would soon be turning six. He wondered if he could get the boy ensconced as a playmate for the royal heir. If Ansel became Cyprian's best friend his son's future would be assured. His wife, Julia, was tying a bib around Diedra's neck, and her burgeoning belly gave Anselmo a flare of pride.

Their Hajin butler was making certain that the Hajin maids trooping in with the breakfast plates were up to his exacting standards. Opening his napkin with a snap Anselmo allowed himself another moment of self-satisfaction. He had picked up a mansion from a minor noble who had gotten into trouble with less than felicitous investments and even better—they hadn't gotten bombed.

Everyone wanted the Consort's right-hand man to put in a good word for them, so the furnishings were far more elegant than they could have afforded. Someday this long, elegant table would be filled with more children and eventually their wives and husbands and their children. Boho had already had Anselmo elevated from *caballero* to baron. It wasn't out of the realm of possibility to think he could achieve *Comte*.

Take that, pops, you withered old espantapájaros, you never thought your sixth son would amount to a damn. Well, I've done better than your precious Guillermo.

The plate of *heuvos con queso* was placed in front of him, his coffee cup filled. Anselmo keypad his ring to check the morning news.

"Oh, Anse," Julia protested. "It sets a bad example for the children when you read at—" She broke off in alarm as he shoved back his chair with a shriek of wood on marble and leapt out of his chair.

He threw down his napkin. "I have to go to the office."

"What? Now?"

He was already running for the door. "Yes! Now!"

"Don't forget Josie's dance recital…"

He read in the flitter to the office. In among the images of Cyprian flinging himself into his mother's arms and her burying her face among his brown curls were images of Belmanor looking out from his shuttle. On the feeds from some of the less savory and more sensational news sites there were pictures of the prince and the admiral set side by side. The headline on one site was a single image.

?

Another headline blared—**"QUIEN ES TU PAPI?"**

All of which resulted in Anselmo bolting from the flitter. Running into the building. Skidding into the bathroom. Where he ended up on his knees in front of a toilet vomiting up the meagre contents in his stomach. After the heaves ended he tottered to the sink, washed the taste of bile out his mouth and tried to calm his racing heart and frenzied breathing. Splashing water onto his overheated face Anselmo stood with a paper towel pressed against his eyes.

He heard the door opening and he ducked back into a stall. Multiple footsteps and then a discussion began among four men.

"Unbelievable."

"What do you think will happen?"

"Nothing. Everyone will turn a blind eye."

"The Consort sure as fuck can't."

"He'll do what he's told. She's got his balls in her purse."

"This is no laughing matter," came a disapproving older voice. *"We don't want another attempted coup."*

Eventually the men left allowing Anselmo to escape the bathroom. He hurried to the office.

"About time you got here," Iris said acerbically. Multiple images from various news and entertainment sites floated over her desk. One particularly disgusting rag had a picture of Boho with the horns of a cuckold photoshopped onto his head.

"No way I don't have to have him killed now," Anselmo muttered.

"I beg your pardon?"

"Nothing. Nothing. Never mind." Anselmo stood silent,

hands hanging limply at his sides.

"So, what do we do?" Iris asked.

Anselmo continued to stand, playing in his head the likely conversation he would have with Boho. Iris waved away the screens, left the desk and came around to face him. "Anselmo." She snapped her fingers in front of his face. "Hello?"

"I don't know," Anselmo said. He clutched at his hair. "I suppose we should draft…a statement…"

"Look, speaking as a woman and a mother I think you shouldn't do a damn thing until you talk with the Empress. Find out how *she* wants this handled."

"Do you think we can delay that long?" Anselmo asked.

"I think we've got to. Right now, we're operating blind and we don't want to make this any worse after we've already made things spectacularly bad."

He gave a wan smile. "Is that even possible?"

"Oh yes. Our species always seems to find a way to dig itself into a deeper hole."

Anselmo keyed his ring and called Mercedes equerry. Jaakon's holograph appeared. Despite being in his mid-fifties he was still dapper and handsome, but right now his expression was so blank he resembled a mannikin.

"Is her Highness available to take my call?" Anselmo asked.

"No. Her majesty is in a private meeting and has left strict instructions not to be disturbed unless it is an emergency," Jaakon said.

"You don't think this qualifies?" Anselmo asked.

Jaakon's inscrutable mask slipped. "I think unless somebody is dying, we let her handle…what she's handling."

Anselmo ended the call. Looked over at Iris. "She's with him," he said dully.

✦ ✦ ✦

IT WAS A pretty room. Sunlight poured through mullioned windows and splashed across the polished surface of the grand piano. Tracy stood studying the mural on the ceiling dome. Apollo with his lyre, Orpheus also with a lyre were the central figures. Around them four females in flowing Greek gowns that he couldn't identify.

There was the click of heels on the stone floor. Tracy didn't turn. He knew her step. "So, who are the *chicas*?" he asked gesturing toward the four female figures.

"Calliope the muse of epic poetry. Euterpe muse of music, song, and lyric poetry. Polyhymnia muse of hymns—"

"Huh, that makes sense."

"And Terpsichore muse of dance."

He turned to face her. "So, what's the difference between epic and lyric poetry?"

"I couldn't begin to tell you," Mercedes said dryly.

While they stood only a few feet apart Tracy made no effort to close the distance. Their surroundings, and how she was dressed in a gown of deep amethyst with a tiara nestled among her silver kissed curls told him that they were gazing at each other across a vast gulf of social status. One that she was not inviting him to cross.

"Why did you have to come back to the capital, Tracy?" she finally asked.

"To ask you why. Why did you lie to me? Because you knew, didn't you? That last morning."

"Not until breakfast. When Dalea had me test."

"You didn't think I had a right to know that I was going to be a father?"

"No. You would have decided to toss me over the front of your saddle and ride off into the sunset. Which was impractical on every level—"

"Especially since I've never been on a horse," he countered and was rewarded by a lip quiver as she suppressed a smile.

"Point being I wasn't going to divorce Boho and marry you. A convicted felon living under a false name and trading with Hidden Worlds? Like I said impractical on every level."

"Well, when you put it like that…" His voice trailed off unable to think of a good counterargument. "So, what are we going to do? Cyprian is my son, and most of the League knows it now."

"Thanks to you."

"Oh, for God's sake, Mercedes, unless you were planning to permanently banish me to a Hidden World or send me on a one-way trip to sector 470—"

"How do you know about that?" Her expression had gone diamond hard, and her tone was sharp enough to cut.

"Jesus, relax. Rohan had me do research on it back when I was in school. Ships go in but they don't come out. And no, I'd never say anything."

She visibly relaxed. "Sorry, go on. You were saying."

"My point being that sooner or later people were going to notice the resemblance. Unless you planned to sequester me in some way. Or kill me…" His voice trailed away. "I'd like to hope you wouldn't have gone that far to protect your secret."

She looked hurt. "Of course not. I would never harm you. I couldn't. But we do need to handle this. It's why I agreed to see you. Why don't we sit down and discuss this like adults?"

She gestured toward the window seat in the mullioned bay window. Tracy followed her over and sat down next to her. Her perfume filled his nostrils. He clasped his hands together to avoid any temptation to reach out and touch her hair, her cheek, to kiss that lush mouth.

Once her skirts were arranged, she twisted around to face him. "The only way out of this is through it. And it needs to be done as quickly and gracefully as we can. We'll say nothing as regards you or Cyprian. Nobility, particularly royalty, do not explain or make excuses. We brazen it through."

"And what form is this brazening going to take?" Tracy asked warily. "As my dad pointed out, every time royalty has decided to get mixed up in my life it hasn't turned out all that well for me…or my dad."

"It's not like you avoided the opportunities to get mixed up with us. And I'm disappointed, I thought you were going to say *I've gotten royally fucked*," she added. "Go for the quip."

"Not feeling very quippy since I have a feeling this time is not going to be the exception."

Then Mercedes stunned him when she thrust out a hand. "Congratulations, you're about to become my brother-in-law and a royal *duque*."

"Wha…wha…what the hell?" He leaped up from the

window seat as if it had become a stove top.

"I've discussed it with Carisa, and my staff is already crafting the tale of your growing romance while under deadly fire. It will be appropriately passionate and action-packed. They are also going to discover an FFH ancestor in your family tree. Right now, Carisa is returning to Ouranos. Once she arrives your engagement will be announced and plans for a royal wedding begun. I'm thinking next month. The sooner the better."

Tracy tried to gain control over his whirling thoughts and emotional turmoil. "And what happens after this picture-perfect fake wedding?" he managed to ask.

"Oh, believe me, it won't be fake."

"It is in terms of the actual emotions of the parties involved," he shot back.

"In my set love has nothing to do with marriage."

"In my set it does." They both fell silent and traded burning looks.

Mercedes looked away and resumed. "After the honeymoon you'll be given a planetary governorship that should occupy a large amount of your time and require very few visits to the capital."

"I see." He paced away from her and stood by the piano. He pressed his forefinger down on a key. A single, sighing, sour note floated in the air. "Your piano needs tuning," he said inanely. Once again, he tried to marshal his thoughts. Turning back to Mercedes Tracy asked,

"Putting aside my feelings in all of this, how does Carisa feel about marrying a man she doesn't love and in fact barely knows—"

"Such was always going to be her fate. She—"

"And with the added bonus of knowing her husband is in love with her sister," Tracy interrupted.

"She understands the necessity to protect the crown."

"And Cullen? Is he on board with this farce or is he going to try and cut off my balls?"

"He'll want to, but he won't. I'll see to that." Another silence fell between them. Mercedes gave a small, twisted smile. "Well, I suppose it's good news that you're not instantly refusing. Last time I made you an offer you threw it back in my face pretty damn quick."

Tracy ran an agitated hand through his hair. "I don't know. I have to think…talk to my dad. Will you give me a day?"

"I'll give you three. It's going to take Carisa eight days to reach Hisselek."

Nausea filled his stomach but whether from excitement, joy, fear, or despair he couldn't say. Tracy stood silent for a few moments then finally muttered, "I'd like to leave now."

"You may." Her voice stopped him before he reached the door. "I hope you'll agree. For my sake, but mostly for Cyprian's."

The words were like a blow between his shoulder blades. Tracy hunched and fled.

7

I DON'T NEED ANY MORE TRUTH

"**W**ELL…DAMN." IT WASN'T one of her more articulate responses.

Jahan stared at Tracy over the rim of her beer stein. He had called her an hour before and asked to meet at a Isanjo restaurant on the edge of Pony Town. Since they had been sitting there, he had gone through five beers, which was totally unlike him. His tale of Mercedes offer had been punctuated by deep gulps of alcohol and now he was staring at her in hopeful anticipation.

"So, what should I do?" he asked again.

"Shit, Tracy, I have no idea what to tell you. And seriously why are you discussing this with *me*?"

He gave her a serious look out of those dark grey eyes. "Because I realized you're probably the closest friend I have."

The statement took her aback. Jahan covered her confusion by taking a long pull on her beer. "Well, if you do become *Admiral Duque high mucky mucky Belmanor* you better not admit *that* to your new social circle. You'll get drummed right out of the FFH." She laid a hand over his. Her golden fur and six fingers set a contrast to his darker skin. "But seriously, thank you. Your friendship means a lot to me too. My husband is my bestest friend, but you are a damn close second, human."

"Thanks. So, what should I do?"

"I can't make that decision for you. What do *you* want to do?" Jahan countered.

He looked away offering her his profile. "I want to marry Mercedes and take her and Cyprian away to Freehold and settle there. Live happily ever after." He sounded sad. Tracy gusted an alcohol laced sigh and looked back at her. "But I know I can't have that, so do I take the sister and occasionally get to see the love of my life and my son?"

"Maybe. I don't think I could do it, being that close to my deepest desire and not having it would drive me crazy. But here is my selfish answer. You are a very odd human. You willingly took on aliens as partners. Let us help in the war as more than just servants." She gave him a smile. "Just admitted that a BEM is your best friend. You could do a lot for us if you had that kind of power. I mean, you'd be in the House of Lords, right?"

Tracy looked aghast at that. "I suppose I would if I were a high mucky mucky." He gave her a sick little smile. "It is going to take all of us, human and alien to rebuild."

"Here is my last question. When you were young, before you knew Mercedes, what were your dreams?" she asked.

"To be successful. To make enough money that my dad didn't have to work so hard. Get us out of the tailor shop. Maybe be an accountant or a stockbroker. Move up on one of the hills or out near the coast. Be respected." He paused. "But I hated the FFH."

Jahan gave him a look knowing he was smart enough to

correctly interpret her unspoken thought.

"Only because I was jealous of them," he admitted.

He stood the caught himself on the edge of the table as the effects of the alcohol hit. "Guess I better go break the news to my dad."

"How do you think he's going to take it?" Jahan asked as she got her shoulder under his arm and helped him to the exit.

"I have no fucking idea."

+ + +

I ACCEPT.

Seconds had passed since he had said the words. The perfect acoustics in the palace music room had let them echo off the domed ceiling. They might have faded from the room, but they were still ringing in Mercedes head. She hadn't expected him to agree though she had certainly *wanted* him to agree—

No, actually she *hadn't* wanted that. Not really, not in her secret heart. *Him with Carisa, skin on skin, his hands caressing her sister's breasts, their bodies entwining, bringing Carisa to shuddering joy, his cries of passion as he murmured* her *name.* The very thought left Mercedes riven with anger and jealousy.

Or perhaps the name he called out when he climaxed on the wedding night would be hers. God knows she had dreamed of Tracy while lying in her husband's arms. It was a comforting thought followed immediately by guilt. How horrible that would be for Cari.

Still her half-sister understood the rules. A marriage of convenience had most likely always been her ultimate fate. So perhaps there would be no pleasure for either of them. Mercedes should have felt badly for them. Instead, the thought brought her a small measure of bitter joy.

"Are you listening? Did you hear what I just said?" His voice brought her back and she realized that in fact she hadn't heard a single word.

"No, I'm sorry. I was thinking about the arrangements. Jaakon needs to draft a notice of engagement—"

A hand went up, palm out to forestall her. "Wait. Slow down. I was saying I agree, but with conditions. I'm not going to accept getting shuffled off to some backwater planet and told to stay there. I want to be assured of frequent visits to the capital so I can see Cyprian. Have some kind of relationship with him, and when he's grown, I want him told. I also have things I want to do in parliament."

"You? A politician?" It came out more incredulous than she wished.

"Yeah. Why not?" came the defensive response.

"Well, bluntly, diplomacy has never been your strong suit. You're hot tempered, Tracy. Admit it."

"Okay, that's fair, but maybe that's what that hidebound institution needs. Somebody to shake things up. If there's one thing the war against the *necrófagos* has taught us is that we need change. We can't go on having well more than half our population living as second-class citizens."

"I gather you're not talking about women," Mercedes said.

"Nope. Alien rights."

She sighed. "I suppose I shouldn't be surprised that you'd want to be a reformer. You know that particular constituency can only vote in local elections."

"Then it's a good thing the members of the House of Lords don't have to win elections." He paused for a long moment. "So, are we agreed or not?"

She cast about for another delaying tactic moving to fluff and rearranged the pillows on the window seat. "How does your father feel about this? I presume you discussed this with him."

"Yes. He's worried I'll fetch up in jail again or something worse. He's also thrilled at the idea of us having a title. You nobles make all of us *intitulados* schizophrenic. We're torn between resenting the shit out of the FFH and craving your privilege and respect."

"You know the more you are here the more often you will have to interact with Boho," Mercedes warned. "How are you going to handle that?" She made it a demand more than a question wanting to be sure he really knew what he was getting into with his requirements.

"Well, I didn't kill him when he challenged me to a duel—"

"*What!*" It emerged as a shriek.

Tracy gave a nonchalant shrug. "After he caught us kissing on Hellfire."

She threw her hands in the air and stormed away. "Oh, you *men*! Must everything be reduced to a dick measuring contest? I am so tired of your bullshit—"

"Hey!" He caught her by the shoulders and a shiver went through her. "It didn't happen. So instead of ripping at me you should be complimenting me on my restraint. *I'm* the one who suggested we table our differences until the war was over. Which sort of proves I can control my temper. And Cullen agreed because he's a—" He broke off abruptly.

"Coward," Mercedes finished grimly. "So you keep telling me."

"Only telling you the truth."

"Well don't. I don't need any more truth in my life. I have people living in the rubble of their cities, trade disrupted, an economy in free fall. What I didn't need right now was all this damn personal psychodrama!"

He stepped toward her, hand out, but then stopped himself, the hand falling to his side. "I'm sorry," he mumbled. "I've made a mess of things. I would never want to make your life harder, but I did."

She sighed and felt her shoulder's slump. "No, it was going to happen sooner or later. People would have noticed the resemblance and the whispers begun. Maybe it's better we handle it now before Cyprian is any older and would understand more. By the time he does figure it out you will have been a presence in his life. He'll see that Boho has accepted you—" Tracy gave a soft snort. "Accepted you," Mercedes repeated firmly. "And Cypri will carry it off as his training and breeding demand."

+   +   +

ONE DAY IN Fold and Boho was already chafing at the isolation. Despite having spent years traveling between worlds in this folded space the twisting grey tendrils like a witch's hair beyond the ship's windows still filled him with a sense of unease as if creatures beyond human understanding were watching, judging…waiting.

Since no messages from tangible reality could reach them in this *not-space*, and thanks to the mysterious glitch in their Foldstream during the time they had been in normal space he had been unable to say farewell to his son or his wife, or his current mistress. Add to that the lack of current news, and he felt like he was going into the mission blind. At least there would be a few days once they translated out of Fold and made their way to Nephilim when he could read the news feeds, consult with Rohan and Rafe, and most importantly talk with Cyprian.

He turned his back on the maelstrom and walked toward the salon where there would be conversation, cocktails, and human companionship. He entered to find Paloma and two of the five diplomatic corps staff and Oldziej playing bridge. As she was the only woman aboard who wasn't an alien the men gathered about her like hummingbirds to nectar. The three men who hadn't managed to secure a seat at the table hung over their comrade's shoulders offering commentary, advice to Paloma, and mocking their fellows.

Constantine Ragsdale caught Boho's sleeve as he entered, and with a jerk of the head indicated they should move away from the group. A Hajin servant drifted by with several glasses of champagne on a silver tray. Boho snagged one and leaned his shoulders against a bulkhead.

"I applaud your efforts, Highness, to engage in trade talks." He jerked his head toward Oldziej. "But I'm not certain it will bear fruit given the fact that Nephilim seemed to have located several more Goldilocks worlds for settlement."

Boho shook his head. "I don't agree. Yes, virgin worlds are valuable, but only in terms of raw materials for building on said worlds, and as an escape hatch for a burgeoning population. First, Nephilim is lightly populated so it's uncertain how many volunteers Talion will actually get. I have found that the romance of being a hearty pioneer ends when the reality intrudes. Also, what Nephilim needs is investment in infrastructure, tech, and luxury goods. None of which will be provided by a newly discovered planet."

Ragsdale nodded. "Those are fair points." The man hesitated a faint frown between his brows.

"Was there something more?" Boho prodded.

"Ah, yes. With respect, Highness, but I was wondering how you intended to explain the presence of Señorita Flintoff."

Boho didn't mince words. "As my mistress."

Ragsdale's eyes slid to the young woman, now laughing, head thrown back at a sally from one of her admirers. "I am assuming that is not her *actual* role."

"No, but we're going to let them think that, and thus discount her. Which will allow the lady to go where we can't. Talk to people that would be closed off to us."

"Such as?"

"Wives worried for their husbands. Mothers for their sons. She gossips with the FFH, and while shopping hears the thoughts of the *intitulados* which can give us insights into the mood of the average citizen. My batBEM will be doing the same among the alien populace."

Ragsdale looked thoughtful and tugged at his chin. "An excellent plan, Highness. Though I do regret the damage it will do to the young lady's reputation," he added.

Apparently, Ragsdale was unaware of Paloma's activities as a honey pot when she had enticed, seduced, and ensnared Boho managing to manipulate him into revealing his half serious rebellion against the crown and his wife. Not one of his finer hours. And yet here she was acting like a virginal nun when it had been clearly established how far she would go. She had traded her virginity for the State and made him a besotted fool.

And still he couldn't stop wishing that she was back in his bed.

✦ ✦ ✦

MERCEDES PACED THE confines of her bedroom trying to outrun her anger, jealousy, grief, and worry. Sapphire tried to wind about her ankles, became frustrated with her perambulations, and removed himself to the bed to stare at her balefully.

She needed to get with Jaakon and craft that damn engagement announcement. She couldn't even tell Carisa that Tracy had agreed since her sister was deep in Fold making her way back to the capital. And in fifteen days she needed to contact Boho and make her confession. The thought made her shiver.

The door to her suite flew open the handle banging hard against the wall leaving a scar on the pale blue paint. Cyprian ran in, bubbling with excitement, and her irritation faded.

The paint and the dent were easily repaired. He flew into her arms and looked up at her.

"Mummy come watch me ride Bouncy."

"Yes, let's do that. And afterwards you can read to me."

He gave her a suspicious look. "That feels like school, mummy."

She almost prevaricated, gave him a soothing answer about how she just wanted to hear a story, but it was time for him to come to grips with the hard reality of life as a royal. He'd learned the hard lessons about war and loss. Now he needed to be trained in duty.

"That's how our life works, Cypri. To be deserving of fun, people must work. Even more so for us because we're royalty." She knelt in front of him and held his shoulders. "We have many pleasant things around us. We live in palaces, have ponies and carriages and way more toys than most people. So, we have to earn those by doing our duty. And right now, your duty is to go to school and study hard, so you'll grow up to be a wise and good ruler."

"This was just school too, wasn't it?" he said seriously.

"I suppose it was." She kissed him and pulled him into a tight hug. "I love you Cypri."

+ + +

EMPTY COFFEE CUPS, half eaten sandwiches, and tap pads littered the surface of the conference table. The Empress's equerry, Jaakon was oddly old fashioned. He had an actual pen and paper pad that was covered with his precise handwriting and lots of scratched out lines. The older man tossed his pen onto the table and dropped his head into his hands.

"God damn the Mormons for doing all this genealogy. Makes it so damn hard to fabricate an ancestor's aristocratic background."

Anselmo swirled his coffee and gazed into the bottom of his cup as if he could divine the future from the dregs. "Maybe we're going at this all wrong," he said slowly.

Jaakon lifted his head and gave Anselmo a suspicious look. "What do you mean?"

"Instead of trying to fabricate an unknown FFH ancestor who somehow fell off the registry why don't we *embrace* Belmanor's *intitulado* status?"

"Because it makes the *Príncipe* illegitimate." As soon as the words left his lips Anselmo could see Jaakon realize his mistake. It didn't stop Anselmo from drawling,

"Well, I'd say that horse has already left the barn."

Jaakon surged to his feet. "You forget yourself, sir!"

"Oh please, it's just us here. Can we cut the crap? The Empress had a little bang on the side with a common citizen. Got knocked up and then passed the kid off as her husband's. Not all that uncommon a story in our set."

"I will not stand here and listen to such crude aspersions cast against—"

"That's going to be the story that's told," Anselmo interrupted. "Hell, it's already being told. So, let's write a different one."

"Not possible"

Jaakon's tone was still censorious, but Anselmo noted that the older man resumed his seat and was looking at him curiously, or perhaps more with the air of a man confronted with a strange and particularly noxious insect he discovered in his bath.

"Look, the Empress is wildly popular right now as is the Consort. So, we tell a story about a couple desperate for a child, but clearly unable to conceive—"

"But the Consort sired numerous children—"

Anselmo impatiently waved Jaakon into silence. "Lots of married couples are infertile with each other. So, going on…realizing that the fate of the League hung in the balance they turned to a deeply loyal and very beloved comrade—"

"The Consort hates Belmanor!"

"Shhh, details…from their halcyon school days at The High Ground. A man who has served with bravery and distinction. We bring up all that shit from back in the day when they all won medals while they were still students, talk about Belmanor delivering the first real victory in the war, etcetera, etcetera, blah, blah, blah."

Anselmo stood and began to pace as he warmed to his tale. "They agreed that with help from medical professionals they would see if perhaps Admiral Belmanor and the Empress would be fertile. And once that was established the Admiral did his duty, donated sperm, the Empress was inseminated and *voila*, our beloved Prince Cyprian Amadeo Marcus Sinclair de Arango was born."

"They would have kept the secret to their graves but for the perfidy of the gutter press turning this act of fidelity, kindness and sacrifice into something salacious when in fact it was a coldly medical procedure."

Anselmo turned back to Jaakon. The older man was staring at him in open mouth astonishment.

"You are a very dangerous man," Jaakon said. "And I salute you." He grabbed his pen and the paper and began to scribble. "However, we need to downplay the artificial insemination. There are many older, conservative citizens who will be reminded of the Cara'ot and their genetic shenanigans."

"Good thing I didn't suggest it was a three way, I guess," Anselmo quipped.

Jaakon glared at him and returned to his writing. Once finished he tore off the page with a flourish, and handed it to Anselmo who read—

Their royal highnesses are pleased to announce the engagement of their beloved sister Princess Carisa Valentina Maite Kiara de Arango to Admiral Thracius Ransom Belmanor. In recognition of Admiral Belmanor's ~~services~~ kindness and offices to the crown he has been granted the title of Duque de Something. The Admiral has always been considered a ~~beloved~~ cherished friend and now that relationship shall change to family.

Anselmo gave Jaakon a grin. "Perfect. Now I'll go whisper the *true*," he made air quotes. "Story into the ears of my less savory journalistic contacts."

"What do we do about the missing fourteen years? Once this engagement is announced the press will drill down into every aspect of Admiral Belmanor's life. Do we admit he was living under an alias—"

"Oh fuck, no. We get Rogers to make a very suggestive statement about clandestine missions undertaken by the dear Admiral in service to the crown, but more cannot be said." Anselmo paused and grinned down into the appalled face of the older man. "Cheer up, we're writing one hell of a soap opera here."

8

JUST WHAT HAVE WE GOTTEN OURSELVES INTO?

I T HAD BEEN a mad ten days filled with fittings and lessons in protocol and deportment supplied by Mercedes stone faced equerry, Jaakon. Tracy couldn't read the man at all. Did he hate Tracy, like him, or just didn't give a good God damn? Since Jaakon had been with Mercedes since she was in her early twenties Tracy had to presume that he had *some* opinion.

Tracy now had a security detail assigned to both him and his father, and Alexander was no longer living in the emergency shelter. They had been given apartments in Rohan's mansion up on the *Palacio Colina*. It was only a few miles from the top of the hill that dominated Hisselek's skyline and where construction equipment was busy clearing the rubble in preparation of rebuilding the main palace.

His rambles through the upper story of the mansion brought him to the entry to the ballroom. He pushed open the massive silver double doors inlaid with mother-of-pearl.

For Tracy it was surreal to once more be in this house. Each Christmas break Rohan had hosted a ball for the students of The High Ground. But the one that most filled

Tracy's memory was the one he attended that freshman year. It was that night when he had first held Mercedes in his arms as she tried to teach him how to dance.

Boot heels clicking on the translucent flooring Tracy made his way to the French doors at the far end of the cavernous room and out onto the balcony where that dance lesson had taken place.

He sucked in a quick breath at the spectacular view glazed by a vibrant sunset and allowed the memories to return. The large ceramic pots were still there but they no longer held roses. Now dwarf orange and lemon trees perfumed the air. Tracy embraced a phantom partner and took a few gliding steps then felt an utter fool. His arms dropped to his sides, and Tracy moved to the balustrade and leaned on the stone.

Eventually he had learned to dance, and years later they had gone dancing during their idyll on Cuandru. That had been their last night together. Cullen's fleet had arrived the next day and taken Mercedes away. No, he thought. If he was going to be brutally honest, she had gone willingly.

Cullen had now intruded into Tracy's memories just as he did every damn time in the real world. Hatred roiled Tracy's gut and momentarily stole his breath. Finding Mercedes in his arms had turned Cullen's contempt for Tracy into hatred, led to a duel that left Tracy with a facial scar he would carry to his grave. Perhaps Tracy had now repaid the pain of that injury a hundred-fold by planting a cuckold's horns on Cullen and being the actual sire of the heir to the empire, but it still didn't feel like enough.

And now I'll have to call him brother. Tracy couldn't help but remember that Cain and Abel had also been brothers. Would the outcome be the same for him and Cullen?

In a few hours he would be going to the spaceport to meet his bride-to-be. It did no good to continue to dwell on the past. Tracy hoped Carisa would hold most people and the cameras attention, and that she was a better actor than himself. Somehow, they had to project the image of a couple deeply in love.

Well, at least we've met a couple of times, he though ruefully.

Limping footfalls and the tap of a cane presaged his father's arrival. Tracy had been avoiding him sensing that Alexander had an opinion about all of this. He forced a smile and turned to face his father.

"Hey, dad." It sounded strained even in his own ears.

A bony had was laid on his shoulder. "Trace, are you all right with all this?"

"Of course, dad. I wouldn't have agreed if I wasn't. You'll like Carisa."

"I don't doubt that, but I married for love. I had hoped for the same for you," Alexander said softly.

"Why do you think I don't—"

"Please, Tracy, I'm not an idiot. You're not behaving like a man in love." He paused, then added, "You don't have to do this."

"At some point it becomes too damn late, and we're way past that point, dad. We have to see this through."

And that is not exactly a ringing endorsement, Tracy thought.

Alexander sighed. "All right. I look forward to meeting

the young lady…the princess."

"Dad, you're going to be her father-in-law. You can use her name."

"I would not presume."

Tracy felt a massive headache coming on.

+ + +

THEY HAD ADDED a new crew member. Another human, so Ernie their engineer wouldn't feel quite so outnumbered. It was the two remaining males who felt outnumbered now: Jahan, Dalea, and Poppy versus Ernie and Kielli. Jax didn't really count. Could a plant actually have a gender? They called Jax a *he* but now that Jahan thought about it she had no idea if that was actually true.

Poppy Greenstein had been a chef and owned a handful of cafes catering to middle class humans before the war, but the fighting had wiped her out. Since the *Selkie* was looking to haul foodstuffs for the hungry citizens of Ouranos and several other League worlds Jahan thought it would be good to have a human helping Jax select the cargo.

From their corner of the battered spaceport, she could see the crowd gathering behind a security fence and another human fence formed by security personal in tactical gear and heavily armed. Camerabots floated overhead, and Jahan realized they had a ringside seat to a royal arrival. Hurrying back up the gangway and into the ship she shouted to her crew.

"*Hoy* looks like the Tracy and The Princess Show is about to begin. Wanna watch?"

"Oh, hell yes," Kielli warbled.

Dalea emerged from the small med bay. There was a shadow of sadness in her large eyes. "I don't know. It seems very sad that he's not getting the woman he loves."

"Why you feelin' sorry for *him*?" Ernie grunted. "She's the one marrying a guy who she knows is in love with her sister.

With a rustle of fronds Jax came gliding off the lift. "I am more concerned about Tracy's inevitable murder at the hands of the Consort."

"I wouldn't bet against our former boss," Jahan said. "He's whip-smart and been through three years of war. It's hardened him."

"Perhaps, but never underestimate the potency of guile and treachery and it seems the Consort excels at those skills. Which are *not* Tracy's skills," Jax said.

"Wow talk about a buzz kill," Kielli said.

Jahan noticed Poppy's wide-eyed gaze and realized they had all been perhaps just a tad indiscreet as regards the enmity between Boho and Tracy. "Umm, don't mind us. We talk a lot of nonsense."

Poppy who was plump and who sported a mop of curly hair dyed in rainbow colors that set off her dark cocoa skin to perfection gave a snort and setting her hands on her hips declared, "Like the Galaxy and the Royal Tattler haven't been all over this. They even have a *very* reputable source inside the palace who says the prince is Belmanor's son, but it was with the consent of the Consort, so I think you're wrong about the Consort wanting to murder the admiral." She reacted to her new cremates looks. "Yeah, I read them. So, sue me."

"Actually, I read them too," Dalea confessed.

"I've been known to take a peek," Ernie added.

Jahan rolled her eyes. "And you believe them? Never mind, let's go." She grabbed up the two sets of binoculars they possessed, and they all trooped outside.

Using the spacewalk handholds, they climbed onto the top of the *Selkie*. It was definitely a ringside seat though at a distance of half a kilometer. Jahan figuring that rank had its privileges used one of the binocular sets first.

"Tracy looks good. In his dress uniform. Medals and ribbons up the yin yang."

Dalea took a turn. "He's lost weight. Makes him look younger. Hope he keeps it off."

Kielli was using the other set. "No Empress," he said, disappointed.

Ernie snatched the binoculars. "Nah, she wouldn't be here. Going to be a reception at the palace. Read about it," he explained somewhat defensively.

"I do see the Prime Minister," Jax offered.

Jahan stared at him. "How can you see that? I mean without…" She gestured with the binoculars.

"My sight is very acute."

She studied the multiplicity of ocular depressions that lined his central stem. "You never told us that."

"You never asked. I also have three-hundred-and-sixty-degree sight."

"Oh, look, here comes the princess," Poppy called.

The two pairs of binoculars were quickly handed from person to person.

"She's in her uniform too," Jahan said.

"Makes sense, she just left active duty." Kielli said.

"Wonder who will design her wedding gown?" Dalea mused.

"Tracy's father made the Empress's wedding gown. Based on a design by his late wife," Poppy offered. At their looks she offered, "It was all in the Tattler."

"They really are playing up his humble origins, aren't they?" Jax said. "Is this planned or beyond their control?"

"I have a feeling anything the royals do has been planned down to the tiniest detail," Jahan opined.

"Oh my, she's running to him. She just threw herself into his arms," Poppy cried. "This is so romantic," she sighed.

At the same moment Jahan whispered to herself, "So fake. Good luck, Tracy."

✦ ✦ ✦

HE HADN'T EXPECTED to receive an armful of woman, so he staggered a bit when Carisa, tiny though she was, launched herself into his arms. She tilted her head up clearly expecting a kiss, and in that moment the full import of what he'd agreed to do hit him with more weight than the actual woman.

He blinked down at her. Perhaps it would ease the awkwardness when they embraced in private. He had to assume that would happen. It couldn't be a completely sham marriage. And God she was beautiful.

He bent and kissed her. Her hand tangled in his hair, and she kept their lips locked almost to the point of it becoming embarrassing. There were a few indulgent chuckles from the waiting dignitaries.

They broke the embrace and Tracy realized that it was his turn to play a role. Carisa had clearly set the tone. He pulled her in close and said, "Ah, my dear, how much I've missed you." He hoped his delivery rang truer to the assembled crowd then it did in his own ears.

"Me too, my love."

Deciding he had reached the limits of his acting ability Tracy offers his arm. "Shall we?" She laid her hand on his forearm, and he escort Carisa to the waiting flitter.

Seconds later they were airborne. Tracy stared at the window at the security flitters that surround them. He felt gauche, awkward, and embarrassed. He forced himself to face her.

"Ma'am—"

"Carisa."

"Carisa—"

"Just out of curiosity…why did you agree?" the princess asked, her tone causal.

"To be close to Cyprian." He hesitated. "And yes, Mercedes."

"Okay. If you had put Mercedes first, I'd be having a lot more trouble with this," Carisa said.

"There's also Cullen. If I'm inside the tent, he can't very well—" Tracy broke off abruptly.

"Murder you?" Carisa suggested with a small smile.

"Yeah, that."

She shifted on the seat to face him. "So, I want to get a few things straight." Tracy stiffened at the change in tone.

Carisa caught it and made a soothing gesture with her hand. "*Calmate*, I don't think my demands will be *too* onerous."

"All right. Hit me," he said.

"That's what I'm trying to avoid. I get that you're in love with Mercedes, but I expect you...actually *both* of you to respect the fact that we will be married. I'm not keen on being humiliated, publicly or privately."

Tracy nodded. "Agreed. And truthfully, I think Mercedes would shoot my nuts off if I even tried to approach her...in that way."

"Well, she'd have to get in line. I watched my father sleep with a line of mistresses, and while my mother may be a loon—oh yes, you have *that* to look forward to—it was still hurtful. I don't want to have my social set whispering *¡Pobrecito!* at every event we attend."

"No problem, but you said things. What are your other requirements?" Tracy asked.

"I want children, so I expect you to do your duty."

That froze him. In some nebulous way he had assumed there would be sex. That there might be an outcome to that sex felt like a betrayal and for the life of him he couldn't figure out why. "I...I hadn't considered...that," he stammered.

"Had a feeling. Pretty sure Mercedes hasn't thought about it either. So, you consider it now and I'll talk to Mercedes later."

He looked out the window at the rooftops passing beneath the flitter to buy himself some time. "I know this makes no sense," he hesitated. "But in some strange way it feels like a betrayal of my..." His voice trailed away.

Carisa seemed to be clairvoyant when she said, "But he's not your son. Oh, genetically he is, and it seems the approach is going to be to acknowledge your...*participation*. But the only father Cyprian has known is Boho, and his papa will return. You seem like a nice man. I expect you will love our babies too. Now I think our kissing needs a bit more practice."

Feeling overwhelmed by Carisa's commanding tone Tracy took her in his arms. It did seem churlish to refuse a princess's command, but as her lips met his he once again found himself wondering just what he'd had gotten himself into.

✦　✦　✦

THE DUST WAS choking, and the roar from the heavy equipment deafening. The noise was the point of being out here, but the dust was an irritant she hadn't expected. Mercedes pulled her scarf across her nose and mouth and led Carisa onto a pile of rubble that was upwind of the construction.

Carisa was still in her uniform and Mercedes felt strange and awkward in her long skirt. She had a flash of memory of her first-time wearing trousers. It had been terrifying, embarrassing and so liberating for her eighteen-year-old self. Before she had gone to The High Ground the closest she had ever come to the feel was wearing a split skirt when she rode. And now she saw human women in slacks everywhere. That memory also contained Tracy. Because of his tailoring skills he had helped Mercedes and her ladies-in-waiting turn their skirts into trousers. His hand had inadvertently touched her inner thigh—

She ruthlessly snipped off that line of thought, and said to her half-sister, "So, how was it?"

"Awkward."

Mercedes pressed for more. "But not horrible."

"No, doesn't mean I'm happy about it," Carisa said. She held up a hand to forestall Mercedes reaction. "Look, I get it, at some point I was going to have to marry. I just didn't think it would happen this soon."

"Cari, you're thirty-six. You're hardly a child bride."

"I know, but I've been enjoying my life."

"Aboard a warship? In the middle of a war? You have an odd definition of fun," Mercedes said.

One of her impish smiles curved Carisa's lips. "Maybe because it kept me from becoming that child bride. And war kept me away from mother." She paused and kicked at the rubble with the toe of her boot. "So, after this fairy tale wedding what's the plan?"

"Tracy becomes governor of a League world. Given his experience as the captain of a trading vessel I was thinking Kronos would be a good choice."

"Because hauling luxury items qualifies a person to run the stock market," Carisa said sarcastically.

Mercedes bristled a bit. "First, he's whip-smart and a mathematical whiz, and he has Jax who is a mathematical genius. I watched that Flute operate. He can give Tracy good advice."

"An alien as an advisor to a royal governor. Are you high, Mer?"

"Well, not officially of course, but be warned, Tracy intends to advocate for alien rights."

Carisa sighed. "Oh, *Dios* I do not foresee a comfortable future. Is he always so nervy?"

Mercedes thought back on the years and the encounters. "Yes, pretty much."

"But enough talk of my future husband. What are you doing about Talion, and won't you want both Belmanor and me back on our ships for the civil war?"

"First, you might want to start using his first name. And second, I'm hoping that Boho can avoid that depressing outcome."

"Because he's going to be in *such* a conciliatory mood after you have your little talk," her sister said depressively.

+ + +

"I'VE GIVEN SOME thought to our escape plan should Talion decide to take us all hostage."

The assembled men looked over at Paloma. The older ones with the indulgent smiles of a parent viewing a precocious child. The younger ones with frowns and resentment. Threatened that perhaps that their wives or sweethearts might begin to evince such independent and unfettered opinions in the presence of their lords and masters. Boho leaned back, took a sip of brandy, and prepared to enjoy the show.

"We're likely to be in disparate places—at various meetings and me at some tea or baby shower so we need a signal that it's time to decamp post haste." One of the young bucks opened his mouth to school her, but Paloma silenced him before the words could emerge.

"Obviously the first thing Talion's security service will do is block our communications so Fred and I have rejiggered your ScoopRings with a private setting that will issue a chime." She keyed her ring and a sharp four note tone emerged.

"And just how are we going to…decamp when our ship will be at the space station and no doubt locked into place, and we're on the planet?" The young man's tone was acidly sweet.

"We're not. There are still loyal subjects on Nephilim, and large sections of the planet are lightly inhabited. We're going to have to live rough for a while until the Empress arrives with the fleet."

"And why would she do that?" another boy asked.

"Because if we stop checking in and we've taken to the hills it will be clear that our mission has failed," Paloma explained with the air of a mother speaking to a particularly slow child.

Boho decided it was time to enter the conversation. "At that point the Empress's only play is to use force to re-establish control."

"And don't worry, Jorge, I made certain the survival packs have a few jars of your favorite shaving cream," Paloma cooed at him. Jorge didn't seem touched by the young woman's solicitousness. Boho bit back a laugh.

The meeting broke up shortly after. Boho caught Paloma outside her cabin. "I do so love watching you bust men's balls," he whispered softly into her shell-like ear.

"Really? You didn't seem too much like it when I delivered said ball busting to *you*."

"Perhaps I've grown and matured since then."

An incredulous look and single raised eyebrow followed his statement. She keyed the door and stepped into her cabin. The door closed in his face. Boho stood and nursed his newly bruised metaphorical balls and struggled to control his growing irritation and frustration.

9

YOU'RE JUST NOTHING

ANSELMO DIDN'T WANT to like the man. Mostly because Anselmo's patron despised him, but now that Anselmo was spending several hours each day with Belmanor he was starting to see why the Empress might have found him intriguing if not attractive. Compared to the handsome Consort, Belmanor was an unimpressive specimen, but there was a keen intellect behind that plain face, and a broad interest in a myriad of subjects. Boho wasn't stupid, but he could be incurious, especially about process and details. Belmanor seemed to thrive on such minutia.

They were currently in a meeting with the Prime Minister, Jaakon, the Chancellor of the Exchequer, Rafe Devris, Rogers who led SEGU, and Naranjo head of the *Servicio Protector Imperial* that guarded the royals. The subject under discussion was security for the wedding, and since it was a royal wedding His Eminence Cardinal Chaughule, Archbishop of Hisselek had also been included.

Everyone was being so very, very polite, but turgid, angry undercurrents wove between the participants. Both Rogers and Jaakon had silently loved the Empress for decades, and now were faced with the reality that this man had won her heart, taken her to his bed and sired her child. It was probably only good breeding and good manners that kept them from his throat. It was probably unworthy of him, but Anselmo couldn't help but enjoy the drama.

The Cardinal, an elegant man in his late fifties with a shock of silver hair setting a contrast to his skin, raised a new issue.

"The cathedral was badly damaged by the bombardment, and I'm concerned about the structural integrity. While we might have at least partial repairs in place by December it will severely limit the guest list."

Rohan gave a grunt and settled his bulk more comfortably. "That's never a good thing when dealing with our set. Whoever is not on the list will view it as a personal affront. Let's not have any more FFH nobles thinking Talion might have a point."

"What about the opera house?" Jaakon suggested. "It was barely touched."

"This already feels like a damn performance," Belmanor muttered. It was the first words he had spoken since the meeting began.

"I also think it sends the wrong message," Chaughule said.

The group of men sat in silence for a long moment then Belmanor stood, clasped his hands behind his back and began to speak.

"Look, since we're playing this Pauper and the Princess *telenovelas* thing to the hilt why not lean into it? Hold this wedding outside in the *Plaza de los Héroes*. Plenty of room, and you can set aside a special section for the FFH so they won't have to rub shoulders with the *hoi polloi*."

Anselmo sat up and studied Belmanor. He had come to recognize his intellect. He hadn't realized Belmanor could be commanding.

"It'll be December. Chilly and it might rain," Rafe said.

"Well perhaps the Cardinal can put in a good word for us about that," Belmanor said and there was a twinkle in those grey eyes that startled Anselmo. He had thought the man only displayed analysis, taciturnity, and grimness.

"Not a problem to rig a canopy if needs be. But only for the participants and the FFH," Jaakon said.

"Of course, covering the entire plaza would just be *too* much," Belmanor drawled. Irritation and embarrassment fought for primacy on Jaakon's face. Irritation won.

Naranjo was looking green. "This was already going to be a security nightmare. You move it outside, and it gets that much worse."

Belmanor turned that intense gaze on Naranjo. "It's a challenge, but certainly not impossible to manage. You order the surrounding buildings closed a few days before the wedding, sweep them the day of to be sure they're still empty. Put security on the roofs and on random floors. Close off the airspace over the plaza, and station police and SPI flitters overhead."

"And frankly the only people who might want to take a shot at Mer...at the Empress at this point would be one of Talion's goons, and I presume you have a list of people who hail from Nephilim, and that you have them under constant surveillance." This was directed to Rogers who gave Belmanor a *you got me look*. Rogers shrugged and nodded.

Belmanor continued. "We came through a bitter war fought mostly by the people who will be standing in that plaza. And we're most likely going to call upon them to fight another one, so let's make this a *fiesta,* food, music, dancing. And make it for everyone."

Jaakon was taking notes writing furiously on his beloved paper. Rogers and Naranjo had gone into a huddle, and the Prime Minister was preparing to heave himself out of the chair.

"And I have one more request," Belmanor said. Everyone looked at him warily. "I want our alien citizens to be not only allowed to attend but invited as well."

Silence.

"Carrying this man of the people thing a bit far, aren't you, *querido amigo,*" Rogers drawled. Anselmo realized Rogers was intensifying his upper class FFH accent. "Since they're not *people.*"

Blood rushed into Belmanor's cheeks, and Anselmo tried to think how to defuse the situation. Then Rohan stepped in. He held out his hand to the Admiral indicating he should assist him out of the chair. Belmanor did so, and Rohan stood clasping the younger man's hand.

"*Madre de Dios,* have you always been this much trouble, *chico*?" he rumbled.

"No, I used to be intimidated by you lot," Belmanor shot back.

For an instant everyone held their breath then Rohan threw back his head and laughed, setting his belly to jiggling with the force of his mirth. "Let's table this for now. It's nearly noon and I'm peckish. I would suggest we consult the

Empress on this issue."

And that's how a master politician defuses a situation, Anselmo thought.

✦ ✦ ✦

THE ROYAL YACHT had barely translated out of Fold near the edge of the Nephilim system and was making the four-day journey to the planet when the priority call from Hisselek came in.

Boho was playing bridge with Ragsdale, Benowitz, and Oldziej, but he handed his cards to Paloma, told her the bid and headed to his stateroom. His boot heels rang on the plasteel flooring as he almost ran so great was his desire to finally get to see and talk with his son.

He keyed the foldstream and Mercedes holographic form appeared before him floating a few inches off the surface of the desk. Even with the distortion of light years and a hologram he could see the tension in her face, and Cyprian was not with her.

A fist seemed to be clenching his heart and lungs. "Cyprian, where is he? Is he all right?"

"What? Yes, of course."

Boho sagged with relief, but his suspicion was not totally allayed. "All right, but again, where is he?"

"We have to discuss something first," Mercedes said haltingly.

"Something political?" Boho asked becoming increasingly puzzled and alarmed.

"Indirectly. In a manner of speaking."

Boho stiffened, ran through his recent activities prior to leaving Hisselek. Had he done something to have Mercedes so on edge? She began to talk her tone a bit high pitched and breathless.

"So, Cyprian got home…you won't believe how much he's grown. I'm so, relieved that Bouncy survived. Cypri was very upset about Myst, so if he'd lost his pony too that would probably have been just too much, but I suppose that's trivial compared with Elizabeth." She was babbling and that was very unlike her.

Boho cut off the words falling from her lips like rapid fire. "What's wrong?" he demanded.

She pressed her lips together, her eyes focusing on Ivoga working in the background, but in camera range. "Please send your batBEM away."

Boho did as she asked. "All right, we're alone now. What the hell is going on?"

She took a deep breath. "I have something to tell you…confess…really."

"All right. Should I sit down?" He asked lightly. She didn't respond to the sally, and he realized something was seriously wrong.

"Seven years ago, after Kusatsu-Shirane you know I was picked up by a trading vessel."

"Yes, I know. I also suspect it was Belmanor who owned that ship."

"How?" It emerged as a gasp.

"Had Anselmo do some digging after I found the bastard laying hands on you. I knew there had to be more to the story. I once caught him engaging in illegal activity which wasn't surprising considering his past behavior—"

"He was framed—" Boho held up a hand to forestall her saying more.

"Anselmo discovered Belmanor faked his death. Add that to a captain who didn't wait to be congratulated for rescuing the Infanta and milk it for all it was worth? That suggested he was a criminal. I was correct," Boho added. "I had a chance to kill him on Hellfire, but I let it go."

"That isn't how he describes what happened," Mercedes said, and her tone was waspish.

A twist in the gut and he demanded, "You've been talking with him? Why?"

"He kept Cypri out of Talion's hands and brought him home to me…us. There was press. Pictures. Thanks to your precious Anselmo…" The name emerged like a spray of acid, but the flicker of anger was quickly replaced with a look of weary dread.

The next words emerged in a rush. "Boho, Cyprian is Tracy's son, and everyone knows it now. The resemblance is just too strong."

For a long moment he couldn't process what he'd just heard. When it finally penetrated, he launched himself out of the chair with such force he stumbled against the desk and his hand swept through her image.

"I *will* kill him now. He violated you—"

"I came willingly to his bed," Mercedes said.

A simple statement with no emotion in the words. Neither guilt nor defiant pride or the throb of passion and infatuation. It was more devastating than a blow.

"You betrayed me."

Now the anger appeared. "Oh *please*, as if you haven't betrayed me for decades with more women than I can count. Not to mention your bastards who have cost the crown *un ojo de la cara* to keep them complacent. The longer we went without an heir it was inevitable that one of those boys would decide maybe it was *their* right to rule the League. We needed an heir, a legitimate heir, to lay all those ambitions to rest."

He gave a snort of disgust. "Right, so *very* legitimate."

"Boho, please." She was pleading now. "You understand duty. We both do. It's not like we were madly in love when we married. It was the right move…for both of us. I wish we could have conceived a child together. I really do, but we didn't, and once I discovered I was pregnant I was not going to terminate. The fate of the League depends on this child."

"What utter bullshit. You didn't keep the baby for the sake of the League. It was all selfishness. To lie to me, to make me look foolish as I lavished love on—" He broke off, unable to continue.

"Let's talk about selfishness! Why should I have been denied the joys of motherhood while you got to rut your way through the world and preen about your bastards? And is it only blood that allows you to love a child? Nothing has changed apart from an abstract issue of genetics. Cyrpi is still the same little boy you taught to ride—" Her voice broke.

"The populace will not stand for this," Boho warned. "They love me, and you've crowned me with a cuckold's horns. There is no way to handle that."

"Yes, there is. We're going to embrace it." And she laid out the plan.

Her voice became a buzz as if heard from a great distance

as the enormity of what she was demanding of him became clear. Stand next to that man. Sit next to him in Parliament. Embrace him as a brother all the while seeing that hated face in the face of his son—no, that boy.

"NO," he burst out. "I WILL NOT STAND FOR IT!"

"Yes, you will." Her voice cracked whip-like through the mic. "The engagement was announced days ago. Cari and Tracy are already giving interviews, plans are underway for a Christmas wedding. The story of how Tracy donated his sperm so I could conceive has been released. After you finish at Nephilim you're going to come home, and we will get on with the business of rebuilding."

"That's assuming we're not at war by then," Boho said, his tone nasty.

"I'm depending on you and your skills to prevent that," Mercedes replied.

"I'm warning you, Mercedes, the people will not accept you passing off *un hijo bastardo!*"

He watched her expression turn to blazing rage. "How dare you? How dare you speak of our son that way."

"Your son," he coldly corrected.

"You're going to reject him? The only father he's ever known?"

"Well, I guess he can just get used to a new one."

"You're angry. You don't really mean that." She paused waiting for him to back down. The silence hung like death between them. She finally said, "Well fine then, because the people will accept, and they'll stand with Cyprian because *I am* the Empress. It's Arango blood in his veins...and you...you're just *nothing.*"

+   +   +

TRACY WALKED AT Carisa's side through the gardens of the *Phantsiestüc*, and clandestinely studied her. Carisa was a diminutive bird, inches shorter than her half-sister, and her collarbones, revealed by her low-cut gown, etched her cocoa skin adding to the sense of fragility. Yet he knew she had fought in a war, shown courage when Talion attempted to capture her. There was clearly more to the woman then just beauty.

She was looking up toward the ruins of the main palace, her expression sad. It took all his courage, but Tracy reached out and with his forefinger he smoothed the soft skin of her forehead where a frown marred that perfect brow.

"Want to talk about it?" he asked.

Carisa sighed. "They were such beautiful gardens. Two-hundred-year-old oaks and a few pines that were planted when the palace was first built four hundred years ago. It will take years for it to be restored. It certainly won't happen in my lifetime."

"Your sister is the Empress. I expect she could arrange for some full-grown trees to be brought in. They might not be as venerable as the ones you lost, but you wouldn't have to wait for them to grow," Tracy said.

"I know." She gave him a sideways look and a smile. "But it feels like cheating somehow. Is that silly?"

Her acuity and perceptiveness surprised and delighted him. It also put into perspective his lifelong discomfort with the FFH. Everything was so easy for them which made the struggles of ordinary people seem all the more onerous and unfair.

"I hope you don't play poker," Carisa said her voice catching a bit on a laugh.

"What?"

"Yes, everything is easier for us, but it's not just rank, money can accomplish the same thing."

"God, are you telepathic?" Tracy asked.

"No, you're just very transparent. So please don't play poker or we'll lose the governor's mansion on Kronos."

Tracy sighed. "I wish it didn't have to be Kronos. I hate the extra gravity."

"I could talk to Mer," Carisa offered.

"No, she's got enough to deal with without my whining."

"I want to ask you a question, Carisa said. "I need someone to escort me down the aisle. Do you think your father would be willing?"

The request shocked him. "Uh, yeah, though he might have another stroke at the very suggestion. And are you sure? What about Rohan or Princess Estella's husband?"

"I think walking that far across the Plaza would give Rohan a heart attack, and Alfred and I barely know each other."

His errant tongue once more betrayed him, and Tracy said, "You barely know my dad."

Carisa gave him one of those looks that for a million years have made men feel that women were tapped into cosmic secrets that the other gender would never understand.

"Your father and I have been having…conversations."

"Oh, God."

"It's all good. Everything he told me."

"*That's* what worries me. What happens when you discover I'm merely mortal?"

"I'll cope."

They walked on in silence for a few more minutes. Carisa was studying his profile. "So, there's clearly something on your mind."

Tracy grimaced, sucked in a breath and face her. "Would it be horribly gauche or cause the government to fall if we had a different priest officiate at the wedding?"

"You have something against the Cardinal?"

"No, but I don't know the Cardinal, and I do know the man who's been my confessor since my graduation…though I did miss a few years in the middle," Tracy admitted. "He's currently the chaplain aboard my flag ship."

"At your request?"

Tracy nodded. "I think he kept me from, well, honestly doing myself harm after I was court martialed and cashiered."

"He sounds quite special," Carisa said.

"He is. He was born into the FFH, actually a noble family that predates the FFH, but renounced his title to become a priest."

"I think the Cardinal would understand. Could they maybe share the ceremony?"

"Sure. That could work." Tracy released a breath he hadn't realized he had been holding. "Thank you for understanding."

"Of course."

Tracy drew her arm through his and they walked on. He

was very aware of the scent of her perfume and her quiet breaths. He broached another subject. "Did Mercedes say anything…about…you know…*the* conversation. I can't very well ask her."

"Not much. Just that it went about how she expected which makes me think it went horribly."

"Of course, it did. It's Cullen." Her expression told Tracy that he had failed to control his tone or his expression.

"You really hate him, don't you?" Tracy couldn't control it. His hand went to the scar that deformed his left eyebrow, a gift from Beauregard Honorius Sinclair Cullen. "Is it just Mer?" she added gently.

"That's a lot of it." He gave her a pained smile. "Like you said, everything's easier for him."

"He was given the women you love."

"That's a terrible thing for you to have to say when you're being forced to marry me. And Mercedes wasn't *given* to Cullen. She chose him."

She slipped her arms around his waist, leaned in close and looked up at him. "And I chose you. I could have said no." She cupped a hand on the back of his head and pulled him down into a soft kiss.

It left him speechless.

+ + +

IT WAS A priority call on a frequency that was reserved for SEGU business only. Before accepting Mercedes keyed the security screens in her office. The hologram sprang to life over her desk but instead of the usual male agent an exquisitely beautiful young woman stood before her.

"Your highness, I know we've crossed paths at various social events, and I believe you were briefed on my activities during the attempted coup d'état, but I'm not sure if we've actually ever officially met. So, allow me to rectify that, I'm Lady Paloma Flintoff."

While circumspect the girl seemed singularly unaffected by those activities which had included seducing Boho when he was flirting briefly with joining in the coup. What Mercedes hadn't expected was for the girl to be so frightfully young. Gathering her scattered thoughts Mercedes said, "Of course I know who you are, but forgive me, you seem very…young for a SEGU agent."

"Very female too," the girl responded with a smile. "I'm also old in spirit. I've been working for the intelligence service since I was sixteen. Mama felt I should be useful despite the heart condition, and old Kemel knew the value of women's eyes and ears. Fortunately, Ian…Lord Rogers has the same attitude. But to business, awkward though it may be. After the Consort's initial…irritation with me it's pretty clear he took the affair seriously, certainly more seriously than I did. Point being he still fancies himself in love with me, so he often says too much."

"I take it he confided in you after our little talk?" Mercedes asked.

"Yes, ma'am."

"You seem very unfazed."

"I'd already been alerted by Lord Rogers, so I knew the part I needed to play. Your pardon, Majesty, but I fear I tossed you out the airlock. I find men always respond well to sympathy and agreement especially where their wives are concerned."

"Quite all right," Mercedes murmured, and found herself eyeing the girl with a mixture of wonder and consternation.

"Bluntly he's mad with jealousy and fury, and I think he's casting about to hit back at you. I'm going to try to be that instrument of his vengeance—"

"You shouldn't have to do that," Mercedes interrupted.

Paloma shrugged. "*No importa.* It's not like I haven't fucked him before, but I'm worried he may do something more…radical if I can't get him to calm the hell down."

"Like what?"

"I don't know. I'll try to keep you posted, but it's going to be much harder once we dock at Nephilim. If Talion is smart, he'll jam our more clandestine transmissions."

"He's smart. And vicious. You need to be very, very careful."

"I expect the Consort will protect me."

"Not if he finds out you've gone behind his back. Boho can be…vindictive."

"He certainly does seem to have a *thing* about the man in question. I best go and offer more coos and brandy and sympathy."

The image flickered and vanished. Mercedes tried to feel as calm and unconcerned as the young agent but found it impossible to quell the fluttering in her stomach, and the fact it seemed very hard to take a breath.

10

DID YOU EVER THINK YOU'D FIND YOURSELF HERE?

T HE ENTOURAGE FROM Ouranos made its way down the long gallery of the receiving room at the governor's mansion. The troops escorting them had continually referred to it as *the palace* attempting to establish Nephilim was no longer part of the League, but rather an equally powerful entity. Boho found it rather stupidly pathetic.

Their footfalls echoed off the arched ceiling some thirty feet above their heads. Massive chandeliers of stark iron marched down the ceiling, and suits of power armor lined the walls. The paintings hung above the armor were all of Talion ancestors in their military finery. The portraits were interspersed with priceless Sidone tapestries displaying scenes of battle, and various types of weaponry artistically arranged.

Paloma, her fingers resting lightly on Boho's forearm, leaned in, put her lips against his ear, and whispered, "Cozy, isn't it?"

Boho gave her a fleeting smile then returned his focus to the figures at the far end of the great hall. Talion's father, José, was a shrunken figure in the massive stone chair. His face was a nest of wrinkles and his hair had gone white.

Talion, half of his face a nest of scars curtesy of his father's training in the art of the duello, and his grey locks the result of the radiation from Nephilim's sun, was at his sire's side seated on a *fusileros* camp chair. The symbolism was glaringly obvious. For a naval officer, an admiral (before he had declared himself a king) to avail himself of a common foot soldier's chair made it clear how Talion, at least, viewed this meeting. Talion was ready for war.

Boho had only four of his security detail with him. The four he knew to be unfailing loyal. The five dip corps drones were behind him and Paloma. Following them Ragsdale and Oldziej. He suspected Ragsdale was armed. He doubted the others were. But was Paloma? He looked down at her, weighing the likelihood. Her dress was a filmy, diaphanous affair offering little place for concealment. Still, he had learned to not to underestimate her cleverness and guile. There was no obvious security in the hall, but it was certain they were present. Boho could almost feel their eyes and targeting lasers boring into his back.

They reached the Talion men and everyone, except Boho, bowed. Paloma dropped into a deep curtsy that was grace personified. Talion's eyes slid across her slender form. Even the old man straightened a bit as he studied her bosom.

"So, Beauregard, have you brought us beads and trinkets to try and convince us that we should once again agree to be serfs indentured to the League?" the old man rasped out.

Delgado who was nominally in charge of the diplomats started to step forward. Boho thrust out his arm and blocked him.

"No, my lord, I've come to offer…me. My knowledge, my expertise, my counsel, my support in your bid for independence."

There was an eruption of conversation behind him. Most of it a babble of confusion. Only Ragsdale's voice came through clearly. "You treasonous bastard!"

Boho pointed at him. "He's SEGU. These others don't really matter," he added as his security detail closed in.

Ragsdale fought and was beaten to the ground. The dip corp men instantly surrendered. Oldziej raised his hands, but the look he bestowed on Boho promised retribution. Paloma slide her hand down to grip his and gave him a limpid look. *Real or feigned?* He wished he could read her.

Once the prisoners were removed the younger Talion gave Boho an amused look. "Of all the things I imagined that was not even in the equation. You never fail to surprise." Boho started to answer, but Talion raised a hand to forestall him. "But let's talk in less austere surroundings."

"Good, this damn stone chair is hard on the hip bones," The old man grumbled. "Young lady, may I escort you to a salon where we can partake of some refreshment while these two young fire breathers plot and connive."

"With pleasure, my lord. Though would you really call them young?" she added archly as she laid the tips of her fingers on his forearm.

He chuckled and patted her hand. "Well, compared to me."

Paloma and the old man disappeared through a doorway on the right. Talion motioned to another door on the left, and Boho followed him to a high tech and very austere office.

A portable heater attempted to hold the chill of Nephilim at bay adding the whir of its fan to the hum of computers. There was no offer of refreshment nor was Boho offered a seat. Instead, Talion dropped into his desk chair and regarded Boho over his tented fingers.

"So, what the hell is going on, Boho?" Talion asked.

Boho declined to be rushed, and he was damn well not going to be treated as an underlying. Instead, he lifted an intricate glass paperweight off the desk and inspected it while musing, "I get the distinct sense your father doesn't totally approve of your actions," Boho said.

"He's nervous. He still thinks of the League as powerful. I've seen the weaknesses—"

"Which you certainly amplified when you absconded with a third of our warships."

"I'd say the fact that certain captains were open to my blandishments rather proves my point. And speaking of, let's get to the point. Why are you doing this? You're married to the Empress, father to the heir..."

"Interesting you should bring that up." And Boho proceeded to tell him what had transpired.

By the time he had finished Boho was gripping the paperweight so tightly that his knuckles had gone white, and Talion had flung himself back in his chair, and was laughing uproariously.

"Belmanor. Well, I always said that *intitulado* would go places. Just didn't expect it would be the imperial pussy."

"Don't be crude," Boho warned.

"You're the one confessing it. Though it surprises me that you did."

"You were going to hear about it sooner or later. I'd rather it came from me and not the gutter press."

Talion stood and removed the paperweight Boho had begun tossing from hand to hand and returned it to the desk.

"Look, Boho, while your declaration of allegiance will go a long way toward legitimizing my little bid for independence, I'm concerned that your devotion might swing again leaving my ass naked in the breeze. And this might also just be a ploy designed to get me to trust you, show you my military assets and my plans, and then you run home and tattle to Mercedes."

"First, you've got my ship locked down. And second, I'm done with that bitch."

"What about the current bitch you're with? What's her story?"

"My mistress." Boho hoped Talion hadn't caught his minute hesitation. "Once the word gets out there's a chance some of my old officers will swing their support to you depleting Mercedes forces further. So, do you want my help or not?"

Talion held out his hand. "Welcome to the Confederacy."

Boho stood and shook. "Mercedes was right about one thing—you need a better name."

✦ ✦ ✦

SHORTLY AFTER BOHO'S arrival on Nephilim a minor noble had managed to get out the word of the Consort's betrayal. At which point Anselmo had been swept into SEGU custody and spent eight sleepless nights and nine miserable days being questioned by extremely large and very unsympathetic gentlemen including Rogers himself. Eventually he had come to the terrifying conclusion that no matter how many times he told them that he had had no idea what Boho had been planning they were not going to believe him, and he was never going to see Julia and his children again.

When the blank metal door of his cell slid open on what he thought was day eleven (though he wasn't certain because he had been ignored for hours and he had lost all sense of time) Anselmo was prepared to be taken for execution or hidden in a deep dark hole for what remained of his life.

Instead, it was Admiral Belmanor who entered. The older man paused and studied Anselmo's bruised face and black eyes. "You've had a tough few days," he remarked.

"Whatever gave you that idea?" He tried to focus through his swollen eyes. "Come to pile on?"

"Actually no. Came to get you out."

Anselmo sat up a bit at that. "Not sure Captain Rogers will agree to that."

"Fortunately for you, Ian shares my view of Cullen. There was no planning to this. It was a purely emotional response on Cullen's part dictated by rage and wounded pride. Nothing more."

"That's rather harsh. I mean, you did fuck his wife." The moment the words left his lips Anselmo regretted them.

Belmanor smiled and it quite transformed his rather plain, angular face. The grey eyes were twinkling as he said, "You know, in situations like this it's usually best *not* to defend your former employer who has just betrayed his oath to his people. Or insinuate that the man who clearly has a very negative view of the aforementioned traitor, *and* who has the power to get you out of jail if you don't piss him off, might be the guilty party in all this."

Anselmo couldn't really argue with that. "You make some excellent points, Admiral." He cleared his throat. "Okay, so you say you're here to get me out. I assume you want something in return."

"Good guess. Yes, I do want something, but it's not all that onerous; I want you to come to work for me."

"Huh?" It was not a response designed to demonstrate his fluency with words. Anselmo rushed to add, "Why would you ever trust me?"

"Because you're ambitious and unscrupulous." Belmanor reacted to Anselmo's hurt and outraged expression. He added soothingly, "You're also clever and a master at crafting a narrative. If we've got to have a wife going to war with her estranged husband while her former lover leads her fleets, it's going to be…awkward. I think you can find a way to make that at least understandable if not palatable."

"She's putting you in command of the Blue?"

"Actually. she'll probably be making me supreme fleet commander with authority over all three fleets."

"Why wouldn't the Empress keep that role for herself?"

"Because she has to focus on rebuilding…and then there's that whole awkward thing. Captain Princess Beatrice will probably have one of the fleets, but that's a discussion for another time. Now, do you take my deal and get out or would you prefer to stay…" He glanced around the cell. "In these charming accommodations?"

Anselmo thrust out his hand. "Oh, I'm totally accepting,

but can I know how badly fucked I am beforehand."

"I'd say you're pretty badly fucked. You're in jail."

"No, no, not that. How hard have you made my job? Did you think to get a news black-out in place?"

"Immediately on getting word of Cullen's betrayal the imperial censures banned all news out of Nephilim, and the palace press office said the news about the Consort was a lie and mere propaganda."

"Okay, you did that right. It's awesome how this beloved friend to the Empress and her husband is going to be heading to Nephilim to free the Consort held prisoner by a perfidious traitor, and reunite him with his family," Anselmo said.

Belmanor gave a bark of laughter. "Yes, you are the right man for the job."

He stepped back and banged on the door. It slid open to reveal Rogers. He looked from Belmanor over to Anselmo then back to Belmanor.

"Knew he'd agree. He's a rat," Rogers said.

"I think I'd call him a pragmatist," Belmanor said.

"Either way we're going to be watching you," Rogers warned Anselmo as he walked past.

"You don't have to worry. I'm sure as hell not going to fucking Nephilim," Anselmo added with an eye roll.

✦   ✦   ✦

"WITH ALL DUE respect, Admiral, I'd wager that I know my husband better than you." Mercedes watched the blood rise in Tracy's cheeks, and he scowled at her.

The men in the conference room in the ad hoc government building all found something profoundly interesting on the backs of their hands or the table in front of them littered with plates displaying the remains of pastries and sandwiches, and cups with the dregs of coffee or tea. They didn't dare look at their TapPads or ScoopRings. She was the Empress, and she was speaking even as no one could be unaware of the currents that flowed between herself and Tracy. Their embarrassment had them all looking as though they wished they could sink through the floor.

The palace press office had put out the tale of loyal subject, sperm donation, artificial insemination, blah, blah, blah, but the message boards on community media were filled with comments about how she and Tracy had totally *done it*, followed by a raft of posts, usually from women, going *why in heaven would you sleep with* him *when you could have the Consort?* It was humiliating, but she would get through it the way royalty always had, with sublime indifference and disregard to something so beneath her. Unfortunately, it seemed her advisers were not as well versed that that particular skill.

As usual her rebuke didn't succeed in silencing Tracy for long. "And with all due respect to you, Highness, your husband won't be in command. It will be Talion, and I think I have a bit more insight into his character having served under him and played on teams with him."

"What is this with you boys and your sporting events?" Carisa asked.

It wasn't intended to be an actual question, but Tracy ignored the sarcasm and answered anyway. "You learn a lot about teamwork, camaraderie and you get the measure of a person pretty damn quick in a game. It would be good if the academy would add a lady's—"

"Women's," Beatrisa corrected sweetly. Mercedes enjoyed watching Tracy blush again this time more from embarrassment than pique.

"Women's league," he corrected, then complained, "You know in the battle of the sexes three on one really isn't all that fair."

Mercedes scanned the conference room ostentatiously counting beneath her breath as her eyes came to rest on first Rogers, Rohan, Gelb, Anselmo and finally Tracy himself.

"I'd say you still have us outnumbered," she drawled.

Moran tried, unsuccessfully, to stifle a snort of amusement. Mercedes' eyes flicked to him, and he subsided. She hated the fact Tracy had included Boho's former chief-of-staff. She knew it was illogical, but she blamed the man for this entire mess. If he'd allowed the reunion with her son to be private Tracy wouldn't be marrying Carisa and Boho wouldn't have betrayed her...at least not right then.

"Perhaps we could return to the topic at hand," Rohan said. "I'm old, it's nearly dinner time and I'm becoming quite puckish."

"You've been eating for the past three hours," Rogers huffed.

Carisa gave the old man a teasing smile. "Besides, you have enough padding to survive for a few weeks," she said, and the old man beamed at her.

Mercedes found it endearing on both their parts. She was also a bit envious. Rohan had never been so indulgent of her, but Cari had that effect on almost everyone.

Would she have it on Tracy too?

Mercedes pushed the thought aside. "Yes, all right. Let us return to the question at hand. Do we wait and allow Talion to make his move or launch a preemptive attack? Carisa, you were in his fleet. Any insights?"

"I was pretty low in the chain of command. He seemed competent. Definitely brave."

Beatrisa spoke up and asked Tracy, "I want to go back to the sports thing." Mercedes rolled her eyes, but Beatrisa ignored her. "It obviously made one hell of an impression on Tracy if he brought it up all these years later. So, what happened?"

Tracy's expression became distant. "It was the final game for the championship. We were getting our ass handed to us because of the Caladonia striker. Jasper weighed his usefulness to our team against the fact this fellow was Caladonia's best player. Jasper decided removing the man was our best chance to win so he deliberately broke the other player's leg to get the fellow out of the game even though it meant he got thrown out too."

Gelb, the other admiral in the room, spoke up, "I remember that game. It was our first year at The High Ground, wasn't it?"

"Yes," Tracy answered.

And then Mercedes remembered it as well. It was the first time she had appeared in public wearing her O-Trell uniform and trousers instead of a skirt. Condemnation in the press had been swift and vicious. And now one saw women in trousers everywhere. Times did change.

Tracy continued, "Even more than the assault it was what Talion said to me afterward that has stuck with me. He said, *winning is everything.*"

Beatrisa frowned. "Don't we all feel that way?"

Tracy shook his head. "Not like he does. Talion will fight vicious, and he'll fight dirty. He'll act without pity or remorse, and he'll risk himself and his troops to attain the victory. Believe me, he'll take the blade so he can shiv you in the gut."

"So, what is your conclusion, Belmanor?" Gelb asked.

"Don't let him set the parameters of the battle. We need to take the fight to him and hope that Flag Captain Princess Beatrisa is correct, and we'll want to win as badly as he does."

"Or we can try once more find a peaceful solution," Rohan said. Everyone stared at the old man in confusion, and Mercedes began to wonder if senility was beginning to cloud his judgment. "The Consort may have allowed his bruised ego to interfere with the diplomatic mission, but there are others with cooler heads who might still attempt it."

"Who?" Mercedes demanded.

"Me."

"You're the Prime Minister. You can't risk yourself like that," Rogers argued.

"Who better? No one will doubt that I have the authority to negotiate."

"And then Talion will have Boho *and* you at which point he has an even better claim to the League than Mercedes does," Beatrisa snapped. "Maybe you'd like to throw in Cyprian too?"

"No, but I would like Admiral Belmanor to accompany

me."

"You know I'd rather like to get married before I become a widow," Carisa said brightly.

Moran spoke up, and Mercedes had to resist the impulse to smash him in the face with her plate. "If we were to try what the Prime Minister is suggesting then we should move up the wedding. That way Prince Cullen won't be viewing the Admiral as a rival."

No was battering at the back of her teeth. Mercedes swallowed hard, noted the nods going around the room. Her eyes met Tracy's and they held each other's gaze for a heartbeat or perhaps it was a lifetime. Then he turned away and looked at Carisa.

Mercedes stood. "Fine. Let's see it done." She swept out of the room.

+   +   +

AFTER MERCEDES' DEPARTURE Rogers, Anselmo, and Beatrisa began a debate about the best date for the wedding until Carisa acerbically said,

"Umm, maybe you ought to include me in these discussions because I have to have a dress made, and no, I'm not going to get married in an O-Trell uniform."

"You could wear an old ball gown," Beatrisa teased.

"I know sororicide isn't as common as fratricide, but I could arrange for it to make a comeback," Carisa retorted.

Rohan waved Tracy over, and relieved to be able to escape the wedding conversation, Tracy quickly joined him.

"We need to discuss how to get to Nephilim. Certainly,

can't use the royal yacht now."

"We could use my frigate."

"I'd like to avoid a military vessel," the old man said.

"And I'd like to have some shielding and fire power. And why in heaven's name do you think this is going to work? And why do you need *me*?"

"Everything in good time, young Thracius. Now help me up." He held out a pudgy hand and Tracy levered the fat man to his feet. "I'll have my office coordinate with the palace about the timing. I think a nice luxury star cruiser would be just the thing."

"Yeah, and the optics on that would suck." It was Anselmo who had clearly been eavesdropping. "We've got hundreds of thousands of people living in shelters waiting for the government to help them rebuild their lives, and you have the Prime Minister commandeering a luxury liner?"

"Well, one would hope they wouldn't know about it," Rohan said. It was clear he wasn't pleased at the intrusion.

"A move that big will get out. Somebody at the company will complain to their Tia Maria or their mistress, eventually it will get to the press, and they'll be all over it like stink-on-shit. And not just about the government waste. They'll be all kinds of questions about why the fucking *Prime Minister* going to Nephilim along with the Admiral of the Green."

"Condé, I fear he's right. If this really is a clandestine effort then we need a more modest mode of transport," Tracy said.

"And it just so happens *you* have one," Anselmo said pointedly to Tracy. It was not lost on Tracy that this was his new employee demonstrating just how much information he had on his new employer.

"Anselmo's correct, I own the majority interest in a small trading vessel that has traded with Nephilim."

"Which means it's going to be recognized as yours. Which could have the Consort requesting it be blasted out of space," Rohan argued.

"Won't be a problem. We'll switch out the transponder. And please don't ask me why we have a second transponder."

"Can I ask you if you have more?" Rohan quipped.

"Once we're aboard."

"All right, you both win, we'll travel on your trading vessel which I am certain will be vastly uncomfortable," Rohan grumbled. He hitched up his trousers and waddled out the door. Anselmo soon followed, and Tracy moved to Carisa's side.

"Do you need me?" he whispered.

"No, go. I'm sure my conversation was giving you hives."

"Not at all," he lied. "But I do have to handle my part of the ceremony. Jaakon keeps badgering me for my grooms-men, so I need to get on finding some."

He left the conference room and found Gelb loitering in the hallway. The other admiral fell into step with him. "Talking about that game reminded me of our school days. When you first arrived at The High Ground did you ever think you would find yourself here?"

"No. Never. I didn't even want to be *there*."

"You deserved it," Gelb said quietly. "More than most of us in the FFH. We're required to go, our acceptance is automatic, and from day one most of us are planning to wash out at the end of the first year. You won your spot."

"As I recall you didn't like me much," Tracy said with a small smile.

"No, I didn't. I was sure you were going to embarrass me, and if you had I'd have lost my position as a prefect. Crazy the things you think are important at twenty." He held out his hand. "Well, allow me to offer an apology for that snot nosed upperclassman who didn't know any better."

"Accepted, but unnecessary. I was stiff-necked little freshman prick who thought my *intitulado* status made me more worthy than any member of the FFH."

Gelb threw back his head and laughed. "Well then, here's to pricks and snots. Wouldn't it be nice if we were able to go back and give our young selves some salient advice?"

"Wouldn't matter a damn. We wouldn't listen. Say...um...I'm told I need groomsmen. I'd be honored if you'd stand up with me."

"And I'd be honored to do so." Gelb bowed and they parted.

Tracy knew that Carisa was going to be attended by a bevy of royal sisters and royal nieces...Or were they a gaggle, a covey, a kaleidoscope, a pack, a pride, a scurry, a conspiracy...?

Tracy found himself choking back a rather hysterical laugh. He ducked into a deserted office and leaned against the wall. He definitely needed more sleep, and some way to release the tension that had his heart hammering and his thoughts in tumbling disarray.

Why the hell was Rohan dragging him off to Nephilim, removing one of Mercedes most effective military commanders when a new war was about to begin? The whole thing was insane.

But it was a mystery he couldn't solve at this moment. Right now, his most urgent problem was locating the requisite number of males to take part in this marital circus. Then he could turn his thoughts to the mysterious Nephilim mission.

11

NEVER A PRIZE TO BE WON

THEY HAD BEEN given an elegant house, or what passed for elegant on Nephilim, near the governor's mansion. Three days had passed without any word from Talion, and Boho was beginning to twitch with anxiety. He had his loyal guards, but Paloma was refusing to speak with him, or interact with him in any way.

Her bedchamber was conveniently connected to Boho's bedroom, but after their arrival she had turned on him and announced,

"*Dios,* you are a petty bastard, and if you think I'm going to fuck you after what you've done then you are stupid as well as petty. And trust me, if you come through that door, I will gut you with a hairbrush, cut off your dick and stuff it down your throat. Are we clear?"

Boho hadn't bothered to argue with her, just warned her to consider herself a prisoner, but now he was lonely, nervous, horny, and increasingly resentful. The silence from Talion made him wonder if he was in fact an ally or merely a convenient pawn? Or worse, a hostage.

Boho had thought Talion would include him as strategy was formulated to counter the inevitable attack from the

League. Boho could be helpful with that. He knew all of Mercedes strengths and weakness. He had also assumed he would be given a ship to command, and he intended to use it to finally remove Belmanor from the galaxy once and for all. Instead, silence.

He keyed his ScoopRing to summon his batBEM, Ivoga, but before he got out the first word he was interrupted by a tapping on the window. Startled he looked over and was even more surprised to see the alien clinging by his tail and feet to a pediment while he knocked urgently on the glass.

Boho hurried over and threw open the second story window. "What the devil are you doing?" he asked as Ivoga swung himself into the room.

"Talion's on his way here. Thought you should have some warning, sir."

"And how the hell would you know that?" Boho asked.

"Went to take Ulrich some coffee. He's pulling security on the roof and it's colder than a witch's tit up there. Anyway, we spotted the flitters. I took the fastest route down."

"All right. Let's be ready. Have refreshments waiting in the sunroom."

"Yes, sir." Ivoga gave him a tooth bearing smile. "Be nice to have him on the back foot for once." Ivoga shot out of the room. Boho paused to adjust his coat in the mirror then followed.

Talion did seem momentarily put out when he was escorted into the sunroom to find Boho already ensconced at a table laden with coffee, tea, brandy, and pastries. He quickly recovered and as he moved to shake Boho's hand, he smiled.

It was a smile that was like ice water down the back. It was equal parts cunning and cruel.

"So good you see you, Jasper. What news?"

Talion settled into a chair and took his time filling a coffee cup and adding a dollop of brandy. The silence continued as he surveyed the pastries before finally making a selection.

"Lots, but I'd like your…mistress to attend."

"Interesting. And why is that?"

"All in good time, Boho."

A hard, cold knot lodged in the center of his chest, but Boho gestured to Ivoga. The Isanjo slipped from the room.

Talion looked around the room. "Are the accommodations to your liking?"

"Very pleasant."

"Excellent. The house belonged to a cousin of mine. He took exception to my plans necessitating his relocation," Talion said.

The rustling of her skirts announced Paloma's arrival. She paused briefly in the doorway and surveyed the two men. She then glided forward and held out her hand to Talion who stood, took her hand, and bowed over it. But the frightening smile was still there, and Boho's anxiety kicked up another notch.

"Coffee, tea?" Boho asked with forced affability.

"Brandy. It's quite cold and I'm a child of Ouranos. I'm not used to such chilly surroundings," Paloma said. Boho tipped some into a snifter and handed it to her.

"I shouldn't be surprised you're not the typical FFH lady," Talion said. Paloma didn't answer, just regarded him over the rim of her glass. "I've been having the most interesting conversations with Señor Ragsdale."

Coffee sloshed into the saucer and Boho realized his hand was shaking. He quickly set down the cup and saucer.

"Gave me up, did he?" Paloma asked.

"I'm afraid so."

"Is he still alive or did your goons kill him extracting that information?" she continued.

"He's alive. We only had to amputate to the thighs before he decided to cooperate."

Boho jerked in horror. Paloma was hiding it better, but her eyes widened in horror before hardening as she stared at Talion. "I'm going to see to it that you pay for every moment of pain you inflicted on Constantine," she said.

"How charming. I'm being threatened by a kitten." Talion's gaze moved to Boho. "I am, however, quite disappointed in you, Boho. As an ally you owed it to me to tell me the truth about this lady. Not continue to pass her off as merely your toy."

"I had her under my eye. I knew she couldn't take any action against you," Boho said.

"You're a sentimentalist and also a roué. Charming but also ultimately disappointing. It begins to support my observation that every action you take is driven solely by emotion rather than reason. Ah well, no matter. It's good to know the weaknesses as well as the strength of any tool."

Rage began to burn through Boho's body. He stared into Talion's Janus-like face, and his hands closed into fists. "The fact you choose not to use this *tool* reveals your arrogance, and it will cost you."

"A threat?"

"No, an *observation.*"

"Touché. Well, this has been delightful, but I fear the demands of governance call." He stood and held out his hand to Paloma. "Come along, my dear."

Boho surged to his feet. "You're arresting her?"

"Of course. It will be useful to cross-check her answers against Señor Ragsdale's"

"No. I forbid it."

"Because she's a woman?"

"Because she is under my protection."

"You only have two choices, Boho. Release her to me…or join her."

That froze him. *Prison.* Potentially torture. His eyes met Paloma's, and what he read in her face curdled his soul. She was afraid, but her contempt for him overrode even the fear. She fully expected him to give her over to this monster in a man's skin. He thought of her crying, screaming, mutilated, and with sudden blinding clarity he realized that he could not bear it. His belly felt loose, shivering like gelatin, but Boho straightened and looked down at Talion.

"So be it. Whatever her fate, I will share it." Somewhere in the back of his mind a small voice was screaming *what the hell are you doing?*

Paloma gaped at him. Talion merely nodded. "So, she's more than just a potential conquest for you. And it seems you can be loyal to something beyond yourself. I needed to know. Very well, keep the girl, but lock her up tight. Ragsdale indicated she's clever and resourceful. You and I need to discuss whether we move against the League or allow Mercedes to come to us. Come to my office in three hours.

I'll have time for you then."

He swept out of the room. One of Boho's security detail stepped up and took Paloma's arm.

"No, I'll escort her," Boho said. The man nodded and retreated. Boho extended his arm and Paloma laid her fingertips on his sleeve. As they mounted the stairs to the upper floor she said,

"Well, that was certainly unexpected. Ironic how a show of loyalty to me is going to enable you to betray your wife and your government."

"I believe we met when I was in the process of betraying my wife and my government. What's unexpected is what I realized today."

"And that is?" Paloma asked as they reached the door to her suite.

"That I love you."

For once she was rendered speechless. Boho closed the door on her and keyed the lock.

✦ ✦ ✦

BELMANOR HAD BEEN given offices in the government building only three floors down from the Prime Minister's suite. Anselmo had pulled strings, threatened, and cajoled to have it fitted out with desks, chairs, couches, a wet bar, and computers so he could do his work, and the space would reflect his new employer's status. None of which the aforementioned new employer had even noticed, much less shown *any* appreciation. Which had amused Iris no end. Anselmo had brought Iris because he needed her, and he figured that Belmanor and the woman would get along. In that he had been correct.

The Admiral came striding in some twenty minutes later than normal and judging from his expression the tardiness had him annoyed.

"Sorry I'm late. The damn rings arrived and mine is too small, so the jeweler is having to resize it. Is no one competent anymore?" Belmanor huffed.

Iris was undeterred by the frown or the tone of voice and recognized a rhetorical question when she heard one. "Prime Minister Rohan would like to see you at your earliest convenience," she said.

"He does know I'm still living in his house, right?" Belmanor said acidly. "He could have told me this at breakfast."

Iris laughed. "Ask *him* to explain the intricacies of FFH etiquette and protocol. I'm just an *intitulado*."

Anselmo stepped in before Belmanor could respond. "Speaking of that. May I have a little of your time before Rohan traps you?"

Belmanor nodded and gestured toward the inner office. Anselmo followed him in. The Admiral settled into his desk chair and silence stretched between them. The man's ability to remain quiet was disconcerting.

"Well?" he finally demanded.

Anselmo sighed. "You do understand that conversation is the grease that lubricates social interactions, right? Normally a person would evince *some* interest in *why* I wished to speak with them."

"What your stalling tells me is that I'm not going to like

whatever it is you have to say. So why don't you just spit it out?"

"Okay, but before I get to that let me give you some context." Belmanor leaned back in his chair, tented his fingers beneath his chin and waited.

Anselmo unlimbered his ScoopRing and TapPad. "So, I've been polling how the average citizen is reacting to this union of a royal and an ordinary citizen. It's through the roof."

"I'm assuming that's a good thing. But your point?"

"Now that the war is over people are going to start noticing how shitty things are. Rebuilding has started, but it's not an overnight process. There are food shortages. People are going to get impatient, angry with the government when they're hungry, living in shelters, and waiting for power to be restored. You get the idea." Belmanor was listening with that particular intensity that he displayed. Anselmo did find it pleasant after years of trying to keep Boho focused.

"You're worried the support for the crown is going to slip."

"Yes. Add to that we may be asking the ordinary citizens to sign up for another war. And this one is between a bunch of FFH..." He broke off looking for the right word. Belmanor supplied one.

"Assholes."

"Maybe not the word I would have chosen, but yes."

"So, what's your solution?"

Anselmo took a deep breath and jumped in. "I know the Empress intends to make you a *duque*, but we're earning so much good will by this embrace of an ordinary citizen, an *intitulado* at that, that it might make more sense to keep you…well…as you are." The look on Belmanor's face had Anselmo hurrying on. "A man who has won high honor entirely due to his own merit, ability and bravery and not by an accident of birth."

Belmanor stood, clasped his hands behind his back, and paced away. The older man stood gazing out the cracked window, his back to Anselmo. "Do you know about the battle of Xinoxex?" he asked.

"Heard of it, can't say I know much more beyond that. I made sure to wash out of The High Ground at the end of the first year."

"The fleet at that particular battle was commanded by Østein Nass. He was a scholarship student, an *intitulado*. He won a title because of his victory at that battle, became Vice Admiral of the Blue, died a Margrave. All three years at The High Ground he was my lodestar. I always thought if I worked hard, succeeded, I'd win high honor too."

"And you did. You're an admiral. Commander of an entire fleet. You've twice been awarded the *Distinguido Servicio Cruzar*. You're marrying a princess—" Anselmo broke off. "Ah, the wrong princess," he said slowly.

Belmanor turned to face him. "When I was young that's what drove me, but age does bring a bit of wisdom." He gave a sad smile "Mercedes is not and never was a prize to be won. That's where I'm different from Cullen. I just wanted to be worthy of her. He assumed he deserved her. So yes, I suppose I can forgo having a title if it will help Mercedes."

Anselmo stood silent for a moment then he bowed to Tracy; the bow one reserved for royalty. "Sir, you don't need a fucking title to establish your nobility." Belmanor's cheeks went pink with embarrassment. Anselmo thought it was actually rather adorable.

✦ ✦ ✦

THE PRIEST WAS waiting in one of the many drawing rooms in Rohan's mansion. Or maybe this was the sunroom, or the lady's morning room or a salon. Tracy couldn't keep them all straight. Father Ken had his hands clasped behind his back, and he was studying the landscape painting over the fireplace.

"That's the Lake District," Ken remarked. "But this was obviously painted back before the Gulf Stream slowed to a crawl. Now the lakes are skating ponds."

"You sound homesick," Tracy said as he joined the priest. Their uniforms set an odd contrast in the room which had a decidedly feminine feel, from the floral print upholstery to the Dresden shepherd and shepherdess on the mantel, and the pretty blue and white Sidone silk carpet.

"At times. No one seems to know how to make a decent scone outside of England. As for clotted cream—hopeless."

"Speaking of," Tracy said indicating the tea tray already set on the coffee table. "Would you like an inferior scone?"

Ken chuckled. "Please."

They repaired to the sofa, and Tracy poured out cups for both. "Carisa is running late. Dress fitting. She apologizes."

Ken gave a dismissive gesture. "Not a problem. And I'm actually glad we have a chance to talk privately."

"Uh oh," Tracy said at the priest's suddenly serious expression.

"Why are you doing this?" Ken asked as he tipped a dollop of cream into his tea.

"Maybe you could be a bit more specific," Tracy replied.

"I'm here for your marriage counseling. Thracius, don't try to avoid this by pretending to be obtuse. The palace press officials have done a good job selling this secret romance, but I've been aboard your ships, and I know damn good and well that you've had almost no contact with this particular princess. The only one you've spent any significant time with is Beatrisa and I'm very sure you have the wrong equipment to hold her interest." He chucked a bit at Tracy's discomfort. "Also, I'm your confessor. I know where your emotions truly rest. So, I ask you again, why are you doing this? And does the princess know?"

"Since she and the rest of League knows that I sired Cyprian I'd say she knows."

"That's biology. I'm talking about emotion. Does she know that you love the Empress?"

Tracy felt a flare of anger. "Yes, of course. I'm not that much of a cad. We're both going into this with eyes wide open. We do it for my…" Tracy broke off before he said *son*. "The boy and the Empress."

"And what if you fall in love with her?" Ken asked.

The question was disturbing. Tracy stood up abruptly and walked away. "I won't," he threw back over his shoulder.

"Then this is a sham and a sin, and I'll have no part in it."

"Come, come, Your Grace," came Carisa's light soprano from the doorway. "Your title dates back nine hundred years. We Arango's are mere upstarts compared to you. So surely you know how this game of thrones is played."

Ken rose to his feet and bowed. "Your royal highness…but I don't hold that title. My younger brother is the current duke. I'm just a simple priest, so I get to be judgmental."

The brown eyes were twinkling, and Carisa responded to the priest's breezy charm with a smile of her own. "You're a rogue Father." She moved to the sofa, sat down then looked to Tracy and patted the seat next to her. An invitation with a hint of command. Tracy obeyed and Ken moved to the armchair opposite the couple.

"Father, Tracy, and I will live as a married couple. We intend to have children and raise them in the church. I believe that really should be the extent of the church's interest, should it not?"

"Am I not permitted to have some concern for the emotional well-being of the parties involved, ma'am? While I haven't had the pleasure of knowing you, I have been a friend to Tracy for some thirty years. I don't want to see either of you unhappy."

"Father, if that were the criterion before the church sanctified a marriage there would be a lot fewer marriages." Tracy stared open mouthed at his fiancée. He had never seen this side of the woman. She leaned forward, hands clasped in an almost imploring gesture. "There is so much at stake, Father, and not just for us. Please, do this for us."

"Ma'am, the Cardinal probably wouldn't be as queasy about this as I am. Why not have him officiate?"

"My fiancé asked for you, and since the groom is rarely considered in these affairs, I thought it was only fair."

Tracy decided it was time for him to get back in the conversation. "It would mean a lot to me if you married us, Ken. You were there for me while I was in jail. You were there for my father after his stroke when I couldn't be because I had to fake my death and live under an assumed name. Please, be there for me now."

"Oh dear, is marriage to me lining up to be as disastrous as all these other events in your life?" Carisa joked then leaned in and kissed Tracy on the cheek.

The priest considered them for a long moment, then shook his head and gave a small laugh. "All right you two, you win."

"Wonderful." Carisa folded her hands in her lap. "So, we're ready to be grilled and counseled by you."

"No need. After watching the two of you interact, I think you might just make a go of this."

+ + +

"LET ME SEE if I fully comprehend the magnitude of this fucked up idea. Jahan was so agitated she leaped onto the galley table so she could be eye to eye with her former captain. "You want *us* to ferry the freaking *Prime Minister* of the Solar League into the heart of an enemy stronghold. Add to that you're going to go along even though you know the man whose wife you boinked and knocked up is there and probably can't wait to cut off your balls and stuff them down your throat. *And* may I remind you the last time the *Selkie* went to Nephilim we barely escaped. So…no."

Jahan noted the trembling lips as Tracy struggled not to

laugh and it just added to her fury. He seemed to realize he was about to take his life in his hands if he had given in to that impulse. He turned it into a cough, and said,

"Get off the table. Dalea would kill you if she saw your feet on the table," Tracy said. "And I still own fifty-one percent of this ship."

"And the answer is still no. You can spout all the legalistic bullshit you want, but I will *not* endanger my crew."

Tracy's grey eyes were dancing with amusement. "Like you didn't endanger them when you helped rescue the prince, or joined me to capture that enemy ship?"

Jahan opened and closed her mouth several times and finally sputtered, "Oh shut up, and stop being right." She hopped off the table. Tail lashing, she paced the small space. "We were going to make a ton of money on a food run."

"You don't think the crown will compensate you…well, royally?" Tracy said.

"Jax gets to negotiate the fee," Jahan warned.

"Ah, so you have agreed."

Jahan felt her fur lift as she realized she had just fucking walked into it. "Well, shit," she muttered.

"Let Jax know he can drive as hard a bargain as he wants since Rohan was going to commandeer a luxury liner before I talked him out of it." Jahan's mood was somewhat lightened with that news.

Tracy continued. "Now let's get down to the details. We'll need space so you need to leave some folks behind. You won't need Kielli, you and I can share piloting and navigation. And your new procurement person, what was her name again?"

"Poppy. Probably won't need Jax either." She reacted to

Tracy's expression. "What?"

"I suppose I was hoping it would feel like…" His voice trailed away.

"Old times?" Jahan suggested gently.

"Yeah."

"No Luis either."

"I could get him. We will need a few aides de camps," Tracy said.

"You really going to endanger the kid that way?"

"He's a soldier, and if this fails and we can't stop the civil war he's going to be in worse danger. So yeah, let's get the band back together."

"We'll still be missing Graarack. Wonder what ever happened to that spider." Jahan mused then reacted to Tracy's expression. "What?"

"Nothing. Just…yeah it was strange how she left. Rohan's going to need his valet, but I can dispense with Kallapus. I'll give you the final number once I have it. And food, Rohan's a gourmand. Have Poppy make sure he won't be complaining about that for seventeen days." Tracy sighed. "Rehearsal dinner tonight…"

"And then the big day."

"Yeah." The flat delivery and his utter lack of expression told her everything.

"Hey, thanks for scoring us a reserved place up front. Press says they expect a capacity crowd for the Plaza."

He briefly closed his eyes. "You're welcome, but some of it was selfish. I desperately need some people I actually know…and care about to be there."

He vanished down the ladder toward the cargo hold, and she muttered under her breath. "Oh, you poor man."

12

HEARTS REALLY CAN BREAK

ORTUNATELY, THE WEATHER was clement enough that the rehearsal dinner could be held in the gardens of the *Phantsicstück*. The dining room at the small palace couldn't accommodate the wedding party, family, friends, and the gaggle of dignitaries who would have been offended if they hadn't been invited. And both Father Ken and the Cardinal were also present. Tracy was just grateful Mercedes hadn't sent for the Pope to officiate as had been the case with her marriage. He was pretty sure his ship's chaplain would not have been allowed to replace the Pope.

The groomsmen, bridesmaids, the father of the groom and the mother of the bride were all at one table with Tracy and Carisa seated side by side at the head of the table.

The rest of the royal sisters had been scattered among the other tables so no one would be denied royal attention and end up offended. Mercedes' table was on a raised dais with only the most senior government figures—Rohan, Rogers, Rafe Devris, other cabinet officials whom Tracy had yet to meet and the Cardinal. Tracy was grateful she wasn't seated with him and Carisa. That would have tested his resolve beyond the breaking point.

Carisa's mother, Constanza, the Dowager Empress sat at the foot of the table, and Alexander, impeccably attired in a tuxedo he had tailored himself, was at her side. Constanza was affecting a series of draperies in shades of dark grey and pale blue that while not actually mourning colors were as close as she could get without offending anyone. But the message was certainly coming through loud and clear. She considered her daughter's marriage to this *intitulado* upstart to be akin to Carisa going to her death.

Tracy's first and thus far only meeting with his soon to be mother-in-law had not been propitious. Tracy had spent a lifetime enduring open contempt from the FFH so Constanza's passive/aggressive digs bounced off him without leaving a scratch, but they had infuriated Carisa who had ended up yelling at her mother, Constanza dissolving into tears, and Tracy trying to vanish into the wallpaper.

But now the dowager was simpering and leaning in close to Alexander as he spoke with her and made certain her every wish was met even going so far as to debone her fish for her.

"Your father is a miracle worker," Carisa whispered to him. "He has mother billing and cooing like a turtle dove."

"He spent a lifetime massaging the egos and sucking up to the FFH. He's the master of obsequious." Tracy reacted to her expression. "I'm sorry, that sounded terribly resentful. Old habits." He took a breath and tried to repair at least some of the damage. "But in this case, it's absolutely sincere. He thinks you all hung the moons."

"It's all right. We're all adjusting to this new normal. Take your very attractive young lieutenant commander," she said nodding toward Luis. "He's not only attending a royal wedding, he's a groomsman, and doing an excellent job flirting with Valentina. Back in the day he wouldn't have been allowed within twenty kilometers of this event...or her."

"Yeah, and what would have happened to me," he joked.

"Horse whipped by my father and thrown into a dungeon," Carisa quipped. Then added at her most deadpan, "Good thing he's dead." A question from the gentleman to her left drew her attention before Tracy could react.

He studied Carisa's perfect profile, and again tried to shake off the feeling of unreality. He was marrying a princess. He was twenty years older than his bride. They weren't in love. They were undertaking a nakedly political act to try and preserve a throne for his son. A child he had conceived with the woman he *did* love.

Tracy looked at Mercedes and felt a stab of agony in his chest. It seemed that hearts really could break.

✦ ✦ ✦

TRACY COULDN'T GET the crew of the *Selkie* into the enclosure where there were chairs and kneelers. That was reserved for only humans, and noble humans at that, but he had secured for them a place in the first row behind the barricaded territory reserved for the FFH. The four aliens had drawn a few frowns, but Poppy had frowned right back, and Ernie had growled, and soon after the wedding mass began, and everyone forgot about them.

Tracy and his groomsmen were already at the altar that

had been erected in the *Plaza de los Héroes*. They were all looking very handsome in their dress uniforms. Well, Tracy was looking as handsome as he could manage. Compared to Luis, Valada-Viers, and Oort he was at a decided disadvantage. Jahan knew him well she could see his tension, and the dark shadows beneath his eyes told a tale.

"He hasn't been getting enough sleep," Dalea said as if reading Jahan's mind.

"Probably isn't going to get a lot tonight either," Kielli quipped. Poppy stifled a giggle, and Ernie bopped the young Isanjo on the head.

The orchestra began to play. The people who had seats all stood as the bride and her attendants entered. There were oohs and ahs as the Princess passed. Jahan checked her program. The entry music was by an ancient human composer Handel, and it was described as Air from the Water Music. Given her grace and the bride's diminutive size Carisa didn't seem to walk so much as float down the aisle.

Jahan approved of the Princess's wedding gown which added to the effect. The sleek lines were offset by chiffon draperies at the arms that made it look like she had wings. The pale gold of the gown would pick up the braid on Tracy's dress uniform, and also perfectly complimented the golden brown of her skin. The attendant's gowns had the same sleek lines absent the wing effect, but they were a rich green that gave the impression they were the green leaves and stalks supporting the golden flower that was the bride. Four of the bridesmaids were Carisa's still living sisters absent the one who was a cloistered nun. Beatrisa, who was Tracy's flag captain, looked decidedly uncomfortable in her dress. The other four were apparently FFH ladies and friends of the princess.

The heir to the throne was also in the wedding party looking adorable in a pearl grey morning suit complete with tails, and he clutched the pillow that supported the wedding rings with elaborate care. Jahan just hoped the seven-year-old was not going to have a meltdown during the ceremony. Catholic wedding masses were *long*.

The little prince struggled a bit with the steps up to the altar and tripped slightly on the top one. Valada-Viers and Beatrisa stepped in quickly and took possession of the rings. There was a moment when Cyprian's face crumpled a bit, but Beatrisa quickly saluted him, Valada-Viers did the same, and the tears were averted.

Jahan finally turned her attention to Mercedes who was the Matron of Honor. A lifetime of public functions and being drilled in deportment and etiquette from birth meant that she looked composed. A gentle smile curving her lips, but Jahan wondered what she was *really* feeling. The father of her child and the only man she had ever truly loved was marrying her youngest sister.

The Cardinal had a rich, sonorous voice as he led them in the opening prayer. After the *amen*, murmured by the several thousand people in the plaza, faded into silence Jahan whispered to Jax and Dalea,

"Do you think Rome makes potential priests submit a voice recording before they're admitted into the seminary?" Dalea gave a tiny chuckle and Jax's fronds shook, the Tiponi version of quiet laughter. The prelate then stepped aside, and the simple priest took his place.

At that point Mercedes' friend Cipriana and her son Hayden took possession of Cyprian getting him settled in a chair between them. Jahan briefly saw the sun reflect off the screen of a TapPad and nodded approvingly. It seemed that Hayden had come prepared with entertainment and had things well in hand.

The ceremony wound its way toward the exchange of vows and rings. The music was beautiful. Despite his diminutive size Father Talbot's voice was as sonorous as the Cardinal's. The rain was holding off, and the press camerabots weren't being too intrusive. Jahan had a moment of picturing millions of eyes watching this event. She hoped Tracy wasn't doing the same. It might send him fleeing. Jahan was very aware that one pair of eyes never looked at Tracy. Mercedes just kept her focus on her sister and the priest.

Tracy accepted the ring from Captain Lord Valada-Viers. Jahan had assisted Tracy in selecting the ring, not that he needed much help. A decade as a trader in luxury items had given Tracy an eye. With Carisa's approval he had selected a straight trillion cut fancy yellow diamond with the base flowing into the actual wedding band. The band was studded with tiny yellow diamonds. His band matched hers, absent the large stone, and looked good against his tan skin.

They clasped hands, and turned to Father Talbot, knelt before him and he laid his hands on their bent heads, and intoned,

"Holy Father, maker of the whole universe, who created man and woman in your own image and willed that their union be crowned with your blessing. We humbly beseech you for these your servants who are joined today in the Sacrament of Matrimony. May your abundant blessing, Lord, come down upon this bride, Carisa and upon Thracius, her companion for life, and may the power of your Holy Spirit set their hearts aflame from on high, so that, living out together the gift of Matrimony, they may adorn their family with children. In happiness may they praise you, O Lord. In sorrow may they seek you out; may they have the joy of your presence to assist them in their toil and know that you are near to comfort them in their need. And after a happy old age, together with the circle of friends that surrounds them, may they come to the Kingdom of Heaven. Through Christ our Lord."

The amen from the assembled crowd once again rose up, echoing off the walls of the surrounding buildings. Tracy and Carisa kissed. Jahan looked again at Mercedes, and Dalea put into words Jahan's secret thought.

"Well, maybe the press will assume those are tears of joy," Dalea whispered to Jahan.

+   +   +

A WHIMPER OF pain pulled him awake, and Anselmo was suddenly aware of the large wet spot in the bed. Julia was sitting up panting, hair falling over her shoulders and beads of sweat breaking out on her forehead.

"My water's broken." She gave a grunt of pain as Anselmo practically leaped out of bed. He began to climb into the clothes he had positioned for just this moment.

"Easy, love. I've got you." With an arm around her

shoulders, he helped her swing her legs out of bed. He carefully slid slippers onto her swollen feet and assisted her to stand. "Let me get you a coat."

As he hurried into the closet, he pinged Jugan. The butler looked sleepy but was instantly roused when Anselmo ordered him to have the flitter waiting at the front door.

It seemed to take a long time to get down the stairs as periodically Julia would have to pause, grimace, and hold her distended belly until the contraction passed.

"I'm so grateful to Admiral Belmanor for freeing you," she whispered. "I couldn't bear to have faced this alone."

He kissed the top of her head feeling the hairs catch briefly in his dry lips. "I know, love."

Grimacing he looked away. He hadn't told her of Belmanor's mission, or the fact that Anselmo had changed his mind and was now determined to go with him. He figured somebody had to be there to keep the two men from killing each other.

✦ ✦ ✦

JAHAN KEYED HER ScoopRing and made the call to Cuandru. Her husband's image sprang to life in the air before her as she sat cross-legged on the bunk in the captain's cabin aboard the *Selkie*. Tageri clocked her expression, and the grey fur around his mouth furrowed as he frowned. "What's wrong, love? It's Ugh O'Clock on Ouranos."

"Nothing. Just wanted to say hi."

"Attending a wedding making you nostalgic?" he teased.

"Little bit. Mostly just sad. Hate seeing people ruin their

lives."

"Belmanor's a big boy. He made the decision. He's got nobody to blame but himself."

"I know, but he's my friend, and you hate to see friends messing up."

"Hasn't he been doing that for thirty years?" Tageri asked.

"Most people would consider his trajectory to have been pretty damn good. From lower middle class to decorated war hero who got to marry a princess."

"Okay, but enough about the human. Why did you *really* call?"

"I miss you." She blinked hard at the sting of tears. "I just wanted to hear your voice. See your face."

"And," he nudged gently. "Sweetheart, you've clearly got something to tell me, so spill," he coaxed.

"How did…?"

"You don't think I know that look after all these years?"

Jahan drew in a deep breath. "We've been hired to take passengers to Nephilim. Part of a delegation trying to stop the war before it starts."

"Oh, sweets, why?" His expression darkened. "Let them use a damn military ship. You don't need to be tangled up in the human's bullshit."

"Military ship sort of sends the wrong message for a peace mission. And we are all tangled up. We've been working for them for generations and now fighting alongside them."

"Against aliens. This fight is entirely between them. It's not our fucking problem."

"You know better than that. We're inextricably linked with them. You work in the shipyards. I sell them trade goods, Shrir is nurse in a human nursing home. Shall I go on?"

Her husband sighed. "No, you made your point. I just hate that it always has to be you taking the risks."

"Hey, I'm a big girl. It was my decision to take those risks."

His quirked smiles revealed his fangs. "Throwing it back at me? No fair."

"All's fair in love and—" She broke off. "I just wanted to call and tell you…I love you, Tageri." And now she did cry interspersing her sobs with human curses while he murmured endearments to her in their own language.

+   +   +

UNABLE TO SLEEP Boho tapped lightly on her door. They hadn't spoken in several days. Paloma took all her meals in her room, and he had been much occupied with meetings as he assisted Talion. They were laying out plans for both an offensive and a defensive campaign against Mercedes and the League. He waited, but there was no response from beyond that blank panel. They had dispensed with the guard at the bedroom door. Paloma had made no attempt at escape and with guards at the entrances and on the roof any escape would be difficult.

The silence stretched on. With a sigh Boho turned to leave then changed his mind and instead rested his back against the door and slid down to sit with his cheek pressed against the polished wood.

"I couldn't sleep," Boho said softly. "I close my eyes and I see my..." He couldn't get out the word son. "Cyprian. But all I see is Belmanor in his face now. I should have known. With my hair color and Mercedes' that amber hair was impossible, but I was blinded by pride. I had done it. I had sired an heir for the League."

There was still nothing, but he suddenly had the sense that she was only inches away, listening. Or perhaps it was only a hope.

"It's hard. I loved Cyprian but when I touch that emotion it feels curdled. Not gone. Not completely, but wrong." He paused trying to gather his chaotic thoughts. "I don't know. Maybe I'm not capable of love. Mother was social, mostly worried about getting the girls married, and father was busy...always. They seemed more like business partners than husband and wife."

He gave a weary snort that was almost a laugh. "Suppose that's rather like Mercedes and me. As for the kids, it was all nannies and tutors and then school. And too many of them. How do you form attachments when you have that many siblings separated by so many years? All of us on different schedules, resentment from the younger brothers, disinterest from the girls except for hoping you'd introduce them to a potential fuck who'd be more interesting than the spouse the parents had arranged for you to marry."

He felt the hot prick of tears against the back of his eyelids. "I don't want to destroy this, whatever *this* is. And I know it may be nothing for you, but I need it, something to center me. I feel adrift, and tonight I realized that I've always been adrift. Trying to make my mark without ever under-standing that it's all meaningless if there's no one to love you while you're here and mourn you when you're gone." He heard a small sound from the other side of the door. A laugh? A sob? A half-spoken word?

Boho suddenly felt a fool. "I'm sorry, I'm not usually maudlin." He went to stand up and gave a brief groan as his back twinged when he climbed back to his feet. "I'll let you get back to sleep."

Her muffled voice stopped him before he'd taken three steps. "Beauregard Honorius Cullen, I cannot be your salvation or form your center. Only *you* can do that. I also know you're a master manipulator, so I have no idea if this is even real. And nothing you've done since I've known you, and nothing you've said tonight indicates to me that you are aware of anything beyond yourself. So, I'm going back to bed. It's only in romance novels that men are saved by the love of women. We all have to save ourselves."

13

CLUTCHING AT A DREAM

THEY STOOD JUST inside the bedroom suite of the hunting lodge high in the mountains twelve hundred kilometers north of the capital. It was another royal home whose isolation had saved it from destruction during the *necrófago* war.

Kallapus and Carisa's Isanjo batBEM had left for the lodge immediately after the ceremony ended to make preparations for the couple's arrival. Now a bottle of champagne was chilling on ice, and there was an assortment of small savory sandwiches. The batBEMs had rightly assumed that the happy couple wouldn't have much opportunity to eat during the reception dinner and the dance that followed the ceremony.

Tracy loosened the collar of his jacket and moved to the table. "Would you like a drink?" he asked.

"Please," Carisa said as she kicked off her high heels and collapsed into an armchair by the fireplace. She looked up at him as she accepted the champagne flute. "You look tired, my dear."

"That's what happens when you marry an old fellow."

"Oh pish, you're just respectably middle aged."

He offered her the tray of sandwiches, and she took a cucumber and cream cheese and began to nibble. His hand hovered over the curried chicken, but Tracy realized his gut was a small knot huddled against his spine. They had come to the moment, and he was frankly terrified.

He settled onto the floor in front of her, pulled one stocking foot into his lap and began to give her a foot massage. She gave a groan of pleasure.

"Okay, you can do that anytime you want."

They fell into silence. Gathering his nerve Tracy finally said, "So, I suppose I have to ask if you're…I mean have you ever—"

"No, I'm not a virgin. If that's what you were trying to ask." She chuckled at his shocked expression.

"Well, yes, and I'm just a bit…surprised."

"We were fighting a desperate war with no guarantee we were going to win, and I was damned if I was going to die a virgin. So, I picked someone and set about to de-virginate myself." She cocked her head to the side and wrinkled her nose. It was one of her more adorable habits. "Is that even a word? De-virginate?"

Tracy didn't respond to the sally instead he said hesitantly, "Did you…do you…love this man?"

She leaned forward and stroked his hair pushing back his bangs. "No, I was in lust with him. Handsome *fusilero* commander. Assigned to a different ship, and we held the same rank, so I didn't break any fraternization rules. And you don't have to worry, I'm not pining."

He stood, took her hands, and drew Carisa to her feet. "I long ago accepted that I could never have Mercedes."

"A very diplomatic dodge." Tracy felt the blood rising in his cheeks. She gave a small shrug. "No matter." She slid her fingers into the waistband of his trousers. His cock twitched as her fingers brushed against the sensitive skin of his stomach. "So, shall we try to make a baby?"

+ + +

APART FROM THE patter of rain against the windows and the moan of the wind through the trees the night was quiet.

Mercedes was alone.

She had tried to sleep and failed. Tried to work and failed. Only a few hours now until dawn.

The palace's alien staff had finally completed cleaning up the remains of the reception, and pulled down the tents that had shielded the guests from the winter rainstorm that had arrived just after the wedding ceremony ended.

Already the tabloid press was gushing that heaven itself looked upon this union with joy and approval because the storm didn't hit until after the wedding. The journalistic love affair would last a few weeks or months, but then they would begin to tear at the newlyweds like the eagle devouring Prometheus's liver. She wondered how Tracy with his quick temper would handle that?

The couple had probably arrived at the hunting lodge by now, and that one errant thought allowed images of bodies sweat slick and gleaming, and limbs entwining to force their way into her thoughts. She imagined panting breaths and cries of pleasure. She shuddered, sensation racing through her body as she recalled the touch of Tracy's hands on her breasts, the taste of his mouth, his head buried between her legs while his tongue brought her to mad arousal. The feel of him inside of her and the shuddering release when she orgasmed.

Mercedes remembered the arch of his rib cage. The way stubble shadowed his jaw. How he slept, one hand tucked beneath his chin. Those impossibly long lashes brushing his cheeks.

Rage drove out grief. Rage at Carisa. Rage at Tracy. At her father. Boho. Rohan. And ultimately, she stood naked before the truth. She alone had made this decision, and all the decisions before it. A sob burst from her.

There was no one else to blame.

+ + +

FORTUNATELY, WE MEN really are simple creatures, Tracy thought as Carisa's fingers trailed down his body, her nails tangling briefly in his chest hair, until she finally gripped his cock, and he began to harden at the touch. *Totally in thrall to our hormones.*

By imperial standards the room was relatively simple. The sleigh bed lacked a canopy and there was a small kiva fireplace in the corner. Kallapus had laid a fire just before the couple had retired to bed. The flames sent shadows flickering over the ceiling formed by diagonally laid *latillas* and massive *vigas*, and the light seemed to dance on Carisa's body.

Beyond the windows wind sighed through the ponderosa pines interspersed with the more palm-like native trees.

Tracy's eyes were caught by his bride's peignoir and night-gown which were all white lace inset with silver glitter. They looked like tumbled snow and ice at the foot of the bed as if the snow currently pecking at the glass had entered the room.

Tracy forced his thoughts back to the woman kneeling over him. He reached up and cupped her breasts in his hands, felt the nipples stiffen as he teased them with his thumbs. She gave a little gasp of pleasure. Tracy ran his hands down her sides to her waist. She was so tiny he could span it with his hands.

The last time he'd had a woman kneeling over him her long hair had been a cloud of deep brown and silver kissed curls, and when Mercedes had bent forward the tips of her hair had tickled his chest.

He wasn't fond of the hair style popularized by the other royal sister, but perhaps it was good that Carisa aped Beatrisa. The short-cropped hair kept reminders of Mercedes to a minimum.

Weren't you just thinking about her?

Shut up! he told himself.

He had to get out of his own head. Be in the moment. Focus on *this* woman. *His wife.* Give her pleasure as well as his seed.

Like all League males he had been introduced to the art of love at sixteen when his father had taken him to the neighborhood brothel. Lisbet had been a few years older, patient, and gentle with a nervous boy.

Years later Tracy and Lisbet had run across each other once again. Lisbet had done well, becoming a madam of her own establishment, and they had engaged in a companionable relationship for a number of years.

But he had never returned to her after finding Mercedes in that life pod. It would have felt like a betrayal of his one true love. In fact, he hadn't touched another woman since Mercedes.

Until now. He wondered if Lisbet had watched him marry Carisa? He remembered what she had said to him the last time they had been together. They had been lolling in bed in a post coital haze when he had decided it would be honorable to marry her. To his surprise she had refused his proposal saying,

"...some men aren't really seeing you...there is something just beyond their reach that still consumes them. Clutching at a dream...that's you."

Was his bride imagining another's face superimposed over his? He was trying not to see Mercedes in Carisa's delicate features, but despite them being only half-sisters there were similarities. In the way Carisa canted her head, the strong line of her jaw, the long, graceful fingers.

Oh, God, this entire situation is a nightmare. Tracy felt his erection starting to ebb.

Carisa leaned down, kissed him, and whispered against his lips. "Where are you? Come back."

"I'm sorry."

He allowed his hands to play across her body, stroking across her shoulders, down her back to cup her buttocks. Her skin was flawless with the richness of cocoa, and her eyes were the sumptuous brown at the heart of a pansy accented by arching brows like a swan's wing.

"You are so very beautiful," he found himself saying.

"*Muchas gracias*, and you are—"

He raised his head to capture her lips, and then murmured against her mouth. "Do not say handsome."

She pulled back, a mischievous sparkle in her eyes. "As if I would start our marriage with a lie." A forefinger traced his jaw line, smoothed across his brow, brushed his lips. "You have beautiful eyes, and I'd give up a year of my life to have your lashes, but the rest of your face just doesn't come out quite right. On the other hand, with your bone structure I expect you won't shrivel down into a garden gnome as you age."

"You always this complimentary?" he chuckled.

"Oh, I'm just getting started."

Her thighs were hot against his as she slid down the length of his body. Her feet tangled with his, and she leaned down to take the head of his cock in her mouth. An electric shock shot up his spine and into his gut and his cock was suddenly aching. He couldn't control the groan that spilled from his throat.

She lifted her head and looked at him. "Now we're getting someplace. I'm making it my personal mission to get you to the point where you can't think or speak or worry anymore."

She took him in one smooth swallow, her lower teeth raking along the underside of his cock. And she was right, he stopped thinking.

+   +   +

AFTER HER SLEEPLESS night Mercedes knew she could not remain in the capital brooding. Paperwork was not going to keep her mind from going constantly to that lodge. It was only two days in Fold to reach Duliahan. The capital city of New Dublin had been hit by the *necrófagos* though not as hard as Kronos where most of that planet's cities had endured bombardment, but there would be reconstruction underway, and it would be a good opportunity to be seen taking action on the rebuilding efforts. She would take Cyprian as well. Let the people see their prince. Know that the royal family cared. Also, it was wise to have Cypri seen in public as a way to show the royals weren't embarrassed by his parentage. They needed to sell Anselmo's lie.

Cypri did not take the news of their impending trip well. His face puckered and he yelled, "NO! I don't wanna go. Bouncy will die if I go away!"

Mercedes dropped to her knees in front of her now sobbing son and gathered him in her arms. "Shhh, shhh, no, Bouncy won't die. Your papa and I killed all the bad men. Nothing is going to hurt you or Bouncy or anyone ever again."

What lies we tell children, she thought. Life was nothing but hurt and pain broken up by brief moments of joy. Well, time enough for him to learn that harsh lesson.

"We're going to get to see your grandmama." Mercedes's mother had gone (*been banished*) to Dulianhan with her new husband after the Emperor had divorced her because she had borne only daughters. The irony was that Maribel had then produced six sons for Hector.

"You'll like that, won't you? Last time she showed you

how to use the pottery wheel. We can do that again. We'll only be gone a few days. Then we'll come right home. Tia Carisa and your new tío will be back by then."

"Will Papa be home too?" Cypri snuffled wiping his nose on his sleeve.

"No, Papa is doing very important things right now." *Stabbing me in the heart.* "With grandmama's help you'll make him something nice as a welcome home present. Won't that be nice?" Cypri nodded, and Mercedes breathed a sigh of relief.

+ + +

LIGHT STABBED HIS eyelids. Tracy groaned and tried to bury his head in his pillow. Even that small movement had sore muscles and bruises screaming to announce their presence. The groan became a yelp, and he opened his eyes.

Carisa stood at the window, one arm outstretched fingers still gripping the fabric of the drapes. Tracy had a moment to enjoy the angles of her shoulders, the smooth skin across her back and buttocks. She turned, smiled at him, and sauntered back to the bed. Her breasts swayed in time to her steps, and he felt his mouth go dry.

"Time to get up," she said.

"Come back to bed," he said. She shook her head. Tracy sighed. "All right, what are we doing today, and don't say skiing." It was the fourth day of their seven-day honeymoon, and if it was a repeat of the third it was going to kill him before he got to seven.

"You did really well for your first time."

"I did not. I spent more time on my ass then on my skies, and I expect I have the bruises to prove it."

"I better make an inspection," Carisa teased.

"Is humiliation also a ritual of marriage?" Tracy asked.

"How else do women remind men that you're not the Lords of Creation."

She lifted the covers and the momentary wash of cold air against his skin had goose bumps rising. She slid back in next to him. Her body was warm and fragrant with a mix of the perfume she wore, and the scent of their love making from last night. He slipped an arm around her waist, and she snuggled against his neck, nuzzling like a kitten seeking milk.

"So, what shall we do today? That doesn't involve killing your husband," Tracy added.

"Why don't we go into the village? Window shop. Maybe actually shop. There's a farmer's market. We could buy supplies and cook our own dinner tonight. Give Kallupus and Binetti the night off."

"The only thing I know how to make it something my crew called Goop," Tracy warned.

"Mmmm, sounds delicious."

"It's actually not bad, noodles, ground beef, green pepper, chili, tomatoes, cheese, lots of herbs. Mix it up in a pot."

Carisa was staring at him as if he had described cooking kittens. She shook off her apparent shock and said,

"Well, I'm a good cook, and there are these things called cookbooks. If you can read, you can cook."

"How in heaven and why in heaven did you learn to cook?" Tracy asked.

"Because the kitchen was the only place my mother never

thought to look for me," Carisa said with a mischievous smile. "The palace chef said if I was going to be underfoot, I may as well be useful, so he started to teach me."

"Okay, we'll shop and cook, but let me grab a shower first."

"Let's grab one together," she said with a heavy-lidded look.

The hot water helped with the sore muscles, but the pounding water on his bruises was less pleasant. Carisa leaned down and gently kissed the vibrant purple and yellow one adorning his left hip.

"Oh, my dear I'm sorry. Perhaps making you learn to ski wasn't the best choice."

The touch of her lips sent a shiver through him, and his cock began to harden. Tracy swept his hands down her body, then returned to cup her breasts. Her breath stuttered and she pressed herself against his body. Resting his shoulders against the tile wall of the shower he easily lifted her up to rest on his hips, her legs wrapping around his waist.

She gave an adorable little giggle as beads of water dripped off her eyelashes and lips. "This seems *very* wicked."

"But fun. Are you game?" Tracy asked.

"For anything." Then with that Arango caution she added. "Well, *almost* anything."

14

THIS IS WHAT HUSBANDS DO

IT WAS A photo op, but that vile little roach, Anselmo wasn't wrong that photo ops had their place. He had been useful in working with the local press on Dulianhan so that the arrival of the actual Empress, the Crown Prince, and one of the dowager empresses was an exciting event. Technically only Carisa's mother Constanza was entitled to that designation. She had still been married to Ferñan at the time of the emperor's death. The other discarded wives had to be content with whatever title their new husbands held. On the other hand, Maribel was the mother of the Empress which gave her significantly more status.

What do you call discarded royal wives? Mercedes wondered as the trio emerged from the flitter to tour the construction site. *Beautiful,* she decided as she looked over at her mother. Maribel was only seventy-two, slim and lovely. Of the three daughters Maribel had borne, Julieta, the most beautiful of the sisters, had been the most like her.

Thinking of her youngest sister was uncomfortable. Julieta had betrayed Mercedes and ended up dying in prison. Mercedes pushed aside the dark thoughts, and assumed the Royal Smile as they were greeted by the architect who had designed the new business district, and the construction supervisor overseeing the building. The men executed very credible royal bows, bouquets of flowers and flowery speeches were delivered to the two women. During this exchange of formal pleasantries Cyprian began to squirm.

The construction foreman clearly had children for he knelt in front of her son, and said,

"Bet you'd like to see the inside of one of those big excavators, wouldn't you, Your Highness."

Cypri gave an enthusiastic nod. "Oh yes, sir. I'd like that very much. Mama, may I?" he asked casting a pleading look up at her. Mercedes sighed and cast her eyes toward heaven.

"Yes of course Señor Belghiti can show you the…machine."

"Boys and their toys," Maribel said softly as the man and boy walked away trailed discreetly by Cypri's security team. Mercedes was pleased to see that Cyprian was keeping his hands clasped behind his back rather than taking the hand Belghiti had offered. He was beginning to grasp royal behavior and apply the proper etiquette.

Maribel continued, "You can give them a baking set or a doll and most of them will still go to the truck and the gun. I think it's wired into their DNA."

The architect gave a tactful cough. "If your Highnesses will follow me, I'll show you the plans and model for the city center." Mercedes nodded her assent, and they moved toward the pavilion that held the massive model and the holograph of the plans.

Press bots and security bots floated overhead. A number of ordinary citizens were gathered at the fencing the surrounded the construction site eager for a glimpse of their Empress. At least Mercedes hoped they were eager. There had been word that a small protest was being held at the other end of this main boulevard. Hopefully none of the press were covering that.

She couldn't worry about it, just had to hope that Anselmo had handled it. Which he probably had. He might be a rodent, but he was a competent one. He had even been back in the office the day after his newest daughter was born. Which was rather terrible for his wife, but such was the lot of women in the FFH. They had two jobs—marry well and then whelp.

"I hope you will not take this amiss, Highness, but I wished to say that my wife has ordered novenas for the safe rescue and return of the Consort. We were devastated to hear he had been detained by that traitor."

"Thank you, Señor Caracas. That is very kind, and I appreciate the prayers and good wishes. And thank you for not mentioning this in front of my son. He is unaware of his...father's imprisonment."

Mercedes suddenly hated herself and the situation. Everything about this visit was a lie. The truth about Boho's betrayal had been buried beneath a lie. Cypri's parentage and how he had been conceived had also been carefully overlaid with a lie. And honestly, she didn't give a damn about reconstruction on Dulianhan. She was here in the hope it would pull her thoughts away from a certain couple and what might be occurring in a certain hunting lodge.

Mercedes realized her thoughts were running down chaotic and meaningless paths, and she tried to force herself to concentrate as the architect began his enthusiastic description of his design; the parks, fountains, shops, and playgrounds that would weave through the towering office buildings and apartments.

She was making appropriately approving noises at the correct times, but Mercedes knew her mother's gaze was on her. When the man showed no signs of running down and was onto describing the type of durasteel and how it was manufactured Mercedes gave him the patented royal smile of dismissal and extended her hand.

"Thank you so much, Señor Caracas, this has been wonderfully informative, but I really should check on the prince and be sure he isn't pestering your workers." Caracas gave a deep bow.

Maribel stepped up and laid a hand briefly on the man's forearm. She was the first lady of Dulianhan since her husband, Hector was the royal governor, a plum dispensation for taking a rejected wife off her husband's hands.

"Your design is exquisite, señor, it will stand as a testament to your creativity for generations to come." Overcome at the praise he bowed again, and the women moved away.

Mercedes scanned the site and spotted Cyprian seated with a burly worker in the cab of a trencher. Maribel's voice broke into her thoughts,

"When will you tell him?" Maribel nodded toward Cyprian.

"When he asks."

"Don't wait that long. By the time he's asking some of his compatriots will already be making snide comments. You should spare him that."

"He's only seven."

"He won't be for long. They grow up so very fast. I know you haven't asked for it, but my advice is to send them away. Otherwise, it will drive you mad."

"He won't go," Mercedes said not needing to use Tracy's name.

"You're the Empress. He damn well better go. If he loves you, he will."

"He wants to know his son."

"Well, perhaps Cari will give him a new son to focus on."

Maribel meant it to be comforting. It wasn't. It felt as if Mercedes very soul was curdling.

+ + +

LATER, AS TRACY was scraping the last of his soft-boiled egg out of its shell, he reflected that he would never have been able to make love to Mercedes in a shower. She was only a couple of inches shorter than his six feet and built far more lushly than Carisa. He couldn't have held her while he drove up into her.

And here he was once again thinking about the sister and not his bride. He gave a quiet huff of annoyance, and Carisa raised an inquiring eyebrow.

"What is it, dear heart?" she asked.

Tracy admired her ability to use endearments that never included *my love*. He only wished he could be as generous, but he found the words catching in his throat as if fighting not to be spoken.

"Just worrying about this upcoming mission."

Her expression told him that she knew he was lying, but Carisa let it go, and soon they were taking the flitter down the mountain while their security detail and surveillance bots flanked them and floated overhead. The entire experience made Tracy feel as if ants were crawling on his skin. He wondered if he would ever get used to the omni-present watchers.

Tracy parked the flitter and assisted Carisa out of the passenger side. Tucking her arm through his they began to stroll down the main market street. Despite the chill the canvas sidings had been rolled up on the spice shop and the heady scent of chili, cinnamon, paprika, ginger, oregano, dried lemon and more that Tracy couldn't identify filled the air. Carisa grabbed a basket and made a few purchases, handing off the shopping bag to Tracy.

He trailed after her as she entered a butcher's and purchased lamb chops. As they made their way down the street various people stopped to offer them congratulations or blessings. They were never intrusive, and Carisa accepted the offered floral bouquets and handshakes with elegant aplomb. Before Tracy could react, a security agent was at his side relieving him of the grocery bags so he too could accept the handshakes and well wishes.

If the security had been uncomfortable these exchanges had Tracy almost writhing with embarrassment. He longed for the days when he could walk down a street and no one noticed him, and he felt a hollowness invade his gut when he realized those days would never return.

A few minutes later Carisa gracefully extricated them from the well-wishers, and they continued with their shopping. Tracy took back the packages and shooed the guard away. Carisa caught him giving her sideways glances.

"What?" she asked.

"How do you know when it's time to…well you know." She didn't help him out and he was forced to add "Tell them to move along?"

"You want to make sure the shyest ones get their opportunity. Once they've had their chance then I thank them all and most people are good about once again giving us our space."

"I'll never learn all this royal protocol. I think you have to be born to it," he said wearily.

"Sure, you will," she called back over her shoulder as she entered a bakery.

By the time they made it down the length of the street Tracy's arms were filled with bags and packages.

"So, this is what husbands do. They're beasts of burden," he teased.

She gave him one of flashing smiles. "Yes, also plate cleaners to finish what their wives can't eat. They are also useful when you don't have a stepladder for reaching things on top shelves—"

"You can't think of *one* other thing?" Tracy said suggestively.

"Hmmm. Well, there are these things called vibrators so not really, no…" Carisa's musical laugh rang out as he felt himself blush.

✦   ✦   ✦

"No, no, no. Taking the capital is the exact *wrong* thing to do."

The look that Talion bestowed on him had Boho repressing a shudder. The man really was a horror with those twisting white scars against his dark skin. Truly a Janus figure. From one angle a handsome man in his fifties. The other a demon. It did match his personality. Talion could be by moments charming and terrifying.

Talion's private office continued the themes that dominated the rest of the palace—martial, cold, unyielding, and frankly ugly as sin. Boho couldn't understand this Spartan attitude. What was the good of being an aristocrat if you didn't live like one? Was comfort really such a sin?

"It is my military to command," Talion said, his voice low enough to qualify as a growl.

"Not disputing that. Just pointing out that the best way to bring the League to its knees is to go after the economy. I would focus on Kronos and New Terra."

Talion leaned back in his chair, fingers playing across the ropey scars. "Hmm, the financial center and the breadbasket."

"Yes. That will pull a lot of the FFH over to your side. While it's considered *déclassé* to sully our hands with trade and commerce, we all have investments through shell companies and blind trusts. You go directly after the Empress and that will give the FFH some heartburn."

"You're quite devious, Boho." Fortunately, the other man's tone was admiring.

"Thank you. It's my specialty." He paused to take a sip of coffee. "Also, Kronos was hit hard. It won't take much to occupy the planet. There's also a major push at rebuilding going on there so you can commandeer those efforts and be the hero who brings the financial markets back online."

"Won't Mercedes make the same calculation?" Talion asked.

"Military tactics and strategy aren't her strong points. She's a great administrator, but a bit of a grind. Flights of imagination aren't in her nature."

"They do seem to be in Thracius Belmanor's nature, and won't he be commanding the fleets?" Talion asked. There was a wicked gleam in his dark eyes. He enjoyed bringing up the hated name.

"I can't imagine the other admirals agreeing," Boho said stiffly. "He's a jumped up little nobody."

"That may be, but they will if they think his leadership will allow them to win. They won't care about him being jumped up or a nobody. Winning is everything." Talion stood and walked to a broad bay window and looked out at what passed for gardens on this harsh planet. As usual the weather was foul with rain slashing against the glass.

"I had a rather interesting communication from Rohan. He wants a face-to-face meeting," Talion said.

"Did you agree?"

"Certainly. It shows weakness on their part."

"Also gives them more time to prepare, and they have what's left of the shipyards," Boho warned.

"Perhaps, but let's see what they offer. I'll want you in the meetings. Your subtlety—"

"And deviousness?" Boho added.

"Precisely…will be useful. You can tell me what is at the

root of this sudden desire for negotiation."

+ + +

THE WEATHER HAD turned to crap, and it managed to dampen even Carisa's inexhaustible supply of energy. The rich and yeasty smell of baking bread floated from the kitchen where the batBEMS were preparing dinner and mingled with the spicy scent off the wood in the fireplace. Occasionally the wind would shriek down the chimney causing the flames to dance wildly sending shadows darting into the corners of room and hiding among the massive beams supporting the ceiling.

Tracy, seated in an overstuffed armchair, looked up from the crossword puzzle he was working on his TapPad. Carisa, on the sofa opposite him, was bent over her TapPad, the tip of her tongue just showing as her fingers flew over the screen as she played a vid game. Their choices of entertainment seemed to encapsulate the age difference. Tracy tried not to feel depressed by the thought.

Carisa gave a squeak of annoyance and tossed aside the pad. "Well, I'm dead again." She untangled herself from the afghan she had wrapped around her shoulders and crossed to him. Taking the pad out of his hands, she set it aside and settled into his lap. Tracy wrapped his arms around her waist.

"Sooo." The way she drew out the word had him stiffening warily.

"What?" he asked.

"Mercedes told me that you are a very good singer."

"I was. I haven't sung seriously in years."

"Would you sing for me?" she asked, doe-eyed, her fingers playing through his hair.

"Only if you show me yours," he teased.

"I think you've not only seen but fondled most of mine," she shot back.

"Oh, come now, I can't believe your mother didn't insist that you learn to play an instrument."

Carisa made a face. "Oh, she did. But it was the instrument *she* chose."

"And what was it?" Tracy prompted.

"Harp." The disgust was evident.

"What did you want to play?"

"Either the trumpet or the flute. She wouldn't let me because she said it would make me look ugly with my face all puffed and puckered up."

Tracy couldn't help it, he laughed. Not only at the absurdity but at the face Carisa was making. "Well, I'm sure you look beautiful seated behind a harp. But seriously, the trumpet?"

"I liked the brazenness of it. The blare. And angels were supposed to play trumpets."

"They also play harps."

"Yes, the wimpy ones. I liked the fiery swords and trumpets variety better."

Tracy threw back his head and laughed again. "You were born to be a warrior, my dear."

"So, will you sing for me?" she asked with a sweetly pleading look.

"For you, I will." He pulled her head against his shoulder,

closed his eyes, and sang a Portuguese love song he had always liked.

When he opened his eyes, Carisa was looking at him in open mouthed astonishment, and the two batBEMS were hovering in the doorway of the kitchen. Tracy gave an embarrassed shrug. "Sorry I'm out of practice."

"Well, if that's you out of practice I can't wait to hear you when you have practiced." She kissed the tip of his nose. "And I guess we know who will be singing the lullabies in our family since I can't carry a tune."

The reminder of the last time he had sung—to his son and the reminder that his bride wanted children of her own—was like a punch to the gut. Tracy looked aside so those too keen eyes of his wife wouldn't see his discomfort.

15

LONG SHOTS & HAIL MARY'S

THEY HAD RETURNED to Hisselek after their seven-day honeymoon, and Tracy was feeling every one of his 56 years. His lower back ached, and he seemed to be catching a cold after the busy schedule that Carisa had set.

They had hosted a small dinner party and Carisa had Luis chortling in amusement as she described Tracy's first and only attempt at skiing. He hadn't minded being the butt of their joke, and even now the memory had him smiling as he oversaw outfitting the cargo bay in the *Selkie* with crash couches for the contingent who would accompany them on their journey to Nephilim.

Jahan was scurrying up and down the ladder as the gourmet food was brought aboard, and Dalea was adding to her medical supplies. Jax rustled about ticking everything off the list making sure nothing had been overlooked. Ernie was in the engine room making a final check. Far from being disappointed he wasn't going with them Kielli was happy to be staying on the capital world. According to Jahan he had met a young female Isanjo and they were making…plans. Apparently, romance was in the air, Tracy thought. A soft female voice broke into his rambling thoughts.

"Admiral." He turned to find young Christina Flintoff standing on the gangway.

"Lieutenant Flintoff, I thought you would be taking advantage of your leave to spend time with your family."

A strange expression flitted across her face and was quickly gone before he could identify it. "We've had our visit, and my favorite sister is stuck on Nephilim with the Consort. Which is why I'm here. I know you're taking some security. Please, Admiral, put me on that detail. My mother is frantic with worry, and it's really important to me to help."

"You're not a *fusiliero*, Lieutenant."

"I know, sir, but I'm fully qualified with a variety of firearms. My mother is always saying something about God not making woman equal, it was someone name Colt. Anyway, she made certain all the girls knew how to shoot, and of course I had to qualify at the academy." She stepped in closer and laid a hand on Tracy's sleeve. Tension was etched in her face, and the tendons in her neck stood out. "Please, please, Admiral, let me come."

"All right. Go talk to Commander Baca. Tell him I authorized adding you to the detail."

She stepped back and snapped off a salute. "Thank you, sir. I can't tell you how much this means to me." Her boot heels clattered on the gangway as she ran out of the ship.

Tracy shook his head and resumed his work. A few hours later he and Jahan were drinking coffee in the galley when Anselmo's head appeared in the access opening. Grabbing a handhold, he swung himself awkwardly into the galley proper.

"That Flute is a real asshole," Anselmo announced.

+ + +

THE FINAL WORD emerged as more of a squeak and a huff as Anselmo tried to catch his breath after the long climb up the access ladder.

"Why, what did he do?" the Isanjo asked.

"He refused to remove some of the crates and allow me to use the elevator."

To Anselmo's annoyance Belmanor laughed. "Once Jax has set a timetable nothing is allowed to interfere. So, what do you need? Another photo shoot? Interview? Tell them I'm too busy, and frankly the Princess would be a better choice."

"Can't argue with you there," Anselmo said a bit spitefully. "Though it would be nice if you'd learn to give more than single word, monosyllabic answers."

"I'm not charming," Tracy replied.

"Really? I hadn't noticed," Anselmo drawled.

While at the same time the Isanjo said in exaggerated unbelieving tone, "*No.*"

Belmanor shot them both a glare. "I hate you both."

"Actually, it's not a virtue, sir," Anselmo said. "But that's not why I'm here. I think you need to take me along."

His boss and the Isanjo exchanged a pregnant glance, and the alien choked down a laugh.

"What?" Anselmo asked. His tone petulant. How dare a BEM behave that way to a member of the royal staff?

"Seems like a whole lot of people want to go along on this Hail Mary mission," Jahan answered.

"If we could speak *privately*, admiral."

Belmanor shrugged. "Jahan has my full confidence. Anything you would say to me, you I can say to her. And I don't appreciate your attitude toward my associates. You travel on this ship you need to get the fuck over condescending to my crew."

"Well, it's actually *my* crew now," the alien corrected, and elbowed Belmanor in the side. "*You're* just a passenger."

"Yes, Captain," Belmanor said meekly, and then quirked an eyebrow at Anselmo. "So, what's *your* rational for coming along?"

"If you insist." It was said in an *it's your funeral* sort of tone, but if that's what his employer wanted then fine. "Back when I was working for the Consort, he ordered me to have you killed."

Belmanor again burst out laughing. It was not the reaction Anselmo had expected. "How typical. Too much a coward to do the deed himself. And he even shifts the job to a subordinate, so his hands are technically clean." Belmanor's tone had shifted from amusement to one of disgust.

"You're not upset?" Anselmo asked.

"Let's just say I'm not surprised. You know, if it had been discovered he would have thrown you into the exhaust of star ship if it would have saved him."

"Well, fortunately I didn't have to test that out because I talked him out of it," Anselmo said.

"Thank you, I guess. But how is this relevant to you replacing a diplomat or more security?"

"*Because I talked him out of it.*" Anselmo repeated, stressing every word. "I can keep him from acting on that impulse again, and God knows he has more reason to want you dead now. I can urge him toward his better angels, and he in turn will probably have some influence over Talion. If we're to have any hope of this mission working, you need me there."

Belmanor brought his hands down on the table. "I'll tell you what. I'll talk with Rohan. If he agrees, you can come. But it won't be comfortable. You're going to be billeted in the hold with the security detail."

"I'll survive," Anselmo said.

Belmanor exchanged another amused look with the BEM. "Well, at least we'll eat well. Rohan's presence has guaranteed that."

+ + +

MERCEDES LOOKED DOWN the length of the long dining room table. It was a dinner *en familia*, as her father would have said. He had loved those times when he got to play patriarch over his large brood. Of course, the fact that all nine of his children had been daughters had *not* been something he loved. His frustration and hatred of his cousin and heir was what had led him to push through a change in the law that would allow her to inherit the throne.

Which had profoundly changed the course of Mercedes life. Emperors had to be military leaders as well as civic leaders which had sent Mercedes to The High Ground. Where her path had crossed with Thracius Ransom Belmanor and led to this current wreckage of her life.

She forced her thoughts back to the present noting that it wasn't strictly family. Only three of her remaining sisters were present—

Estella with her husband of thirty years.

Beatrisa accompanied by a good *friend*, a pretty little girl from a moderately well to do *caballero* family who taught kindergarten. Bea's waggling eyebrows had Mercedes rolling her eyes in exasperation.

And Carisa…without Tracy. The *Selkie* had departed eight days ago and was now deep in Fold and out of contact.

Mercedes had included her best friend Cipriana McKenzie, her teenage son, Hayden, and Ian Rogers. She had also brought Cyprian to the table. She had been away from her son so much during the war that she was willing to risk a childish melt down over the main course. The little boy was seated between herself and Hayden. Between them they could probably keep the seven-year-old entertained for the duration of the meal.

The doctors had assured her that Cyprian's nightmares and occasional temper tantrums were completely normal given the trauma he had endured. Which just added to her guilt. Somehow, some way, she should have prevented that trauma.

Another black mark against Talion. Her rational mind hoped that Rohan's peace delegation would succeed. The vengeful mother reptile side of her brain wanted to beat the man into a mewling, bloody pulp. Mercedes pulled her thoughts back to the conversations around her just in time to hear Hayden saying to Rogers,

"If we are about to have another war, we'll need all the people we can get. I'm seventeen. There is no reason why I can't go to The High Ground now."

Mercedes and Rogers exchanged amused glances over the

heads of the boys. *Fire breather*, Rogers mouthed to her, and she felt her smile deepen. The head of intelligence gave the boy—*no, young man* Mercedes amended—an indulgent smile.

"There's a very good reason…you're not eighteen."

Hayden gave an exasperated huff and turned to Cyprian to help the little boy cope with cutting his pork chop, but the child was staring at the older boy with terror in his eyes.

"No, Haydy, you can't go. I don't want you to die too!" His voice spiraled higher and higher with each word.

Mercedes quickly pulled him into a hug. "Shhh, it's all right. Hayden is not going, and this will all be settled *long* before he has to go."

Cypri started up at her out of large golden eyes. "Promise?"

"Promise." Her response had Hayden frowning down at his plate.

The crises averted, Estella leaned over to Mercedes and asked quietly, "Do you think they'll succeed?"

Her Madonna-like face was placid, but Mercedes knew this last living full sister well enough to hear the strain in her voice. She knew why. Both of Estella's children were in uniform. Her son Benjamin had just graduated from The High Ground and had started his five-year mandatory tour of duty. Her daughter had only seven months before her five-year tour was over. If they failed Estella's children would be in the thick of it. *Along with a lot of other children of far less elevated families*, Mercedes added to herself.

"Rohan is a clever old fox," Mercedes said gently. "And I've authorized him to offer a number of sweeteners to facilitate the talks."

"Just don't let Tracy start talking," Carisa said with chuckle. "We'll be at war instantly." Mercedes felt herself bristle, and Carisa patted the air with a hand. "Relax *hermana*. Just teasing. And yes, I am starting to see there's more to the man than just frowns and the quick temper."

"So, how was the honeymoon?" Estella asked.

"Good. Nice."

"That wasn't what she meant," Beatrisa said with a knowing look. "What she really wants to know is how was the sex—"

"Bea, you're going to shock our more sensitive male guests," Cipriana said. She had registered the appalled looks from the men, and Mercedes stricken one.

"Oh, all right. We'll wait until we've withdrawn to allow the men their port and cigars in peace, and a chance to fulminate about how it's positively criminal how women behave today."

"It's certainly dreadful how *you* behave," Estella said, and gave the unrepentant Beatrisa a light slap on the arm.

But Mercedes was looking at her youngest sister's face and saw the nervousness and excitement. The meal she was eating became a painful lump in her stomach.

"Actually, somewhat indirectly on that topic…" Carisa took a deep breath. "I'm…I'm pregnant."

The words were rushed, and Cari's brown eyes met hers as if her youngest sister was both apologizing and begging for forgiveness. Beatrisa jumped up and ran to hug Carisa. The men raised their glasses in a toast, congratulations flew about the table.

Mercedes pushed aside the tumbling emotions. They could wait for a private moment when she could recall all the desperate years of trying, hoping to be able to say these words to Boho. And when she finally could it was lie because another man had given her the gift of her son. The man, the love of her life, who had just filled her sister's belly with a baby. Trying to cover her emotions Mercedes reached out to brush Cyprian's curls.

"How lovely. Cypri, you're going to have a new little…" She stuttered to a stop. This child would not be some sort of distant cousin given that she and Carisa were only half-sisters, but instead her son's half-sister or brother. A thought flashed past. *My God the imperial family was a mess.* And she could just imagine how the gutter press would report that. Well, she had survived worse from them. The throne would survive this too.

Cyprian looked up at her, his expression serious and she saw Tracy in the frown that furrowed his brow. "Mama, I'm mostly grown up now, and I wanna be called Cy. Cypri's a baby name."

The adults around the table indulged in gentle chuckles quickly muted at the little boy's offended look. "All right, *Cy,*" Mercedes stressed. "But you have to be patient with me if I slip and accidentally use your other name."

"I'll forgive you," he said with aristocratic hauteur and this time the chuckles were outright laughs.

Mercedes was so grateful to him for changing the subject and helping them get past this most awkward and painful of moments. She looked down at him and saw something in her little boy's eyes that made her think this had been his plan all along. He might not know why, but he knew his mama was upset and he had tried to help. Mercedes felt her throat tighten, and she hugged him close, burying her face in his curls.

16

THE LESSER OF TWO EVILS

THERE WASN'T A lot to do when a ship was in Fold. They were fifteen days into the journey to Nephilim, and the cramped conditions and the sheer numbers of people on the small trading vessel made for an uncomfortable voyage. There was no way everyone could fit into the *Selkie's* galley. So, they heated meals on the personnel deck and carried the food down to the cargo bay where everyone ate at long trestle tables that could be set up and broken down with relative ease.

Jahan and Tracy had tried to alleviate the boredom and keep tempers from wearing thin by arranging for board games and card games, and evenings spent playing Charades. They had returned to their old pattern of reading aloud after the evening meal, and Rohan had pushed for impromptu concerts. Much to the surprise of the original crew Tracy could sing. Really well. They had never known that during the fourteen years they had worked with him. When they thought his name was Oliver Randall. Turned out the pretty young lieutenant, Flintoff, had a lovely voice as well, and their duets were especially charming.

Jahan was taking her time climbing the ladder up to the

bridge as she ruminated. She eschewed the elevator because it was tough to get enough exercise on a ship at the best of times, and right now the security detail and military personnel were hogging the workout equipment. She supposed that was fair. If things went pear shaped, she wanted them at their deadly best.

She hopped up on to the floor of the bridge and found she was not alone despite the late hour. When she saw the shadowy figure, she assumed it was one of the *fusileros*, they tended to be more alert—*paranoid*—her mind supplied then the navy officers or the politicos.

But it wasn't a soldier she found on the bridge. Instead, it was Rohan's valet. He was standing at the navigation station, hand resting lightly on the console and gazing out the front viewport at the twisting fog of Fold. Like all Isanjo she was soft footed and the shoes they wore that allowed them to use their prehensile toes were equally quiet.

Since she hadn't used the elevator, the man didn't realize he was no longer alone, and not wanting to cause a heart attack she cleared her throat and said,

"Excuse me?"

She hadn't meant to make it sound quite so accusatory, but it was odd to find one of the support staff on her bridge. Actually, the more she thought about it the odder it seemed.

He turned quickly to face her. "Oh, captain, forgive me. I had no intention of intruding."

"So, why are you up here?" she asked as she joined him.

She gave him a sideways glance. Like most humans, apart from their children, he was significantly taller than her, and couldn't be more unlike his master. Where Rohan was all bulging curves from his pendulous belly to his double chins, and broad buttocks this man was spare, and now that she was studying him, she noted the bulge of muscle in his arms and thighs and the taut abdomen. *So not just a prissy manservant,* she thought. This one could probably do some damage. An odd choice for a man as sybaritic as Rohan.

He turned to look down at her, his silver hair setting a sharp contrast to his dark skin. "There are no viewports on the lower levels. I wanted to see…well outside." He gave a brief smile. "Not that there is much to see."

"That's the truth." She noticed that his hand kept stroking across the console though he seemed unaware of it. "Um, maybe you ought not do that."

He snatched his hand back. "Ah, quite. Sorry." A brief pause and he added, "Not even many messages flashing past," he said referring to the fact that Fold transmissions showed up as streaks of rainbow light through the twisting dirty cotton of Fold.

"Not surprising given that we're about to go to war." She sighed.

"If it's any comfort I think it will be avoided," he said.

"Your lips to God's ears," she said and crossed herself.

"Amen. Well, I best get back downstairs. Good night, Captain."

"G'night," she muttered.

The entire encounter and been strange and she found herself looking down at the navigation console. Then it struck her. He had avoided all the touch controls that could have interfered with the smooth operation of the ship. As if he knew their pattern and placement.

A shiver ran through her. She'd definitely mention this to Tracy when the day cycle began.

+   +   +

THE PLASTEEL WALLS of the cargo hold bounced sound, so breakfast on this final day before they reached Nephilim seemed chaotic. Maybe the voices weren't actually louder, but Anselmo didn't think it was his imagination. People were nervous. They had every right to be. Hell, *he* was nervous. They had no way to predict the outcome of this crazy ass mission. They might arrive and find themselves immediately imprisoned…or worse. He eyed the platters of steaming sausages and reconstituted eggs and found himself nauseous. Maybe he'd skip breakfast.

Once people had settled, Rohan at the head of one of the tables stood and held up his glass of juice. Everyone followed suit.

"A toast and perhaps a prayer. Tomorrow we will embark on an effort to heal the rifts in our beloved League. Thank you all for being willing to volunteer for this mission. And may God give us the wisdom and foresight to accomplish our goals."

There were murmurs of *hear, hear*, and a few amens. People drank though Anselmo only pretended too. They were down to <u>balci</u> juice, a particular favorite of Hajin and Anselmo hated the stuff. People returned to their seats and began to eat.

Anselmo reached for a carafe to fill his coffee cup when the man seated next to him collapsed face first onto the table.

Anselmo gave a yelp of alarm.

"Hey! Medic! This man has—" He broke off in terror when he realized that *everyone* was collapsing. Falling face first into their plates or falling out of their chairs and onto the floor of the bay.

Only Rohan, the Hajin doctor and Rohan's valet were still conscious. *Or alive*, Anselmo thought. His gut trembled in terror. Kicking back his chair he bolted for the elevator though where the hell he thought he could go on a ship in Fold he didn't know. He just needed to get away. Rohan's valet moved with lightning speed and intercepted him. Anselmo struggled against the iron grip. The valet raised a fist, but the Hajin doctor ran up before the blow could land.

"I've got it!" she snapped.

Anselmo had only seconds to register the syringe in the alien medic's hand before it was driving into the side of his neck.

Darkness washed over him.

+   +   +

POUNDING PAIN BEHIND his eyes and pressing his skull was the first thing Tracy registered. He forced open his eyes and moaned when the light hit them. Dalea's soft voice said,

"I've given you something for the headache. It should kick in soon."

"What the hell? What happened?" Tracy managed to croak past a dry throat and a tongue that felt too large for his mouth. Once he could focus, he realized he was on the mid-deck seated at the galley table. Rohan and his valet were sitting across from him with no indication they had been unconscious or were in pain. *Drugged*, Tracy realized and felt his muscles tense.

Dalea moved to Jahan and gave her an injection. A few seconds later the Isanjo came bolt upright, and yelled,

"What the fucking fuck?"

"Yes, that is the question," Tracy said and leveled a glare at Rohan, Dalea and the valet.

"We wanted to be able to talk with you without the chance of anyone else overhearing," Rohan said.

"What did you do to them?" Tracy demanded.

"Nothing serious," the Hajin said. "The drug will wear off in three hours and they'll have no memory that they were unconscious."

"We've reset the chronometers, so they won't notice the time discrepancy," the valet offered.

"And the food in front of them will be fresh," Rohan added.

Trust Rohan to think about the food angle after they've just admitted to assaulting everyone, Tracy thought sourly and then noticed there was a platter of scrambled eggs, sausage, and pastries on the table in front of them. He gave a small head shake and was relieved it didn't result in an explosion of pain.

Tracy forced his spinning thoughts to center. "Okay, what the fuck is this about? Are you working for Talion? Planning a coup? What the hell is going on?" The final sentence emerged far less forcefully than he'd hoped. In his own ears it sounded rather plaintive and whiny. Tracy gritted his teeth and his hands closed into fists.

"Talion? Oh, good God no. He's thrown rather a large spanner into our plans," the valet said.

Tracy blinked at the manservant in confusion. A servant, human or not, speaking up like this in front of the Prime Minister and a *Condé* to boot? It was bizarre.

"Which is why I proposed this delegation." Rohan said placidly as he filled a plate with food. "But it's going to be up to *you* to find a way to convince Talion to drop this foolishness and join forces with the League against what's coming."

"What's coming?" Jahan asked, but for Tracy it felt like ice needles ran down his spine.

For an instant he was eighteen, back at his first ball, eating oysters for the first time when Rohan had joined him at the table, and talked to him about Sector 470. The place where ships disappeared. Tracy's dawning understanding must have shown on his face for Rohan nodded and said,

"Ah, good. I see you understand."

"Well, *I* goddam well don't understand," Jahan yelped. Her fangs were showing a bit as she spoke.

"There's a sector where ships go in, but they don't come out," Tracy said tersely. "Rohan had me research it years ago." He looked back at the older man. "But I don't understand why you had me do that work when the way you're talking now seems to indicate that you know an awful lot about it."

"Yes, we do, but we wanted to begin to have certain...individuals also become more aware of the dangers. Certain individuals who could possibly be useful to us going forward. You did rather derail things when you got yourself cashiered, but we do appreciate what you did for us that led to your conviction."

Tracy's lungs seemed to collapse, breath stuttering in his chest. For an instant the room swam around him. "That was…are you saying…?"

"Yes, we're Cara'ot." Rohan paused and indicated Dalea. "Well, she's not. But she is one of our assets."

Tracy felt Jahan shrink against him. He had to fight the urge to grab her hand for comfort.

"But…but, you're human," Jahan squeaked.

"I've only done it for the past three years." The valet jerked a thumb toward Rohan. "He's been at it for almost sixty. Gotta say, the two legs two arms thing really sucks," he added, and his tone made the statement significant.

Jahan immediately understood. "You were Gaarack," she whispered. "*That's* why you were on the bridge."

"Yeah. Stupid of me but I couldn't help being a bit nostalgic maybe even a bit sentimental." He looked at Tracy. "I was also Donnel." The valet smiled at Jahan's look of utter confusion. "I was Tracy batBEM when he started at The High Ground. Back then I didn't have to hide my species."

Tracy leaped out of his chair and retreated halfway across the galley only stopping when the small of his back slammed against the counter. He found his hand desperately patting the counters, opening the drawers as he searched for a weapon. His hand closed on the hilt of a knife in one of the drawers.

"I met the real Rohan, didn't I?" Tracy rasped. "Back on Wasua on my first posting."

"Yes. That was unfortunate. Most people dismissed him as a crazy drunk, but we worried when he button-holed you.

I knew how curious and thorough you can be," Rohan said.

"Fortunately, you were so busy feeling sorry for yourself you never did," the valet added.

Tracy ignored the valet, former batBEM, navigator, *spy*. "So, what happened to him?" Tracy had to force the sound through a throat that was threatening to close.

Rohan sighed. "We dislike doing this, but it felt like the safest choice, so we…ah…removed him."

At almost the same moment the valet said, "Killed him."

"Is that what you're going to do to us?" Tracy demanded.

Rohan looked confused. "Why in the galaxy's name would we do that? We *need* you."

"Somehow I suspect that means something more than just talking Talion down from secession," Jahan said and gave a rather hysterical giggle.

Tracy understood it was a panic reaction from the Isanjo, but it still made him want to slap her. They were trapped on a ship with aliens who had an agenda he could not fathom, and who had just admitted to murdering a man whose life they had stolen.

Sucking in a deep breath he dropped his desperate grip on the knife handle and willed his hands to stop shaking and his heart to stop racing. He walked slowly back to the table and sat down. Dalea laid a soothing hand on his back. He couldn't control the flinch, and she immediately stepped away.

"Yes, we do want more than just an end to this nonsense with Talion, but that will require a bit of explanation. So, do get yourself a nibble," Rohan said. "This is going to take a while."

Jahan began to fill a plate. Tracy sat still. The valet sighed, stood up, and filled a plate for him just as Dalea returned with a cup of hot tea and pressed it into his hands.

Rohan's look of sympathy was like acid on Tracy's soul. The old man…*no, alien, Cara'ot*…sighed. "This was not how we would have chosen to make these revelations, but the situation is dire, and time is of the essence."

"Why are you talking to us and not the Empress?" Tracy demanded.

"We will in due course, but the first and most immediate issue is this idiotic civil war you children are contemplating. It is imperative that you preserve your strength, rebuild, and prepare for what is coming."

"Second time you've said that, so just what the fuck is coming?" Jahan demanded. "And please, just get to the damn point."

Rohan and the valet exchanged a glance. Rohan sighed and began. "Some two million years ago we became aware of an intrusion into our galaxy by creatures out of intergalactic space. We were uncertain of their origin, suffice it to say they weren't from around here. As we Cara'ot had done with any emergent race we attempted contact. To no avail. This assemblage of entities merely transformed our ships and moved on doing the same to anything they encountered— asteroids, comets, planets even a few dying stars."

Tracy and Jahan exchanged horrified glances. Tracy didn't need telepathy to know what the Isanjo was thinking. What could possibly have the power to affect a *star*?

"Transforms them into what?" Jahan managed to ask.

Rohan nodded to the valet indicating he should pick up

the story. Tracy realized that the man…thing…needed a name. "What the hell should we call you," he demanded putting voice to his thought.

The valet looked up. "How about Donnel? For old times-sake," he suggested as he keyed his ScoopRing.

"Jesus, all right. Fine."

An image sprang to life in the center of the table. It was a recording of a League scout ship, an older model by the design. Tracy tried to read the designation on the hull, but it was too indistinct. The ship seemed like a toy against the massive crystalline structure spinning in space before it.

"It's beautiful," Jahan breathed, staring wide eyed at the alien form.

"Beautiful and deadly," Rohan said grimly.

Tendrils extended from the structure toward the ship. Missiles were fired but there was no explosion rather the crystals crawled across the missiles, and they changed into the same form as their attackers. The ship's engines fired as it tried to flee, but the crystal lances speared it. The image changed to the interior of the ship, and they watched as the alien life form oozed through the walls turning them to crystal. Men were shooting desperately, but nothing could hold back the tide and they too became particles of crystal. The image shivered and vanished.

"How…how could you have images from inside? This is a fake," Tracy stuttered.

"We embed cameras in almost all your ships," Donnel said. Tracy and Jahan looked wildly around the galley. "Oh, not a junker like this." Tracy and Jahan glared at him. "Military ships, luxury liners. Places where we might get useful intel from important people."

Jahan looked over at Tracy. "Guess we know how we rate."

"Oh, you rate," Rohan said. "That's why we put Donnel aboard."

"Because of Tracy," Jahan said.

"Correct."

"Why? This is crazy. My dad was a tailor. I'm an *intitulado*."

"Well, for starters we look for brains and talent," Rohan said.

"Don't preen," Donnel added, and Tracy's heard the echo of his impertinent batBEM from all those years ago.

Rohan laid a hand on Donnel's arm to quiet him. "But sometimes random chance plays a role. As in the case of a young scholarship student meeting and befriending the heir to the empire. We had arranged things so Mercedes would take the throne, but she had to get through The High Ground, and anyone who could assist her in achieving that goal was going to have our attention."

Tracy had lost all interest in why the Cara'ot thought he was special. All his focus was on a single casual statement.

"Wait. What did you mean about Mercedes and the throne? How did you *arrange* that?"

"Made sure the emperor never sired a son," Donnel said.

"Why? What difference would that have made?"

"We needed to make sure you begin to utilize *all* of your population."

"What does that even mean?" Tracy demanded.

"They wanted women in the military," Jahan said quietly.

Rohan gave her an approving nod. "We were quite startled when the humans went backwards as a species. Woman had been in all walks of life including the military prior to the discovery of the Fold technology. We had thought that would continue."

"We also needed you to allow aliens to serve." Donnel shrugged. He pierced Tracy with a look. "You started that, and now that you're connected with the royals you can carry it the rest of the way." The valet looked at Rohan. "Maybe it wasn't a spanner in the works when Tracy got cashiered. Put him in close contact with aliens. Changed his outlook."

Rohan chewed and swallowed, considering then nodded. "Interesting. You could be right. Once again random chance intervenes," the old man mused.

"Lucky for us random chance seems to be on our side," Donnel said, the words dripping with sarcasm.

"Perhaps it isn't so random," Dalea said softly. "Perhaps there is a plan." Tracy recalled that Dalea was religious.

Donnel gave a derisive snort. "Which deity we talking about here? Pukke? Nihan? The threesome the humans venerate. Or is it four? Does Allah count? How about that pantheon that the Sidone worship?"

"Can we please stay focused?" Rohan huffed. "Tomorrow, we reach Nephilim and you must find a way to end this war before it starts. You may show Talion and Cullen the recordings of the *ke'luukale'tulaslatea'chakutra'hhakt'ne-nana*—"

Jahan's eyes widened at the explosion of sounds. "*Gesundheit*," she said. "What the fuck was that?"

Rohan looked miffed. "What we call the creatures."

"Yeah, that's not gonna fly," the Isanjo said.

"Well, what would you suggest?" Rohan asked stiffly.

Tracy was watching the ship and crew die on an endless loop. "A nightmare," he whispered. He shook off the dread and met the alien's eyes. "Let's wake up Anselmo and put him on it. I can guarantee you he'll come up with something."

"All in good time. For now, let us please keep this just been the five of us," Rohan said.

"Sounds like you are going to help us," Donnel said.

"Yeah," Tracy said. "Because right now you bastards are definitely the lesser of two evils."

Donnel just smiled at the snarled delivery. Tracy longed to wipe that smile away...preferably with his fist.

17

GENERAL IDIOCY

T HEY WERE WAITING in the long gallery of the governor's mansion now renamed Heaven's Palace. The martial decor set a rather ironic counterpoint to the new name, Boho reflected, but then Talion was not a particularly subtle or thoughtful man.

The sound of boot heels on slate floor was ear splitting as the League delegation approached. Boho's eyes ranged across the group, and he stiffened when he spotted Belmanor who had been partially obscured behind Rohan's bulk. The gall of Rohan bringing Belmanor to this meeting had Boho fuming.

He leaned over and whispered to Talion, "It's a damn affront! Does Rohan want these talks to fail before they even start?"

"What? You're not delighted to greet your new brother-in-law, Boho?"

"Damn it, Jasper, I will not tolerate this. Send him packing."

"It's not *my* wife's lover in the party, so I don't really care." Boho's teeth ground together with enough force to send a flare of pain through his jaw. "And these talks are going to fail. I have no intention of again bending the knee to your wife. I'm just winning the perception war by showing how open and reasonable I am." Talion shrugged. "It should reassure any of my citizens who might be a bit queasy over our independence."

"Fine," Boho muttered, and he tried to calm his racing nerves by studying the rest of the delegation.

It was an odd mix. In addition to Rohan and fucking Belmanor there was the Isanjo pet of Belmanor's, and Rohan's valet. *Why the devil were they there?* And adding insult to injury—Anselmo was among the crowd. Boho's eyes narrowed in fury, and the man, after catching Boho's withering look, had the temerity to just shrug as if his betrayal was a mere nothing.

There was the usual security detail, but Boho's eyes widened when he spotted Paloma's foster sister, Christina, among them. She was navy so her inclusion with the trooper detail was unusual. On the other hand, her sister was trapped here. Perhaps that was why she had been included despite not being a *fusilero*.

Rohan was all hail-fellow-well-met as he waddled forward to meet Talion, his plump, soft hand outstretched. "Jasper, dear boy, what a pleasure. And Boho. Seems like only yesterday I was watching you both graduate from The High Ground."

Boho was amused by the old man's obvious ploy to belittle and infantilize them, but he wondered how Talion would handle the obvious insult wrapped in bonhomie.

"You do understand that I have your ship locked down, and an entire military at my command, Danilo. You'd be wise to show some respect," Talion said to the old man.

Boho approved. The use of the *Conde's* first name, the reminder they could easily become prisoners, (and if Boho had anything to say about it that was going to be Belmanor's fate) turned the ploy back on Rohan.

Rohan gave a deep belly laugh, and an errant wave of his hand. "All right, we've both thrown a few elbows and registered our disdain, but the time for games is past. If we are to survive, we must put aside our differences and join forces."

Talion gave a slow, mocking clap. "Bravo, Danilo, I hadn't expected you to go to such a pathetic argument quite so quickly."

Belmanor elbowed his way forward, mouth pulled down in a sulk, frown wrinkling his forehead. "Oh, for fuck's sake. He's not kidding, but we need privacy for this discussion. So, can we dispense with all this aristocratic posturing and dick waving and get on with it?"

Removing his glove as he stepped forward Boho said, "Be silent. Your betters are speaking."

He was ready to slap that homely face and issue his challenge when from the corner of his eye he caught sudden movement from among the *fusileros*. It was Paloma's sister, shoving forward, her face twisted in fury, teeth bared. Her pistol was in her hand.

"You bastard! You monster! You killed my mother!" she screamed as she brought up the pistol.

The room erupted in shouts of alarm, guards from both sides tried to grab at her, but she deftly dodged them. The muzzle of the gun seemed enormous as Bobo gaped at it, a yawning darkness waiting to spit death.

And here I always thought I'd be shot by a jealous husband, not an angry sister, Boho thought before panic froze both his mind and his body.

+   +   +

HE'D HEARD OTHER soldiers say that time dilates when you're in a crisis. Tracy had never experienced it. Until now. He had been shot at many times over the course of his military career, and in those cases, time had seemed to speed up leaving him breathless, heart hammering, and his sphincter clenching in fear. But in this moment, everything had slowed down as his mind raced along branching futures.

I stay still and let Flintoff kill Cullen and free Mercedes.

But what of Carisa? Leave her after not even a month of marriage?

Would Mercedes ever forgive me?

What would Cullen's death do to Cyprian?

But fuck, Cullen's a coward, a bully, a philanderer...I hate him...He doesn't deserve...

And he can rally the populace in a way I can't.

Cullen might make the difference between survival or death.

For the people I love...

Tracy flung himself in front of Cullen.

+   +   +

IF THE FOOTFALLS had been loud in this ugly room, then the two gunshots were deafening. Particularly with her sensitive

Isanjo ears. Add to that that everyone was screaming, shouting, and cursing. Jahan realized she was doing the same and clamped her teeth together to quiet herself. Right now, the only thing that mattered was getting to Tracy.

She grabbed the belt of one of the troopers and pulled herself onto his shoulders. He yelled in alarm, and tried to clutch at her, but before he could get a grip, she had launched herself off him and onto the shoulders of another. From there she jumped straight up and caught the finial at the base of one of the iron chandeliers. She swung for a moment to build up momentum then released and went soaring toward where Tracy lay bleeding on the stone floor.

During her leap she looked down and saw two *fusileros* wrestle Christina to the floor and disarm her. Luis was shoving aside aides and soldiers to reach Tracy. Then she had to prepare for her landing.

Despite bending her knees to absorb the force she landed hard and almost toppled onto Tracy. Jahan's abrupt arrival startled the Consort who was staring opened mouthed at his wounded rival.

"Well don't just stand there!" Jahan snapped at the human. "Get me something to staunch the bleeding. We gotta get pressure on these."

She was trying to sound authoritative and calm, but her stomach was quivering for one bullet had hit Tracy in the chest and the other in the stomach. Cullen continued to just stand staring down at Tracy.

"For fuck sake, snap out of it, you *pendejo* motherfucker! He took the bullets that were meant for *you*." She was screaming at him.

Jahan watched the conflicting emotions flowing across Boho's face. Talion was on his ScoopRing calling for medical help. Then Luis was at her side, pulling off his uniform jacket.

"Here," he said and shoved it into her hands. Jahan used her claws to rip out the arms and folded them into pads that she laid over the wounds.

"I need a way to secure them." Tracy's blood was sticky against her fur, the sweet sickly smell nauseating. Talion and Luis pulled off their belts and hooked them together. Then the men lifted Tracy so she could reach underneath him and tighten the belts on the pad on his chest. Rohan removed his belt, and Jahan used that one to hold the pad in place on Tracy's belly. She noticed that Rohan was holding up his trousers with one hand.

That's all we need…to see the Prime Minister's heuvos and pinga. Didn't the Cara'ot replace those too? Must have or his wife would have noticed. She bit back a hysterical giggle.

"Medical is on the way," Talion said. He was grimacing which pulled the scars on his right cheek into a gargoyle's mask.

Jahan was embarrassed to suddenly find tears flooding her eyes. Luis's hand was on her shoulder offering comfort. "Please don't let him die. We need him," she whispered, and to her eternal shame she began to sob.

✦　✦　✦

MEDICAL STAFF RUSHED into the grand hall and began working on the Admiral. The soldiers were pulling Christina to her feet. The rage that had twisted her face was gone. Now she looked lost, young, and devastated.

"I didn't mean to. I didn't mean to. Why did he do that? I didn't mean to. He deserves to die," she sobbed.

Anselmo shook his head trying to sort out the various *he's* in her hysterical babble. Tracy was loaded onto a stretcher and rushed away. The young lieutenant commander and the Isanjo captain accompanying him. Talion was issuing orders to his security forces to take the woman into custody, and the head of Rohan's security detail was indicating quite firmly that Lieutenant Flintoff was their problem and would remain with them.

Rohan and his valet were looking very grim as they went to join Boho whose confusion was evident on his face. Anselmo decided to see what the powerful and well connected were going to discuss and he drifted into their orbit. Oddly enough the Consort was echoing the distraught girl.

"Why did he do that?" Boho said. "We hate each other. I was going to challenge him. Kill him. Why would Belmanor do that?"

"Because he knows that we need you," Rohan said. His voice had dropped several octaves and seemed to come rumbling from deep in his gut. "Without you, *all* of you there may be no hope for any of us."

At another time Anselmo would have rolled his eyes and shrugged thinking this hyperbole. Sure, a civil war was never a good thing, but there was something in Rohan's voice, and the valet's stance that felt like he wasn't talking about Talion's little tinpot kingdom, but something much more deadly and dangerous. Something that had fuck all to do with their mission. A prickling ran down Anselmo's spine as if ice spiders were nesting in his flesh. He shivered and started to back away. He didn't want to know.

But Rohan spotted him before he could make his escape. "Oh, no. No, no, no. Thanks to your general idiocy we don't have Belmanor for this meeting, so you can fill in." At his valet's incredulous look, the Prime Minister added, "He probably needs to hear this anyway. Like Tracy said, he's the closest thing we have to a minister of propaganda. We're going to need him."

"Hey!" Anselmo cried.

"That was a compliment," the old man growled. "Now come along."

✦   ✦   ✦

"YOU ARRANGED THINGS, so the League went without an heir for twenty years," Boho said slowly, almost thoughtfully.

That tiny detail had slipped out during the surreal briefing that had been delivered by Rohan and his valet. Boho's own voice sounded like a strangers' to him. But as he sat with what he had just learned the rage began to flick along his nerve endings. These fucking aliens had essentially cock blocked him for two decades. If they hadn't, he and Mercedes might have had a quiver full of kids by now. Mercedes might never have gone to Belmnor's bed. The chair screeched across the marble floor as Boho leaped abruptly to his feet, and he found his voice.

"You fucking BEMs ruined my marriage!" he bellowed.

Rohan and his valet were unmoved. Boho's traitorous

former chief of staff shrank back in his chair. Talion raised an eyebrow and gave him an incredulous look.

"Really?" Talion drawled. "We've just learned the Prime Minster is an alien who stole the identity of the human Chancellor of the Exchequer fifty odd years ago. We're about to be invaded by an alien threat that could destroy all life in our galaxy. And *this* is where you place your focus?"

"Shut up, Talion. You've got your passel of kids and maybe they're all yours." Talion tensed at the implication and started to come out of his chair. "I will not be insulted. I will have—"

Anselmo interrupted. "Maybe less dick waving more sphincter clenching are in order?" he said wearily.

The reminder of what the three human men had watched moments before had both Boho and Talion dropping back into their chairs. A deep quiver settled into Boho's belly as he gazed again at the hologram of a ship's death that was suspended over the center of the desk in Talion's office and playing on an endless loop.

Boho had known all the men who had been aboard the last ship sent into sector 470. He knew it was the place where emperors sent troublesome individuals. It had even been used once by Mercedes. She had packed a ship with the men who had schemed with Boho to sell promotions and captaincies and sent them off to a fate unknown while still keeping her royal hands nice and clean. But now their fate was no longer unknown. Boho knew just how they had died. It sent another shudder through his body. He could so easily have been among them if Mercedes hadn't been merciful and protected him.

And then that damn valet had said something about how the Cara'ot harvested, pruned, grafted, and seeded DNA to get the desired results, and Cyprian had been mentioned, and Boho didn't need to be a genius to grasp that the Cara'ot had decided *he* was not an appropriate stud to sire the next emperor of the Solar League.

"Look, we needed the right heir," the valet said as if reading Boho's thoughts.

Anselmo huffed in disgust, threw his hands in the air, and threw his body against the back of his chair. "Really, we're going back to that?"

Rohan smiled at the younger man. "Do give poor Boho a chance to come to grips with all of this. The threat is not yet on our doorstep."

"Just doorstep adjacent," Anselmo muttered.

Rohan turned back to Boho. "You have gifts. Very different from Tracy's, but gifts none the less. And you have progeny. We wanted to see how your bastards developed before we removed the block on the Empress's fertility." Rohan stretched out a hand for another sandwich. "Unfortunately, the results were less than satisfactory."

Boho leaped up and slapped the sandwich out of the old man's hand. "But you decided Belmanor was the appropriate cock and balls to do the job?"

"Well, actually we were more interested in his DNA than his junk," the valet piped up.

"And his morals and ethics," Rohan added.

"Meaning mine are lacking," Boho ground out. "*Muchas gracias.*"

"Well, you said it, but…yeah," the valet said.

"I can't believe this," Boho muttered.

"*I* can't believe it either," Anselmo said. "Could we please get back to the *giant alien threat advancing on us.*"

Boho once again flung himself, muttering, back into his chair.

"So, just what *do* you want?" Talion asked Rohan.

"For you to stop all this nonsense. Take your stolen fleet back to the capital. Swear fealty to the Empress, and all of you start planning on how to save us. *All* of us. If you don't, it's quite likely that this galaxy will become a lifeless husk filled only with *that.*" Rohan pointed at the crystallin form. He stood. "We'll be returning to Ouranos as soon as your fleet is assembled."

The valet laid a hand on the old man's arm. "Tracy probably shouldn't travel for at least a few days. Assuming he doesn't croak."

"Well, let us hope he doesn't." Rohan thought for a moment. "The little Isanjo can bring him back in the *Selkie.*"

"What makes you think I'm going to agree to any of this?" Talion asked.

"The very large ships we have stationed all around your little toy kingdom," Rohan said and gave them a bright smile. "And more importantly…*that.*" He pointed at the holo of the League ship being endlessly consumed by the aliens.

"If you've got all these ships why not whistle one of them up and take it back to the capital?" Talion challenged.

Rohan sighed, and Boho found himself irritated by Talion's obtuseness as well. Boho spoke up. "The supposed human prime minister of the League can't come cruising back to the capital in a Cara'ot ship. Especially since every

Cara'ot in known space vanished over twenty years ago. Also, Rohan has to brief Mercedes before they reveal themselves."

"And then I get to figure out how to explain this as a good thing. Oh, joy," Anselmo muttered while at the same time the valet was saying to Boho,

"You may be a skunk, but you were always a clever, cunning skunk," the valet said admiringly. He glanced at Talion. "And you, you're a blunt instrument. But don't take it personally, Baron, hammers have their place."

Talion smiled though it was more akin to a snarl. "And what's to stop me from contacting the Empress, and spoiling the careful rollout of your news? And maybe contacting the press while I'm at it?"

Anselmo spoke up. "Because she won't believe you. She'll think it's some kind of ploy. Also, there's a complete press blackout concerning anything about Nephilim, and the press is more afraid of SEGU then they are eager for a scoop. And finally, I don't think the Consort is going to back you up. He understands the value of a face-to-face meeting. Look, it's all very sad, but you aren't going to get to be the potentate of your own little kingdom.

The valet jerked a thumb toward Anselmo. "I like this one."

"Fine, take him under your wing," Rohan said to the valet. He turned back to Boho and Talion. "Now we need to bustle. Call back the ships from the new systems you've discovered. I want to leave as soon as possible. We'll travel with you aboard your flagship."

The two men left. No, aliens, Boho amended. The three human men exchanged glances. The flickering images from the hologram played across their faces.

"Do we believe them?" Talion finally asked.

"Do we dare not to?" Boho asked.

18

OUR PERSONAL MATTERS WON'T MATTER

"WELL, THIS RATHER sucks," Carisa said calmly as she unconsciously laid a hand over her belly. Even this early in pregnancy it seemed that nature and instinct had taken over.

Mercedes sat, stunned, trying to process what the little Isanjo had just imparted to them. Tracy shot. *Twice.* He was in surgery. *What if he dies?* She had already lost him by giving him to Carisa. If he died Mercedes would never see him again. Register the warmth in those grey eyes when he gazed at her. *But if he died, he might never have the chance to fall in love with Carisa.* Hateful, horrid little thought. Self-loathing was a taste on the back of Mercedes tongue.

"Thank you for letting us know," Carisa continued when Mercedes remained silent.

"Yeah, well, all the boys ran off to have their important talks." Sarcasm dripped off the words. "I had a feeling nobody had bothered to tell you. Or even thought about it. Fucking men."

"Just out of idle curiosity, who did shoot my husband? It wasn't Boho, was it?" Carisa asked as she approached the hologram as if proximity could bridge the light years.

"No, though he was getting ready to challenge Tracy to one of your stupid duels. No, it was Christina Flintoff, but she wasn't gunning for Tracy. She was trying to kill..." The alien looked over at Mercedes with embarrassment. "Well actually, your husband."

That snapped Mercedes out of her frozen state. "What? Christina? Why in heaven would she want to kill Boho...? And Tracy..."

"Yeah, did some heroic shit. But Flintoff was yelling about how Cullen killed her mama." Something niggled at the back of Mercedes' mind, but it was gone before she could grab the thought. "So, yeah, things are going *just great here*. And there's some other stuff too, but Rohan doesn't want me to say anything. Said he should be the one to explain...well, everything. Look, I'm at the hospital, I won't leave until Tracy's out of surgery. Oh, the surgeon is a Doctor Riley Chen. He'll probably call you once it's all over. Bye."

"No, don't you dare!" Mercedes was on her feet shouting as the hologram flickered and vanished.

Carisa stepped to Mercedes side and took her in her arms. "He'll be all right," she said gently.

Mercedes drew in a shaking breath. "I'm sure he will. Tracy's too damn stubborn and annoying to die." She cast a sideways glance at Carisa. "And this is ironic. I should be comforting you. He's your husband."

"And you love him. I just like him." Carisa led Mercedes to the sofa and got her to sit down next to her. "So, I don't know Christina Flintoff well, but why would she want to kill Boho? Jahan said she was talking about her mother. Last I checked Sumiko is fine."

Mercedes jumped up and paced a circle around the sitting room wending her way between the coffee table, armchairs, and the sofa. "But Sumiko isn't her mother. Christina is a fosterling." And then the elusive thought came into focus. "Oh, God." Mercedes quickly tapped her ScoopRing and began flipping through records.

"What?" Carisa asked.

"Now I remember. Christina was born on Sinope. A Hidden World, and a weird one. Only women. I'll explain that later," she said in response to Carisa's confused look. "Boho and I were part of the mission that assimilated the planet into the League. There were some issues when we began to remove the children. Some women tried to hide with their children rather than allow us to take them. Boho and I stumbled across a couple and their little girl. There was a struggle. I can't remember all the details. I just remember that frightened child." Mercedes gave a defeated shake of her head.

"I gather the girl was Christina and Sumiko adopted her."

Mercedes nodded an affirmative. "I guess I talked to her about the girl. I can't remember, it's been so long ago. Apparently, I did feel guilty." She paused then burst out, "I should have seen this coming."

"How? How could you possibly have seen this coming? You couldn't know Christina would remember enough to nurse her anger for all these years. And why now? It's not like Christina hasn't been around Boho. She could have shot him any number of times."

Mercedes shrugged. "Maybe because she thinks of him as

a traitor? Because he was about to challenge Tracy? Because of Paloma? Because the opportunity presented itself?" Mercedes pressed a hand to her forehead. "God, does every choice we make have to have such venomous consequences?"

"Given my current gravid situation…I'd have to say yes," Carisa said dryly.

Mercedes rushed to her and embraced her sister. "Oh, Cari, I'm sorry. I didn't mean to ruin your life."

"Well, it's not ruined yet. Tracy could still pull through." She glanced down at her waist. "And if he doesn't, I can marry again so this baby won't grow up without a father." Carisa reacted to Mercedes expression. "Um…yes, sorry, that probably wasn't all that comforting."

They sat in silence for a few moments. Carisa cleared her throat, an uncertain little sound. "May I ask you something?"

Mercedes gave her a little hug. "Of course."

"If the girl had succeeded. If she'd…well, you know. Would you have taken Tracy away from me?" Mercedes felt hot blood rise in her cheeks grateful that her dark skin hid her guilt. "I just would like to know if I'm going to have to…I just don't want this baby not to have a father."

Mercedes held Carisa by her shoulders and looked her straight in the eye. "You gave up any plans you might have had to help me. I won't repay you by betraying you. How could I? *What God has joined let no man take asunder.* He's yours as long as you want him."

+   +   +

"HEY, GOOD NEWS. You're not dead."

The voice seemed piercing. Tracy slowly became aware of his surroundings. Unfortunately, he also became aware of his body. *Pain.* That was the first thing he registered in his chest and abdomen. He tried to speak, but nothing emerged. His mouth felt like he had been chewing on a wool sweater dipped in piss. He struggled to conjure up a bit of a saliva and swallowed. His throat erupted in fire, and when the spit hit his stomach it sent nausea churning through his gut. He started to retch, and then Jahan was there, helping him onto his side which made him hurt even worse, and holding a bedpan as he vomited up the little that was in his stomach.

Jahan helped roll him back onto his pillows. The action tugged at the various tubes running into his body, and the sources of pain in his chest and belly and he gave a yelp.

"I think I'd prefer to be dead," he croaked. "What's happening? Where's Flintoff? Cullen? Did Talion agree?"

"Whoa, whoa, whoa." She picked up a cup, inserted a straw and held it to his lips. "Drink and I'll catch you up."

But before she could begin a nursing sister came bustling through the door. "Ah, I see you're awake. Let's see how you are doing."

A thermometer was run across his forehead, she checked his bandages then lifted the covers and checked a receptacle that seemed to be attached to the tube that was crammed up his dick.

"Hmmm, still not making any urine." Tracy's face was burning. "We're going to have to work on that. Keep drinking water, but if you haven't peed by tonight, I'll ask doctor to start you on a diuretic. Hopefully we can avoid dialysis. If you feel like you need to defecate ring me and we'll help you onto a bedpan."

Jahan was trying, unsuccessfully to stifle her giggles, and Tracy had a feeling he had gone as red as a tomato. "I'll have nutrition services bring you up a tray. Liquid only, but it might get things moving in there," and she lightly tapped his abdomen with a forefinger which pulled a groan from him. She left like a tornado in a habit and wimple.

"Where were we before I got a look at your private bits?" Tracy glared at her. "Oh yes, Flintoff. She's locked up on the *Selkie*. Cullen is fine. You saved his aristocratic ass. Talion, Cullen, and our alien overlords are leaving in a few hours for Ouranos to talk with Mercedes—"

"So, the war is over."

"No, the war you're talking about never started. They're going to be talking about the new one that's about to start. Whee."

Tracy tried to sit up but fell back with a groan. "I need to go with them," he panted.

"We'll catch up. Well actually, we'll get there a few days later. I'm going to take you back aboard the *Selkie*. Dalea will look after you."

He turned his face away. "No. I don't want her too. She lied to us. Betrayed us."

"Well, since we all now seem to be on the side of the evil, manipulative alien overlords I guess we'll just have to forgive her."

"You know you're an alien too."

"Yeah, but I'm a *good* alien and from my perspective *you're* the alien," Jahan said.

"And you're giving me a headache," Tracy groaned.

"Welcome to my world, you given me a headache for the past eighteen years…give or take a few months." She paused for a moment. "If you feel up to it you might want to call your wife. I told her you were out of surgery, and going to be fine, but she'd probably like to hear from you directly."

"My wife," he repeated slowly.

"Yes…her."

"Bring me my ScoopRing."

Jahan slid off the bed where she had been perched and headed over to the closet, but before she could comply the door to the hospital room opened. Tracy was startled to see Cullen standing in the doorway.

"Are you up to talking?" he asked. Tracy noted he had lost some of his aristocratic swagger.

"Yes."

Cullen advanced into the room and stood at the foot of the hospital bed. Tracy used the controls to sit up a bit, so he didn't feel at quite such a disadvantage.

"Do you need me to find you a glove?" Jahan asked Cullen as she secured Tracy's ScoopRing from the packet that held his personal effects. Sarcasm dripped off the words.

Cullen shut her down with a glare then looked back at Tracy. "I came to thank you. I know why you did it. I know it wasn't for me. But I'll take it. Otherwise, I might be laying in that bed or in a box. I don't like you. And I'll never forgive you. But I'm willing to put aside our differences until we've dealt with…" He made a vague gesture. "And if we fail our personal issues won't fucking matter. So, that's all I came to say."

"You're welcome?" Tracy said though it emerged more as

a question than a statement. "And let's assume we'll win so I can cross blades with you again. I still owe you," he said and touched the scar that distorted his left eyebrow.

"I think you've done far more damage to me than I ever bestowed on you," Cullen said through clenched teeth. He turned on his heel and left the room.

After the door fell closed behind him Jahan returned with Tracy's ScoopRing. "He's not wrong," she said quietly. She held out the ring. "Now call your damn wife."

19

ACCEPTABLE TRADE OFFS

"R OHAN! I'M SO glad you're back." Mercedes leapt up from behind her desk at the temporary government offices, and almost ran to the old man. "And successful as well." He enfolded her in a massive hug. He smelled of fresh citrus from his aftershave, though stubble rasped against her cheek.

Rohan stepped back and rubbed the cheek with the back of his hand. "Sorry for the sandpaper. I came straight here and didn't shave first. Should have planned my time better, but things are hectic."

"Any sign that Boho is rushing? Home? Here?" They stared at each other for a long moment. "Where is he, Rohan?"

"I believe he escorted Lady Paloma home."

"Oh, I see." Mercedes forced a smile. "Well, there was no reason for you to rush. You could have gone home first. I had a message from Talion. He says he'll publicly swear allegiance, so crises averted, but as to why he changed his mind...he told me I had to talk to you." She drew him toward the sofa and armchairs in one corner of the office. "So, since you're here, tell me."

But she didn't give him a chance to answer just rushed on as her thoughts danced from topic to topic like a maddened flea. "When can we expect Tracy? I know he's talked to Carisa and is recovering, but I'd like to have him in the hands of the palace doctors. He did say he was bringing the fleet which does rather alarm me. Talion, I mean. And of course, I have to decide what to do with Christina. Is she with you? Sumiko is devastated. Will Boho come back to the palace? If not, I must think of something to tell Cyprian—"

Rohan gripped her shoulders. "Mercedes, slow down. All in good time." Gentle pressure had her sinking down onto the couch. "Right now, I have something I must impart to you. Boho, Tracy, Talion, Anselmo and Jahan already have some of this information, but I felt it best if you hear it directly from me. And once you do, I need you to remember that I have known you since you were born. And that I love you and that I have always been there for you."

Something in his tone sent a tendril of dread through her gut. Mercedes gave him an apprehensive look. "So serious. All right. Should I send for refreshments?"

"No."

"Now I know this is serious," she quipped mostly to cover her nervousness.

"Security up, please," he said as he settled his bulk into the armchair opposite her.

"If it's that secret, shouldn't we be in a SCIF at SEGU headquarters?" Mercedes asked losing the teasing tone.

"No, too many people around, and Rogers will want to join in. I would rather leave it up to you when and how much you tell him," the old man said.

Acquiescing, Mercedes keyed her ScoopRing to shut and lock the office door, and then brought all the security protocols on-line. The security screens grinding up over the windows and the low hum of white noise generator to disrupt listening devices made the space seem suddenly threatening.

She folded her hands in her lap. "All right. What is so sensitive or dangerous that we have to go to such lengths?"

"Sector 470," Rohan said grimly. The old man set a data cube in the center of the coffee table. A holograph sprang to life.

Mercedes watched with sick horror as the ship and its crew died. Crawling horror ran down her nerve endings and clenched in her gut. She fought back nausea, but ultimately the guilt overwhelmed her. She had sent men there. *This* had been their fate.

She couldn't control it. Bile climbed up the back of her throat. Leaping up she ran into the bathroom attached to her office. Falling to her knees she vomited until there was nothing left to come up. She heard heavy footsteps, running water and then a cool cloth was laid against her forehead.

"Breath," Rohan said quietly. He offered a glass of water, and she rinsed her mouth. He leaned past her and flushed the toilet. "All right?" he asked.

"No. But calmer. What *are* those *things*?"

The old man assisted her to her feet. "That's what we've been unable to ascertain," he said as they returned to the office. Mercedes throat burned. She forced herself to study the League ship. "That scout is decades old. How is it *you* have this and O-Trell doesn't? And did my father know?"

"What became of the ships and the people aboard them? No, none of you knew. We saw to that. It was your great-grandfather who stopped trying to discover the cause of the disappearances and put the sector off limits. But he also saw the advantages in terms of removing occasionally inconvenient people. *That* we hadn't anticipated."

"Wait. We? Who are you talking about?"

Rohan sighed. "Mercedes, I'm not really Rohan Danilo Marcus Aubrey, the Condé de Vargas. I am Selaa'ka Karro. And I'm Cara'ot."

She stared at him. Was it a joke? Should she laugh? Roll her eyes? Instead, she slowly moved her hand toward her ScoopRing ready to send the signal that would summon armed guards to protect their empress.

"Please, Mercedes, don't do that. You're in no danger from me. Like I said, I've been in your life from the moment of your birth, and if we wanted you dead, I've had plenty of opportunity to escort you into that state."

Mercedes pulled her hand back. "All right." She was pleased that her voice was steady. "Let us assume for the moment that I believe you, and don't assume senility has set in. Why did the Cara'ot vanish? Why reveal yourself now? Why keep the knowledge of this..." She gestured at the hologram. "Secret from us?"

"You know why we vanished, that little matter of the massacre of the half-human, half-Cara'ot children on Dragon Fly. Which to your credit, you and Belmanor did stop before they were all killed. It also gave us the perfect excuse to ratchet up your paranoia about aliens by our vanishing act. Helped give us time to finish setting up for the next step in our plan. Unfortunately, the very things that make you such effective Janissaries for us can also lead you to…well, frankly, nearly fuck everything up."

"Meaning Talion?"

"Yes," he said. "Which is why we decided we had to step back out of the shadows and take control."

"Which is why you wanted to lead the delegation. You told him all this! You told Talion the crown has been extra-legally executing people this way? I'm surprised the war didn't start immediately."

"No, no. Why would we mention something so trivial? We made it clear there is an existential threat to all life in the galaxy from an alien threat of immeasurable power. We don't know if these creatures are sentient or not, or merely a weapon unleashed by an unknown race in a neighboring galaxy. God knows the central mass shows no sign of intelligence, and all our efforts to communicate have been useless. But I lose the thread. This thing doesn't just kill ships and crews. It also destroys planets, comets, asteroids, and even dying suns. Thus, adding to their armada. That is why we need you humans, why we nurtured you. This galaxy and all life within it are under grave threat."

"Nurtured us? We conquered you," Mercedes snapped.

"We let you. What better way to guide your development then as a humble, defeated people infiltrating all aspects of your lives?" He smiled at her horrified and outraged expression. "But allow me to explain." He paused and gestured toward the small bar in a corner of the office. "May I? This will take a while. You might like a drink too. Honestly it might be better to face this drunk rather than sober."

"Fuck you. But help yourself."

Rohan…no the *alien* crossed to the bar and poured himself a brandy. "I do enjoy your human comestibles." He returned to his chair and took a sip, gave an appreciative sigh. "You always had excellent taste, Mercedes. So, a history lesson."

"You know we Cara'ot have always traded in life—DNA—because it's ultimately the most precious commodity. It's from life that everything else springs; art, music, literature, scientific advancement. So, we're always on the lookout for promising new species, and some million years ago we spotted just such a species on a small backwater world on a spiral arm of this great galaxy."

"Earth," Mercedes supplied bitterly.

"Yes. We watched and what we saw was a species that excelled at violence, but also shared rather startling similarities with this deadly foe that was approaching."

"Why do I get the feeling that's not a compliment," Mercedes said from behind gritted teeth.

"It's not. You both expand quickly and use up all the available resources. But unlike the creatures who seem completely emotionless in their destruction you humans are aggressive, suspicious, murderous, and cruel."

"And that's meant to be a compliment?"

"It's what we believe is required to counter this threat. We snipped off any branching evolutionary shoots that might have been more peaceful and tolerant. We wanted you to be the meanest species in the known universe. We knew you were going to kick the shit out of any alien race you met, but we felt it was worth the cost. Fortunately, you opted for subjugation rather than extermination. You'll need the Isanjo, Hajin, Flutes, and Sidone of you are to succeed."

"And what if we hadn't been magnanimous?" Mercedes asked. She thought she knew the answer but wanted to force the creature to say it.

"We would have started over. If you had taken the path of genocide, we might have had to either intervene or make other plans."

"Meaning snip us off like those other evolutionary threads?"

"Well, fortunately it didn't come to that. You managed to control your blood lust and opted for conquest. No, we're stuck with each other. All our eggs are in the human basket, and we have to make this work. The fight for our very existence is upon us."

Mercedes couldn't stay still. Fear, anger, and confusion drove her to her feet, and she paced the confines of the office. "God damn it! Why did this have to come now? Why did it have to fall to me? I just wanted a life. A normal life. I never wanted…" She gestured wildly. "*Any* of this! I wanted a husband, children, grandchildren. I didn't ask to be Empress." She was embarrassed that it emerged almost as a wail.

"Initially we didn't care so long as some female took the throne and opened the military to women. But now I'm very glad it was you. You are strong enough, brave enough and wise enough to lead us, Mercedes. My gens might call me fanciful, but I think it was fate, perhaps some higher power that ensured it would be you." He gave a rueful head shake. "And I've clearly been going to your Catholic masses for far too long."

The praise, and what seemed to be intended as humor washed past her without making any impression as a suspicion became certainty. "Nine daughters…that was you."

He looked inordinately pleased with himself. "Yes, and I was the one in close proximity to make sure that Férnan only shot girl bullets."

"Well, fuck you very much. You ruined my mother's life. My life—"

"Your emotional pain verses certain annihilation? I'd call that an acceptable trade off, Mercedes."

"And me? Are you the reason I was barren?"

"Yes. Our analysis indicated a high probability of narcissistic tendencies in any child conceived by you and Boho. We considered alternatives—Rogers, Jaakon—but you never evinced any interest. Then fate once again took a hand and brought you and Tracy back together. We lifted the block on your fertility."

"How? Who?" Mercedes broke off thinking back to the events nearly eight years ago. Remembered that odd insistence that they had to meet so the Hajin could give her a B-12 shot. "That medic. Aboard Tracy's ship."

"Yes, Dalea. One of our assets. We got word to her that we wanted the block lifted and provided the necessary treatment." He blinked at her expression. "You seem…upset."

"Do you think?" she gritted.

"But you have your son. Why would you be upset?"

"Because you took away my agency. My rights as a human being."

He grunted as he stood. "Oh Mercedes, we took away the

agency of your entire species. You just happened to be a somewhat more special case."

She could think of no rejoinder as she watched him leave.

+ + +

LUIS AND A *fusilero* brought Christina to Tracy's cabin. She was in handcuffs, there were dark circles beneath her eyes and her pale blond hair was limp and greasy. Apparently, she hadn't been offered a shower since her arrest. It was the first time Tracy had had a chance to talk to the girl since they had left Nephilim on their way back to Ouranos. Dalea had severely limited his visitors and kept him confined to the bunk in his old cabin.

They were only two days behind Rohan and the rump fleet that Talion had constructed out of the traitorous captains who had abandoned the League during the final battle against the *necrófagos*. Any officers, *hombres* or *fusileros* who hadn't gone along with their captains' betrayal had mercifully only been imprisoned on Nephilim and not executed. They had been freed and restored to their ships. Tracy could only imagine the atmosphere aboard those vessels as men rubbed elbows with the men who had betrayed them. There was probably going to have to be a major reshuffling of crews once they got back to Hisselek to address these tensions.

"Leave us," Tracy said to Luis and the guard.

"Sir, I have to protest—" the *fuisilero* began.

"I'm in no danger from the Lieutenant, sergeant."

"Sir, I'd like to stay," Luis said. "I've served with Lieutenant Flintoff. I want to offer testimony."

"This isn't a court, Commander," Tracy said. He found himself trying to suppress the smile that threatened to reach his lips. How far they had come from the vain young peacock who had been a crewman back when the *Selkie* was a barely legal trading vessel. Back then all Luis cared about was getting his ashes hauled and buying new clothes. *Bloody war and sickly season did tend to focus the mind*, Tracy thought recalling the old toast.

"I know, sir, but that decision will have to be made at some point and I'd like to offer reasons why she doesn't deserve to be cashiered or imprisoned."

Tracy looked at Christiana who did not lift her eyes from a rapt contemplation of the deck beneath her feet. "Lieutenant…Christina." Her head jerked up to look at him. "Do you have any objection to Commander Baca remaining?"

"No." It emerged as a whisper of sound.

"All right." Tracy shifted the pillow behind his back. "So, why don't you tell me why you wanted to kill the Consort?"

The mention of Boho roused her from her crushed flower aspect. Her head jerked up, and her face was twisted in fury. "He's a murderer."

"Lieutenant, one could argue we are all murders," Tracy said.

"We kill soldiers. He killed my mothers when the League *assimilated*," her tone turned the word into an epithet. "Sinope."

The years peeled back, and memories returned. A strange Hidden World of Amazon women procreating through parthenogenesis in violation of League genetic laws and to the horror of the predominately male military who came to seize their planet. Christina went on with her story.

"I was almost three, but I remember. I didn't know what I was seeing then. I remember marmee screaming as she hugged mama's body. Now I know what blood and brains look like, and the Consort beat marmee bloody too. A few years ago, I checked to see if he had at least left marmee alive, but she was dead too. The same day they tore me away from my family. The same day he killed mama."

"They?" Tracy asked.

"The Empress was there too."

"Do you want to kill her?" The question seemed to stump the girl. Her mouth fell open in shock at his question. "And what about me? I was part of that invading force. I wasn't there for the taking of the children, but I helped in the conquest." He paused for a moment. "There's a gun in the dresser. Want to finish the job?"

She was shaking her head so violently that tendrils of hair escaped from her braid. "No, of course not. It's different with Cullen. He's a snake. I'm not supposed to know, but Paloma told me. She seduced him so they could catch him plotting against the Empress and then forced him to work against the conspirators."

Luis was shocked. "He was part of the coup attempt? Against his own wife?"

Christina's strange white skin showed her every emotion, and pink washed through her cheeks and turned the tips of her ears red. "Well, maybe he was only toying with the idea," she grudgingly admitted. "But he did think about it," she burst out. "And then he did betray her...all of us...when he joined up with Talion."

"It's not like he didn't have provocation," Tracy ruefully admitted.

"But the news said you all—"

"Oh, you sweet girl," Luis said. "That ain't how it happened. I was aboard this ship when we brought the Empress aboard."

"What?"

Tracy bestowed a furious frown on the young man. "That is a story for another time…as in never. Christina, whatever sins may have been committed we've got to put all that aside and unite. We need every soldier. I can't explain why until the Empress has been briefed. As for your situation, Anselmo will come up with some bullshit to explain all this away. You're a good officer and I don't want to lose you. Also, your…" Tracy hesitated then said it. "Your mother was…is a good friend to me. We're not going to tear up her family by putting you through a trial. You're dismissed."

She came to attention, snapped off a text-book perfect salute, spun on her heel and left. Luis gave an eye roll followed by a rueful smile and followed her out. Tracy stared at the blank panel of the closed door though in his mind's eyes could still see those two young faces.

Heavenly Father, please keep them safe.

The last time he had been in this cabin it was his son who had lain in this bunk gazing up at him with trust, but not love because Tracy was just another adult, not his father, not the person to turn to for comfort, advice, love.

Which inevitably brought him back to memories of Mercedes resting in his arms in this very bunk. Guilt seized him and Tracy forced his thoughts to his bride. In their one brief conversation in the hospital Carisa had said she had news and asked that he hurry back to her. He was no fool. He suspected the news she was going to impart. And he didn't know how he felt about it.

Especially now. *How do you bring a child into a world where only death awaits?* But wasn't that the fate of every living creature? Rohan, Donnel and presumably all the rest of the Cara'ot believed the humans, together with the other alien citizens in the League, could stop the advancing threat.

For the sake of all the people Tracy had ever loved and still loved he was going to do his damnedest to prove the fucking Cara'ot right.

20

VARIATIONS ON THEMES OF GRIEF

URING HIS BRIEF absence Carisa had found them a home. It wasn't one of the big FFH mansions up on the *Palacio Colina*, but instead a penthouse apartment in a neighborhood that before the war had been a magnet for the young and hip among the FFH and wealthier non-noble citizens.

Despite Jahan calling him an idiot, and Dalea's scolding Tracy was determined to walk through the door under his own power. Though to be honest his *own power* meant leaning heavily on Luis's arm while his right hand desperately gripped the head of his cane.

Carisa herself threw open the door at the chime. They stood regarding one another for a moment. Then she gave a tiny shake of her head and bestowed on him a fond but rueful smile.

"You really are a noble idiot," she said. At his gaped mouth expression, she chuckled and added. "Though I honor you for it. Come in and sit down before you fall down."

As Tracy hobbled in, he took in the surroundings. Unlike the destroyed royal palace and the *Phantsiestück* which had favored the carved and the gilded, this space was rather spare, the furnishings tending toward then modern rather than the lush. The touches of color were provided by floral arrangements and a few paintings.

"It's beautiful. As are you," he added and releasing Luis's arm he lifted her hand and bestowed on kiss on the back. He tottered and Carisa quickly pulled his arm through hers and assisted him over to the white leather sofa that faced a wall of windows.

Luis braced and saluted. "I'll leave you then, Admiral."

"Please Commander, do stay for tea," Carisa said, and Tracy couldn't help but notice how her eyes lingered on Luis. The entry of Kallupus carrying the silver tea tray and Binetti with the flatware, china and napkins into the living room broke the younger people's intense gaze.

Tracy added his voice to the invitation. "Yes, stay, Luis." He glanced at his wife. "Where's my father?"

"He has the floor beneath us," Carisa answered. "But he said he would stay with Rohan for the time being, so we have some privacy. Your papa is a treasure. Also, he's volunteering at the refugee centers, and he's pretty much taken over handling the clothing drives. Like I said…a treasure."

Tracy's gut twisted at the news of Alexander's choice of lodging. It was irrational, Rohan had given no sign he was going to behave any differently than before, but it still made Tracy nervous to have his father functionally in the alien's hands.

Carisa dismissed the batBEMs and played mother, pouring, and handing out the teacups. It did not escape Tracy's notice that Luis and Carisa's fingers touched and lingered. Tracy busied himself filling a plate with an assortment of savories, sandwiches, and cookies. After everyone had had a few sips and nibbles Carisa set aside her plate and said to Tracy,

"So, the war is over and you its only casualty."

Tracy studied the two young faces both smiling brightly at him. He intended to tell them the truth, they deserved to know, but he hated to destroy their joy and cheerful optimism in this moment of homecoming.

Carisa read his mood and quickly came to sit next to him on the sofa. She brushed her fingers softly across his forehead, "So grim, my dear. What is it?"

"Please pull up the security." Luis and Carisa exchanged a glance but obeyed. "There's something I have to tell you."

"And I have something to tell *you*."

Her tone was arch, and doubt shook him. Should he reveal the truth? That death might be coming for them all; even the new life she was carrying? If he kept silent and allowed her to speak, he wasn't sure he could feign joy and excitement. Which would hurt her, and she would think it was because of his divided heart. Perhaps if she knew the approaching danger she would understand and forgive him. Tracy hated himself for making this about his needs and feelings, but truthfully, he hurt and hope, and happiness seemed like distant memories.

His long silence had Luis and Carisa exchanging glances. "Sir, forgive me, but it seems like you've been under a heavy burden even before you got shot."

So, he told them.

+ + +

Kielli had returned to the *Selkie* and was now staring at Jehan in consternation while she sobbed inconsolably. He nervously scratched at the back of his head while his tail lashed about his ankles then shot up to flick against the top of his upturned ears.

"Uh, Captain? Jahan? *Nenuknuk* he said reverting to their native language to say the diminutive *auntie.* "What's wrong? Did something happen to *Sejekul* Tageri?"

"No, no, he's fine. I'm going to call him later." She furiously swiped at the tears. "Once I get control of this bullshit!" She forced a smile. "Were you with your girl?"

"Uh huh."

"You really like her?" He nodded. "Then you should grab her now. Take her home to meet the family. Has she ever been to Cuandru?"

"Nope, she was born on Ouranos."

"Then you should definitely take her." Jahan left the table and crossed to the counter to busy herself making a cup of coffee she really didn't want. Her stomach felt like it was filled with battery acid.

"Yeah, like that's gonna happen. I couldn't afford one ticket much less two."

"You wouldn't have too. I'm taking the *Selkie* back home."

"Wait? What? I thought we were doing a food run now that you're back."

"It can wait."

She felt his hands close on her shoulders, claws pricking at her flesh. The fact they had unsheathed showed the depth of his worry and alarm. He forced her around to face him. "*Nenuknuk*, I'm not a little kit any longer. You can tell me what's wrong."

"It's not my secret to tell," she whispered. "At least not yet." She pulled him into a desperate hug as static drew their fur toward each other. "Go. Go to your girl. Be with her. Then bring her."

"Okay. I'll go ask her if she'd like to meet all my crazy relatives." He flashed her a smile. "Maybe I won't phrase it quite that way." He started toward the ladder than paused and looked back. "You gonna be okay?"

"Yes. Never better. Now go!" She made a shooing gesture. He gave a mock salute and darted down the ladder. Jahan sank back down in a chair and began to cry again.

+ + +

MOMENTS BEFORE LUIS had walked out of the apartment muttering *"I need a drink."* Carisa was now in Tracy's arms, head resting on his breast, her tears dampening his jacket. The pressure on the bandages over his chest and belly wounds was painful, but he said nothing and made to attempt to shift her. He had just dealt her a devastating blow.

She finally lifted her head and looked up at him. Tears glittered on her eyelashes and streaked her warm brown cheeks. He couldn't help but reflect that she was the only person he had ever seen who could weep and *still* look beautiful. Tracy used his thumbs to wipe away the wetness beneath her eyes.

"*Perdóneme*," she whispered. "Apparently being overly emotional is also a symptom of pregnancy." She pushed herself upright. "Not how I wanted to impart my news, though I expect you had already guessed."

"Yes, I had. Even through a holo I could see you were glowing," Tracy said and softly kissed the top of her head. "And it's all right to react. I've had more than a few moments of railing against fate."

"I should terminate."

That shook him. "What? Why? You want children."

"How monstrous would it be to bring a child into this world at this time. Knowing that if we fail, they die."

He felt his jaw tighten. "Then we won't fail. The Cara'ot seem to have confidence in us. Besides, we're not engaging this thing yet. You must have heard the lecture at The High Ground about how *space is really big*." The reminder made her laugh. "That's better," Tracy said, running his hand through her tight curls where her hair was beginning to grow out. "Have your…our baby. We have a lot to do before we can even think about fighting."

✦ ✦ ✦

ANSELMO HELD QUINTANA. He had been gone only a little over a month, but his new daughter had transformed from an angry-faced, wrinkled homunculi into a baby girl whose skin was like rich cocoa and who already had a mass of curling black hair. Her plump little legs kicked at the blanket in which she was wrapped, and one tiny hand reached up toward his nose.

An image of that soft body turning into unyielding crystal filled his mind and without warning a sob escaped him. He clutched his daughter to his chest. Apparently with too much force for she began to wail. He quickly loosened his grip, and frenziedly kissed her petal soft cheeks breathing in the scent of milk, powder, and baby.

"I'm not going to let it happen. I'll never let anything happen to you. Not to any of you," he whispered as he thought of all his darling *bebés*.

He felt a momentary flash of guilt that he had deliberately washed out of The High Ground at the end of his first year. If he'd graduated, done his five-year tour of duty he would be trained, if not currently ready to do battle. Instead, he was a soft bellied, middle aged man. The best he could do was prepare the populace for the knowledge that the Cara'ot had returned and were their necessary allies in this fight for survival.

Honestly, in this moment it all felt beyond remedy. Against such a foe did they have any hope at all? He wondered if he ought to tell Julia what he had learned rather than have her wait for the calculated bullshit that he would soon unleash on the gullible press.

He gazed down at his daughter's innocent face. Thought of his wife currently tucking Deidre, Andrew, Josephine, and Ansel into bed. Kissing their foreheads. Smoothing back errant curls. She did not deserve to share his fear and dread. Not yet. He would keep it from her for as long as he could. And tonight, he would hold her and make love to her, and inwardly rail against the coming of the darkness.

+ + +

DESPITE THE ARMY of servants, and the guards Mercedes felt utterly alone as she roamed the *Phantsiestück* palace. These late-night rambles were starting to take their toll. Her image in the mirrors of the small ballroom showed a woman with slumped shoulders, bags beneath her eyes and a grey cast to her skin.

What drove this current bout of insomnia was her missing spouse. Boho might have returned, but he hadn't come home. She knew he probably hated her, would be grateful if he never had to lay eyes on her again, but Cyprian…he had adored the little boy. Was genetics really all that mattered? Tracy hadn't comforted the child when he scrapped his knees, taught him to ride, read him bedtime stories, carried him on his shoulders.

That had all been Boho. In every way save one he was Cyprian's father. So far, the little boy didn't know his papa was back, but little pitchers had big ears and sooner or later he would hear some servants or soldiers gossiping and he would know and wonder why his papa hadn't come home.

She had Jaakon inquire of Boho's mother, the dowager duchess. if her son was with her. He wasn't. It made her feel pathetic, but she asked Rodgers to use the assets of SEGU to find out where her husband was staying. It turned out to be the Royal Mark the only five-star hotel that had survived the bombardment, though with significant damage.

The question was what did she do now? Did she send a request that he come to her? What if he refused? What then?

Arrest him? Kidnap him? Humble herself and go to him? As if they hadn't already had enough personal drama with the royal family. All they would need was for her to be caught standing outside his hotel room door yelling and cursing like one of those *putas* on vid shows that trafficked in dysfunctional families, missing fathers, and errant wives…

Mercedes gave a bitter laugh. Actually, the house of Arango would fit right in. She should propose it to Anselmo. The payment they received might help defray the cost of the coming war.

Finally, she acknowledged that this was not something she could fob off on an underling, and there was a middle ground. Mercedes keyed her ScoopRing to their private channel and called him. Minutes passed without a response, and she was about to give up and cancel the call when he answered.

"Can't sleep?" his holographic image asked.

"No."

"Guilty conscience?" Boho suggested.

"Yes, among other things. Rohan told me…everything."

"I don't want to talk about that," Boho said. "Let's stay on your guilt. I like that topic better."

"Fine. Yes, okay, I lied to you. You can be angry at me, hate me even, but don't take it out on Cyprian. He misses you. He needs his papa."

"You didn't even let me see him before you sent me away."

"I know. That was wrong of me. I was panicking. With Trac…Belmanor back I knew you'd see the truth in our son's face. I was a coward."

Silence gripped them as they regard each other. "What do you want from me, Mercedes?" he finally asked.

"Come home. Please. We're facing a desperate threat, Boho. If we fail, we all die. I don't want Cypri to die crying for his father."

"You love Belmanor."

"I do. For thirty years." She paused then added. "But I married you."

"I've fallen in love," was Boho response. His image reacted to her expression. "And no, this isn't one of my *inamoratas*."

It landed like a blow to her chest. "It's the girl, Sumiko's daughter, isn't it?" Mercedes said her voice heavy with grief and regret.

"Yes."

"So, what does this mean? You won't come back?" Mercedes asked.

"She doesn't want me. She despises me." Regret hung like shadows off his words. It was the most honesty that had ever existed between them. "I have no place to go."

"I need you, Boho. I need you here. I can't face this alone."

"What about him?"

"Carisa will need him. She's pregnant."

"Ah."

The silence again. "We can't just give up," and she wasn't sure whether she was talking about their marriage or the alien threat.

"All right. I'll come back."

"Thank you," Mercedes whispered as he broke the connection.

✦　✦　✦

THE CAPITAL CITY was a ghost of itself. Once Hisselek had hummed and bustled with nightlife. Crowds in the streets after ten when the heat of the day had dissipated. Little boys like darting schools of fish kicking soccer balls in the courtyards while fathers looked on indulgently and mothers schooled their youngest daughters in proper deportment. The older girls played come hither games with strutting young men. There had been music spilling from the cafes and nightclubs. The aroma of a thousand cuisines, human and alien, tantalizing the nostrils and sometimes causing one's eyes to water at the fire and spice.

Now it was all shadows and grief that twined through the rubble still waiting to be removed. The sound of cats fighting tore the night only to be silenced by a shouted curse from the window of a damaged building.

A pair of *policías* paced the cracked sidewalk, nightsticks swinging, and holsters unsnapped. Boho watched as they rousted a homeless man out of his makeshift tent. Apparently, he was squatting too close to the *Palacio Colina* where the FFH dwelled. They did at least help him take down his tent and bundle his meager belongings into a large duffle bag.

One of the cops spotted Boho watching, and crossed the street with that bulking, threatening gait of authority figures the galaxy over. Boho's ever vigilant security started to melt out of the shadows, but he waved them back.

"Eh, *Señor*, you're out late."

"Sorry, officer, I didn't mean to add to your burdens." Boho blinked and looked away as the policeman flicked on his flashlight illuminating Boho's face. "Just doing a bit of reconnaissance."

The man froze realizing just who he had accosted. "Your Highness, *Dios*, please forgive me."

"Nothing to forgive, officer." Boho clapped him on the shoulder. "Thank you for keeping our good citizens safe. And for being gentle with that *hombrecito*," he added gesturing at the homeless man who was shuffling away down the sidewalk.

"So many people are hurting, Highness, no point being a dick about it."

"Very true, my good man. Please give your partner my greeting and my thanks."

"Yes, sir. Thank you, sir."

The *policía* hustled back across the street and began an animated conversation with his partner who clutched at his head, then turned to face Boho and gave a deep bow. Boho inclined his head in answer and walked on.

The encounter had given him a momentary respite from his bleak thoughts and black fears. Eventually his path would bring him up the hill to the small palace where his son…where a *child* slept, and his wife wandered the halls. *Restless is the head that wears the crown*, Boho thought.

He lit one of the thin cigars he enjoyed the pale smoke dancing before his eyes before being swept away in a breeze off the bay. *Just as we will be swept from the galaxy*, he thought.

If he was honest with himself, he would admit that he

was afraid to die. Did it hurt when those things consumed a person? Would memory or emotion remain once you had been joined to that alien mass? He found himself thinking about the five children he had sired. God, most of them were grown by now, and he knew them not at all. They too believed that other men were their fathers. Those fathers kept quiet and plaint because of monthly stipends paid by the palace into their bank accounts. Were those happy families?

What if he tried to see them? Form some sort of relationship with his children before death came for them all? Furious at himself Boho flung the cigar onto the pavement and ground it out beneath his shoe. This was maudlin crap. Why would he do that? So he could prove to Mercedes…to Paloma…to himself that someone could love him and would mourn his passing? That he was capable of love?

One of agents stepped to his side and said quietly. "Would you like me to summon a flitter, sir?"

"Yes. There's nothing worth seeing out here. And it's time for me to go home."

21

NOW WE NEED A PLAN

*A*ND THUS, WE *have come full circle* Mercedes thought as she disembarked from the imperial shuttle in the docking bay of The High Ground. Thirty-eight years ago, she had arrived on just such a shuttle, preparing to take her first step on the path that would ultimately place her on the throne of the Solar League.

In addition to her ever-present security detail she had invited Beatrisa, Cipriana, Ian Rogers, Narrano, and Rafe to join her and Boho aboard the Imperial shuttle.

A second shuttle carried the rest of the complement made up of Tracy, Talion, Rohan and his valet, and Gelb along with various other military officers and dignitaries. They would all have fit aboard her shuttle, but Mercedes was still deeply uncomfortable in the presence of Rohan, bloody well didn't want to make small talk with Talion, and she felt that keeping Tracy and Boho separated was in everyone's best interest.

Cyprian's joy at seeing Boho had pierced her heart, and the little boy's love for his papa had melted away the momentary reticence Boho had displayed when he first saw the child, but Mercedes saw no reason to tempt fate and male pride and tempers.

On balance the fact it had taken eight days for her most senior advisors to arrive hadn't been a bad thing. The individuals who had been cursed to know the information she was about to impart to a wider circle had probably needed time to reflect and mentally prepare. Mercedes knew she had certainly needed that.

Once the call had gone out to Ernesto on Hellfire and the various royal governors, the question of where to meet became the issue. In an abundance of caution Mercedes had decided to hold this meeting off world, on the space station that housed the military academy. Within the confines of The High Ground there was no danger of a snooping reporter or nosy servant catching wind of this extraordinary gathering.

Vice-Admiral Baron Tarek El-Ghazzawy, Commandant of the academy waited to greet her and Boho. The shining blue-black hair was now streaked with grey, and crows-feet surrounded the deep brown eyes, but he was still the slim, upright figure who had trained them in combat flying all those long years ago. He delivered an impeccable bow to her and Boho. He then offered a salute to the gaggle of high command officers and political figures who trailed after them.

"Welcome, Highness. We have prepared a lecture hall for the briefing. The students, professors and support staff have been ordered to leave the premises. Which is why I recommended you provide the refreshments," he added.

"Which you'll be glad to know *I* handled," Rohan said, and Mercedes flinched.

Her reaction was not missed by the sharp-eyed El-Ghazzawy who shot her a curious look. Mercedes wished she could be as good an actor as the Cara'ot imposter. He was continuing to behave like the man they had all believed him to be, and Mercedes found it disturbing and horrifying.

"What excuse did you offer to furlough the students and staff?" Boho asked they left the docking bay.

"An infestation," El-Ghazzawy said with a smirk.

"Well, I suppose an invasion of admirals and politicians could certainly qualify," Mercedes said with a small laugh.

El-Ghazzawy continued. "Fortunately, we'd had some acid ants escape the biology lab." Mercedes couldn't suppress the shudder. The insects were native to the Sidone home world, and a bite often necessitated amputation of the affected limb. More than three and a person was dead. "Oh, not to worry, ma'am, we got them all rounded up, but I told the staff and students we were fumigating today."

Boho engaged the Commandant in conversation leaving Mercedes to her thoughts. The long hallway rang with the tread of men and the only three women present.

She sensed Cipriana's gaze and their eyes met. All those long years ago there had been four young women who had made this walk. The princess and her three ladies-in-waiting—Sumiko the smartest of them. She had left before the end of the first year, devastated by the loss of the young man she had loved, and had quickly married and proceeded to pop out babies for her drunken fool of a husband. Mercedes suspected that Sumiko still blamed her for Hugo's death.

Cipriana the…Mercedes couldn't quite decide how to

encapsulate her friend. She had been the party girl who never took anything seriously. Ironically, she was the one who had taken the most damage both physical and emotional in war.

No, Mercedes amended, that would have been Danica—sweet and biddable Danica who had paid the ultimate price. She had been killed along with the rest of her family by Mercedes' father for siding with the conservatives in the FHH who opposed his plan to place a woman on the throne.

Black thoughts, and Cipri, sensing Mercedes mood, moved to her side, looped Mercedes' arm through hers and pulled her tight against her side.

"What a long, strange journey it's been," she whispered.

✦   ✦   ✦

THE DAYS OF rest had helped, but Tracy was still moving slow. Fortunately, Rohan's girth meant they were all matching his ponderous gait. Tracy stiffened when Donnel fell into step with him.

"This is the hallway where you and I first met," the valet said fondly.

Tracy made a disgusted noise. "These hallways all look the same, and it's been decades, you couldn't possibly remember."

"No, no this is the one, you had just left the quadrangle after assembly on that first day."

Tracy stopped and glared at him. "Excuse me, but why this stroll down memory lane? You think I remember this place fondly? This place was nothing but humiliation and pain for me." His hand went instinctively to the scar at his eyebrow. "One of my few friends died here and to this day I wonder if I could have done things differently and prevented that from happening." His gaze went to Mercedes. "And—" Tracy clenched his jaw to prevent any more words from spilling out.

"And you didn't get her. I get it, but Jesus, my *hombre*, you came out okay. Try to have a little perspective."

"Shut up," Tracy snarled and hobbled away.

It did feel like ghosts were walking the echoing halls with him. He had made only four real friends during his years here. Two of them were dead, Hugo and Davin, and the third, Sumiko, was a bitter, angry woman who had walked away after Hugo's death. *So, I have to save her daughter*, he thought. And the fourth…once again his longing gaze went to Mercedes.

Tracy wished he could be like Mozart or that character from a children's book. When they couldn't have their first choice, they married a different sister and were happy. Why couldn't he do the same?

Because the universe never seemed to cut him a break, he decided. Maybe it was just his injuries making him feel so hopeless, but he wasn't certain he could muster the energy to fight another war. But he had to. Mercedes was counting on him, and Carisa and his unborn child deserved that he give his all to see them safe.

+ + +

LIFE HAD BEEN so simple back then. Boho knew he would graduate. Knew he would be the best at everything that mattered. That actually hadn't turned out to be the case. Mercedes was the top pilot in their class and Ernesto and Belmanor had been his superiors in the intellectual pursuits. But ultimately none of that mattered for he had won the prize.

His father had made it clear to him that since the emperor was set on this mad scheme to make Mercedes his heir Boho had to make damn sure that he would be the man at her side when she inevitably failed. Truthfully Boho would have preferred Cipriana. They had enjoyed more than a few trysts when they were all just heedless teenagers, and she had been far more beautiful than Mercedes. But ambition is a jealous mistress. When Mercedes had proposed he had accepted.

Boho had assumed that he would be the actual power behind the throne and Mercedes just a figurehead. When that had turned out not to be the case boredom had driven him into other women's arms, gambling dens, and legally questionable schemes.

Boho was not a man much given to self-reflection but returning to this place, at this time had him wishing for those less complicated and more peaceful days. The one thing he did acknowledge was that he was a coward. Yet here he was being forced to walk these halls, back stiff, head erect presenting a picture of calm bravery and determination. When all he wanted to do was grab Paloma and flee to the opposite side of the galaxy well away from this advancing horror. Space was big. They could live out their lives before the monster would ever reach them. But of course, Paloma would never agree, and by placing himself at Mercedes' side escape was now impossible.

✦   ✦   ✦

IT HAD TAKEN an hour for Rohan (Mercedes kept telling herself she ought to use his Cara'ot name, but a lifetime of knowing him as Rohan made that virtually impossible) and the valet to lay out the information. The initial outrage at the admission that the man they had worked beside for decades had been an alien imposter had quickly passed when the room was shown the recordings of ships dying, and the slow camera pans across the surfaces of planets and asteroids, whole solar systems turned into crystalline structures.

Indignation tried to reassert itself when the Cara'ot made it clear that they viewed humans not as their masters, but as Janissaries serving the needs of the aliens. Several of the governors and a couple of the older admirals started to walk out.

Mercedes surged to her feet. "Sit down!" she snapped. Five hundred years of devotion and obedience to the throne won out over wounded pride, and the men slunk back into their seats.

"I summoned you to this meeting because once we go public with this information we must transition from rebuilding to preparation for war and it will be up to you," she nodded at the governors. "To explain the reasons to your citizens and keep unrest to a minimum. I do think…hope…that once people understand the dire threat that we face we will all pull together."

"Ma'am." It was Tracy.

"Yes, Admiral Belmanor?" Mercedes said.

"What exactly are we going to build? We've seen how ships and weaponry are ineffective against this threat. We need a lot more information if we're to destroy this thing…things." He glared at Rohan and the valet standing behind the lectern. "You've had thousands of years to analyze it. You've got nothing?"

"After several failed attempts we were unwilling to risk anymore ships and bringing aboard a reconnaissance buoy that was in the process of being transformed resulted in the ship and crew being infected and mutated," Rohan answered.

Tracy fell back into his chair with a whuff. Ernesto raised his hand as if being back in this lecture hall had returned him to their school days. "Yes, Vice-Admiral?" Rohan said.

"That word, infected, raises interesting questions, is there any point where the object is safe to examine?"

"Once the transformation is complete the object becomes inert," Rohan replied.

Ernesto nodded thoughtfully. "Interesting, however I'd like to set that aside for the moment and revisit a bit of recent history."

"Oh please, let's not re-litigate the Expansion Wars," the valet said, his tone acid.

"Not planning on it," the scientist said. "I'm talking about our most recent war. With the *necrófagos*."

Mercedes noticed how Rohan and his factotum exchanged a glance. There was something in Ernesto's question that clearly had them on alert.

"Yes? What about them?" the valet said.

"I'd like to understand your reasoning for pitting them

against us?" Ernesto asked. "Why weaken us when you knew the real battle was yet to be fought?"

"And why do you think we had any connection at all with the *necrófagos*?" A smile was hovering around the old man's…the alien's mouth.

"I had questions regarding their unnaturally homogeneous society and culture which I expressed to the Empress. After I received her message summoning me to this meeting and revealing that the Cara'ot had returned I went back to my study of the bodies but on the molecular level. It wasn't a mass suicide, was it?"

Icy claws seemed to grip Mercedes chest. She struggled to draw in a breath. What Ernesto was suggesting…No, it was too monstrous.

Rohan gave the scientist an approving look. "Commander Westfield always said you were the brightest student to ever pass through his exo-biology class," he said. "We didn't do it to weaken you. We gave you an opponent designed to toughen you up for the coming battle. You had become far too fat and complacent after your final victory over…well, us."

"A JV team? You created a fucking junior varsity team and threw it at us!" Boho burst out.

"And once we had sharpened our skills and won, you killed them," Mercedes said her tone betraying both disbelief and horror.

The valet shrugged. "They had served their purpose."

"You cold fucking bastards," Tracy whispered. "And stupid too. You don't think your toy soldiers could help us against this…this thing? They were tough bastards."

"We would have had to redesign them," the valet answered. "They had been engineered to hate you on sight. Changing that programing wasn't worth the time or effort."

Rohan nodded and said, "We're pragmatists and we always take the long view."

Talion spoke up. "If you wanted us at peak, you shouldn't have stopped *our* upcoming scrimmage." He shot a glance at Mercedes.

Rohan gave a firm head shake. "No, you would have done too much damage to each other. We could not allow your little civil war to continue," The remark again infantilized the humans by both tone and words. He looked at Ernesto. "So, have I answered your question?"

"Yes, thank you."

"So, now this is in your hands. We've done all we can over a million years of evolution to prepare you mentally, emotionally, and physically for the battle to come."

"What? You're not going to help? You're just going to disappear again?" Mercedes gasped.

"No, of course not. We will help in any way possible, but you were bred for this, and in this desperate hour *you* will lead."

And with that Rohan and his servant settled into seats in the front row of the lecture hall, Rohan having to uncomfortably squeeze his bulk into the space between chair and desk.

Mercedes sat still for a few moments fighting the almost overwhelming desire to run. She then stood and moved to the podium.

"All right. We know what we're facing. Now we need a plan."

22

POLITICS AND ORATORY

"**I** NEED YOUR help."

Boho looked up from the report he was reading on his TapPad. They weren't words he had ever expected to hear. Certainly not from this man. Belmanor hovered in the door of Boho's office, weight shifting from leg to leg as if uncertain whether to advance or retreat.

"Wait. I need to make a call and see if *El Diablo* is skating in Hell."

"Ha, ha," Belmanor said as he finally entered.

He glanced around the office, and Boho could see the judgment in the grey eyes at the opulent surroundings. The hanging spider lights that had replaced the harsh lighting panels, the day bed, the bar topped with an array of liquor bottles, the deep, soft armchairs and coffee table near the windows, the art adorning the walls.

"Yes. If I'm going to be spending sixteen to eighteen hours a day here, I wanted it to be comfortable. So, fuck you and your bourgeoise judgment. And by the way, when are you returning my chief-of-staff?"

Belmanor settled gingerly into a chair opposite Boho. There were dark circles under his eyes, and he looked gaunt.

Of course, over the past three weeks no one had been sleeping well and he was still recovering from his injuries. "Not my call. That's up to him, so talk to him yourself."

They exchanged glares. "You said you needed my help," Boho finally pressed.

"Yeah. With a piece of legislation. Well, two actually. I can swing the commons, but the lords are going to be a bitch. That's where you come in. You're one of them. Actually, the first among them. You can get the votes."

"And what is this legislation?"

"Rohan isn't wrong, we need everyone for this fight. That means the Hidden Worlds. I can go to them, but for them to give us more help than they did during the fight with the *necrófagos* we need legislation. Legislation that promises them that the League is forever renouncing our policy of assimilation. That they can stay independent once they reveal themselves. Also, warning them about the danger is the right thing to do. They need to know this…this thing is coming."

"Aren't they all a bunch of nuts who set off to try and create some utopian society? What possible help could they be?"

"Yes, some of them were riding particular social, religious, or historical hobby horses, but a number of them are highly advanced, and we need all the brain power and fire power we can muster right now. So, will you help me? Back the legislation?"

"You said there were two…" Boho allowed his voice to trail away suggestively though what he honestly felt was suspicion. What was Belmanor up to?

"Yeah." Belmanor rubbed the back of his neck nervously.

"The second one. Well, the second one—"

"Oh, get on with it!"

"We need to allow BEMs into the military," he said so quickly that he almost slurred the words.

"Jesus! You don't ask for much. And what the fuck are they going to do—what the fuck are *any* of us going to do—against an enemy that can't be hurt and just absorbs you?" Boho realized his voice had risen several octaves and he was shouting.

"You may be right. But maybe some Tiponi or Sidone or Hajin or Isanjo will find the answer. Or some bright boy or girl on Freehold will develop the weapon we need. We've got nothing to lose."

"Just our culture. Our very way of life. If we take these steps everything may change."

"And if we don't everything may end."

They measured each other, a long look. Boho tried to muster the hate he had felt toward this man, but it was a flickering ember next to the fear, sadness and regret that gripped him. He sighed and ran a hand across his face.

"All right. We'll work together. I'm sure that will delight our respective wives." Good manners reasserted themselves. "How is Carisa?" Boho asked as he escorted Belmanor rose from the chair.

"Not enjoying morning sickness. Truthfully neither am I."

They shared a look, a moment of male bonding, but the moment passed quickly when Boho suddenly saw his son's features reflected in Belmanor's. His jaw clenched painfully as emotions too chaotic to process swirled through him.

"Get me a draft of the bills so I can look them over and prepare my arguments," he said curtly. "Now get out."

✦   ✦   ✦

ENDLESS MEETINGS. THAT was her life now, and this one had turned contentious with everyone blaming everyone else for why they seemed to be going around in circles. As usual it was Tracy who was yelling. The current recipient of his ire was that little toad Anselmo though Boho was also getting some of the anger.

Tracy thrust a finger into Anselmo's face. "*You* say you can't craft a statement for the Empress informing the people of this threat until we have all the pieces in place." He turned on Boho. "But *you* won't get the legislation passed which means *I* can't approach the Hidden Worlds and the Empress can't talk with the alien plenipotentiaries which means Anselmo won't prepare the statement."

Boho surged to his feet and glared at Tracy. *What else was new?* Mercedes thought wearily.

"I can't risk it until I know the aliens are actually going to agree, and I don't know that because Mercedes hasn't spoken to them about it."

She didn't mean to respond, but the accusation stung. "And I can't very well talk to them until I know this is actually going to happen. How many times have we made promises to the BEMs and never followed through on them?"

"So apparently *nobody* can do fuck or all!" Tracy snapped.

Anselmo was pouting. Talion was amused. Rafe was

doing calculations on his TapPad and ignoring them all—typical economist. Gelb looked like he wanted to fall through the skyscraper's fifty-five floors. Rogers and Beatrisa were nodding in agreement with Tracy's tirade.

Ernesto raised his hand. "I could do something. I could go out and take a look at this thing. Get readings. We can't fight it if we don't understand it."

"Didn't the Cara'ot give you their research?" Boho asked.

"Yes, but I'd prefer to do my own analysis. And fresh eyes might offer a fresh perspective."

She nodded at Ernesto. "Thank you, Vice-Admiral. So nice to have a useful proposal."

"And we could have more fresh eyes if we had experts from the Hidden Worlds and alien allies," Tracy growled. Mercedes shot him a glare and Tracy subsided back into his chair.

"More brains are always good," the scientist agreed mildly.

Mercedes sighed and ran a hand through her hair. "I've also reached a decision. We should stop all work on rebuilding the palace."

Anselmo reacted as if he'd been jolted with electricity. "No, no, no, no. *After* we get the news out. You do that now and the press will start digging. Things might come out in a piecemeal manner. That will kill us."

"And here I thought it was the aliens that were going to kill us," Talion drawled his fingers playing with his tap pad stylus.

Rafe finally looked up. "Where do you want the money we'll be saving to be spent? Ships? Weapons?"

"Well, we won't know where to spend it until we have a better idea of how to fight this thing," Mercedes admitted.

Boho slapped Ernesto on the shoulder. "And it's all back to you, my man."

"The Cara'ot said it's at least one hundred and eighty years until this…creature…thing—we've got to come up with a name for it," Rafe said in frustration.

"I've been mentally calling them Star Ants," Tracy offered.

"That is a terrible name," Anselmo said.

"Then come up with something better," Tracy snapped back.

The exchequer's Chancellor loudly cleared his throat. "*As I was about to say*, it's a long time before it reaches any of our planets. Why are we rushing? Why not rebuild? Have our economy secure before we face this?"

"Because if we fail, I'd like to give our children and grandchildren time to see if *they* can come up with a solution," Mercedes said.

"And you don't wait until the barbarians are at the gates," Beatrisa said almost at the same time.

"And we need to control the shape of the battle," Boho added.

"And pick the battlefield," Talion concluded. Rafe subsided.

"Also—" Mercedes broke off and adjusted the security measures one more time. She had called this meeting that deliberately excluded Rohan and his factotum. She could only hope none of the other people in the room were Cara'ot changelings. "Ernesto in addition to everything else, I'd like you to try and figure out how the Cara'ot…" She hesitated, looking for the right phrase. "Turned off. Shut down—"

"Killed," Tracy said.

"Did whatever they did to the *necrófagos*. It makes me nervous when an alien race is powerful enough to grow an enemy like Cadmus sowing dragon's teeth, and then just toss them aside once they served their purpose."

"Will do," Ernesto said.

She turned to Anselmo. "Work with Jaakon and let's get this speech written. Boho, get the legislation passed, and Admiral Belmanor you may as well begin your mission. Hopefully when you come out of Fold at your first stop, we will have everything in place."

"Yes, ma'am."

Anselmo raised his hand. "One last thing. The timing on all of this is critical. We can't have the press covering long debates in parliament over these bills. They're not stupid, we start talking about Hidden Worlds and BEMS in the military and they're going to fucking know something is up." He turned to Boho. "This all needs to be classified and the discussions held in secure rooms." He next looked to Mercedes. "And when the laws are passed your speech needs to immediately follow."

"Who knew a fight for survival would depend so much on politics and oratory," Mercedes said with a sigh.

"Always does," Boho grunted.

+ + +

IT WAS A soft summer night in Shuushuram, the capital city

of Cuandru. The family had rolled up the screens so the breeze could play shyly through the rooms of the tree house. As with all family gatherings a massive amount of food had been prepared and the rich and spicy aromas played tag with the breeze. The word had gone out that all entertainment channels would be pre-empted for a speech by the Empress, and Jahan had convinced her mother, who had taken over leadership of the family when old Pelan had died, to call a family gathering. Jahan knew what was coming so she selfishly wanted her loved ones around her.

Jahan leaned back against Tageri, his arms wrapped around her, his breath tickling the tips of her ears. Their youngest had whined about missing a party at university, and Tageri who had always spoiled their only daughter was inclined to let her off, but Jahan had insisted in such forceful terms that it had him holding up his hands and backing away up one of the climbing beams in their home. He didn't press for details, but her reaction told him that something serious was at stake, and he had ordered Lilala home in terms that brooked no argument. The two boys had immediately agreed and now all three of their children were clustered nearby.

The patriarch of the family had died this past winter so Jahan's mother, Foss had taken the role of matriarch. She was ensconced in a large chair that gave her an unobstructed view of the E-cube, and Dulac's long suffering wife was waiting on her hand and foot.

Kielli sat with his girlfriend who was staring wide eyed at this generational gathering, and her surroundings. Raised on Ouranos, Silala had only lived in human designed apartment buildings in Hisselek. This home nestled in the branches of a massive Tinagu tree was an utterly new experience. Kielli's father, Jahan's bother Dulac, looked at the couple with fond yet regretful eyes. Jahan knew what that was like when you realized your baby was all grown up.

Jahan's sister, heavily pregnant, was trying to get her restless toddler to sit still. Her new husband took the kit and placed his stepson on his shoulders where the little boy happily pulled at Eoca's ears. Jahan was glad Lenna had remarried. It had washed away the bitterness over the death of her first husband.

The E-cube projected a (muted) panel discussion of human journalists all probably speculating about the upcoming speech. Then the screen shifted to the Imperial flag, and Dulac turned up the sound. Only to find silence. The imperial anthem that usually played prior to any royal speech was notably absent.

Yes, Jahan thought, *Mercedes is definitely letting everyone know this isn't the usual Christmas or Establishment address or an announcement of a royal birth or wedding.*

The image of the flag faded to show the quadrangle at The High Ground, a dais, and a podium. Mercedes, wearing her O-Trell dress uniform, and a circlet rather than a crown emerged from a doorway at the back of the dais and walked to the podium. The unusual setting and the uniform screamed that this was *serious*. She was alone on the platform.

"Citizens of the League, *all* citizens. I come to you tonight with grave and somber news. Your government and your military have recently learned of an approaching threat that imperils all life in our galaxy." She paused to let that sink in.

"That is not hyperbole, so let me emphasize that again. I am talking about Every. Living. Thing. Every human, every Isango, every Tiponi Flute, every Hajin, every Sidone all gone. All dead. This force destroys all life leaving behind only cold and sterile crystal. No animal, no bird song, no insect, no rose will survive its arrival."

Mercedes vanished and there was a replay of things Jahan had already seen—ships and men dying, planets reduced to crystalline forms. Jahan looked around the utterly silent room. Registered the wide eyes, elevated breaths, felt her husband's arms trembling around her. Lenna let out a small moan and hugged her swollen belly.

The cameras once again returned to Mercedes. "I can't tell you if this thing is a living creature or an unknown space anomaly, but I can assure you that even as I am speaking to you, human and Cara'ot scientists are observing this phenomenon to try and determine its nature and more importantly how it can be destroyed."

"And yes, the Cara'ot did not die or vanish forever. In fact, they have been monitoring this approaching danger, and it was they who bought us the warning. Thanks to them we have time to prepare, to fight this menace, and survive. And for that we are eternally grateful."

"I can't offer assurances. I can only tell you that every member of your government will work tirelessly to find a solution and stop this threat, and I will give every full measure of my life to see you all safe." She paused and stared directly into the camera. "But I need more than just my cabinet, the MPs, military leaders and our brave starmen & *fusileros*. I'll need every citizen." She paused and added with emphasis, "*Every citizen* to join us in this effort."

Mercedes lifted a sheaf of papers on the podium. "Which is why tonight I am signing into law two bills just voted on by parliament. The first is the Human Right of Return bill that establishes that any Hidden World may open trade, diplomatic relations, form military alliances with the League, but will be allowed to maintain their autonomy and independence if they so choose. Human citizens who because of League policies regarding Hidden Worlds have been unwilling to step forward and greet their brothers and sisters will no longer have to hide in the shadows. My brother-in-law Admiral Thracius Belmanor is currently on a diplomatic mission to these various worlds bringing our offer of unity in the face of this shared threat."

Jahan noticed that Mercedes didn't elaborate on just how the hell Admiral Thracius Belmanor knew about these Hidden Worlds. Hopefully nobody else would want more details but given the rapacious press she wasn't holding out much hope. Jahan just hoped that she and *Selkie* could somehow be kept out of it.

Mercedes continued. "The other bill is the Full Citizenship and Service Act which grants to our alien brothers, sisters and non-gendered the right to vote in all League elections, and all the rights and privileges of citizenship. It also opens O-Trell to any individual whatever their species who wishes to serve. Our recruitment centers stand ready to accept your enlistment because we need your help."

That caused an eruption of conversation much of which amounted to *holy shit*, and Dulac's wife stating in no uncertain terms to both her husband and her son,

"You are *not* joining."

"The fuck we're not!" Kielli shouted back.

Kielli's girl laid a hand on his arm. "If you're joining so am I. If I have to lose you, I'd rather be with you if it happens."

Mercedes had laid down the papers and was still talking and all the gabble had obscured her words. "Shut up!" Jahan yelled and amazingly they did.

"…have dreamed of the stars probably from the first moment we looked up. We populated the heavens with gods, believed that these diamonds in the sky could control our destinies. Once we understood their actual nature we wondered if there were worlds orbiting those distant suns, and if they might hold other creatures who also looked to the stars and dreamed?"

"Unfortunately, some among us did not view that potential meeting with anticipation and excitement, but rather with dread. To our shame when first contact did occur, we humans didn't see our shared dreams, or the things we all had in common. Instead, upon discovering we were not alone in the universe we reacted in fear and allowed our distrust of The Other to drown all that we might have shared in blood and conquest."

"So, now as the representative of humanity allow me to offer my deepest apology and ask that you will join with us as equals and fellow citizens to save all that we love."

Mercedes paused for what seemed like a long time staring down at the podium while her hands tightly gripped the sides.

"When I was a child, I never imagined that I would stand

in this place. That I would be given the privilege to serve as your Empress. The throne would have gone the brother I never had…should have had. There have been moments when I've been afraid. When I've hated that this fell to me." She lifted her head and Mercedes' expression sent a shiver down Jahan's spine.

"But not today. Today I feel none of those things. Today I know we will stand together, and our suns will not shine on a galaxy devoid of life. Our joys and loves, and yes, even our grief and sorrows will not be lost to cold crystal, but instead be remembered. In the songs and poems, paintings and sculptures we hand down to our children and grandchildren and on to descendants beyond counting."

"We will not falter, and we will not fail. With the grace and mercy of our gods we will have victory."

The camera returned to an image of the Imperial flag and now the Imperial anthem was played. Jahan felt the tips of Tageri's fingers sweep away the tears that clung to her eyelashes and had begun to run down her cheeks.

23

I'M AFRAID TOO BUT YOU GIVE ME STRENGTH

THEY DROPPED OUT of Fold at the edge of the El-Nafud system. Tracy nodded to Luis who opened a communication link, and Tracy blasted a message to the capital city.

"Amir Nazimuddin, this is Admiral Thracius Belmanor in command of the dreadnaught *Sutāburezā*. Before you assume this is a hostile action on the part of the League, please let me assure you it is not. We are bringing you an urgent warning, and a personal message from Empress Mercedes Adalina Saturnina Inez de Arango. I'm familiar with your world and know its coordinates because I'm known to various parties on El-Nafud as Oliver Randall formerly captain of the trading vessel, *Selkie*. My crew and I traded in goods out of League space with you for twelve years. You can check my bona fides with Hakeem Satam, Madiha Qureshi, and Fatima Touma. We will hold at a discreet distance until you give us leave to enter orbit."

The bridge crew were giving Tracy very odd looks. Fortunately, Beatrisa raked them all with a look that clearly said *what?* indicating that this was not new information for his flag captain.

A prick to Tracy's index finger from his ScoopRing reminded Tracy that it was time for dinner with his senior officers. Luis, having gotten the same reminder, turned over his station to young Ensign Havers. Beatrisa leaned in as he stood and said quietly,

"I'll hold down the bridge while you go satisfy your officers curiosity."

"Hopefully no one will decide to mutiny over the dirty *intitulado's* criminal past," he murmured back.

"I expect you've transformed from low born scum to exciting rogue for most of them," she whispered back, and she slid into the command chair.

Tracy and Luis entered the lift, leaned against opposite walls, and stared at each other. "Seems so weird to be back here," the younger man said.

"Well, you better get used to it because we've got five more stops," Tracy replied. The younger man was looking uneasy. Tracy stifled a smile. "So how many broken hearts have you left on these various worlds? Am I going to be fending off outraged papas, unwed mothers, or jilted women?"

Luis glared then relaxed into a smile. "I was careful back then…mostly, but there might be a little problem on… well, we'll burn that bridge when we reach Geneva."

"Wonderful, and I was counting on your charm to help me convince the Hiddens to look past all this chest candy on my jacket."

"How's Carisa?" Luis asked in a tone so casual that it became conspicuous.

"Fine. Saw the doctor last week. First ultra-sound. Turns

out she's carrying twins."

"Oh, wow."

"Yeah," was all Tracy offered.

The lift sighed to a stop on the personnel deck, and the men walked to the door to the captain's mess. Kallapus bowed as they entered, and handed Tracy his preferred cocktail, an Aperol Spritz. The buzz of conversation cut off abruptly at his entrance and Father Ken gave him an amused glance. Tracy's command staff all came to attention and saluted. Their expressions were so studiously blank that they could have been mannikins. Cipriana gave him a wink. Tracy surpassed a smile and waved them to unbrace.

"Gentlemen, madam please." With the arrest of Christina Flintoff only two of Tracy's top officers were now women. He regretted that. Tracy gave them a mischievous look. "So, what were you discussing?" he asked casually.

"Admiral don't be a brat," Cipriana said. "They're about to *expire* from curiosity.

"Wondering about that reprobate Oliver Randall, were you?"

The officers exchanged confused and uneasy glances. Only Cassutt who commanded the weapons division and was knows as a sharp-tongued cynic had the nerve to speak up.

"You can't tease like that and not put out, sir. Look, we'll even buy you dinner first," Cassutt said.

"I believe *I* fund these captain's table dinners, but I take your point. Shall we?"

Tracy moved to his chair at the head of the table. Most O-Trell command officers favored heavy wood paneling, crystal chandeliers, and lots of paintings of military engagements. Tracy preferred a simpler aesthetic in his dining room. The walls were lined with ice blue wallpaper, the chandelier over the clear Lucite table was a series of crystal rods of varying lengths and the only decoration were three vases in Celadon green with Asian style flower arrangement, and a single watercolor painting of a grey and white cat against a stark white background.

They all stood behind their chairs. Kallapus, and various other officer's batBEMs filled the wine glasses and Tracy led the toast. "Her Majesty, the Empress."

A rumble of male voices and one woman's rose in answer. "Her Majesty, Empress Mercedes the First."

The little priest said grace, a murmur of amen went around the table and they all crossed themselves followed by the scrape of chair legs on plasteel. There was the clink of flatware on plates as the batBEM's began to serve. Not wanting his food to get any colder than it already was (the galley was not close to his private mess) Tracy ate for a few minutes before setting aside his fork.

"So, here's the story. Got cashiered. Raided an abandoned Cara'ot warehouse at the spaceport in Hisselek. Stole a bunch of Phantasm gems. Used them to fake my death, buy a new identity, and a trading vessel. Hired a crew and became a legitimate businessman trading in luxury goods, gourmet foodstuff and medicines."

"So, how the hell did you end up trading with Hidden Worlds?" Chief Babcock who commanded the *fusileros* asked.

"How did you even learn their coordinates? Given the fact they were like…hidden?" Lieutenant Vaughn asked.

"O-Trell couldn't find them. How did you?" the physician Afumba added.

Luis spoke up. "Aliens. They'd been trading with them for decades. We had an alien crew. They trusted us."

"So, you were part of the Admiral's crew?" The tone was a bit accusatory, and Tracy studied the new lieutenant who had replaced Christina. Carson was heavy set, of medium height and would probably run to fat by the time he was fifty.

Tracy stepped in. "He was indeed. Commander Baca joined the crew when I was forced to replace my first crew."

"And why did that happen?" Ken asked though he knew the answer.

He and Tracy had had many long conversations both when Tracy was in jail prior to his court-martial, and in the years since over games of chess that Tracy usually won. Tracy was grateful to the priest for acting as the social lubricant and helping steer the conversation away from dangerous shoals.

"About seven years into my new life the Fold converter blew. I didn't have the Reals to pay for a replacement, so I offered shares in the *Selkie*. Only person who took me up on the offer was a Tiponi Flute. I only had two choices, sell the ship as scrap, and go back to tailoring, or take him on as a partner. Jax wanted to travel with us, not be a silent partner and my human crew at the time objected. They quit as I was firing them, and Jax proved to be more useful than any of them ever were. He took over the bookkeeping, analyzed markets, tailored cargos, and increased our profits. Meanwhile I went looking for a new crew."

Luis picked up the story. "I had just finished up two years as a *fusilero*, had gotten myself in bad credit spike debt, so when Oliver…Tracy…the Admiral offered me a job I would have shipped with him even if Jax had been a Sidone. And I really hate spiders," Luis added. He then shot Tracy an aggrieved look. "Of course, then he went ahead and *hired* a Sidone."

"You should thank me. Bet you don't mind spiders now." Tracy paused for another bite and a sip of wine. "Anyway, Jax recommended the Isanjo who became my first officer, she brought in our medic who was a Hajin and the medic brought us Graarack. The Sidone," he added.

Who of course had turned out not to be a Sidone at all, Tracy reflected, but instead a cuckoo in their nest, abusing their trust and lying to them, but his officers didn't need to know anything about that. Tracy forced his fingers to relax around the stem of his wine glass.

"They had coordinates for various Hidden Worlds, so we augmented our legitimate income with—"

"Very illegitimate and highly illegal black-market trade," Luis concluded with a bright smile.

"Which is why it makes sense and was very wise of the Empress to have you handling the outreach to these planets," Ken said.

"I don't disagree, but I do wish we were doing it aboard the *Selkie* and not with an imperial flagship. Doesn't exactly scream *we come in peace*," Tracy said with a sigh.

"Probably for the best," Ken said mildly. "We are carrying formal documents from the government of the Solar League. Wouldn't do to turn up in a private vessel."

"And no offense, Admiral, but the *Selkie* isn't exactly a beauty. This ship." Cipriana twirled a finger to indicate all the *Sutāburezā*. "Screams *legitimate*."

Tracy looked around in feigned open-mouthed surprise. "Huh, guess that means I've arrived."

Chuckles ran around the table, and his officers raised their glasses to him. Ken laid a hand on his shoulder, leaned in close and said softly.

"That you have."

+ + +

"WELL, THE HOARDING and price gouging has started," Anselmo announced as he hovered in the doorway of her office.

Boho and Mercedes, huddled over her desk and pouring over a collection of TapPads, looked up at his announcement. His former boss gave him a smile that was more of a snarl and Anselmo blanched. Boho looked pleased and Anselmo wished he was a more violent man. He decided to deliver some additional bad news instead. Show how much they fucking needed him.

"Oh, and more good news, meaning bad news—stores are refusing to sell to BEMs," Anselmo added.

Boho looked at Mercedes. "Back to parliament?" he asked.

She sighed and rubbed at her forehead. Now Anselmo felt bad for adding to her troubles. While it was clear she didn't like him, but she always treated him with courtesy.

"Yes. We'll need legislation, and I suppose I'll have to make another damn speech." Her shoulders slumped and for an instant her weariness was evident.

Anselmo spoke up. "Yes, ma'am, we'll need both of those, but if I may make a suggestion."

Boho's response was a glare while Mercedes looked suspicious, and at the same time he said *no,* she said *yes.*

Anselmo continued. "Let the Consort make the speech. Shows that you are a team working side by side and trust each other to do each other's jobs."

"And what, exactly, is going to be *my* job?" Mercedes asked. Her tone was a mix of curiosity and distrust.

"Taking a squad of *fusileros* and raining down hell on the shop keepers that I've identified who are engaged in this naughty behavior."

"And you will, of course, tip off the press," Boho said.

"Of course."

"You are such a weasel, but fuck you are good at this," Boho groused.

"*Gracias.*" Anselmo paused before he stepped through the door. "And by the way, sir, I have a ton of great footage of you on the floor of Parliament making your speeches. Iris is cutting together a kick ass montage. We'll add in the Empress leading the troops and run it after your address to the League. Now I have to get back to the office and put the final touches on your speech."

"You were so sure we would agree?" Mercedes said, a smile barely bending the edges of her lips.

"I'd be a pretty shitty spinmeister if I didn't know how to spin you too," he shot back with a grin, and whisked himself out of the office.

+ + +

SOUNDS SURROUNDED HER. The clash of boot heels on the pavement and echoing off the buildings. The click and hiss of radio communications as the *fusileros* exchanged orders and updates made tinny by their helmets. Overhead was the drone of flitter engines as security flew in guard formation to make certain the woman leading the squad was not in any *actual* danger. And of course, the whirr of the ever-present camerabots because ultimately this was nothing but a publicity stunt.

Which was why Mercedes wasn't wearing her helmet. Anselmo had stressed that she had to be recognized. All in all, she felt a fool decked out in her battle armor quick marching at the head of a squad of soldiers, their rifles held at the ready. *And all of this martial display to intimidate a grocer*, she snorted to herself.

They rounded a corner in a commercial district of Hisselek and headed toward the market midway down the street. In her ear she could hear Boho delivering his speech.

"Life will go on. Parents will hug their children and send them off to school. Lovers will steal kisses and plan weddings. Grandparents will walk on beaches and bask in the sunset's glow."

There was a clot of assorted aliens spilling off the sidewalk while a tall, skinny man flanked by a pair of private security guards berated them. Behind him human customers were passing in and out of the doors of the market, but they were being closely monitored by four more rent-a-cops.

"Because we will not panic. We have faced down danger and adversity before and arisen stronger from those tests. I believe in all of you, human and alien alike."

Mercedes gave a mental eye roll. She was now close enough to hear the shouted threats and insults being hurled by both sides. Bystanders hovered on the sidewalks gawking while a few offered their own opinions of the grocery store owner or the aliens demanding entrance. Tribalism was already rearing its ugly head.

"…and it will be my honor and my privilege to fight beside you for the safety and survival of all we hold dear."

Customers, gawkers, and the private security at the door of the market had become aware of the approaching *fusileros*. A little girl in the crowd of onlookers pointed and cried out excitedly.

"Look mommy, look! It's *la Empresa!*"

"That's why I know I can depend on all of you to do the right thing."

Not without a little help from me, Mercedes thought, *And a group of very heavily armed men.*

People were starting to cheer, calling out God save the Empress. *Viva, la Empresa.* Three cheers for Her Majesty! Mercedes acknowledged them with a raised hand but didn't slow her advance on the now gaping grocer.

"Ma…Majesty," he stuttered and attempted a low bow with all the grace of a crane attempting a curtsy.

But know this—there will be no hoarding. No unreasonable price hikes. No individual, no matter their species, religion, or planet of origin, will be denied service.

"*Ciudadano.*" Mercedes had deliberately picked the colder, more officious, and less polite *citizen* form of address rather than *Señor.* "Why are these League citizens." She gestured at the clot of Isanjo and Hajin. "Being denied entrance to your establishment?"

His mouth fell open and his eyes flicked nervously side to side. "Uh…um…Highness…Majesty…my Empress—"

"I am aware of my titles," Mercedes snapped. "Please answer my question."

"Yes, yes, well, I have limited supplies and I was attempting to…to…limit how much any one individual…can…buy." His voice trailed away.

Everyone will be able to shop and care for their families."

"Yet I see only humans entering and leaving your market. Why is that?" He hung his head. "No answer. I thought not."

"We are setting up the Fair Treatment Bureau to investigate any reports of such activity, and we urge all citizens to report any violations on any planet to the FTB."

Boho had concluded and Mercedes assumed that Anselmo was busy splicing together visuals from this encounter into segments of the speech. It made her skin crawl, but she imagined he would want more material, so she turned to the private security guards.

"You may ensure that entrance and exit are orderly and respectful, but you will not deny entrance to any individual, human, or alien. Have I made myself clear?"

One of the men had the courage to raise his eyes to her. "Yes, ma'am, very clear."

She turned to the sergeant in actual command of the squad. "And sergeant you and your men will assist these gentlemen in these efforts."

"Ma'am." He snapped off a perfect salute.

"Excellent." Mercedes raised her voice to address the growing crowds on the street. "As my husband has just announced, there will be no hoarding, no price gouging, no discrimination. We're all in this together and we will not lose this fight." She concluded with the motto of the *Orden de la Estrella.* "May we touch the stars with glory."

A roar of approval went up from the now massive crowd that had gathered. One of the security shuttles descended to carry her back to her temporary office, but Mercedes took her time opting to move through the crowd. The sergeant and several of the troopers accompanied her as she moved through a kaleidoscope of outstretched hands, desperate eyes, and fear filled faces. She maintained her soft smile, the serene expression that had been drilled into her through years of deportment lessons.

The florist down the street was doing a rousing business selling bouquets. Mercedes arms were soon filled with flowers presented by shy young children offering awkward bows and curtsies.

Then a young pregnant woman with tears running down her cheeks approached, curtsied, and told Mercedes that her husband served about her flagship. Mercedes handed off the flowers to the sergeant and gave the younger woman hug.

That had not been part of her deportment lessons, but Mercedes knew she had to project calm and confidence and comfort even if inwardly she longed to call out to them, *I'm afraid too. So very afraid.*

Then she realized their faith and belief in her was the thing that gave her strength, made her all the more determined to save them, and they deserved to hear that.

So, she said it. What she hadn't expected was for the sergeant to be crying too.

+ + +

"WHO IN THE hell calls at this hour?" Tageri groaned as Jahan's ScoopRing signaled an incoming call. He threw an arm over his eyes as she snapped on the bedside lamp. His fur was rumpled, and he had slept funny, so one ear was folded at an odd angle. Jahan's heart squeezed with love for him.

Jahan glanced at the clock. *3:12 a.m.* She forced back a thrill of fear, calls at this hour usually presaged bad news. She grabbed for the ring and sent it tumbling toward the floor but managed to catch it with her foot. She finally got it into her hand and keyed the signal.

And promptly sat bolt upright and yanked the covers up to her chin when Mercedes' hologram appeared in the air over the bed.

Tageri, arm still across his eyes, growled out. "Who the fuck is it? And tell them somebody better fucking be dying."

"It's…" Jahan cleared her throat. "It's the Empress, dear."

"Jahani, I am not in the mood—"

"No. Really. It's the Empress."

"Oh, fuck."

Mercedes image showed she was struggling between laughter and chagrin. "I'm so sorry, Jahan. I should have had Jaakon look up the time difference. I can call back later."

"No, no, it's fine, ma'am. Let me get up, put on a robe

and give my husband some oxygen so he won't die of embarrassment. Say five minutes?"

"Perfect. I'll call back then," the Mercedes hologram said, and her image flickered and vanished.

"How did this become our life?" Tageri asked plaintively.

They then said in chorus. *"Tracy Fucking Belmanor."*

Sleep was impossible now, so they swung down from their bed suspended in the branches of the home tree. Jahan snagged her robe off a branch as she leaped from branch to branch and onto the platform that served as their bedroom. The wall screens were rolled up allowing the warm summer breeze to carry the gentle cry of a night bird to Jahan's nervously twitching ears.

She slid into her robe and grabbed a brush to smooth her fur. Tageri kissed the tip of one ear as he swung past her.

"I'll be down in the kitchen making cocoa, and when you join me, you will tell me why the Empress of the Solar League has your Scoop number."

"Yes, dear," she said because he had his high school principle voice on.

A few minutes later Mercedes called back. "I'm so sorry."

"Really, it's fine, ma'am. How may I serve?"

"You know about opening O-Trell to—"

"We all listened to the speech, ma'am."

"Oh, thank you. Well, anyway there hasn't exactly been a run a recruitment centers by our alien citizens." Jahan opened her mouth to speak but was forestalled when Mercedes held up a hand. "And look I understand why that is. We conquered you, made you second class citizens while relying on you to clean our homes, build our ships and buildings, tend our gardens, pick up our trash. You're an indispensable part of our lives even if we humans don't acknowledge that, but right now I need your skills and your brains and your bravery. I need aliens to enlist, and I think you can help with that."

"What? Me?"

"Is that so surprising? You were Tracy's XO, now you're a captain. You've got a Tiponi and a Hajin among the crew. I need you and your crew to be the face of our recruitment efforts. You'll be an official member of my government, paid for your work and sent out to talk to alien communities. We also need you to reach out to the scientists and researchers in your communities. O-Trell has a powerful R&D division. I'd like to have input from all of you. We've got to find the answer. The solution."

In that moment Jahan saw the human woman's exhaustion, fear, and desperation. "Of course, we'll help," she heard herself saying.

Mercedes thanks bordered on effusive, and she requested that Jahan and the *Selkie* return to Hisselek as soon as was convenient.

Jahan closed the connection and sat staring at the leaves trembling delicately in the breeze. Now she just had to find a way to tell Tageri that she was once again leaving her home and family.

24

NO SONG TO REMEMBER US BY

"BUILDINGS ARE ALL collapsing. Nobody's lived there for years, maybe decades," Luis' holo image, face obscured by the helmet of his spacesuit, hung in the air in front of Tracy as he sat on the bridge. "There's a cemetery. Lots of graves and a skeleton lying on one grave with a shovel at its side." The image of Luis vanished replaced by the melancholy picture of gave and skeleton.

"Roanoke," Tracy murmured.

"Sir?" Beatrisa asked.

"Sorry, thinking out loud. It was another colony that didn't make it." Tracy indicated for Luis to continue.

"Lieutenant Mehetia has run tests. The planet didn't kill them. It's a perfect Goldilocks."

"Well let's be sure. I'll send down a sealed container for the skeleton. I want Afumba to figure out what killed them before we investigate further."

"Yes, sir." Luis snapped off a salute. "Paranoid is always better than dead."

The *Sutābureza* had made its way to this distant solar system because of a call from the imperial governor of Earth, Henrick Rothchild. From Mercedes speech he knew of Tracy and the dreadnaught's mission and had set his people to scouring records dating back six and seven hundred years. Their mission, to search for information about any long view ships that might have set out on their quixotic missions to give humans a foothold in the galaxy. They had located three that weren't previously known.

Fortunately, there had been press accounts about these various undertakings, and the interviews provided trajectories, and which stars the colonists had pinpointed as possible locations for Goldilocks planets. The *Sutābureza* had made their way to the first two and found no trace of the ships and passengers, and only one system showed an even marginal planet. Clearly their gamble hadn't paid off.

This final system had seemed far more promising with a lush, world bursting with life, and a few pieces of the cannibalized ship still in orbit, but radio silence from the surface of the planet. Because paranoia was now only second to cleanliness and godliness for Tracy, he ordered that the shuttle crew should wear spacesuits, and all contamination methods would be observed upon their return. If the planet proved to be toxic to humans like Paradise Lost, they could warn off any future colonists.

Assuming we survive our current threat, Tracy thought glumly.

Several hours later the ship's doctor appeared on the bridge. "Male victim. Cause of death starvation," Afumba said without preamble. "Perhaps there will be records on the planet as to why they were so woefully ill prepared to survive, but everything else checks out as fully habitable."

"Well, let us go and see," Tracy said and levered himself

out of his chair.

"Long damn detour only to find no help," Cassutt grumbled.

The weapons office wasn't wrong. They had spent thirty-seven days in Fold to reach these coordinates.

"We can at least give them a benediction," Father Ken said gently. "They were our brothers and sisters. They reached for the stars and fell short, but their hope and bravery should be honored."

Tracy selected the landing party while Ken went off to gather his stole, missal, and holy water. The shuttle ride to the surface had been made in almost utter silence. Even the normally cheerful Luis was subdued. Tracy wondered if the younger man was remembering another Hidden World where they had found only death?

Now they stood in what had been the central plaza of the only town on the planet where the local vegetation was reasserting control. A large tree had burst through the roof of what appeared to be a public building, the walls of the houses were starting to collapse. In front of one house a lone Earth rose bush defiantly spread its bright red blossoms to catch the light of an alien sun.

Tracy wondered if it was the only survivor, but then the soft calls from a flock of winged creatures in a tree were suddenly replaced with shrieks of alarm and the thunder of wings as the bird-like things took to the air. Tracy caught a glimpse of orange tabby fur as a cat bought down one of the creatures.

"Naturally the moggies survive," Cipriana said with a snort.

They followed an overgrown path to the cemetery. "Gone to graveyards everyone," Tracy murmured and suppressed a shudder.

"On which grave was the skeleton found?" Ken asked.

"Here, Father," a *fusilero* said and showed him the grave. They all bent to read the faint script etched the wooden gravestone.

"Matilda? Marianne? Can't quite make out the surname." Ken pulled aside a vine that had grown up over the marker. "Beloved wife," he read aloud, his voice dying away into sadness.

"He was the last one standing," Tracy said quietly.

"And chose to die near the woman he loved," Luis added softly, an odd look on his face.

It was a sharp reminder for Tracy hadn't spoken to his wife in over a month. It wasn't fair to her especially when he had already been gone for five months, and they still had to visit Freehold. She would be three quarters of the way through her pregnancy by the time he returned.

He whirled on Luis. "Tell Afumba we need the body sent down. We'll see him laid to rest next to her."

"Yes, sir." Luis stepped aside and keyed his ScoopRing.

It was going to take a while for his order to be affected. The landing party scattered into the various buildings to see if they could locate a manifest, a journal, a recording, anything that would detail the fate of these people. Cipriana went in search of the cat, luring it to her with pieces broken off a protein bar.

They found most of it, and it was a harrowing tale of awakening from cold sleep to discover the livestock embryos had died, and a puncture in the cargo area during their long journey had allowed much of their seed stock to be lost to the vacuum. Judging by the names it seemed they were primarily people out of the European Union.

The skeleton of the last survivor arrived, and Babcock who commanded the *fusileros* had the foresight to include entrenching tools. They all joined in digging the grave, and through a process of elimination they thought they had the man's name. *Luciano Ricci.*

Father Ken kissed his stole and placed it around his neck, opened his missal and read—

"Eternal rest grant unto them O Lord and let the perpetual light shine upon them. And may the souls of all the faithful departed, through the mercy of God, rest in peace. Amen."

A murmur of amens whispered to the wind sighing through the alien pines. Tracy crossed himself and laid the rose he had cut from that one scrappy bush onto the newly turned earth.

It was a silent and pensive group that made their way back to the shuttle. *If we fail,* Tracy thought *there will be no attestation that we ever existed, no song, no book, no work of art to remember us by.*

+ + +

IT WAS LATE when Mercedes finally crawled beneath the covers. She had spent over an hour listening to her youngest sister wail about…well, everything and nothing. Intellectually Mercedes knew Carisa was dealing with the hormonal storm of being six months pregnant with what the couple had discovered in an ultra-sound to be twins rather than the single baby they had been expecting. A husband who probably wouldn't return for at least another month. All of which left Carisa feeling abandoned, abused and overall, very poorly treated.

Estella had been a saint, having Carisa over to her and Alfred's home, insisting she stay for several days, and generally petting and cosseting the younger woman who was now going into the most unpleasant period of any pregnancy. Swelling ankles, aching back, the constant need to pee and starting to feel trapped in an ungainly swollen body. It had to be hell for someone as tiny as Carisa and there was no one there to tell her that pregnancy made her even more beautiful.

Mercedes snorted into her pillow. As if that wasn't a lie if ever there was one. Sapphire chirruped at the odd noise and nosed her chin. She slipped a hand free to stoke the cat's soft fur.

"I suspect it's more than that," she told the cat. "We're all suffering under this miasma of dread. How do you live when you know death is coming?" She shook her head at her own question. "Well, I suppose that's just the human condition, but annihilation isn't normal, and it isn't fair. How do we even comprehend the death of *everything*, hmm? How do we do that? How do we keep going?"

The cat's response was to purr. It was as good an answer as any. She was just dozing off to the lulling rumble when her ScoopRing signaled an incoming call. Every muscle in Mercedes body tensed. Calls at this hour.

She stumbled out of bed, threw on her peignoir and answered. It was Ernesto, and he looked exhausted.

"So, sorry to disturb you this late, Highness," he said. *So, it was going to be one of* those *conversations.* The scientist rarely used her title.

"Quite all right. What have you got for me?

"May I be crude, ma'am?" She nodded her assent. "Fuck and all."

"You've been observing it for months," Mercedes snapped.

"I know. I've tried every way I can think of to test this monster, but I can only get remote readings since anything it touches it transforms."

"And?" she prompted.

"And nothing makes sense. It's like the fucking thing doesn't belong here."

"Well, the Cara'ot did say it seems to have originated in a different galaxy."

He ran a hand wearily across his head, fingers snagging in his greying curls. He shook his head and the single gold earring that he'd worn the entire forty years she had known him caught the light. "Yeah, but physics should be physics, all the universe around, and this thing seems determined to defy physics."

"Well at least it hasn't figure out how to transcend light speed," she said. "Gives us a bit of breathing space."

"Talion's got some thoughts on a military strategy, but we'd like to return to brief everyone in person." Ernesto paused. "Also, I think we'd all like to see our families." His voice went very quiet on the final word, and Mercedes felt a stab of fear beneath her breastbone, and her breath went short.

In case that military strategy fails and most of us die. Her mind supplied what Ernesto had left unspoken.

"Of course. Travel time for both you and Admiral Belmanor is roughly similar. I'll inform high command and set a meeting that takes that into account, and also arrange shore leave for everyone."

"Thank you, ma'am."

+   +   +

BELÁN WAS A lovely world. If you liked grasslands. Lots of grasslands. Lots and lots of grassland. Endless grasslands. Having grown up on Cuandru in the midst of that world's massive forests the expansive vistas made Jahan nervous as a cat in a room full of rocking chairs. No place to hide, no way to go high and get away from danger. It was primal this fear speaking to evolution more than reason.

Even the damn buildings were squat. All single story built from stone with sweeping canvas roofs that resembled bird's wings. Only the imperial embassy in the capital city of Talis was multi-storied.

To be fair it was evolution that had allowed the Hajin to develop on this world, to go from peaceful grazing herbivores a million years ago to a bipedal race with a large brain and opposing thumbs.

Jahan forced her attention back to the royal governor. He was of course a human, and he was clearly not thrilled by their visit. Only the royal credentials provided by Mercedes had mollified the man.

"I'm supposed to offer you any assistance you might require," Margrave Clark Bennington Kunst said with an added sniff at the end indicating his feeling about that.

"Actually, we don't need much," Dalea said quietly. "I grew up here, still have family and connections. We mostly just want the local constabulary to not overreact if they see a herd of Hajin congregating in the cities we'll be visiting."

"Wise, very wise," Kunst admitted. "There have been increased incidents of rioting and violence on some worlds and the *policía* are…tense."

"On predominately human worlds," Jax trilled as he slid down the hallway on his root tendrils.

"Which is exactly why the Cara'ot picked you lot to lead the big fucking fight," Jahan muttered under her breath. Unfortunately, the man heard her.

Fortunately, he was amused. He smiled. "True that. Though I haven't picked up a rifle apart from bird hunting since I finished my military service."

"Yeah, but you were a swordsman."

Kielli's remark surprised Jahan. "How would you know that?" she asked her nephew.

"I read up on him. He was the president of his dueling society at The High Ground, and he's got the dueling scar. I always thought it would be cool to—" Kielli hopped about pretending to wield a sword. "You know, buckle and swash."

"Well, perhaps you'll get your chance. Only a matter of time before your kind will be allowed to attend," Kunst said with a smirk.

Everyone tensed, and Jax smoothed over the awkward

moment by asking, "Will you be returning to active duty?"

"I have thirteen children. Seven of them are aboard ships. So yes, I'll be returning to active duty." Kunst's tone was grim, and he strode ahead of them. "I'll see to it the authorities in the cities are informed of your arrival. I hope you recruit a lot of your people."

"We will," Dalea said and concluded softly, "They have children too."

+   +   +

SINCE TALION HAD returned his purloined ships back to Ouranos it had been easy for Paloma to avoid Boho by traveling aboard a different ship. When Boho had suggested she travel with him on the flagship she had refused. It had hurt more than Boho had expected.

Once back in Hisselek the rush of events had kept him from even attempting to contact her. He wondered if she was afraid after Mercedes had made her speech. Like all of the rank and file she had had no idea why Talion had given up his dream of a throne, and until Mercedes speech none had known about the return of the Cara'ot. Rohan had felt it best that the revelation to the League as a whole should come only from Mercedes.

Then there was Paloma's personal trauma. Her older sister arrested for attempted murder, and still in jail because dealing with Christina was the least of the issues currently facing them.

And now Boho and Cyprian were visiting the orphanage where she worked. Another of Anselmo's stunts designed to fill the vid screens with heartwarming moments of the royals bringing joy and comfort to average citizens. Boho tried to concentrate on the tour being conducted by the administrator but found himself glancing down hallways and through open doors to see if he caught a glimpse of the girl.

They reached a large playroom where children were engaged in finger painting, playing with toys, bouncing on a trampoline while adults kept careful watch on all four sides. Paloma was in one corner helping a group of children assemble a castle out of plastic blocks.

The woman who ran the orphanage leaned down to Cyprian. "Would you like to join the children, your Highness?"

Cyprian looked up at Boho. "May I, papa?" There was a hitch in the child's voice, and a shadow deep in those golden eyes. Had the boy caught Boho's faint flinch when he said *papa*?

"Of course."

Cyprian ran off to where a clot of boys and two girls were playing with models of spaceships. One of the younger children tripped and fell, and the administrator excused herself to deal with the wailing child.

Boho signaled his security detail to hold back, and he made a slow circuit of the room drawing ever closer to Paloma. Her eyes tracked him, and he had a fleeting thought about hunters and prey. But he was truly the prey being lured closer and closer. Boho forced himself to stop near the water fountain. Took a drink to cover his nervousness.

"Hello, Boho." Her voice. She was at his elbow.

"Ah...hello." An awkward silence ensued. This was so unlike him. "Family all right?" He winced even as the words emerged.

"Not really. Sister in prison. My brother, Shadrach is getting a divorce. Daddy's wrecked another flitter, and has cirrhosis, oh, and impending doom. You?"

The jab should have either enraged or amused him. Instead, Boho found his eyes burning and fought to hold back the tears. He couldn't interpret Paloma's expression but found himself gripped by the sleeve and dragged out a door into a small courtyard that held a sandbox, a slide and a swing set. The late summer sun was brutal, and Boho felt sweat beginning to bead on his forehead.

"What is it? What's wrong?"

He shook his head, uncertain how to even begin to catalogue the fears, regrets, sadness, loneliness, and guilt he felt. She caught a tear that had managed to escape with her knuckle.

"This isn't your normal feeling sorry for yourself."

"Do you ever not insult me?" he asked honestly curious.

"I was trying to be sympathetic. I suppose I must work on that."

She pulled him over to the swing set and seated herself. The chains creaked softly as she propelled herself with one dainty foot. Boho leaned on one of the uprights.

"My b—Cyprian. Mercedes keeps throwing us together. As if it will…" He broke off and shook his head. "And it should. What's changed, really? And he doesn't know. People are careful around him and he's too young to have read that farrago of nonsense that Anselmo put out. But he senses that something has changed."

He went silent again, squinting up at the sun, smelling

the spicy sent of the chaparral being carried into the city by the sirocco winds. "I was so proud of him. My son. Heir to an empire. So bright and verbal. At two he was speaking in complete sentences. I took all the credit. This was *my* boy. But now I know the truth, and if I'm honest with myself all of those traits, those things that make him special…they're due to *him*."

"Well, Mercedes did help a little," Paloma said.

He shot her a glance but found himself unable to stop the confession that was demanding to be spoken. "I'm hurting a child who is innocent in all this. He shouldn't bear the weight of all the sins his mother, that man, and I have heaped on each other. I want to be better, Paloma, but I don't know how."

Paloma stood, shook out her skirt that had attracted a bit of pollen from the flowering chamisa. She then stepped in close, went up on tiptoes, rested a hand on his shoulder and startled Boho completely when she kissed him gently on the cheek.

"That is the most honest and self-aware I have ever heard you be. I could…like this man."

He gazed into her deep brown eyes and felt a fierce desire to protect her. Forever and always.

She placed her hand on his back and gave him a gentle shove toward the door. "We should go back inside. There's a little boy who needs a papa."

25

LIFE GOES ON, HOPE ABIDES, AND WE WILL WIN (WE HOPE)

"I'M SORRY. I'M sorry. I'm sorry." It was a mantra as he rubbed his hand across her back while Carisa wept onto his chest. They weren't tears of grief or joy, however. It was pure rage that fueled the waterworks.

Tracy had stepped through the apartment door, met the blazing eyes of his *very* pregnant wife. She had waddled up to him and punched him hard on the bicep. Now he was awkwardly trying to hold her while the swell of her belly seemed to be trying to push him away.

Carisa joined in her belly's effort and succeeded in forcing him back a step. She glared up at him. "You better not leave me again. Until *this*," she gestured at her swollen belly. "Is over."

"I'm here now, and I'm not going anywhere."

He almost mentioned that they had to figure out to integrate the ships from the Hidden Worlds into O-Trell, get new recruits trained and the entire process was going to take months. Then he thought better of it. He had a feeling she had precisely zero fucks to give about military affairs at this moment.

A handkerchief was procured from his pocket, and he gently wiped her eyes. "You carry a handkerchief?" she asked and from her tone it didn't sound like approval.

"Yes, because I taught him to," Alexander said. "For just this type of situation. You never know when a lady might need assistance." His gentle tone broke the tension and Carisa visibly relaxed.

Alexander crossed to them. "Welcome back, son," he said and hugged Tracy.

"I'm sorry this took so long," Tracy said. "Especially when three of the stops were a waste of time."

"Yes, we know. Luis kept us informed," Carisa snapped.

Tracy's mind stuttered on that for an instant, but he recovered and continued, "Good news Freehold has a sizable fleet and is a highly technologically society. They're going to be a big help." He looked down at Carisa. "You'd like it there. In fact, once this is over, I was going to see if we could be the ambassadors to Freehold."

"Sure, fine. You have to win first." Her tone was bitter and hopeless, and she walked ponderously to the sofa, sat down with a groan, and rubbed at her distended belly.

"You look wonder—"

"*Don't*! I look like hell. I've gained almost fifty pounds. These babies kick all the time, and I can't sleep, I have to pee all the time, have indigestion, and I'm miserable."

Tracy looked desperately to his father who had as much expression as a store mannikin. No help there.

"It will be over soon." Another glare so clearly not the right thing to say. "Did you find out the sex of…our…babies?"

"Yes."

"Do you want to tell me?"

"Do you want to know?"

"Yes, I think I do. Easier to work on names, right?"

"Little girls."

"So, identical twins," Tracy said trying to wrap his head around that.

"Yes."

His father was beaming at him, and Alexander clapped him on the shoulder. "I'm going to be an *abuelo*."

"I'm going to get out of this uniform and relax. Do you need anything, my dear?" Tracy asked as he bent solicitously over her.

"Some cranberry juice over ice, please." She gave him a sideways glance. "And I'm sorry I'm being such a harridan. Mercedes…she looks like a ghost, Estella, Beatrisa, Izzara, Delia, they're all doing their part to help us prepare, and I'm just being a lump." She blinked hard holding back tears.

There was a tightening in Tracy's chest. "No, you are doing exactly what you should be doing. Caring for yourself and our children. You've given me a gift, Cari, yourself and the children I never thought I would have. I'm unworthy of your devotion, but know how deeply I…I—"

She laid a hand over his mouth. "I know. It's enough. I am content without you saying…well, you know."

A jumble of conflicting emotions shook Tracy to his core. "I'll…I'll get your juice," he said and fled.

✦   ✦   ✦

THERE WERE CLEARLY too many people in this meeting. High command from O-Trell and command staff from Freehold's SpaceCom matched shouts with officers from Al-Nefud's *Qiadat Alnujum* and Geneva's *Stern Befehl* bellowing out agreement with remarks made by Freehold's officers. Rohan and his valet set along the wall as passive observers and Mercedes wanted to slap them both. They were the puppet masters here they could at least give an occasional tug on the strings.

The main auditorium at the *Ministerio de Guerra* in the giant octagonal building on and below the surface of Hellfire was the scene of this shitshow. And the shit had started flying even before the actual meeting.

When Mercedes had decreed that the military briefings would be held at the League's main military headquarters her high command staff had had a white-hot meltdown. The admirals and generals had huffed about possible espionage, cyber warfare by the military officers from the Hidden Worlds, and the dangers of unrepentant republicanism.

Boho had quipped that soon there would be women and aliens in the military, cats and dogs living together, mass hysteria. The senior staff had *not* been amused. Mercedes had wanted to kiss him, and the arrogant valet had had the temerity to give her husband a thumbs up, and murmur *"Right on."*

A new voice had joined the din, Gelb was yelling. "All you lazy damn Hiddens sat back fat and happy while we fought the *necrófagos*."

"We protected *your kinder*," a general from Geneva yelled back.

"So, you are wonderful babysitters," Valada-Viers shouted back.

"Maybe we shouldn't blend them with our forces. They'll just weaken us. They've never actually fought," Talion added.

Admiral Tina Vasquez, supreme naval commander of the Freehold SpaceCom, glared at the League officers. "You should be so lucky as to have my people, but I'm damned if I'll see any of them under the command of a bunch of aristocratic *pricks*."

Tracy who was present only as a hologram since Carisa was days away from giving birth spoke up. His tone was both weary and supremely irritated.

"Here's a thought. Maybe we all could stop arguing over who gets to lead the goddam parade and instead focus on…oh, I don't know…*winning* so we can *have* a fucking parade?"

Now Mercedes wanted to kiss *him*, and the *intitulado's* disgust and sarcasm seemed to remind everyone of the stakes. The room went quiet.

"Admiral Baron Talion has developed a possible attack strategy," Mercedes said taking control. "Perhaps we could hear his proposal."

There was grumbling assent. Talion stood up and keyed a hologram that offered a three hundred and sixty degree and three-dimensional view of the deadly phenomenon.

"There is a certain cohesion to the object, but thus far it's only had to react to single ships or a handful of ships all dropping out of Fold in the same quadrant. My thinking is that if we encircled the thing dropping out at numerous points and firing our weapons simultaneously the creature wouldn't be able to react to all of them, and restructure and assimilate every missile and rail gun slug."

"The calculations for all those ships translating, and weapon trajectories would have to be so precise. Otherwise, we're in a circle shooting at each other, and just as likely to blow each other out of space," Tracy pointed out.

"I'll work with the officers and crews to hone the translation and firing calculations," Talion said.

Mercedes spoke up. "No, Admiral Belmanor should do that. He was top of our class in orbital mechanics and math."

Talion acquiesced with a bow of his head. "Very well."

"I'd like to pull in professors from Tiponi universities to help with that. The Flutes grasp of mathematics dwarfs ours," Tracy said.

Ernesto stood. "And Admiral Belmanor is correct. This isn't a single entity. It's tiny, discreet pieces that somehow form a whole. Like a swarm of bees or an army of ants—"

Tracy made a choked sound, and Mercedes rolled her eyes. "All right, we'll call them the Star Ants." She glanced at the others in the room. "My brother-in-law has taken it upon himself to name the enemy."

"The Admiral and his crew have a tendency to do that. One of our lieutenants named the *necrófagos* too," Valada-Viers said with a chuckle.

Boho scowled. "Perhaps we could return to this briefing and stop handing out participation awards." He nodded to Ernesto who continued.

"The point is that assuming the missiles and slugs aren't transformed and might detonate and tear through a portion of the creatures, I'm not certain the destruction will actually weaken the overall structure." Ernesto gazed at the newcomers from the Hidden Worlds. "I'd really like to take any of your xenobiologists out to view the creature. See if any of you see something we've missed. I've added Hajin, Isanjo Sidone and Tiponi scientists."

"What about the Cara'ot?" Vasquez asked.

Rohan shifted his bulk and lifted his head. "Oh, we've been studying the…er…Star Ants for millennia, and everything we have learned has been given to the League. I'm sure they'll provide our research to your people."

"Which actually raises an interesting question," Boho said. "My impression is that our alien citizens, and that's not limited to the Cara'ot, were very aware of the location of your worlds, but kept that information from us."

"Yes," Rohan said, and Vasquez nodded in assent.

"Which makes me a bit uncomfortable with this new attitude that we're all in this together. Clearly the five civilized races weren't all that loyal to the League," Boho continued.

"They were making a Real," Tracy said. "Money was the lure not sedition."

"And did the Hiddens know that the Cara'ot disappearance was a giant crock of shit?" Boho asked, his tone like acid.

"No," the admiral from Geneva said. "We were as much in the dark as you, and it made us damn nervous when the big trading ships stopped arriving."

"Which was the whole point of the disappearing act," Tracy said. His holographic image was focused on Rohan and the valet. "Wasn't it? To add to our paranoia."

"Yep," said the valet. "You humans are snake mean when you're scared, and you better fucking be scared now."

+   +   +

IT WAS VERY late. The only sound piercing the darkness the drone of police flitters patrolling the city. Occasionally there would be the sharp bleat of a siren, and every time Anselmo would stiffen, yanking pain from his agonized back muscles. Was this it? Had the aliens arrived? Was death coming? Then his rational mind would take control, force his tense body to relax and he would return to his task—cutting together propaganda vid designed to comfort and sedate populations across the League.

Here was footage of Mercedes touring a munitions factory on Dragonfly. The grateful staff all standing in line, bowing, scraping, and tugging their forelocks while in the background missiles on the assembly line slid past. Anselmo had had the camera crew do a rack focus from Mercedes calm expression to the worshipful face of a young woman worker, to a close up of the missiles. Message clear—leadership is not worried and we're going to blow the shit out of our enemies. We got this!

Pausing for a sip of coffee Anselmo waved screens aside until he found the images from Captain Princess Beatrisa's visit to a recruiting station. Looking trim and efficient in her uniform she walked up the line of young humans and aliens waiting to enlist shaking hands, pausing for pictures. Once again, he thanked God for royal training that had her expression equally as calm and determined as her sister's. He spliced a few cuts into the vid.

Next up Boho dressed in battle armor, tall, handsome, the silver at his temples only adding to his aura of gravitas and composure. He was drilling *fusilero* recruits on an obstacle course and firing range. Of course, it was all bullshit. The soldiers weren't going to go hand to hand against the Ants, but it looked impressive as hell.

Anselmo had forced Belmanor onto the bridge of his flagship for some shots of him studying holograms of navigational plots and weapon trajectories. Anselmo had no fucking idea what all the numbers and lines meant. Most of the people who viewed the vid wouldn't either, but it all looked very technical, and Belmanor was known as the man who single handedly—Anselmo rolled his eyes and mentally added *with three ships and a fuck load of fusileros*—captured a *necrófago* ship.

The other sisters—Estella, Izzara and Delia—he had touring hospitals and medical labs because Anselmo did not want the general public to assume this was going to be a cakewalk. While the Star Ants weren't going to reach any League or Hidden Worlds for almost two hundred years there were going to be losses in the fleet. The husbands, brothers, wives, sisters, and children serving aboard those ships were going to die, and they couldn't have the populace going wobbly on them, and deciding their current leadership wasn't up to the task.

The best news in terms of his task was that there were going to be several lovely life affirming events in the next few days. Right now, Princess Carisa was under the care of palace physicians as she gave birth. Naturally Belmanor had absolutely refused to allow Anselmo to have a camerabot with the anxious father-to-be and grandfather-to-be, but there would be a photo op when the happy family left the hospital with their little bundles of joy, and Anselmo was already planning how to make certain Quinta would be a companion to the two little princesses. He then realized that those banal thoughts belonged to a different time and pulled his thoughts back to his task.

Despite Belmanor's attitude toward propaganda he wouldn't be able to ban cameras from the christening ceremony. It would be broadcast, and Anselmo would nicely spin it to deliver the message that life goes on, hope abides, and we will win.

He only hoped it was true.

+ + +

"WILL YOU RELAX. First time mother. Twins. Oh, and labor. It takes a while." As soon as she said it Jahan realized she hadn't been all that soothing or comforting.

Even in a hologram she could see Tracy's exhaustion and panic. On the other hand, she knew it probably wasn't as great as Carisa's exhaustion, so her sympathy was limited. She said as much to Tracy.

"I know, I know," he stuttered. "But it's been twenty-seven hours. She's so tiny. What if I've killed her?"

"The doctors are not going to let that happen. If they decide the babies are in distress or Carisa is in danger, they'll do a cesarean. Trust me, they're not going to let anything happen to a princess royal." She paused then asked, "Is

Mercedes there?"

His expression twisted into something she couldn't identify. "No." He then hastened to add. "She's off world. I'm certain she'd be here if she wasn't."

Would she Jahan wondered? Cyprian's half-sisters were being born. And wouldn't they also be some kind of cousin to the prince since their mother was Mercedes half-sister…The whole thing was head spinning.

"Tracy, stop being such a pussy. Go back in her room, hold her hand. Tell her you lo—Well, tell her something fond and affectionate. Look, are you happy?"

He ran an agitated hand through is already messy hair. "I don't know. Dad says when I hold them there will be this rush of love, but it all feels…"

Jahan thought she could supply the final word, but she didn't say it. Instead, she gentled her tone and said, "I know this situation is weird. Far from ideal. But I know you. You're a good man, and you're going to love these little girls, and respect and honor their mother. And your dad is right. I know Tageri would fight off the Star Ants with just his teeth and claws to protect our three. Now go do you husbandly job and hold your wife's hand."

He gave a hurried nod and his image vanished off the galley table.

✦   ✦   ✦

TENSION WAS ETCHED in every line of his navigator's shoulders. Boho sympathized. His own muscles felt like they were cracking, and a trickle of sweat was tickling his sideburn. All the bridge crew were hyper-focused on their instruments ready to take the ship back into Fold at the merest hint that the Star Ants were moving their way.

He was in sector 470. He supposed he should be grateful it was under these circumstances and not because he'd been sent here to die, but death could still happen, and he couldn't still the frenzied pounding of his heart.

There had been some initial questing tendrils when they had first dropped out of Fold, like curious snakes drawn by motion, but the activity had ceased as the creature continued to encircle a gas giant unfortunate enough to be in its path.

The *Vencedor* had been tasked with bringing a gaggle of Isanjo, Tiponi, Hajin and Sidone scientists along with a few Hidden World experts to observe and take measurements on the Star Ants. Some were aboard the flagship, but the majority were in two shuttles that were taking readings. All except the Isanjo. Naturally those crazy fuckers had their observation team clinging to the skin of one of the shuttles their equipment strapped to their spacesuited backs.

Boho could not imagine being outside the protective walls of the dreadnaught. Not that it would make any difference, but it at least offered the illusion of safety buried as they were deep within plasteel and shielding, but he could feel his skin crawling as he studied the phenomenon.

He hadn't wanted to lead this mission. Mercedes had of course said she'd lead it, but no one was going to risk the Empress on mere reconnaissance. Boho had suggested Belmanor and been overruled by his wife who said that the *intitulado* was a new father and he needed to spend time with his wife and their babies. Talion had his own tasks, so it had, perforce, fallen to Boho and he fucking hated it.

He had never intended to remain in the military after his five-year stint. He wanted the resume, but his real goal had been a royal governorship with a planet to squeeze financially and the opportunity to fuck his way through the provincial nobility's wives and daughters. Instead, he ended up the imperial consort and now alien monster bait.

It was as if his bitter thought had affected the fucking thing for horrifyingly the swirling, glittering mass abandoned the planet, heeled over and began to move toward them.

"It's gaining speed, sir," the officer on sensors reported. "It will reach us in fifty-seven minutes." He watched, fingers flying across his console. "Make that forty-two minutes."

"It must sense us," Boho's flag captain murmured.

"Not a comforting thought," he muttered back. Boho keyed his radio and broadcast to all the scientists. "Gentle beings, this thing has decided we're interesting and is coming for us at increasing speed. So, whatever you're doing, do it fast and get back here. We'll keep you apprised of its progress."

"Thirty-one minutes."

"How the hell is it accelerating?" Boho muttered. "It's not like it has engines or thrusters." He keyed his radio again. "Citizens, you've got fifteen minutes then get back here. Use that time to try and figure out its means of propulsion." He cut the connection, then reopened it and added, "And don't be late. We're not waiting for you."

26

WE'LL FINISH THIS TOGETHER

PART OF THE roof of the cathedral had yet to be repaired so dust motes like silver glitter played among the golden sunlight. Camerabots circled overhead, and the Cardinal was waiting to baptize Tracy and Carisa's daughters. Having been denied the honor of marrying the couple Mercedes had indicated it might be politic to allow him to officiate at this sacrament.

They were all gathered around the baptismal font, and Cyprian was peering down into the face of Syna. Her long lace christening robe trailing across Carisa's arms like a waterfall of snowflakes. Her older, by two minutes, sibling Sidra was in Tracy's arms, and fussing a bit. He stuck the tip of his little finger into her flower bud mouth, and she settled. The look he bestowed on his daughter both melted and shattered Mercedes heart.

"She doesn't have much hair, does she?" Cyprian observed critically.

"Not right now, but just you wait, soon she'll have lots of pretty curls like yours," Carisa said.

"I'm a boy, I don't have pretty curls," he said with disgust, and looked indignant when all the adults laughed. He looked up at Mercedes and asked, "So, Syna and Sidra are my…aunts, even though they're babies, like Tia Carisa is my aunt?"

Everyone froze, Tracy most of all. Cyprian's brow furrowed as he gave it more thought. "Or are we cousins? I guess we're cousins like Aurelia and Issac and Halton, and Emery—"

Before he could go through an exhaustive list of all his cousins Mercedes slipped an arm around her son's shoulders. "It's complicated, Cy, I'll explain it later."

She shot an intense glare at Anselmo who circled a finger in the air and drew it across his throat to indicate that he had gotten the message and none of that sound would ever be broadcast. Still, she wondered how much longer the truth could be hidden from Cyprian.

+ + +

BOHO SAT SLUMPED; hands clasped between his knees. Mercedes was rubbing soothing circles on his back. It felt nice, but he still felt cold horror even though he was safely away from the creature.

"It wasn't my fault. One shuttle got too close. I told them to come back, but they went to pick up a scanner buoy. Goddam thing threw out a tendril, it was like a whip and hit the shuttle. Radio channel was open. I heard them…sounds they made as they…as they…and it was all for nothing." He flung himself off the sofa and began to pace. Frenzied steps, breath hitching as the fear returned. "And it was all for nothing," he repeated. "The BEMs and the Hiddens have no more clue than we do."

The staff had thrown open the windows in the sitting room, and the breeze carried the scent of flowers from the garden. A night bird called softly. The peaceful beauty pierced him, and Boho trembled. Soon all of this would be like the lifeless worlds they had visited so the scientists could take their useless samples. Boho had been terrified to allow them to even touch the transformed objects for fear the contagion could spread, but the Cara'ot hadn't been wrong. It was only mid-process or the creature itself that could affect the change. What it left in its wake was just cold, inert death.

Mercedes remained silent and he could see the fear in her face. "The damn thing is just so fast," he said trying to excuse himself again. "It became aware of us virtually the instant we translated back into normal space. We just thought we'd have more time."

"We knew there would be casualties. And what choice do we have? We can't just wait passively to die."

He once again joined her on the sofa. "And it won't be passive. Unrest is going to increase." Mercedes shifted closer to him, and Boho put an arm around her shoulders. "And even if this plan works things will never go back to the way they were, back to normal," Boho said.

"What do you mean?"

"Your ascension to the throne meant that women started jostling the elbows of the average *hombre* vying for what he considers his God given place. Then we went and made the BEMs full citizens. Up until now an ordinary *ciudadano* could think that no matter how abysmal his life might be he was still better than those alien *pendejos*. Now we've said *they* are his equal too. So that citizen is going to cast his eyes upward and wonder just why the fuck the FFH is superior to him?"

"And what will he decide?" Mercedes asked. He sensed she probably had a pretty good idea but wanted to let him spool this out.

"That we all put on our trousers one leg at a time, and that maybe we're a bunch of parasites living off their hard work and industry. Democracy, republicanism, populism, maybe even revolution are going to rear their ugly heads. We need to find a way to get ahead of it, or at least blunt the effect."

Mercedes gave a sigh that seemed to come from the depths of her soul and laid her head on his shoulder. "Would it be awful of me to admit that I wouldn't mind that one little bit? To be simple Señora Arango might be nice. Because sometimes I think I shall shatter into a thousand pieces under the weight of it all." Her voice was muffled, thick with unshed tears.

Boho turned his head and pressed a kiss onto her temple. "No." He found himself unable to hold back the words. "Sometimes I wish I could just run—" He broke off abruptly before he said too much.

Mercedes pushed herself upright and stared into his face. "Run. But not away." Her tone was musing, analytical. Surprise washed across her face. "To *her*. You want to run to her." Her expression was open, wondering, and held no hint of anger or accusation. "Oh, Boho, my dear. You *do* love her."

He studied his hands. "Yes."

"We're a pair, aren't we?" Mercedes said with a small sad smile. She abruptly stood. "Well, I've made a mess of my situation, but there's no reason for you to have to live with this lifetime of horrible decisions. We may not have all that much time so I think you should use what remains to find your happiness. I think we should divorce."

"What!" He surged to his feet. "I was just talking about how unstable the political system is right now and you want to add this on top of everything else? Besides, there's no guarantee she'll even have me."

"So, go find out. Paloma might feel differently if she knew you weren't just offering the position of inamorata."

A surge of excitement, of hope, the first he'd felt in months pulsed through him. "Thank you." He gripped Mercedes' hands. "You could do the same."

"No. He has too much integrity. He'll never leave Carisa and his daughters."

She didn't seem to realize that once again she had insulted and demeaned him, but honestly, didn't he deserve it? He studied her, the crow's feet around her eyes, the amount of silver now running through her hair. Over thirty years of marriage, battles fought, and battles won. Unlike him she had never betrayed him publicly, and she had even spared his pride when the truth emerged about Cyprian claiming she had used artificial insemination rather than hanging a cuckhold's horns on him. Could he really walk away and leave her to carry this burden alone?

The answer came quicker than he had expected, and he found it surprised him.

"No," he found himself saying. "We'll finish

this…together. We can reassess then. Assuming we survive."

+   +   +

"No, I'm not going to help you enlist. You're too old." Tracy said.

Jahan had mandated that the *Selkie* would stop at the capital on their please-enlist-for-the-good-of-the-League tour because she wanted to enlist Tracy to help her well…enlist since she kept getting turned down. Unfortunately, she had found it impossible to get through the thicket of secretaries, and assistants to set a meeting with Tracy at his so she had just gone straight to his apartment.

Fortunately, the *fusilero* commander in charge of security had served with her when they took down the *necrófago* ship, so he let her take the elevator up to the penthouse. They now stood in the elegant living room. Down the hall she heard the tinkling of a music box playing a popular lullaby.

"I'm younger than you," Jahan shot back. "And you're going. Going to be right on the fucking front lines when you try this Hail Mary."

"I'm an admiral," Tracy responded. "We're supposed to be old shits, and on the front line. You'd be enlisting as a da—" He cut off the curse word. "An *estrella hombre*, and you'd hate it. You've been the captain of the *Selkie* for years now. How are you going to take orders from some snot nosed lieutenant fresh out of The High Ground? You'd be busted for insubordination in three days…" He considered. "Probably less. Besides, I need you to protect my wife and my daughters."

"And just how the fuck am I supposed to do that?"

He cast a panicked look down the hallway, and whispered, "Please don't curse so much…the girls."

Jahan stared at him in open mouthed amazement, "They're five months old."

Tracy gave a rueful smile and rubbed at the back of his neck. "All right, I admit it, I'm besotted."

"And God knows they heard enough cursing from their mother while I was trying put push the little buggers out," Carisa's voice came from the doorway.

She glided into the room, a baby in each arm, and handed one off to Jahan. She cooed at the infant who focused on the stripped fur on her face and reached to touch it. Jahan nuzzled against the infant human.

"Looks like they are taking after their mother," Jahan said.

"Thank God," Tracy murmured as Carisa handed him the other infant, along with a quick peck on the cheek, and then gave Jahan a hug.

"And to echo Jahan, just how the fuck is she supposed to do that? Protect us, I mean?" Carisa asked as Tracy winced.

He answered. "If this plan fails, I want the people I love as far from this thing as it's possible to be. The girls could live out full lives before—"

Carisa gripped his shoulder, her hand like a claw. "No! If this plan fails, you'll fall back, we'll regroup and come up with another plan. My children are not going to grow up without a father, without knowing their brother, without family."

"What she said," Jahan echoed.

+ + +

"AND WE COULDN'T have this conversation via Fold-stream…why?" Tracy asked as he entered Ernesto's office on Hellfire. "Really didn't need to spend five days in Fold when I'm trying to do orbital mechanics for several hundred ships and have new-born daughters."

"You should be grateful. When my kids were infants, I couldn't get a damn thing done at home. At least you had some peace and quiet."

"True and I got to foist off attending the opening ball of the season onto Luis. He's going to escort Carisa to the Poni's."

"So, you see, win/win," Ernesto said.

They were both grinning, and Tracy pulled the other man into a tight hug, but Ernesto's bonhomie was gone by the time they broke the embrace. Deadly serious now he set about engaging every security measure available to guard the office.

It felt oppressive as heavy inner walls slid closed, and the sound deadening measures made Tracy feel as if he were trapped beneath deep water. Irritation gave way to anxiety and a formless sense of dread.

"All right, Ernesto, why *did* you pull me all the way out here when we're in the final planning stages of a major military operation?"

The other man's head jerked as he glanced from side to side as if expecting intruders. "You have to delay it."

"What?"

"Because if you succeed, we all die," Ernesto responded.

Tracy was beginning to wonder if the pressure had begun to affect Ernesto's mind. He tried to pass if off with a light quip. "I thought if we *didn't* succeed, we all died."

"I'm serious, Tracy. Come here, look at this." Ernesto brought up a hologram of an intricate DNA strand."

"That doesn't look human."

"It's not. *Necrófago*. Their genome is vastly different from ours, but I kept digging trying to figure out how they were switched off, and I discovered these DNA segments that are very difficult to identify, but there was something about them that kept nagging at me. So I went back to our human genome, focusing on our archaic genes. Most of them are superfluous. They just sit there, holdovers from our evolution that didn't manage to get deleted. And there hidden deep I found *the same marker*." Ernesto ran his hand through his hair. "It's an off switch. I'm sure of it. And it's in both the *Necrófagos*, and in—" His voice caught.

"Us," Tracy finished. A yawning pit seemed to have replaced his stomach.

A jerking nod. "Rohan said we were bred to fight for them, and that while they prize our violent natures, they also deplore it."

Unable to stand still Tracy began to pace. "This must be why the Cara'ot never objected when we placed the ban on genetic engineering because they were afraid we'd discover this." He ran an agitated hand through his hair. "God we're such fools when we let our fears govern our actions."

Ernesto knotted his fingers together over and over. "I'm supposed to be studying the Star Ants, not the *Necrófagos*. I think I'm being monitored so I've been doing this research in secret. Given the urgency of the research on the Ants I was afraid a sudden trip to the capital might alert the Cara'ot. And I was *not* going to put this out over the Foldstream."

"So, if…when we win against the Ants, they're going to trigger this," Tracy said slowly. Fear and anger warred within him. "And why wouldn't they? They think we're unruly, violent children. We take care of the threat. Then they remove us, and they have their nice peaceful galaxy back again with them grooming and pruning the remaining species." Bitterness and rage were a bad taste on the back of his tongue.

Ernesto gave a snort of disgust. "But I'll bet they keep a little human DNA on ice just in case they need to whip up some soldiers again."

"How much time do you think you'll need to counter this thing?" Tracy asked. "Because we can't delay too long or the Cara'ot will begin to suspect something."

Ernesto turned back to the hologram, drummed his fingers on the surface of the desk. "I'll have to develop a gene knockout. Question is whether I use plasmid, a DNA construct, or a biological chromosome."

"All very fascinating, doesn't tell me how much time you need."

"I can't rush this. The very survival of the human race depends on it," Ernesto snapped.

"Is there anyone you can bring in to help?" Tracy asked.

"Given that our patron at The High Ground turned out to be an alien…no, I don't trust anyone any longer," Ernesto said.

"Fair point."

"I think I can do it alone. It will just take a little longer."

"Give me something, I have to come up with plausible excuses."

"Maybe three months to develop the knockout another two to test it, but then we have to get it distributed to billions of people. It's going to be a logistical nightmare, and we'll need a cover story for that."

"Don't suppose you can just put it in the water?" Tracy asked at a poor attempt at humor.

Ernesto sighed and rolled his eyes. "No."

"Sounds like you need nine or ten months."

"That will probably do it. When will you head back?" Ernesto asked.

"Not for a few days. We need this to look casual. I'll talk to high command, go over requisitions. You and I should go out drinking—two old friends catching up."

"Not two men laboring under a deadly secret," Ernesto said. He began to shut down the security protocols, but Tracy forestalled him with an upraised hand.

"Once you have the treatment, we need to give it to the military first," Tracy said.

"Why?"

"I want the Cara'ot to know that if they try this, we'll grind them into dust. They think we're dangerous and aggressive now? Just wait."

27

THE LEAST BAD OPTION

MERCEDES HAD MADE a great show of inviting Rohan to join them on the royal sailboard, the Spindrift, for an afternoon of game fishing. The alien had declined saying an afternoon in the cramped confines of a sailboat was not his idea of a pleasant outing. Mercedes had indicated she felt the same, but that Talion desperately wanted to match his strength and wits against of the great leviathans of Ouranous' oceans. She added that it helped maintain that sense of normalcy to have the FFH engaging in such frivolities. Kept the simple folk calm. *"I mean if the elites weren't worried, perhaps they didn't need to be either."* As Mercedes had uttered those words, she felt like her face was cracking as she worked to maintain her smile.

They were far out to sea now beyond the protective reefs that kept the waters of the bay around which Hisselek was built so smooth and glass-like. Spray damped her face, and the smell of brine and seaweed filled her nostrils. Mercedes surveyed the group.

Tracy was bent over the railing puking his guts out while Beatrisa laughed at him even as she patted him sympathetically on the back. It hadn't occurred to Mercedes that Tracy had never been on a boat, but of course he hadn't, and she should have realized that. Everyone else had been born into the FFH, so there had been dance masters, ski instructors, riding lessons, music lessons, art and archery. They learned to sail and swim. If they were male, they were taught to fence and shoot, and perhaps a martial art as well. And for all of them was the ever-present etiquette. It was a testament to how diligently Tracy had applied himself to present as a gentleman that she sometimes forgot.

Talion, seated in the bow, gripped his fishing rod the line spooling out with a whirring sound and shifting from side to side as the leviathan sought to escape. The muscles in Talion's forearms bulged as he battled his catch.

The sails began snapping as the wind changed. Boho, standing in the stern spun the wheel to catch the shifting gusts. His feet were planted wide, and there was a wild smile on his lips as he controlled the sailboat in this dance with the waves and wind.

Ian Rogers was manning the rigging shifting the yard on the mainsail to adjust for the change in direction.

Tracy moaned as the boat heeled over and shipped what had to be the last of his lunch over the side. He cast Mercedes a miserable and accusing look as she walked past. She was easily adjusting to yaw and pitch of the boat.

"I'm sorry," she said. "Once we've talked, you can go below and lie down. Can you manage?"

"The only thing left in my stomach is my stomach, and it's threatening to leave as well," he groaned.

"Hey, problem solved, right?" Beatrisa said brightly and Tracy's look threatened murder.

"I'll take him now," Mercedes said to her sister.

Beatrisa gave him a final pat on the shoulder. "Try not to puke on your Empress." Tracy gave her a rude gesture and Bea grinned. "Okay, looks like he's going to live." Bea rested her elbows on the railing and gazed out at the cresting waves, the sea birds floating overhead sending their raucous cries into the wind.

Mercedes slipped an arm around Tracy's waist, and he placed his arm over her shoulder. Despite his wobbly legs, and unpleasant breath the presence of his hip pressing against hers sent fire along her nerve endings. Mercedes knew from the trembling of his hand on her shoulder that he was equally affected. It was understandable, the last time they had been in such close physical contact had been on Hellfire years ago. A moment when they had lost all control and begun madly kissing in a men's bathroom. Then Boho had caught them. It had not, Mercedes reflected, been one of her finer moments.

"Next time we have to hold a private meeting away from the prying eyes and ears of the Cara'ot I'll try to find some other form of noisy activity," she said.

They moved to a position just behind Talion as if they were watching his efforts to land his prey. Mercedes keyed on the tiny headphone and mic nestled in her ear.

"Everybody linked?" she asked softly, and immediately felt foolish for whispering.

It wasn't as if that would help. They had scanned the sailboat and found listening devices in the cabin below. Which is why they were putting on this pantomime. Their quiet conversation wouldn't be heard over the noise on deck, and any watchers in the sky would only see people enjoying an outing.

There were murmurs of assent, and she began. "Rohan is becoming suspicious of the delay. He knows we have three hundred new ships, and have mounted lasers on half of the fleet, and have stockpiled both missiles and slugs. I used the excuse that crewing all these new ships takes time and pointed out that it's not like we can re-up former O-Trell *hombres* and officers. We already did that for the last fight. Bottom line I'm running out of excuses."

"Where is Ernesto on creating the...vaccine?" Beatrisa asked uncertainty edging the last word.

"It's actually a CRISPR," Tracy said weakly.

"It's been damn near forty years since I was in a biology class, xeno or otherwise," Talion grunted as the leviathan gave a strong tug on the line. "What's a CRISPR when it's at home?"

"A gene editing tool," Tracy replied. "Ernesto's building a tool to cut out the...the..."

"Let's cut the strings of our little human soldier puppets so they all fall down dead," Boho supplied.

"What's going to be the fail rate on this CRISPR thing?" Rogers asked.

Tracy answered again. "About two percent."

Mercedes processed that for a moment. "We have a total human population of one trillion spread across fifteen planets." She did a quick calculation and stared at Tracy's profile. "You're telling me that we could have up to two billion people die?"

"Yes," he said, his voice low.

"That's unacceptable!"

"It's more acceptable than all one trillion of us dying," Talion countered.

"No medical treatment is one hundred percent effective," Boho said gently. "The question is whether Ernesto can improve those numbers if he's given more time?"

"Probably, but he has been working virtually alone to keep this from any Cara'ot spies," Tracy said. He shrugged. "We trapped between two bad choices, and if the Cara'ot are alerted they may prevent us from saving as many of us as we can. I think we've got to take the shot at the Ants while Ernesto is disseminating the CRISPR."

"And just how are we going to do that?" Rogers asked. "Our military ships are going to be engaged in the assault on the Ants."

"We use the independent traders," Tracy said. "There's more of them then even O-Trell ships, and we need to involve the doctors and nurses on New Hope. I have friends who can organize that."

"And we've got the Hiddens to help now," Beatrisa added.

"Also, the luxury liners. They all have medical personnel aboard who can be enlisted," said Mercedes.

"The good news is that it will be easy for us to get the treatment to the military, and probably won't arouse any suspicion," Talion said.

"The more people who know the more likely it will leak," Rogers warned.

"Let's hope the Cara'ot are all going to be too busy watching us fight the Ants to notice," Mercedes said grimly.

"Wait, we're going at this all wrong. Trying to hide this is the absolute wrong approach," Boho said.

Mercedes felt Tracy tense up next to her, and a sneer curved his lips as he turned to face Boho. The old enmity was probably never going to fade she thought with a mental sigh.

"So, you want to tell the Cara'ot that we're going to undermine their plan to kill us all? Sounds brilliant," Tracy said. HIs tone was withering.

"Don't be dense, Belmanor." It emerged as a drawl, Boho FFH accent firmly in place.

Sensing an explosion was about to occur Mercedes hurried into speech. "So, what are you proposing?"

"We lie. I go to Rohan and that toady of his and report my concerns about growing unrest among the populace. I propose that we tell the citizens that we have a vaccine that will protect against the Ants. I then roll my eyes and declare that of course it's all nonsense, just a ruse to keep the yokels quiet which will amuse Rohan. Then we proceed to disperse the CRISPR out in the open and right under the noses of the Cara'ot."

There was stunned silence for a few moments then Talion said, "Goddam, Boho, whatever you lack as a military mind you make up for as a conniving politician. That is fucking brilliant."

Mercedes walked toward the stern of the boat and blew a kiss to her husband. "You are a genius."

Boho gave her a bow and a smirk. "*Muchas gracias, querida.*"

Tracy's voice rang out. "Before you break your arm patting yourself on the back, you've got a problem, Cullen, a big one." Boho stiffened, his hands clenching on the wheel, and Mercedes cast her eyes up to heaven. "If the ruse is that this cure protects against the Ants then we have to inject a placebo into every Isanjo, Sidone, Flute, Hajin and Cara'ot, and I'm pretty damn sure there aren't enough doctors and nurses to get that done. Also, if the Cara'ot discover that what's being given to humans differs from what's being given to the aliens the gig is very much up."

Silence apart from the cries of the birds, the snap of the sails and creak of rigging, and the rush of waves against the hull fell over the group. The solution was obvious, but Mercedes hated to even contemplate it much less say it, but there was no choice.

"So, we announce that the scientists have developed an antidote for humans and are working diligently on treatments for the other species," Mercedes said. "A good many of our alien citizens already think that we favor humans over them—"

"They're not wrong," Tracy muttered.

Mercedes ignored him. "So, this won't come as a surprise. We'll just have to accept the backlash and outrage."

"There will be riots, violence," Beatrisa said. "They'll turn against you."

"Probably, but right now there are no good options. We'll just have to live with the least bad one," Mercedes said.

+ + +

LINES OF PEOPLE wound down the street and around the block. They were on Dullahan in the capital city, New Dublin and it was a hot and humid day. Jahan was rolling a small hand cart down the street and handing out bottles of cold water to the humans waiting in line. The acrid smell of human sweat, and the blossoming musk trees that were native to the planet was almost gagging. At least the crowd was patient and grateful as they accepted the water. Like most BEMs Jahan was always on alert around large crowds of humans.

Over the years there had been violent episodes, and bad times tended to bring out bad behavior. But it seemed everyone was too scared to be turning on their alien neighbors right now.

Instead, over the past few weeks it had been the BEMs turning on the humans with a predictable outcome. Law enforcement had come down hard on alien communities, and in places where the police hadn't been sufficient the military had been called in. Now curfews and travel restrictions were in place which were weakening an already rocky economy. Alien enlistment had collapsed. It felt like everything was falling apart, and she badly wished she could just go home and hold Tageri and her kids and forget about the wider galaxy, but Tracy had begged her to help in this effort.

Thinking of the former captain of the *Selki* had her remembering a human poem that Tracy had once read back when he travelled under a different name and none of them had known they were doomed.

Things fall apart; the centre cannot hold;
Mere anarchy is loosed upon the world,

The blood-dimmed tide is loosed, and everywhere
The ceremony of innocence is drowned;
The best lack all conviction, while the worst
Are full of passionate intensity.

Passionate and fucking pointless as well, Jahan thought as she handed out the last bottle.

She went rattling back up the street, cursing a bit as the wheels caught in the cobblestones. Verisimilitude and memories of home were all well and good, but this was carrying tradition too damn far in her opinion. Why not some nice, smooth paving?

Back at the head of the line she watched as Dr. Engelberg, his wife Kathy and their team were administering injections. Younger children wailed in anticipation of the injection, and babies wailed when they were smacked on the butt before the pressure gun was applied to the still stinging spot.

The governor and his lady were present, the husband assisting in unloading cases of water from a flitter while his wife wielded a knife to cut open the tight plastic. Jahan dumped another bag of ice into her pushcart while taking surreptitious glances at the wife because this was Mercedes actual birth mother who had been set aside after producing three daughters for the emperor. Jahan didn't see a lot of resemblance. Apparently, Mercedes had taken more after her royal father.

Rolling the cart over to the Duchess Jahan bobbed a quick curtsy though she always felt stupid doing it in her coveralls with the cutout for her tail, and her soft shoes with their six toes so she could use her prehensile feet.

"So good of you to bring these physicians to us," Maribel said, and then Jahan found the resemblance. Mercedes had her mother's rich, husky voice.

"It's our pleasure, ma'am. We're all united in this fight." *Though it'd be nice if we got a cure too*, Jahan thought.

"Indeed, we are," the woman said as she handed Jahan several bottles of water.

The Isanjo shoved them deep into the ice. It felt really good on her fur. They worked together to fill the cart, and Jahan began to trundle back down the line when she heard a woman's scream of horror and despair. Fear and conspiracy joined hands and went capering through the crowd. Murmurs and rumors whispered from person to person. *Someone turned into crystal! A baby died! It's a plot by the BEMs. They're angry because there's no cure for them yet!* Jahan began to back away when she heard that.

The governor scrambled onto the top of the delivery flitter, and one of his aides handed him a bull horn. "Please, please, everyone be calm. One individual has had an adverse reaction to the injection, but the doctors are handling the situation. They have assured me this is a very rare occurrence so please, everyone, stay in line. We're all sophisticated enough to know that any medical treatment carries some risk, but the alternative is death. So please, let's all stayed calm and focused."

The murmurs subsided, and only a handful of people left the line having surrendered to their fears.

They worked until late into the night, the governor's staff bringing in food for the people still waiting in line, and flood lights so the doctors would keep going. Jahan was worried about Doctor Engelberg, he was not a young man, but he seemed more chipper than some of the younger physicians that he and Kathy had brought from the hospitals on New Hope.

Her feet and back aching from the constant walking on the cobblestones Jahan went looking for Dalea. The Hajin had been relegated to working behind the scenes refilling pressure guns with the serum. The powers-that-be had felt that having a BEM administering injections wasn't going to go over well. Jahan hoped that other planets would be more rational, but she didn't have a lot of hope.

Dalea took a look at Jahan and shook out three aspirin and handed them to her. She swallowed them dry. They had run out of water hours ago.

"So, what happened that caused the freak out this afternoon?" Jahan asked.

"Baby had an adverse reaction. Went into anaphylactic shock."

"Are they okay?"

"No, she died." Jahan shivered and guessed Dalea's lack of reaction was something they taught in medical schools.

"Does the press know?" Jahan asked.

"No. It's one of the advantages of state media," the Hajin said dryly. "I expect the parents will be sequestered until we've gotten this job done."

+ + +

MERCEDES WATCHED AS Carisa tried to corral the twins who had gotten quite speedy as they crawled about the floor of the drawing room. Their plump little legs were a pleasant cocoa against the lemon-yellow rug, their little diapered behinds sashayed as they crawled and scooted around the gilded room. They were almost ten months old and had begun to pull themselves up on furniture or the legs of adults. They would be walking soon.

A yell of delight from Cyprian drew her attention to where Tracy was seated at a small table with the boy making a hexaflexagon. Cyprian was enchanted, coloring the various panels with different colored pens without realizing his father was teaching him geometry while they played. Mercedes wasn't surprised that Cyprian took to it so quickly and easily. Tracy had been the math wizard in their class at The High Ground.

She greedily studied his profile, committing it to memory. The aquiline nose, the prominent cheekbones, the way the corner of his mouth quirked up when he smiled at the child seated next to him, the scar that pulled at his eyebrow.

There had been a number of social events that had included both Tracy and Boho over the past few months, and she had been relieved that they two men were managing to at least suffer each other's presence. She supposed Tracy taking a bullet for Boho did help mitigate the hate…at least a little.

Whatever the reason the truce was a welcome relief as she monitored the progress of the vaccination efforts, dealt with the occasional outbreaks of panicked violence on various League worlds all the while spinning excuses for the Cara'ot about why they weren't yet ready to move against the Ants.

Finally, she had reduced it to the emotional and the personal. She "confessed" to Rohan that she was terrified, and that she wanted just a few more months with her child in case she died confronting the Ants. He had looked indulgent and condescending and she had longed to rip his face off, but mercifully it had worked. Possibly because it wasn't entirely untrue.

Mercedes noticed the nurse and her assistant were carrying the twins out of the room. Sidra was nodding off, but Syna was fussing, her little hands reaching out, fingers grasping at the air.

Tracy murmured something to Cyprian, got up, crossed to his daughter, stroked her silky curls and gave her a kiss. She grabbed his nose and he chuckled. A charming moment that was again a knife to Mercedes heart.

She was interrupted by Carisa's soft breath brushing across her ear as she whispered, "We haven't talked about it, but I give you both my permission and my blessing should you and Tracy wish to…you know, before the battle…"

Mercedes leaned her head against her sister's. "Thank you," she whispered back. "But I won't do that to you."

Cyprian's voice interrupted them. "*Tio* Tracy, please. We're not finished and I'm more interesting than babies," Cyprian said imperiously. Tracy choked on a laugh, and the three adults exchanged amused glances. Cyprian stiffened in outrage. "I am *not* funny, and you shouldn't laugh at an emperor."

Tracy started to respond, but Mercedes gestured for him to let her handle it. She walked over to her son and looked down at the eight-year old. Her serious expression had him wilting a bit.

"First, you are not emperor. And second what have I told you about the duties and responsibilities of royalty?" She folded her arms and waited.

Cyprian looked down and mumbled, "The sole duty of a ruler is to serve the people and put their needs above his own." It emerged as a sad little sing song. The tawny eyes were lifted to meet hers and he whimpered, "Sorry, mama."

It felt like her heart was trying to leave her body. Mercedes ruffled his curls and kissed the top of his head. "It's all right, my darling. It's easy to forget when we live in a palace. Which is why I want you to listen to your…to Tracy because he didn't grow up in a palace and he can help you grow up to be a very good ruler."

Once again, the three adults exchanged a glance, but this one was far more fraught.

28

INTO GOD'S HANDS WE RESIGN OURSELVES

EARTH'S CURRENT CAPITAL city, Vladivostok, was on fire. The Pope had put out statements pleading for calm. Baron Henrick Rothchild, royal governor of Earth had made reassuring statements about efforts being underway to protect every League Citizen from the effects of the Ants but had also warned of harsh consequences if their alien citizens didn't *get a grip*. Well, he hadn't actually said that, but that was Jahan's interpretation of the modulated political speak of the human.

She and the team of doctors and nurses were huddled in a hospital hoping calm would be restored so they could continue with their work. Sirens wailed in the streets outside, and through the glass front doors Jahan could see the ring of police surrounding the building. Beyond them was a seething mass of Hajin, a handful of Sidone, Flutes swaying agitatedly, and naturally a gang of her people were leading the rioters.

Engelberg limped up to her, leaning heavily on his cane. "If the authorities can't get this under control we may as well move on to Wasua. We don't have time to waste."

"They're pissed, and honestly, I can't blame them. Once

again it feels like the only people that matter are humans, and the rest of us can just go get fucked or crystallized or whatever." An odd expression flitted across the human's face. "What?" Jahan demanded.

"Come here. Got something to tell you." He grabbed her elbow, and pulled her into a hallway, huffed when he found it filled with people who had been in line for the vaccine before the rioters arrived. He moved down the hall until he found a supply closet and pulled her inside.

"And you have to do it in a closet?"

"This is big. I need your word you'll keep quiet."

The smell of the cleaning materials in the small space was irritating her nose and causing her eyes to water.

"Fine." The doctor hesitated, mouth working as he contemplated. "Do you want me to pinky swear?" She allowed her irritation to show. She didn't have much patience for bullshit right now.

"You know how I feel about governments," Engelberg said.

"Yeah, you think they are staffed by idiots and are mostly evil and are always doing something sneaky. My question is how they pull off all these conspiracies if they're really that stupid, but whatever."

The doctor looked offended. "Well, in this case I was right. Kathy and I tested this so-called vaccine. It's not a vaccine and it will do fuck all against the Ants. It's a placebo designed to mask something else which I think is a CRISPR."

"Which is what when it's at home?" Jahan asked.

So Engelberg explained. "I haven't got the training or the equipment to determine exactly which gene or genes are being targeted by this thing, or why it's being snipped-out, but I imagine the reason is pretty damn dire," Engelberg concluded.

Jahan gave a whuff of amazement and dropped down onto a convenient crate of bleach. "So, whatever this thing does it's only for humans, and the fact the crown is spending a fucking fortune for us to administer it means—"

"We need to fucking get it done," Engelberg concluded grimly.

"Which we can't do when BEMs are rioting," Jahan said wearily. "Okay let me see if I can knock some heads together."

She jumped off the crate and hustled out of the closet and down the hall. She went in search of Jax. She wished Kielli was still with them, but as he had promised his mother he had enlisted and was now serving aboard a ship. Once she found her shipmates, she outlined her plan.

Jax's fronds shivered. "So, you're going to yell at them?"

"Well, when you put it like that that does sound stupid, but we have to do something."

"If you get me killed, I'm going to be very put out with you," the Flute huffed as he followed her to the doors of the hospital.

Dalea stroked one of his fronds. "We'll make sure you have a really nice funeral."

"Not helping."

They reached the front entrance and Jahan paused for a moment studying the twisted, angry faces, the waving fists. She flinched a bit when a rock hit the glass of the doors, and then got pissed. She grabbed the handle, and a security guard intervened.

"I can't let you go out there. We can't risk opening the doors."

The tap of Engelberg's cane announced his arrival. "I'm authorizing it. She's going to try and turn this around. She'll be quick."

The man shrugged in an *it's-your-funeral* sort of way, stepped back, and released the lock. Jahan pushed the door open and she, Jax and Dalea hurried out as the crowd surged forward. Jahan held up her hands.

"NOW JUST HOLD ON A DAMN MINUTE!" Perhaps it was her captain's voice or maybe they were just tired of standing out in the sun for this many hours, but the advance slowed and then came to an untidy stop.

"Look, I get it. We're tired of always being told to step aside, be patient, wait our turn, but this is not the time to start some big revolution. Everybody's spooked and scared and seriously, don't we all know what happens *to us,*" she gestured at the crowd of aliens, "When human's get scared."

"They kick the crap out of us," someone from the crowd yelled.

"Exactly, and they're really good at that which is why we—"

"We gotta hit 'em first!" a burly Hajin roared.

"Wrong answer! They're out there right now preparing for the biggest battle of our lives. For *all* of our very lives. We should be praying for them to succeed because it's not just humans on those ships. My nephew enlisted. He's aboard a *destructore* right now. I bet some of you have family aboard ships. Why don't we wait and see if they win before we lose our shit and burn everything down?"

Dalea stepped in. "Right now, there is a treatment for the humans, but you can be sure our scientists and doctors are working on this too."

Jax picked up the thread. "And we've got the Cara'ot on our side, and we all know they're a hell of a lot better at this than the humans." There were nods and murmurs of agreement at that.

Jahan too over again. "So, let's all get home. Hold our loved ones close and wait to hear word." She gave a lopsided smile. "And let's hope the humans kick the shit out of some different aliens for a change."

There was laughter, a few cheers and the crowd began to disperse. A hand closed on her shoulder, and Jahan looked up into Engelberg's bearded face.

"I see a bright future for you in politics," he said.

"Bite your tongue," she responded.

+   +   +

ANSELMO SLIPPED FROM the bed, paused to study Julia, hand tucked beneath her chin, a small moue of displeasure pulling down the sides of her lips. He wondered what she was dreaming about. Gathering up clothes and a pair of boots Anselmo crept into the hall and after dressing he checked his chronometer. Right about now the armada should be preparing to drop out of Fold and engage the Ants.

The nursery where his four eldest children were sleeping was just down the hall. He moved to the door and slipped inside. The light from the nebula twisting in Hisselek's night sky cast rainbow colors across their slumbering faces. He bent and kissed their cheeks.

Josephine, his thoughtful little professor-to-be, awoke at the touch of his lips, and blinked up at him. Anselmo laid a finger on his lips, then on hers, and she gave a nod of understanding.

"Bad dreams, daddy?" she whispered.

"No," he whispered even as his mind said. *The worst because it's a waking nightmare.* "Go back to sleep, princess."

He went next to the new baby's room. The nursemaid they had hired was snoring in the small adjoining room. Propelled by the ceiling fan cooling the room, the mobile hanging over Quintana's crib was spinning softly. The mobile was an indulgence, the strings were spun silver, and they supported glittering snowflakes formed out of diamonds. Leaning down he inhaled the scent—talcum powder, lotion, and baby. Her plump cheek was so soft that he feared his rough, dry lips would hurt her, but she continued to sleep.

At three a.m. the streets were deserted. The construction cranes, many sporting the flag of the Solar League, seemed like prayerful pilgrims stretching their arms toward the swirling colors of the nebula. The spire of the cathedral was draped in metal scaffolding for the repairs, but some workman had placed a lit star atop the bent cross at the top. Anselmo felt his breath catch in his chest, and he fought back tears.

Climbing the steps, he went past the great carved doors to a smaller door on the side. As expected, it was unlocked. He had anticipated being alone, and thought he wanted the solitude, but when he found the pews nearly filled, the tears flowed freely. They were all here to pray for the men and women who somewhere out in the darkness of space were going to fight for all their lives.

An old *abuela* motioned to him and scooted closer to a middle-aged woman making room for him in the pew. Anselmo slid in next to her, and gratefully accepted the handkerchief she offered him. He wiped his eyes and tried to compose himself. The kneeler was already down. He slid onto it, rested his elbows on the back of the pew in front of him, and folded his hands beneath his chin.

He didn't know if he actually believed there was a higher power. Maybe the higher power was this. Good people from all walks of life coming together to share hope and humanity…and rail against an uncaring universe.

+   +   +

THE BRIDGE CREW kept sneaking surreptitious glances at him. Tracy forced a yawn and fought to maintain a bland, bordering on bored, expression. He knew his face often (*always*) revealed his thoughts and emotions, but this was one time when he had to keep it under control. They were seventeen minutes and twenty-one seconds from dropping back into normal space, and immediately engaging in the deadliest battle of their lives. They would be fighting not only for their own survival but for the lives of everyone they loved. Hell, they were fighting for *life itself.*

He hadn't slept during the preceding night cycle. Instead, he spent it reviewing his calculations for their coordinated translations out of Fold. There were four hundred and twenty-three ships involved in this action, the maximum that could be utilized. He had coldly anticipated that three ships might be lost during translation. It wasn't common, but it did happen where ships never emerged from not-space, and he had to assume the worst. He believed, hoped, that he had accounted for any lost firepower, but then he reminded himself of the Prussian commander Helmuth van Moltke's adage that *No battle plan survives first contact with the enemy.*

Well, they would know in…he glanced down at the chronometer embedded in the sleeve of his battle armor…*Thirteen minutes and forty-two seconds.* Tracy keyed the radio and contacted the weapons deck.

"All ready down there?" he said softly.

"Yes, sir," Cassutt responded. "We've turned fire control over to the computer, but Commander McKenzie is ready to take manual control if necessary."

"Excellent." Tracy looked to Luis seated tensely on the edge of his chair at navigation. "You ready to get us out of here?"

"Yes, sir. Computer is ready to calculate a translation moment to moment once we engage."

Tracy ended with a report from engineering. He didn't bother to contact Afumba down in medical. If this all went tits up there was no medicine known to human or alien that would save them. He glanced down at the chronometer again. *Nine minutes twenty-three seconds.*

He contacted Father Ken who had spent hours hearing confessions, praying with the *hombres* and officers, and holding a final Mass.

"I think a prayer would be in order, Padre."

"I thought you might ask," Ken replied.

Tracy turned to his comms officer. "Please pipe it to the entire ship."

"Aye, sir."

The bridge crew fell silent the only sounds the pulse of the Fold engines, and the faint sounds of electronics. It was so quiet that Tracy could hear Ken's indrawn breath over the ship's intercom.

"Oh, merciful God, maker of love and of peace. To know you is to live, and to serve you is to reign. Through the intercession of St. Michael, the archangel, be our protection in battle against all evil. Help us to overcome war, and to establish your law of love and justice. Into God's hands we resign ourselves and the just cause which is entrusted to us to defend. Grant this through Christ our Lord. Amen."

A chorus of *Amens* whispered through the bridge. Tracy crossed himself and felt Beatrisa's armored hand close on his shoulder. The servomotors in the armor increased the grip. He turned his head to glance up at his sister-in-law and flag captain and laid his hand briefly over hers.

Four minutes five seconds...

+ + +

"Amen." Boho crossed himself as the chaplain concluded his prayer.

He glanced at the chronometer in the arm of his command chair. *Two minutes and fifty seconds.* He hadn't bothered with battle armor. What was the point? If the creatures reached his ship nothing would protect him. He also knew he cut a more impressive figure in his dress uniform, and he felt like the armor might give his people an unrealistic sense of their chances. They needed to be prepared to beat a hasty retreat if this battle went the way he feared it might.

He wished he could speak to Mercedes, but ships were beyond contact when they were in Fold, fragile shells holding life within their walls as the traversed the seething grey nothingness. And once they emerged, they would be in the fight of their lives. No time for personal communication between the ships. All the ships computers had been linked with the firing and tactical information set to be shared within a zeptosecond of their translating out of Fold.

He knew from his military history classes that back in the atomic age when most the world's population had feared annihilation in nuclear fire the military had predicted wars that lasted mere minutes. This one was going to last a few seconds at most.

He had obsessively checked in with his navigator to be sure he was ready to translate them the hell out of there if things went badly. O-Trell had drones shadowing the mass of the Ants and once they were in interstellar space and far from any stars or planetary systems, they had decided the moment had come to attempt this mad venture.

And now it was mere seconds.

Mercedes.

Paloma

The counter clicked to zero.

+   +   +

HER STOMACH SEEMED separated from her body for that moment of indrawn breath as they translated out of Fold, and immediately fired retro rockets so every ship was held in place. As she studied the display, she noted that two ships had failed to translate. Perhaps they had re-entered real space at another location or perhaps they were lost forever.

The *San Francisco de Asis* shuddered as missiles began launching from their silos. The massive laser that had been mounted on the hull painted red across the black on interstellar space.

The other League ships lasers were also firing, creating a web of destruction around the massive crystalline object that was the body of the Ants. The flare of the rockets on the missiles were like fire arrows heading for the heart of the cluster,

But then suddenly there was no cohesive center to the mass of crystals. It was flying apart like slow motion images of a bullet shattering glass. Shards flying in all directions and at terrifying speed. Even as the lasers seemed to burn sections of the expanding mass it was not enough to stop their advance. It was as if the Ants had sensed each ship and was targeting each of them with terrifying accuracy.

Panicked calls for orders were coming in over her radio. For an instant Mercedes mind felt frozen as she contemplated the disaster that now confronted them. They had risked everything on a single throw...and lost. She slammed her hand down on the controls opening a channel to every ship.

"Abort! Abort! Everyone translate *now*!"

She had studied the battle plan in frenzied detail during their eight-day journey to reach the creature. She knew every ship, its location, and its captain. So, she knew that Boho had blinked out of reality even before she gave the order. The sense of abandonment was like a knife in her chest, but there was no time to grieve. She had to cover the retreat.

Talion's voice cut through the terrified racket and filled her earpiece. "Mercedes be ready to bring up your Fold engines. You'll know when to translate.

"Talion! Jasper! What are you doing?" Mercedes cried as she saw the marker that represented the Nephilim Baron's flagship begin to move out of its carefully calculated position on her battle screen.

"Dragging the scent for the bastards. Buying you time." For an instant the hunting allusion baffled her and then she understood.

"Jasper," she breathed, "Your people."

"You didn't actually think we were getting out of this unscathed, Highness. Now prepare to *GO*." The final word was a guttural yell.

"All ships calculate for rendezvous at Hellfire, and prepare to Fold," she ordered.

Scanners measured the massive acceleration of Talion's dreadnaught. Anyone aboard the ship who hadn't prepared undoubtably had broken bones now, Mercedes thought. Such injuries would soon be nothing to what was coming if Talion's plan worked, and he pulled away the bulk of the crystal structure. And the movement did seem to attract the Ants. Most of the whip-like structures curved away from the encircling ships, and nosed toward the Nephilim ship arching like curious, questing elephant trunks snuffling after a treat.

But not all. Four of the tendrils reached stationary ships, and the sound of screams replaced the competent voices giving updates as navigational courses were plotted.

She identified the ships. The Saber, the Panther, the Santa Barbara, and a Hidden World ship the Corsair. Panic beat in her chest, fragmented her thoughts. Was it time? Should she give the order to translate? Talion said she would know when. But she didn't. She didn't. They were all going to die because of her. Because she didn't know what to do.

A massive explosion rained fire through the pursuing crystalline structure as Talion detonated his ship's engines and armory.

"All ships, translate," she ordered and felt the atoms of her body twist as they fell into nothingness.

29

THE DUTY OF A RULER

"So, what's the final butcher's bill?" Mercedes asked. Her voice was hoarse with weariness, and her eyes seemed to have sunk deep into her skull.

Gelb answered. "Five ships taken by the Ants. Two more never emerged from Fold." He lifted his eyes to meet Mercedes. "It could have been worse."

They were in a secure room at the Octagon. Present were only high command. The captains and crews of the remaining ships were on lockdown, with strict orders that no information regarding the battle was to be disseminated until the crown, meaning Anselmo, had crafted their response.

"I'd still call that pretty fucking bad," Boho said.

"Seven ships out of four hundred and twenty-three? I'd call it a bloody miracle and a testament to great leadership that it was only seven," Beatrisa shot back. Boho thought it was odd that she was present and not Belmanor.

Mercedes raised a hand. "Please, the last thing we need is sniping among ourselves. What we need is a plan."

"How about this for a plan?" Boho said. "We build massive ships, pick a galaxy, point ourselves in that direction and Fold. Save as many of us as we can."

"I'd call it a shitty plan," called that hated voice from the doorway.

"So glad you could bother to join us, Belmanor," Boho gritted. "However, if you have nothing constructive to add why don't you just fuck the hell right off?"

The usual scowl and pout that usually appeared during most of their interactions failed to appear. Instead, Belmanor looked almost manic. His boot heels beat a quick tattoo on the hard flooring as he hurried to the front of the room. Ernesto was trailing after him. The other man looked shell shocked. Belmanor's focus was completely on Mercedes.

"Merce—Highness, I think we have an answer," Belmanor said.

Mercedes shot an inquiring glance at Ernesto. He gave a shrug. "This is all on the Admiral. I just helped him analyze the data."

"What data?" she asked.

"I didn't just release missiles when we came out of Fold. I also seeded in some scannerbots. Until they were absorbed, they were recording, taking readings and sending the data back to Ernesto as well as to my ship. I studied the information during our trip back, but I wanted to see if Ernesto concurred before I said anything."

Belmanor inserted a data spike into the conference table, and an image of the central body of the Ants sprang to life, rotating slowly in the air.

"What am I looking for?" Mercedes asked.

"Watch how it moves just seconds after we've emerged from Fold. Does it remind you of anything?"

Boho was sure Mercedes would have gotten there, but his

aversion to Fold, the fact he studied it like it was a monster waiting to envelop a ship and its inhabitants got him there first.

"It moves like the tendrils in Fold space," he blurted out.

Belmanor turned to him, a broad smile on his lips. "*Exactly!* We've thought it was drawn to the ships, but I don't think that's it. I believe it's drawn to the brief tear in reality when a ship comes *out* of Fold."

Ernesto spoke up. "We've been baffled at how it transforms matter and haven't been able to determine the method or the underlying physics. Well, this might explain that. If Admiral Belmanor is correct, it's because the Ants aren't natural to our four-dimensional universe."

"When Rohan said they're not from around here he didn't know how accurate that was," Belmanor added with a sharp laugh.

"Okay, assuming you're correct, what do we do?" Mercedes asked. "How do we get them out of our universe and back where they belong?"

"We need to construct a…gateway, if you will," Ernesto said. "Set up Fold engines in a sequence that will allow a large enough opening for the Ants to pass through."

"And we need a fox for the Ants to chase. How did Talion put it…dragging the scent," Belmanor added.

"That could be a one-way trip if the thing catches the fox before they're through the gate," Gelb said. "And what happens when it gets back home? Does it magically turn back into that fog or hair, or whatever it is? That could affect the fox too."

"This could be a one-way trip." Tarek El-Ghazzawy

voiced what everyone was thinking.

The men and two women gathered the room exchanged looks. Boho dropped his eyes and studied the toes of his boots.

Of course, Belmanor spoke up instantly. "I'll do it."

"No," Mercedes said. "You have a relationship with the Cara'ot. When the time comes to deliver our warning—"

"More like our threat—fuck with us and we'll kill you all," Beatrisa said with a snort. Mercedes shot her a stern glance.

"It should be you to deliver it," Mercedes concluded. Belmanor looked mulish, but then gave a sharp nod.

Ernesto said. "I would be honored to take this duty."

"No, not you either," Mercedes said. "We need you here continuing to oversee the CRISPR, and to help oversee the construction of these Fold generators."

"But when I'm done with that I can easily—"

"No!" Mercedes snapped out again.

"I am just a soldier, Highness. Allow me to undertake this task," Gelb said.

"You're my flag captain, and we're not assigning any crewed ship to this task. Our fox to the hounds will be an *Infierno*."

It felt as if people's gazes were on him, and that each look fell like a blow across Boho's shoulders. Eventually he would no longer be able to keep silent.

"They don't have Fold capability," Belmanor objected.

"We'll do a retro-fit. There must be some bright engineer who can accomplish that task." Mercedes said.

"It won't be necessary," Ernesto mused. "If we open up

this gateway the *Infierno* can just go through along with the Ants."

"But then we have to close the gate, and we have to give that pilot at least a *chance* to get back out," Belmanor practically snarled.

"Oh right. Sorry." Ernesto ran a hand nervously through his hair. "I'm still trying to wrap my head around all this."

"Why should there be a pilot at all? The fighter could be pre-programed, or remote piloted," Boho said, and felt the tension in his shoulders lessen a bit.

"Having all that as redundancy would be good," Ernesto said. "But—"

El-Ghazzawy jumped in. "But we're talking about an effort that could literally save all life in our galaxy. I'd really like to have a human mind behind those controls able to react to changing circumstances."

Beatrisa said quietly, "I'll fly it. I'm the most expendable person here."

Mercedes jumped up and hugged her younger sister hard. "Not to me you're not, and no." Boho watched her draw in a deep, steadying breath, and felt the word *NO* battering against the back of his teeth."

There's a reason why the League always required the person holding the throne be a war leader. This is the duty of a ruler."

The room broke out in a storm of objections, denials, arguments.

Say something. Say something! You promised you'd finish this together. Say something. Shame choked him and no words emerged.

"Enough!" Mercedes voice was a whip. "I am your Empress. The decision is made."

Silence. Everyone bowed. Boho thought he saw tears in Belmanor's eyes.

+ + +

"YOU CAN'T. I won't let you. Please, Mercedes. I can't lose you." He was frenziedly gripping her shoulders.

Tracy had followed her into a woman's restroom, a reversal of the last time they had met clandestinely at the Octo.

"We have to stop meeting this way," she teased gently.

It didn't work. Tracy gave her an angry, desperate look, and took an even tighter grip on her shoulders. "Let me do this."

"It's going to take a very talented pilot, and I'm better than you. Always have been," she said lightly trying to ease the tension that crackled between them.

"That's nonsense and you know it. Right now, there is some twenty-two-year-old lieutenant who can fly circles around both of us."

"And they're not the Empress. How would it look if I lay that burden on some young officer?"

"Then at least let me come with you." Tracy's voice was ragged.

She laid a hand on his cheek. His skin was hot against her palm, blotchy red showing on his paler skin.

"No. I will not have your children left fatherless and my sister without her husband."

He clutched at his hair, paced away, and paced back to

her. "You talk about my daughters. What about our son? You're going to abandon him?"

"No, I'm going to hope to come back, but if something happens to me, I'm going to instruct the privy council that you and Carisa are to raise Cyprian. You can tell him the truth whenever you think he's ready."

"Cullen will never agree to that."

"I expect Boho will marry this little girl he's entranced with and be relieved not to be constantly reminded of my infidelity."

Her memories flew back to a dimly lit cabin on a battered old spaceship, and a too small bunk where she and Tracy had finally made love. It seemed his thoughts had gone there too for the look he gave her almost shattered her resolve.

"You're my life." His voice was thick with unshed tears. "I can't—"

She laid a hand over his mouth. "I need you here to handle the Cara'ot, and to oversee the military. Boho will take control of the government. He'll be very good at that. Especially with you to advise him."

Tracy snorted. "Like he'd listen to me."

"I actually think he will. And this may go perfectly, and I'll nip in and out of Fold and be back before you know it."

"You're going to be on the wave front of an alien creature that we don't...can't understand. Who knows what will happen to that not-space when this much matter enters from our universe? You could be thrown God knows where."

"Maybe I'll find all those lost ships," she said with a faint smile. "Perhaps there's a Bermuda Triangle or Sargasso Sea in there, and I'll come home leading a motley fleet."

He buried his face in her shoulder and gave a laugh that sounded suspiciously like a sob. "My pirate queen," he murmured.

She stroked his greying hair for a long moment, feeling his panting breaths against her neck. Finally, she said,

"Life has never been fair to us. There's no reason that should change now. We just have to accept what we cannot change."

✦ ✦ ✦

HE STILL GOT nervous around the Empress. Anselmo knew Boho, knew all of his weaknesses, his insecurities, Anselmo even had dirt on the Consort. *I mean the man had ordered him to have Belmanor* killed. But the Empress?

Anselmo tried to picture her naked, sweaty, and gasping in Belmanor's arms. The credulous might believe the bullshit he had put out about artificial insemination, but he knew or at least suspected the truth. But try as he might the image just wouldn't stick. All Anselmo could ever picture was her height, her elegance, the distant expression, and focused calm. Anselmo doubted the woman *could* sweat.

And now he was in a room in the small palace (first time he'd ever been invited there) with just Boho and Mercedes, and his bowels felt like they could let go at any moment for the Empress had added grim to her repertoire of expressions.

"With respect, Highness, you've been back for two days, and the people need to hear about your glorious victory."

"We've actually been back for thirteen days," Boho said. "We were at Hellfire."

"Sooo," Anselmo drew out the word. "Not a glorious victory?"

Mercedes just shook her head.

"It could have been worse," Boho said.

"Not the best P.R., sir. The people are getting restless. We wait too long to put to a statement, and they'll be revolting. It's not going to cut it for us to be telling people to show up for work, go shopping, get married and make babies without giving them some hope that it's all going to be okay, that we've got a plan." He paused, but they didn't fill the silence. "We do have a plan, right?" he asked hesitantly. "That's why you were at Hellfire." It emerged sounding more pathetic than cocky.

"We returned to Hellfire because we could keep all the ships and communications on lockdown," Boho said.

"Oh shit." He froze. "Oh, God, *Perdóname,*" he rushed to added.

Mercedes spoke up for the first time. "No need to apologize. It seems a very apt response. But yes, there is a plan." And she outlined it, concluding, "The best estimate is that it will take eighteen months to two years to construct these Fold generators that will operate on what is virtually empty space."

"Why is it going to take so long?"

Boho spoke up. "I don't fully understand the physics...actually I don't understand the physics at all, but apparently the Fold technology needs to grab onto something in order to translate out of normal four-dimensional space."

"Usually, the thing a Fold engine grabs is the ship and

occupants," Mercedes said.

"The tech and brainy boys are figuring out how much and what to seed in space around the generators. It has to be large enough that an opening will be created but doesn't offer the Ants something to grab onto and transform."

"Instead, it just has to open up a tear in reality large enough that they'll be lured into," Mercedes concluded.

"Lured by what?" Anselmo asked.

Mercedes waved him off. "That will be a discussion for another day. There's also the scale up factor. Nobody's ever built Fold generators this large. Certainly not five of them.

"For right now you need to craft a publicity campaign that will calm people," Boho said.

"Also, it's my understanding that you have a degree in political science?" Mercedes asked. Anselmo nodded. "I want you to work with the Consort, Admiral Belmanor and others analyzing our governmental system to see what changes need to be made. The granting of full citizenship to our alien subjects will require some adjustment. There will be disruptions, and I want us to be ahead of things, and not reacting after the fact. That's how revolutions get started. Particularly in times of fear and uncertainty. So, I'm depending on you to give our citizens some certainty and security."

She held to her hand. He was clearly dismissed. Anselmo bowed over it and backed to the door. A final bow and he left. The two guards just outside the room gave him the side-eye as he passed.

Soft-footed servants stepped aside and bowed to him as he passed. Outside he took a deep breath and descended the stairs to his waiting flitter.

"Everything okay, sir?" his driver asked as he opened the door of the vehicle.

"Yeah, just great, Henry," Anselmo said, and then he began to laugh hysterically as he reached for his flask.

30

WE'LL GET THIS DONE – FOR HER

J AHAN JUST STARED at Tracy's holographic image after he'd delivered the news. Inside she was wailing. Wanting to beat her fists against the walls, tear at her own face. Instead, she gave a rasping cough. In an emotionless voice she said, "Thank you for telling me. Odd my brother didn't give me this news."

"I'm sure he'll call you later. His wife is…well, not taking it well, and I didn't want you to read it on a casualty list."

That reminded her she was not alone in her suffering. "Oh God, Jieki didn't want them, either of them, to join up, and Keilli's little girlfriend…" A sob rose up, and she fought to push it back. Tracy looked away not wishing to embarrass her as she struggled to hide her grief.

Tracy pinched the bridge of his nose. "I'm sorry. I should have insisted he be assigned to me," he said.

"Could have been your ship that got hit, and he knew the risks," Jahan said gruffly.

"Kielli was a good kid." He winced. "I'm sorry, what a banal, stupid, thoughtless thing to say."

"It's okay." A fist seemed to be crushing her chest. How could emotions have such weight? "I wish you could have gotten to know him better. He would have knocked some of the pompous out of you."

"Pompous?" Tracy repeated, pretending to be offended.

"Yes, very. Probably because of O-Trell putting a stick up your ass, but also because you're a human." Rage warred with grief, and she couldn't hold back the words. "You all walk around draped in it. Even the good ones, like you."

He looked ashamed and devastated at her words. "I'm sorry," he said again.

An uncomfortable silence hung between them like cobwebs. Finally, she asked, "Did he die well?"

She watched as conflicting emotions chased themselves across his face. "I don't think there's any such thing as dying well in war," he said, his voice harsh. "We chew up the young and the poor. And we call on them again and again and again." He cut off the words, breathing hard through his nose.

"Tracy, what's wrong?" Jahan asked gently.

"We may have a solution, a way to save us, but Mercedes..." He choked momentarily, cleared his throat, and continued. "I'm trying to find a way around it, keep her safe—"

Jahan interrupted him. "Sometimes there is no fix. No way out. You just have to get through it and accept the goddam consequences."

"I don't think I can," he said brokenly. He hung his head, fighting to regain control.

Her grief flowed back, and anger though she knew it to be misplaced. Her nephew was dead, and all he could think about was his own damn pain—

No, he's thinking of the woman he loves. Would she behave any differently if it was Tageri in danger?

He apologized again. "I'm sorry. I bring you devastating news, and then I lay my suffering on you. I'm an ass."

"Yeah, sometimes," Jahan agreed. He gave her a hurt look. "But it's okay, we can share our misery. Might be easier to carry that way."

✦   ✦   ✦

PALOMA'S BACK WAS against the hotel room door, arms folded protectively across her chest as she eyed Boho suspiciously. He gave her what he hoped was an encouraging nod and keyed his ScoopRing. The moans, gasps, grunts, muttered endearments, and the sweat slick sound of skin on skin filled the room. She rolled her eyes and relaxed from her defensive posture.

"Really? You recorded porn?" she whispered.

"No, I'm just playing it live, directly off Clit Bait," he whispered back. "Should be loud enough to cover our conversation, and I expect our Cara'ot listeners will dip in, hear what's happening, consider my reputation and move on to spying on someone else."

"And if they're watching as well as listening?"

"They can't bug every hotel room in Hisselek, and I verified this one was clean. It also caters predominately to aliens. Not a place one would expect to find me."

"All right. So, what is it you want to discuss?" Paloma asked.

"The next few months are going to be critical," Boho said

as he led her over to the bed and pulled her down next to him as the woman in the recording cried out *Oh Dios! Yes, yes, there! Right there!*

The light citrus perfume she always wore reminded him of other times and other rooms when she had been the one making those sounds of pleasure as he had taken her body.

"Are we assuming success or failure for the purposes of this discussion?" Paloma asked.

"Success," he said.

"Then what's the worry?"

"Have you been briefed about the real nature of the vaccines?"

The woman nodded. "Well, not officially. Ian told mother, but she broke protocol and told me."

"Good, saves me the trouble. Point is once the Cara'ot realize we've managed to protect most of the human race they are not going to be happy. We might find ourselves back in another war," Boho said.

"Why would they risk that when we beat them so decisively last time?"

"Because they weren't really trying to win," Boho explained. "They made it look good, but they always intended for us to become the masters of the galaxy. But I'm not just worried about the Cara'ot. I'm worried that our alien citizens might decide to throw in with them despite the concessions we're granted to them. We need them to side with us over those manipulative fucks."

"I take it you have a solution." The man on the recording let out a bellow and groaned out. *So close. Gonna cum God, God, God.*

Boho stood, ran a hand through his hair and paced a few steps away. "I hope. I think. No, I'm right, this is the only way." He turned back to her. "We're going to have to completely restructure our political system. Do away with the aristocracy and hereditary rule."

"*Querido Dios*, that's extreme." The woman on the recording let out a scream of pleasure. "You were a royal *duque* even before you married Mercedes. You'd be willing to do that?"

"To keep power, absolutely."

"Why not a constitutional monarchy?"

"No, we need to do something radical if we're going to keep alien support. We've got to allow them into parliament, or a congress if we go that route, and we will have to abolish the monarchy."

She cocked an eyebrow at him. "Are you sure this isn't just to punish Mercedes...and by extension Belmanor? To deny him the honor of being the actual father of the emperor. And what about Cyprian? It's not his fault he's..."

"A bastard?" Boho snapped. Her lips pulled down in a moue of disappointment, and a frown wrinkled that perfect brow.

Chagrined Boho stared into Paloma's large brown eyes. He had wanted to lie, but instead allowed his fury and wounded pride to reveal himself. But if he ever wanted her to love him, he had to acknowledge it. He sensed she hated his lies—to himself and to others—more than she hated the pettiness.

"Yes, I'll never stop hating Belmanor, but I can acknowledge that right now we need him. And Cyprian's eight, it's not like being emperor has been the focus of his life. He'll recover. But more to the point I honestly feel like this is the only solution. We can never go back to the way things were before."

"You're going to need bigger changes then just at the capital," Paloma warned. "Instead of planetary governors being appointed by the crown you're going to have to allow for direct elections. No more plums and lucrative graft. I don't have to tell you how that will go over with our set."

"Oh, I know." He gave a twisted smile. "Bit ironic. That had been my life goal when I was younger. Get rich on the backs of a planetary population."

"Instead, you married rich and it still wasn't enough. So, what are *you* planning to get out of this?" Paloma asked.

"A chance to lead in a way that I'm actually good at, meaning politics not war. I'm very popular with the people, so I'd prefer a direct election which suggests we go with a separation between the legislative and the executive rather than me having to wheedle and curry favor with a parliament."

"What about the House of Lords? What are you going to do about them? You're not elected. You're just in by virtue of being you," Paloma said,

"It's going to have to be abolished. And mostly we just existed to stop any liberal legislation coming out of the commons. I've been looking at the old Earth American systems. I do worry about the two houses of congress solution. It often ended up in gridlock, so that might not be the best choice. We'll have to work on that."

"So, no titles of nobility at all?" she asked.

"I think people can keep them. They just won't be an automatic ticket to power and wealth. As it is, they're not achieving that now for the fourth, fifth, sixth, seventh and eighth sons."

"Would this also mean that we can stop trying to out-breed the aliens?" she asked. Something in her tone had his warning antenna going up.

"Well, hopefully we'll all be such good friends—aliens and humans alike—that it won't be necessary," Boho answered cautiously.

"One more question. So, you're going to allow aliens into your new congress or parliament or diet or whatever you're going to call it; and women don't have to be baby factories any longer…so, do we get to stand for election too?"

They stared at each other his shock slowly giving way to amusement. "You'd run against me, wouldn't you, you little vixen." She took the insult in the spirit it was meant, as a compliment.

"I just might. But it would be more fun to sit in the legislature and bedevil you that way." She stood and shook out her long skirt. "For right now you best agree to full rights for aliens *and* women. Otherwise, I will be leading the suffragette movement."

She gave him that heart stopping smile, and he couldn't stop himself. "Paloma. I love you."

"I know. And I think even with your vaunted stamina we'd be done by now." She tapped his ScoopRing and the sound of the frantically fucking couple on the porn site went silent. She then stood on tiptoes and whispered in his ear, "And for what it's worth I think you're absolutely right and

I'll support you. Not that my voice carries much weight."

He crooked a finger under her chin and tilted her face up. "I suspect everyone will be hearing from you in the not-too-distant future."

✦　✦　✦

CULLEN'S EXPRESSION WHEN Tracy arrived at the Consort's office with two dueling rapiers had Tracy struggling to hide a smirk.

"What's this then?" Cullen demanded.

"I did promise you a rematch," Tracy said with a shrug.

"Fancy another scar, do you?" Cullen drawled.

"Fancy returning the favor," Tracy drawled back in his best FFH accent.

Cullen snorted. "This is not how it's done. No challenge, no seconds. You really are a peasant."

"We don't need any of that bullshit. This is between us. We've been ordered to work together, and the only way I can see that happening is if we settle things between us." He tossed one of the rapiers to Cullen who managed to snatch it out of the air by the hilt.

"I'm going to hurt you," Cullen warned as he shrugged out of his coat. "You fucked my wife and saddled me with a bastard."

"Well, you won't have to be reminded of that much long-er," Tracy said as he was removing his own jacket. "Mercedes wants me and Carisa to raise Cyprian if anything should—"

Cullen let out a roar of fury, and Tracy barely got his blade up to parry the unexpected attack. He shook his arm out of the last sleeve, and then threw the jacket in Cullen's face while he danced away.

"Should have known you'd cheat," Cullen growled.

"*Intitulados* fight to win," Tracy replied as he moved in with a flurry of attacks that forced Cullen back a few steps, but the taller man's parries were executed perfectly. Tracy felt the quiver from the blades clashing go vibrating up the length of his arm. The fucker was not only big, but he was also *strong*.

"Why isn't my security in here arresting you right now?" Cullen gritted as he lunged. Tracy spun away, but the tip of the saber caught in the material of his shirt and ripped a hole in the material at his side.

"I sent them away to get lunch for our working meeting," Tracy panted.

Tracy recovered and began a fast assault. Cullen parried and followed with a quick riposte. The sound of metal on metal was punctuated by their huffing breaths. They both stepped back and circled each other looking for openings, evaluating the other. Tracy was grateful for the chance to regain his wind.

Cullen had the reach on him and outweighed him, but Tracy realized he was faster and more agile. He'd had several openings where he could have cut Cullen's face, and while that might feel satisfying to pay the other man back for the scar that twisted his own brow it would only increase Cullen's hatred of him.

Despite being in one of the poncy dueling societies at The High Ground, Cullen had never received a dueling scar. Partly because he was that good, and mostly out of vanity

Tracy suspected. Cullen had never wanted to mar that handsome face. No, what Tracy needed was to find the opening to disarm Cullen and take this down to where this needed to be—a bare knuckled brawl.

The fight resumed. Retreating from a series of thrusts Tracy lost track of his surroundings and slammed into the bar. Bottles and glasses teetered and a number of them fell to the floor. A couple broke making the footing slick and adding the pungent smell of spilled alcohol to the air.

A painful stitch was stabbing up his side, and Tracy's arm felt numb from the effort of parrying Cullen's powerful blows. And then luck smiled on him. Cullen leaped back from a lunge by Tracy, stepped onto a rolling gin bottle and lost his footing. Tracy tossed away his rapier, ran forward, and gripped Cullen's wrist forcing him to drop his blade. Tracy kicked Cullen's rapier out of reach.

"What the devil are you doing?"

Tracy stepped back arms spread wide. "I'll give you the first one for free." He tapped his own chin with a fist. "I probably deserve it. But after that, let's get down to the business of beating the living piss out of each other. It won't make us friends, but it might allow us to get on with what we have to do."

Cullen, sweat running down his cheeks and glinting on his forehead, stood panting and glaring. He seemed genuinely confused. "Then why the hell did you come in here with a sword?"

"Vanity, I wanted to show you I'd learned how to fence. That I could hold my own against you. Now, are you going to take your shot or are we just going to shake hands and call it even?"

"Oh, fuck no," Cullen said and there was the light of sadistic pleasure in his green eyes.

He stepped forward and delivered an uppercut that sent Tracy staggering back to crash into the abused bar again. More bottles fell. Grabbing the seltzer bottle Tracy directed a spray of water into Cullen's face blinding him momentarily. Tracy rushed in to deliver three hard punches to Cullen's torso. He tried to drive his knee into Cullen's balls, but the man quickly shifted so the blow landed on his thigh instead.

Cullen butted him in the head and Tracy saw stars as their foreheads connected with an audible *crack*. Tracy got his shoulder under Cullen's arm, flipped him onto the floor, and kicked him in the ribs. Cullen scissored his legs around Tracy's and tripped him. Tracy landed hard on his hip and groaned in pain.

Cullen rolled on top of him using his greater weight to pin him while he punched Tracy over and over in the face. Tracy felt his nose break and hot blood spurting onto his upper lip. He licked it away the copper and salt taste were gagging. Cullen had straightened a bit which allowed Tracy to bring up his knee and slam it into Cullen's kidneys. The bigger man let out a yell of pain, and Tracy was able to push him aside.

Climbing to his feet Tracy moved in as Cullen used the edge of the desk to pull himself upright. They were in a bear hug now swaying back and forth, panting in each other's face, sweat flying off their tousled hair. Then at almost the same moment they broke away and staggered a few steps apart.

Tracy leaned on his knees. Each shuddering breath felt like it was filled with knives, and the pain from his broken nose was dizzying. "Enough. Peace, *Paz. Pace.* I'm done for."

"Me too," Cullen gasped then added, "Fuck. We're old,"

"Yeah," Tracy agreed.

Cullen surveyed the ruins of his office. "How the fuck do I explain this?"

"Poltergeist?"

"You bled on my carpet!"

"Sorry."

"Oh, get out of here, Belmanor."

Tracy nodded and limped over to recover the swords. He hobbled toward the door, but was stopped when Cullen called out,

"Wait."

The taller man walked over and held out his hand. Tracy stared at it for a moment then accepted the offer. They shook.

"This is only a truce. I still despise you, but we'll get this done. For her," Cullen said gruffly.

"For her."

31

IT'S NOT LIKE WE HAVE ANY OTHER OPTIONS

T HEY WERE DEEP in interstellar space well away from any League or Hidden World for this final essential test of the scaled-up Fold generators. It was also where they had located a large asteroid that had been knocked from its planetary system by some catastrophe millions of years ago, doomed to lonely wandering. Best guess it had roughly the same mass as the main body of the Ants. It had been seeded with thrusters and a tracking system so it would follow an *infierno* into Fold.

Mercedes had wanted that fighter to be flown remotely, but had been overruled by Commander Declan Kelly, the new *infierno* instructor at The High Ground. An *intitulado* and scholarship student to The High Ground, he had been O-Trell's top pilot during the war with the *necrófagos,* but lost the sight in one eye during that final, desperate battle over the alien's home world. The loss affected his ability to finely control the high-tech fighter, so he turned his skills to training the next generation.

His argument against using a drone was that they needed an actual human to report back from Fold how the entry of so much mass affected that not-space. Mercedes had countered that machines could bring back that information. Kelly said redundancy was safer, and she acceded because he was right. But now looking at that young, serious face of the pilot all Mercedes' doubts returned.

When are we ever not going to stop throwing our young people into the maw of the next damn war? Mercedes thought wearily as she and Ernesto approached the Commander and the young lieutenant. The boy looked scarcely older than Hayden who had just left for his first year at The High Ground.

Unable to bear looking at that young face Mercedes turned her attention to the *infierno*. The dome was raised awaiting the pilot who would fly it into the vortex. The Fold engine awkwardly grafted onto the saucer shaped fighter made it look awkward and off balance. Mercedes knew that shape didn't matter in space, but there was something in human nature that wanted their ships to look sleek.

Ernesto had been quietly apologizing to her as they rode down in the lift to the shuttle bay, reminding her that he was primarily a xeno-biologist so the task of redesigning Fold engines into Fold generators, linking them, and making them large enough to open a tear in space large enough to accommodate the mass of the Ants had fallen to mathematicians, physicists and engineers, human and alien. He'd done his best to facilitate the team's work, but—

"I'm sorry this has taken so long," he said for what felt like the hundredth time. "But it hasn't been easy. Scaling up wasn't just hard, it was dangerous, a lot of our attempts had a distressing tendency to melt down and explode."

"I know. I get all the fatality reports," Mercedes said, and hoped it hadn't come out as nasty and critical. Judging by Ernesto's expression she had failed.

"I understand your frustration at the time this has taken, and I assume full responsibility."

She laid a hand briefly on his shoulder. "No. I'm sorry, I know this has been a daunting undertaking. It's just every time we lose a lab team or a ship…" She couldn't continue.

The ship had been lost when they were trying to ascertain how much matter was needed to trigger the generators to actually Fold and create the opening into that not-space. They had to use the minimum amount of material. Too much and they might attract the Ants, and indeed it was during that first experiment they had tested with too much material, the Ants had taken notice, and the ship and crew had been lost. Intellectually Mercedes knew that they had to test in proximity to the creature, but sometimes she thought the cost in human life would crush her.

"They didn't die in vain. We were able to fine tune the amount of material. Now we just have to judge the effect on a fighter and…"

Ernesto looked at the young lieutenant dressed in battle armor his helmet tucked beneath his arm getting his final briefing Kelly.

"Our guinea pig," Mercedes said grimly, and she walked to the two men.

The boy snapped to attention and gave her a textbook salute. "Majesty!"

"At ease. Thank you, Lieutenant Lord Dupres for your service and for bringing your skills to this critical test."

"It's my duty and my honor, ma'am."

Kelly laid a hand on the younger man's shoulder. "He was top of the class in his year, Highness." He gave Mercedes a crooked grin. "Had even better scores than yours in flight training, ma'am."

That news seemed to delight Dupres. "That's brilliant, ma'am. I confess I always liked flying more than class work."

Mercedes leaned in and whispered. "I felt the same way. God speed, lieutenant."

He bowed, locked his helmet, and climbed into the *infierno*. All personnel retreated through the airlock into the body of the transport as the bay doors opened and the fighter launched. Mercedes watching the screens in launch control offered up a silent prayer and crossed herself. She and the two men then headed for the bridge.

The captain of the transport started to vacate the captain's chair, but she waved him down choosing to stand. She was too nervous to sit still.

In addition to the giant asteroid there were six other big transports in the immediate area. Five of them had brought the five Fold generators and put them in place. Much of that construction work had been done by Isanjo contractors recruited from the shipyards. Mercedes murmured a reminder into her ScoopRing to make sure that Anselmo singled out their efforts in press releases. The sixth transport was loaded with the amount of sand and crushed rock deemed necessary to achieve Fold.

The Fire Lance frigate, Swiftsure was also present to provide security. It probably hadn't been necessary, but Mercedes had become paranoid as it seemed like the crises and disasters of her rule had continued to pile up.

Ernesto gave the order to the transport carrying what they had come to call the catalyst material. It began to wend its way through the formation of Fold generators spreading its cargo like a terraforming drone seeding a planet. The light of the distant sun caused some of the detritus to sparkle. It was an uncomfortable reminder of the Ants and Mercedes shivered.

Some forty minutes later Ernesto gave the order to engineering to fire the engines mounted on the asteroid. He followed up with a command to the communications officer to link the homing device on the asteroid to the signal coming off the *infierno*. The fighter seemed like a tiny gnat pacing a whale as it shot past the lumbering mass of rock leading it toward the configuration of Fold generators that formed a Reuleaux triangle. Mercedes checked the chronometer in the sleeve of her uniform jacket.

"Nothing to do for fifty-three minutes until we fire the generators. Coffee anyone?" she asked the bridge officers.

There were smiles and a minute relaxation of spines which had been her intention. Several people expressed an interest. Mercedes sent for Venia and had her and several other batBEMs arrange for the beverages.

The minutes passed with agonizing slowness. The head of the engineering group that had built the generators joined them on the bridge when they were at the twenty-minute mark of the countdown. He had a couple of physicists with him as well as a very tall, very leafy Tiponi Flute. It delighted Mercedes to see the alien being included.

The final moments passed in utter silence except for a bit

of hushed conversation between Kelly and Dupres. As the countdown reached one minute the Flute said,

"Let us hope opening a translation point this large does not cause out entire universe to fall in."

"Wait! What?" Mercedes heard herself hiss.

"There's an infinitesimally small chance that could happen," the engineering head said. Tension stretched his voice to the point where it almost cracked.

"We didn't include it in our briefs to you," Ernesto said soothingly. "Since the chances were so small." He paused then added. "And it's not like we have any other options."

The countdown reached zero and the generators fired. Mercedes had watched as other ships made the translation into Fold that strange mind bending, stomach lurching image of lines and folds and twists as space, time and reality were warped, but she had never seen it on this scale. Fortunately, it only lasted for a split second and then the *infierno* and the asteroid were gone. The Fold generators were immediately shut down. Space and Mercedes body and mind settled.

One of the physicists patted a leafy frond on the Flute. "See. All good. We didn't fall into another multiverse."

"How long until Depres emerges?" Mercedes asked Ernesto and Kelly quietly.

"We told him to give it five."

But Dupres didn't emerge even as five minutes became five days. Eventually Mercedes gave the order to pack up. She ordered them to leave a sentry buoy in case the lieutenant should find his way home.

+ + +

"Jahan?"

"Do you have any idea what time it is on Kronos?" Jahan said as she wearily rubbed the sleep out of her eyes.

"Yes. Which is why I'm calling at this time. I know you'd be alone," Tracy's holographic image said. He seemed very unrepentant.

"You can't know that. I might have a hot young lover in bed with me."

"Well, kick him out. I need to talk to you."

"Fuck you for not believing me," she grumbled as she went ahead and keyed the visual on her ScoopRing. "So, what's so important that you have to call me at this hour?"

"Go someplace where you can be noisy and bring up your security protocol."

Alarm began to flicker in her chest like a small animal trying to beat its way out from between her ribs. She slipped out of bed (how she hated the beds in these human hotels they didn't sway) and went into the bathroom. After turning on the shower and the faucet on the sink she brought up the security measures on her ring.

"Okay. Can you still hear me?" Jahan asked with false sweetness.

"More important that you can hear me." His eyes flicked nervously about him. Jahan could see he was in an office. He opened and closed his mouth several times. It felt like hours had passed before he finally took a deep breath and said,

"How would you feel if every human in the galaxy died?"

"Relieved. I might be able to get some sleep if you were one of them. Wait. What? You're…serious."

"As a heart attack," he said grimly.

By the end of his explanation bile was burning its way up the back of her throat. For twenty-three generations no Isanjo had lived in a world that wasn't dominated by humans, so she had no frame of reference beyond the history books. And to achieve that world Luis and Hayden, Ernie and Poppy would die. The nice man who owned that restaurant she liked on the San Pedro space station. Not to mention the man who's imaged wavered in front of her. And Mercedes. Jahan remembered the faces of Tracy's baby girls or the young prince.

"So, I ask you again, where do you stand?"

"You know the answer to that. You may be arrogant assholes, and *you've* been a particular pain in my ass, but we're all in this galactic boat together, and frankly the fucking Cara'ot have always acted like they were superior to all of us. So no, I don't want you all to die. And that's what we've been doing, right?" A new thought intruded. "Thank God Engelberg didn't try to find out what that shot was actually doing or the Cara'ot might have noticed. And speaking of how the hell did the Cara'ot *not* figure out what you were up to?"

"Sort of what you said. They feel superior to us, and Cullen and Mercedes sold them a story about how this was all just an attempt to keep the violent humans pacified and mollified until the Star Ants were defeated." Tracy shrugged. "They have such a low opinion of us that they bought it."

"Look, I appreciate you telling me the truth, but I expect

that's not why you called," Jahan said.

"It's not. Do you think you can pull together a representative group of Sidone, Flutes, Isanjo and Hajin who would stand with us? Character witnesses if you will? Be willing to confront Rohan and the Cara'ot when they go to trigger the off switch? Because we haven't managed to protect everyone and if they pull the trigger a lot of humans are still going to die and that isn't going to sit well with the survivors."

"Which means you'll want to kick the crap out of the Cara'ot—'cause you actually are kind of violent—and then yay, we're in another war."

"Exactly."

"Yeah. I can do that. When do you need us?"

"Soon. Once you have them gathered get to Hisselek."

✛　✛　✛

THE WORK WAS done. After twenty-three months of sustained effort the Fold generators had been towed out to a location in sector 470 from where they could use drones hoping in and out of Fold to draw the mass of the anomaly into range of the gate. This time Mercedes had won the argument, and the drones dragging the scent would be unmanned.

The frantic effort to protect every human in the League had continued, and they had close to ninety-eight percent vaccinated with the CRISPR. There were some holdouts. People whose religious beliefs forbid medical treatment, some who believed vaccines were dangerous, and criminal elements who suspected this was just a ruse by the authorities to lure them in and arrest them.

Now the only thing left was to set the date. Mercedes had asked that they wait until after Cyprian's ninth birthday party. Since the Ants were still a century or more away from League space no one had demurred.

It had been a beautiful September without the usual blast furnace heat of a normal Indian summer. She and Cyprian were seated on the patio of the *Phantsiestück* drinking lemonade and nibbling on sugar cookies.

"So, how would you like to celebrate your birthday?" Mercedes asked her son.

He looked serious and took a long drink of lemonade before answering. "I've been thinking a lot about that…" His voice trailed away, and he gazed out across the garden.

The sunlight drew out red and gold highlights from his tawny brown hair. She greedily studied his profile, the long-fingered hands so like his father's, the rather lush lips, and the Arango nose that she had bestowed on him. He had lost his baby fat and had sprung up in the past six months as evidenced by the fact his Isanjo valet kept having to order new trousers. He would be tall and slim.

In twelve days, he would turn nine. It was hard to believe that so much time had passed, and he had grown so much. It was only yesterday he had been an infant in her arms, then a chubby toddler.

He had been contemplating her question, and now turned his head to look at her. "I think I'd like to have one of those mystery games. Where we all play parts and have a dinner and a murder and stuff."

Mercedes chuckled. "All right. I think we can do that."

He turned to face her his expression solemn. "But before the dinner I'd like the kids and me to volunteer at the orphanage or at one of the construction sites where they're building apartments for poor people."

The statement had her off balance. To buy time she brushed back a lock of hair that had fallen into his eyes. "I think that's a lovely idea." She hesitated then added, "But what brought this on?"

"Well, papa's been taking me to help him and Paloma at the orphanage and I really like it. I've been teaching them how to play *fútbol*." He gave a brief puzzled frown. "Though Paloma makes me teach girls too which is kind of silly since girls don't play *fútbol*."

"Girls are doing a lot of things they didn't do before. Like be soldiers and—"

He gave her a saucy look from beneath his long lashes. "Empresses?"

"Rascal." She smacked the top of his head with her napkin. He grinned, but soon looked sobered again. "But you didn't answer my question."

His smile faded and he looked very serious. "You're going to do something. Something dangerous against the Ants. So, I may need to start being an emperor soon."

Fury rose up to choke her. Mercedes finally forced out. "Who told you that?"

"Hayden. Just before he went back to The High Ground after summer break. He said he thought it was wrong not to tell me."

"And just how did Hayden get this classified information?"

Cy rolled his eyes. "All you grownups think you're being so sneaky, but we kids aren't stupid."

Mercedes sighed. "No, no you're not."

He left his chair and came to her, wrapping his arms around her neck. "Mummy, were you just going to go away and maybe not come back, and not tell me?"

"No, my darling, I was going to tell you, but I wanted you to enjoy your birthday before I did."

Tears filled the amber eyes. "I can't enjoy it if you're going to die."

"I'm not planning on dying, sweetie. In fact, I'm going to try very hard *not* to, but I can't tell you this won't be dangerous. And if something should happen to me your *Tia* Carisa and *Tio* Thracius are going to look after you."

He pulled back and studied her. She could almost see the question trembling on his lips—*Why not papa?* But he never voiced it. Instead, he hugged her again, burying his face in her shoulder. She waited for tears to moisten her blouse, but they never came.

I and life have made him grow up too quickly

32

LO QUE SERÁ, SERÁ

H IS HANDS WERE trembling. Tracy studied them as if they were foreign objects that had somehow become attached to his body. Anticipation? Or terror? Tracy wasn't sure. Was meeting on this beach silly? Stupid even? What if she didn't remember? How would that make him feel?

He had been surprised to discover that the public beach, through a series of dubious actions by parliament, had been turned into private property and sold to a wealthy FFH family who had built a *"cottage"* on the land. Apparently, it had outraged large numbers of people, so an investigation was brought by the crown prosecutor, and the property was seized.

In the aftermath of the *necrófago* war it had been used as a refugee center, and now almost four years later the mansion stood empty while parliament discussed if it should be razed, and the beach made public again or be repurposed for public use.

Its location had relevance for Tracy—*please God, let Mercedes remember*—and its abandoned state made it perfect for their…He mentally fumbled trying to find the right word. *Tryst? Liaison? Dalliance? Affaire de coeur?* No, it was none of those, just an opportunity to say farewell. An opportunity she had requested, leaving it to him to make the arrangements.

For a brief moment Tracy had considered having them return to the hotel on Cuandru where they had spent those last idyllic days before it all turned to heartbreak. When Mercedes had left him and returned to Cullen.

Fortunately, Jahan's incredulous look, and his own good sense had intervened, and saved him from that mistake at least. In one of the aeries on Cuandru they could only be reminded of that parting, and Tracy had learned from Dalea that it had been on the Isanjo home world where she had been instructed to remove the block on Mercedes fertility. While they both loved and rejoiced that Cyprian had been conceived during that interlude, the reminder of how they had both been used and manipulated by the Cara'ot probably added to all the *other* reasons why Cuandru was a terrible choice.

Anxiety overcame him. He took a final look at the arrangements he had made in one of the upstairs bedrooms. Champagne, some food, the bed made up with silky sheets, windows open to allow the boom and whisper of the waves to enter. Rogers and Naranjo had made sure that the airspace above the beach and the mansion were off limits for the next eight hours, and Luis had volunteered to take Carisa and the twins on an outing to an amusement park on the other continent. And most importantly Carisa had given not only her permission, but her blessing.

Unable to find anything else to do Tracy headed down the stairs and out the front door to stand at the water's edge.

The late September day was beautiful. Sunlight glittered on the softly lapping waves, and a warm breeze caressed his face. Tracy resented it. In ten days, he would lose Mercedes again and this time perhaps it would be forever. A vise closed around his chest and Tracy struggled to breath. The goddam weather should reflect his emotional anguish, he thought.

Ever since the disastrous test run, he had tried, to no avail, to convince her to let him take over the mission, and had only stopped when she burst into tears, and told him his constant hectoring was just making this all the harder for her.

Devastated that he had added to her fear and worry Tracy had gone silent on the issue though he had insisted that in addition to retrofitting the fighter with a Fold generator he had the engineers turn the small cockpit into a life capsule. In the worst case it would put her in cryo-sleep and engage the autopilot to bring her home. *Please God, bring her home!*

The drone of a flitter engine rose above the sound of the waves and the calls of sea birds. Tracy shaded his eyes with his hand to watch a nondescript flitter come in for a landing next to the mansion. The landing struts of the vehicle crushed the sea grass sending a sharp pungent scent into the air.

Tracy walked up the hill as the door of the flitter opened. "What? You're not going to land down on the sand?" he called.

"No," Mercedes responded. "Because if I did some very insolent and very rude boy will tell me the tide is going to swamp my flitter, and that I'm an idiot."

"So, you remember," Tracy breathed into her ear as he

took her in his arms.

"I'll never forget," she whispered back as her body seemed to melt into his.

The admission eased the tension in his chest. For Tracy their first meeting had been life changing. Apparently, it had been the same for her. They had both been eighteen. Both hating the fact that life had forced them to attend The High Ground. Both ultimately ending up attending. Both falling in love.

"Shall we go in?" he asked.

"Yes." She tucked her arm through his and they walked into the house. Mercedes studied the furniture draped in sheets, the darkened places on the walls where pictures had once hung. "So, do we just get right down to the fucking?" she asked.

He felt his face heat as he blushed. "What romantic things you say. I thought you'd at least buy me dinner first," Tracy teased. She looked embarrassed, and he smoothed her hair off her face. "My love, my heart, whatever you want, but we have the entire night."

"And it won't be long enough," she whispered as her fingers dug desperately into his shoulders. She abruptly released him, and moved away hugging herself, anxiety etched in every line of her body. "I'm very much afraid we will be quoting Romeo and Juliet to each other come morning," she said as she circled back to him. "Though I expect the roles will be reversed," she added softly as she twisted a button on his shirt.

"Stay...and live or—"

She laid a hand against his mouth holding back the

words. "No." She choked on the word, and her voice was thick with tears. "Make love to me, Tracy."

He gave a groan that was part grief and part passion, swept her up into his arms, and began carrying her up the stairs.

"Are you going to drop me?" she asked as he began to pant halfway up.

"Never."

"You're panting."

"Don't…make me…talk."

She buried her face in his neck her breath tickling his skin as she giggled. He started to laugh and managed to stagger up the final three steps and collapse onto the floor with her sprawled in his lap.

"Well, this was awkward," Mercedes said.

"It was supposed to be romantic," Tracy sighed as he traced her lips with his fingertips.

"Not really your forte," she said.

"What is?" he asked trying not to feel hurt.

"Always being there," she said softly.

They helped each other to their feet and clasping hands, walked into the bedroom.

Tracy cupped her face between his hands and gently kissed her. The months and years of stress had stripped the flesh from her. She felt fragile in his hands as Tracy gently removed her clothing. With each button undone, each layer removed he murmured endearments, worshiping the woman and the body that had filled his dreams for nine lonely, empty years. He felt a momentary flare of guilt for his wife, but resolutely pushed it aside. This night was for her, for whatever comfort he might be able to offer her before she did as she had always done and always would – her duty.

He watched the play of muscles in her back and buttocks and legs as she walked naked to the bed and settled against the pillows. Mercedes held out her arms to him, and he quickly undressed and joined her. Burying his face against her neck he breathed in her scent, felt the curls of her hair caressing his shoulders.

Her hand slipped down his side, gripped his hip. He stroked the line of her jaw, brushed the palm of his hand across one breast and she gave a small gasp as her body arched against his. Heat lanced through him bringing him to full arousal.

His hands and lips trailed across her body as he worshiped her while trying desperately to memorize every line and curve. There was so much he wanted to say, but words eluded him. He finally managed to choke out her name, but it emerged more as a sob. She brushed the hair off his forehead. The dark eyes lifted to his were glistening with unshed tears.

"Shhh, I know my love. Words are unnecessary."

After that their bodies said it all.

+ + +

HOURS LATER TRACY lay on his back with Mercedes curled up against him. Her head was resting on his shoulder, and her fingers played in the greying hair on his chest. He had an arm around her, his hand cupping her breast. Her breath fluttered against his neck as she asked,

"What would you have done if this house hadn't been built?"

He turned his head to smile at her. "Gotten a tent." At her look of feigned indignation, he laughed and added. "Not to worry, Highness, I'd have set up an air mattress. Put a feather mattress on top of that. Gotten your favorite pillow and blanky from the palace."

She gave one of his nipples a hard pinch. "You are such an ass," she said, her voice catching on a laugh. "Though at our age this bed was probably the better choice."

He smiled and kissed the top of her head her crisp curls catching a bit on his lips. "I love you, Mercedes. I've loved you from that first moment on the beach."

She chuckled. "It took a little longer for me. You really were terribly rude."

"And you were very haughty." They shared a chuckle. Tracy cupped her cheek and turned her face toward him. "So, when? When did you know?"

She stroked her hand across his cheeks, his brows. "I think that night you helped us tailor our skirts into trousers. You were measuring and touched the inside of my thigh. I thought I would never catch my breath again."

He pulled her even more tightly against him. "Will you not let me at least be there."

"No. You need to be here, ready to confront Rohan. We can't take the time for you to travel back to Hisselek. Besides, if you're watching from the scout ship isn't going to affect the outcome. It's just going to hurt you more, and I can't risk being distracted…or losing my nerve. *Lo Que será será,* Tracy."

"I'm not good at that."

"I know, love."

She glanced toward the window.

✦   ✦   ✦

HE WASN'T HER personal confessor. That would have been Cardinal Chaughule. While she thought he was a godly man Mercedes knew he was also a political man, and when politics and God collided oft times the affairs of men won out. She wanted to be sure she could trust that her final messages would be delivered.

Father Kenneth Robin Herbrand Francis Russell, had formerly been the Duke of Bedford before he had renounced the title in favor of his younger brother, and taken on the duties of a humble priest. Which meant he understood the FFH, but also was very aware of its drawbacks and dangers. He had apparently been a support to Tracy during Tracy's court-martial, and later he had served as a chaplain aboard Tracy's first command. And of course, he had married Tracy and Carisa. Mercedes assumed that meant he was familiar enough and forgiving enough with the utterly fucked up Arango family that she could trust him.

The press and camerabots were always lurking about the palace. Registering who entered, how long they stayed, when they left. Having a priest come to the *Phantsiestück* and the less savory outlets would have her dying, or Boho dying, or Cyprian dying. Or perhaps the more conservative rags would have her losing her mind since clearly no woman could handle the strain of governance and war—even though she'd been doing it for some thirty-five years.

Her irritation led her to squeeze a bit too tightly with her lower leg sending Vento bounding forward, legs swishing through the chamisa and sage that grew on the chaparral. She heard pounding hoofbeats coming up behind her. Glancing over she saw it was the good father, leaning over his rented horse's neck and reaching for Vento's left rein.

Mercedes laughed and gave a half-halt that had the white stallion immediately slowing until he was nearly catering in place. The priest and his horse shot past, and it took him a few minutes to rein in his mount and come trotting back to her. She set Vento passaging toward them, then slowed to a piaffe and finally halted.

Father Ken shook his head. "I should have known it wasn't a runaway situation."

"Oh, if only I could," Mercedes replied. "Thank you for meeting me this way," she said as he turned his gelding, and they went walking down the trail side by side. Vento was snaking his head toward the rental stable horse establishing his dominance. She gave his neck a slap. "Be nice."

"Probably good they didn't give me a mare," the priest remarked.

"Oh, he's very well behaved. He just expects deference from everything, and everyone." Mercedes gave the horse's almost iridescent white neck a stroke.

"As he should. He's being ridden by an empress." Ken smiled at her. "So how may I serve, ma'am?"

"I do want you to hear my confession, but I have things I need delivered, and I think I can trust you to see that done, and not sneak a look at those messages."

"You can," he said simply.

The simple response startled her with its odd power. So often when people gave her assurances it was accompanied by flowery periods and effusive promises, promises they rarely kept.

They were far out on the chaparral now, her security very distant. She reined in and pulled a handful of message spikes from the equestrian wallet that was hooked to her belt. "I have prepared messages for my all of my sisters, but there is an extra one for Carisa. There are private messages for Cyprian, Boho, Paloma Flintoff, and Admiral Belmanor. They're clearly marked. They are to be delivered after, well, after it's over."

"You're not coming back," the priest said his tone and expression both so neutral as to make him seem like an automaton.

"No. We lost a pilot on our test run. I expect that to be my fate as well. We then went to drones. They didn't come back either."

"You know there are hundreds, probably thousands of people who would willingly take your place."

"Yes, and none of them are the head of state, and First Star Lord of the military. This is my duty, and Cyprian will have competent help until he reaches his majority."

"This could topple the League as it's currently organized," the priest warned.

She shrugged. "He'll still have competent help, and appropriate role models whatever his future may hold."

"You're very sanguine about this, ma'am."

She gave him a twisted smile. "In a very short time, father, it won't be my problem anymore."

+   +   +

THE ENTIRE LEGISLATURE was assembled in the upper house of the newly rebuilt parliament building. In addition to the lords and the commons were high government officials—Rogers, Devris, and various other cabinet officers. Belmanor was also present the glittering ribbon and jeweled cluster that designated his new rank glinting on his breast. His face was locked in a rictus of anguish. Fortunately, Anselmo had noticed and was making certain *none* of the cameras focused on the newly promoted First Star Lord. They didn't need Belmanor making a spectacle of himself, Boho thought as he stood next to the throne and at Mercedes side.

In the gallery were the wives and children of the assembled lords and parliamentarians and the remaining royal sisters, including Beatrisa in her O-Trell uniform. It did seem absurd she was barred from the floor of Parliament while other, male, O-Trell officers were allowed, and Boho was forcibly reminded of his conversation with Paloma about opening politics to women. He found himself searching for the girl among the gaggle of women and spotted her. She gave him a knowing, cynical smile as if she knew where his thoughts had taken him.

And finally, among all the dignitaries there was Rohan. As Prime Minster he held a prominent position in the first row. Only a select few among the ruling elite knew that Rohan was not actually human. Everyone with knowledge had deemed it safer that way. It had been hard enough to

418

spin the return of the Cara'ot as anything but paranoia-making to an already skittish populace. The idea that the man who had been first Chancellor of the Exchequer and now the Prime Minister had not been a man at all, but instead a secret alien would have led to riots and murder of BEMs across the entire League.

Boho's hope was that Rohan would shuffle off the public stage after the Ants were stopped, then arrange for an appropriately tragic death, and then the bastard could go back to whatever monstrous form he wanted. Assuming the Cara'ot peacefully accepted that they weren't going to be able to kill every human. Even thinking about what the Cara'ot had planned had Boho's hand tightening into a fist. Personally, he would like to make Rohan's faked death a reality, preferably getting to kill the alien himself, but he knew it could not be. All they needed was another damn war.

Boho glanced down at his wife. Mercedes, seated on the throne, was in full imperial regalia. Elaborate gown, an ermine trimmed robe, and the imperial crown rather than her O-Trell uniform and the small circlet she usually wore. The ribbons on the bottom of the impressive parchment document were trembling slightly because Mercedes hands were trembling.

Was she actually afraid, Boho wondered? Once again that feeling of deep relief that it wasn't going to be him swept over him. If only it could have been Belmanor. The thought brought a wave a rage. Two nights ago, she had spent the night in the arms of her *intitulado* lover. Carisa had pretended this hadn't happened which left him with no recourse but to follow suit. Boho had secretly believed that Mercedes would think better of it. He had been wrong.

It shouldn't have had the power to affect him any longer, but it still did. It was no longer a visceral hatred where he wanted Belmanor dead by his own hand, but God he still wanted Belmanor dead. Instead, he was going to have to work with him…if the worst happened.

His gaze went to Cyprian who was seated a step below them. He wore a small circlet as opposed to a crown, and there was a grey tone to his amber skin. Last night they had told him that immediately after this meeting Mercedes and a small crew aboard an *explorador* would leave for the coordinates of the Fold generators. The child had known his mother was going to attempt something dangerous, but now he had the details. Boho had expected a hysterical reaction considering the trauma that boy had witnessed when he was five. Cyprian surprised him by keeping his composure as Mercedes outlined what was expected of him as the imperial heir. Then in a choked voice he had asked his parents if he might be allowed to cry now? That had almost broken Boho's resolve to emotionally distance himself from the boy. Mercedes had allowed Cyprian to cry but been very firm that he had a duty to fulfill, and he was not to embarrass her before parliament. So far, the boy was handling himself admirably.

Once Boho would have been preening with pride at the child's bravery and dignity. Now it was like ashes in the mouth. *And you're planning to deny him his birthright if Mercedes should be lost*, an ugly little voice whispered.

Not my child. Not my problem. I have to think about what is best for our human hegemony, not one individual child.

Keep telling yourself that. Compartmentalize, it's what you do best.

He pushed aside the discomfiting thoughts as Mercedes began to read from the document that had been meticulously prepared by royal lawyers, the document that made Boho regent and head of the government until such time as her Royal Highness should return. It also elevated Admiral Thracius Ransom Belmanor to the rank of First Star Lord again until her Royal Highness should resume those duties or Cyprian achieve his majority and have graduated from The High Ground at which point the regency would end and Cyprian would become emperor.

At the end of the proclamation every member of parliament and the cabinet came forward to swear fealty to the regent and the heir apparent. After that tedious ritual the entire assemblage had stood and Rohan boomed out,

"God save and protect our beloved Empress!"

The shout went up from the men in the room. Mercedes accepted the encomium with a regal bow of her head, and the royal family left the building.

Outside a small nondescript flitter was waiting next to the royal flitter. Anselmo and Gelb stood at the door of the smaller vehicle. Gelb had transferred his command from Mercedes flagship to the small scout that would take them into sector 470, and the propaganda chief was there at Mercedes request. The younger man looked a bit green. Boho was relieved that Belmanor wasn't there, but also wondered at his absence.

Boho and Mercedes exchanged a hug and a kiss to each other's cheeks. She then turned to Cyprian. He gave a little hiccupping gasp but held back the tears.

"Be safe, mama. I love you."

She gathered him into her arms. "I love you too my brave, wonderful boy."

She shrugged out of the elaborate embroidered cloak, took off the imperial crown and handed both to Boho.

"I don't think the Ants would be impressed with my pomp and pageantry," she said with a crooked, uncertain smile. He bent and gave her a ghosting kiss across her dry, trembling lips.

She paused one more time to press Cyprian against her side, then she and the men stepped into the flitter. The door cycled closed, and Boho and Cyprian watched as the flitter dwindled into a dot against the sky and was gone.

It was then the boy's control snapped. He let out a desperate ragged sob. Boho stood for a few seconds before dropping an arm over Cyprian's shoulder and pulled him close.

33

FOR THE ASHES OF OUR FATHERS AND THE TEMPLES OF OUR GODS

"TRACY, TRACY, MY boy. What can I do? How can I help?"

The touch of his father's hand carding through his hair only brought a fresh rush of tears. One part of him felt a fool, damn near sixty and weeping with his head in his aged father's lap. But he had no strength left, no emotional surplus. He had given it all in support of others. First to the child he and Mercedes had made together, then to men who had served Mercedes for decades and loved her too, then the remaining sisters who were checking in from various homes on distant planets, and one aboard a ship of war, and finally for his wife, sister to the woman he actually loved.

In front of Carisa, he could not reveal the full depths of his anguish. To do so would reveal his twisted and confused emotions toward her, and she didn't deserve that. She had already borne him spending a night in her sister's arms. But her sorrow rubbed at his taut nerves and emotions. He had always been quick tempered and prone to a bluntness that had caused many of the problems in his life, so it had been a struggle for him not to rip at her. For not being Mercedes, for not taking Mercedes' place on this mission, for giving him children who were not Mercedes', for being the wife he never wanted, but had married to protect the woman he loved.

But he hadn't said any of it and thought he had hidden it from Carisa. After he had held her and comforted her, she had wanted to go to the cathedral to pray. He had suffered through that, gazing up at the suffering Christ figure on the cross, and hating a God who would not save his love.

They had returned to the apartment and eventually Carisa had drifted off to sleep. Tracy was unable to rest. He paced the flat, snapped at his batBEM when Kallupus had checked on him, awakened by the clink of glass on glass, and the hiss of soda being added to Tracy's whisky.

Eventually he had gone downstairs to the suite that Carisa had prepared for Alexander so Alexander could have his own space. She had been unfailing kind. Tracy was a brute for resenting her on this night, but he couldn't help it. His father had seen the depths of his emotional struggle reflected in his tear-filled eyes, and devastated expression.

Alexander had pulled him inside, the stroke damaged right arm and hand like a claw on Tracy's shoulder and supported him as Alexander guided him to the couch where he now sobbed into his father's lap like goddam child.

"There's nothing...nothing anybody can do. I'm going to lose her, dad. And I can't bear it. Even when I didn't see her for all those years just knowing she was in the universe made it bearable. Knowing she's gone—" He choked unable to continue.

There was a long silence and then his father said, "I felt the same when your mother died. I didn't think I could bear it either, but I had you, and it gave me focus. I knew I could never love anyone the way I loved Teodora, but you were my tangible link to her." He paused then added softly, "You have that too."

Tracy sat up and wiped away the tears. "Cyprian."

"Yes. And the girls. And a wife who is her sister. Whatever grief you feel you must push it down, put it aside. You have to be strong for them."

"The way you were for me," Tracy said.

"Well, I tried." Alexander sighed. "Perhaps it was selfish of me not to remarry. To raise you alone with only grandfather and me, and no mother to love you—"

Tracy pressed his fingertips to his father's twisted lips. "It's all right, dad."

They sat silent for several minutes. "You're assuming the worst," Alexander finally said. "Perhaps this will all go perfectly, and Mercedes will be back in just a few days after having saved us all."

Tracy just looked at him, and Alexander read the truth in his face.

"Oh *Dios*." Alexander crossed himself. "This is too cruel."

Tracy nodded in agreement, and his father gave his back a hard rub. "You best get back upstairs."

"Yes, I have to be ready to comfort..." He couldn't continue past the ache in his throat.

"I'm here whenever you need me."

✝   ✝   ✝

ANSELMO DID NOT want to be here. Yeah, he was scared this

crazy plan wouldn't work, and the Ants would destroy the ship and its crew and him with it. It didn't help that the voice of the navigation officer kept coming in over the intercom reporting on the location of the approaching Ants. But most of his discomfort was because he did not want to watch this woman whom he had come to respect and admire undertake a suicide mission. He was grateful she had trusted him with the truth, but it wasn't making it any easier to accept.

They were all gathered in the shuttle bay as Chapman-Owiti gave a final briefing to the Empress. She was wearing battle armor, the helmet tucked beneath her arm. Her back was ramrod-straight, the long hair confined to a braid. Her shoulders were back, chin high. She was an imposing figure at any time, in the battle armor she was like a figure out of legend.

Anselmo couldn't hear what was being said, and the fact they had positioned themselves so no lip reader would be able to reveal the conversation implied to Anselmo that this was private and not mission specific. That's why he had switched off the sensitive microphone on the camerabot that was recording the moment.

He understood why Mercedes had asked for him to be present. There had to be some record of the events that were about to transpire, and she had felt that, deserved or not, he was viewed as an honest broker and spokesman for the palace. Which was pretty ironic since the truth was that he was really just a very cynical propagandist for the crown.

When he'd told Julia, he was going on this mission she had screamed at him, wept, threatened to divorce him if he went. He had surprised himself by saying, *fine, do that if you want, but my Empress has called upon me and I will serve.*

Now he felt stupid, the only civilian among all these military types. Admiral Marqués Chapman-Owiti had been in the location for weeks prior to the arrival of the *explorador* overseeing the setup of the massive Fold generators, and the seeding of the material that would enable them to open a rift in space.

After the conversation ended Anselmo clicked back on the microphones. Mercedes walked down the line of technicians, *hombres*, officers and the Isanjo construction workers, shaking hands and murmuring thank you's for their hard work and efforts on behalf of everyone. Anselmo made sure the camera caught the tears that ran down more than a few faces. But not the Empress. Her expression was calm and serene.

There was a moment when Anselmo wondered and hoped that Belmanor might come sweeping in and rescue this woman from the fate that awaited her. It was a foolish hope. The Admiral was light years away on Ouranos awaiting word like every other League citizen. And beyond that was the sure knowledge that no one would defy this woman's commands. They would all do their duty no matter how much it might crush their hearts.

The thank you's had concluded and Mercedes moved toward the modified *infierno*. Anselmo trailed after her filming. Ernesto joined her at the foot of the ladder and took the helmet from her gloved hands. She looked to Anselmo and gave him a small smile.

"Make it a good one."

"I will, Highness."

"And if this doesn't work be sure to erase it," she added.

"Of course. It's going to work," he added.

She gave him another smile as a voice over the intercom reported that the main body of the Ants had entered the plane of the generators. Mercedes nodded to Chapman-Owiti who helped her lock down the helmet. She then climbed the ladder and dropped down into the cockpit of the fighter and plugged in. The ladder was pulled away as the dome lowered hiding her from view.

Everyone retreated out of the shuttle bay. The great doors ground open, and the *infierno* shot into space. Anselmo had mounted cameras to catch that moment. Chapman-Owiti rested a hand on Anselmo's shoulder.

"Let's get to the bridge. I'll be monitoring from there."

"Will we be able to see in real time? I mean are there cameras?"

"Mounted on the generators. Until she's inside their effect we'll be relying on graphics." At Anselmo's expression the Admiral gave a short, unhumorous laugh. "Sorry not to have planned to make this more exciting for you."

Embarrassed, Anselmo ducked his head and followed Chapman-Owiti to the lift. Once on the bridge the captain of the Swiftsure motioned Anselmo to a position where he wouldn't be in the way. He continued to film focusing on the faces of the bridge crew as they gave reports on the Ants location and studied their consoles.

Forty minutes later, when Anselmo's back and knees had begun to ache from standing so long one of the bridge officers, his voice thin and tight, reported.

"They have detected the *infierno*. They are in pursuit."

The admiral keyed the comm. "Highness, maximum acceleration now."

The officer at the sensor array spun around in his chair. "It's just a tendril they sent after her. Not the entire body of the creature.

Chapman-Owiti knuckled his chin. "Ma'am, it's not what we planned, but we need to activate the generators earlier. The mass of the fighter is only giving a limited response to your presence."

Her voice came back labored as she struggled to speak against the gee forces pressing her into the acceleration couch. "Do what you need to do."

The Admiral crossed himself and gave the order. "Initiate Fold generators.

The main screen came on-line showing the effect of five massive generators focused on a point in space. The sand, dust and pebbles that had been seeded early in the week seemed to explode in waves of incandescent rainbow light. The effect was disturbing, and a massive headache settled behind Anselmo's eyes. He heard someone retching.

Chapman-Owiti was panting as he ground out, "Majesty, the main body is responding, moving toward translation point." Silence. "Highness?"

Anselmo stared, mesmerized at the screen as the fighter raced toward the rippling veil of an opening in time and space. Horrifying close behind was the crystalline structure, light coruscating off its diamond bright pieces. It rotated like a galaxy in miniature.

The Admiral, voice rising with fear and tension, said, "Ma'am?" There was no response. "Mercedes!"

Seconds passed, and then faint and labored they heard her speaking though she could hardly be heard over the groan and rattle of plasteel being stressed beyond the point of endurance.

"Death come to every man, sooner or late. There is no better way to die than facing fearsome odds for the ashes of our fathers and the temples of our Gods."

Then they were gone. The fighter, the woman, and the crystal thing.

"Shut down! Shut down generators!" Chapman-Owiti ordered. The rending of space vanished. The empty blackness returned with only the massive structures to mark what had just occurred.

Silence. Anselmo waited for someone to sob, to react. God knew he wanted to, but in that stoic silence he wouldn't allow himself. Chapman-Owiti relinquished the command chair back to Gelb.

"With your permission, Captain, may I use your office to inform the regent and cabinet that we were successful?"

"Of course," Gelb said thickly.

Anselmo hurried onto the lift with the Admiral. The descended several levels in silence then Anselmo gathered the nerve and asked,

"That thing she said, what—"

"A poem by Lord Macauly. We're required to memorize it before we graduate." The older man stalked away his back so rigid that it looked like it might snap. He seemed uninterested in whether Anselmo followed or not.

Anselmo stepped off the lift. "Glad I didn't graduate then," he muttered to himself knowing that the flippant remark was only to cover for the sorrow that was threatening to drown him.

+ + +

"THEY'RE GONE. SHE'S gone."

It was just Ernesto's disembodied voice briefing the room where the leaders of the empire had been tensely awaiting this report. Boho suspected that the military scientist had not keyed the hologram because he wanted no one to witness his tears. But Boho could hear the stretched quality of his voice and knew that the man was fighting to hold back his emotions.

There was a murmur of relief tinged with grief from the seventeen men assembled in the room then silence. Boho tried to analyze the emotions washing through him. Relief, he would not have to face this threat. Hope, that the League could be preserved in some form. Sorrow, she had been in his life for all of his life, first as one of his set, then as his wife. Fear of what the future held, could he really remake the League? Confusion, was he really going to hand off Cyprian to Belmanor and Carisa? Joy and cautious hope, how long did he need to wait before he could approach Paloma?

Ernesto had regained control of his voice and proceeded to offer a more substantive report. "A tiny number of scattered remnants from the edge of creature didn't make it through before we closed down the generators, but they have lost cohesion and are dissolving." A pause and then Ernesto concluded, "First Star Lord, permission to wait 120 hours before returning in case..." His voice trailed away.

"Permission granted," Belmanor said his voice dead level and utterly emotionless. Boho appreciated that; he'd endured about all he could stand because of his wife's infidelity with this man. He didn't need Belmanor reminding everyone assembled of that.

Rohan gave a grunt of satisfaction and slapped his knees. "Well, that's it then." He stood with Donnel quickly following suit. "Expect it's time for me to announce my retirement." He gave a nod of his head to the men. "Well done, all of you."

Boho knew it was meant for more than just these political and military leaders. It was a commendation to humanity in general. Which was pretty damn rich knowing what the Cara'ot had planned.

For an instant Belmanor's eyes locked with his, and Boho gave an imperceptible nod. When the door closed behind Rohan and his slimy aide Belmanor went after them.

✦   ✦   ✦

ROHAN AND DONNEL were striding down the hall. Tracy hadn't expected them to move that quickly. Apparently, Rohan's waddling gait was another affectation. Tracy watched in horror as Donnel reached into the pocket of his jacket and pulled out a small device. He hesitated, bouncing it on his palm. Tracy kicked into run, his footfalls pounding on the stone floor.

Rohan snapped out, "Now!" There was again minute hesitation from Donnel, and Rohan snarled and reached for the device. Tracy realized with a sickening sense of dread that he wouldn't get there in time.

A door on the left was flung open and Jahan came flying out like a fur covered harpy, claws extended, and fangs bared, tail rigidly upright.

Her claws raked at the Cara'ot's faces while her tail snaked out and knocked the device out of their grasping hands.

Donnel pressed a hand against the bleeding cuts on his cheek, but Rohan attempted to dive for the device. Jahan landed on the old man's back, grabbed his hand, and pulled it back just as Tracy skittered to a stop and drove his boot heel onto the device crushing it into its component pieces.

Panting a bit Tracy pushed back a lock of hair that had come loose and said, "Sorry, actually not sorry. You just couldn't wait to trigger your kill order, could you?" The two aliens wearing human skins exchanged glances. "You didn't think we'd figure it out."

"So, how did you?" Rohan asked sounding genuinely curious. He glanced back and up at Jahan still perched on his shoulders. "Madam, if you please." Jahan looked to Tracy, and he nodded his assent. She jumped off and Rohan with help from Donnel maneuvered his bulk until he was standing. "We tried to make sure you were atrocious at genetic research."

"You shouldn't have admitted to shutting down the *necrófagos*. Or being quite so condescending about how you'd bred us to be cannon fodder. Vice-Admiral Marqués Chapman-Owiti went looking and found your little killer gene," Tracy said.

"Son of a bitch," Donnell breathed, and surprised Tracy

by chuckling. "So, I take it those weren't placebos you've been administering to the human citizens." Tracy nodded and couldn't control the smirk.

"There are other ways to kill you. Ways that aren't so pleasant," Rohan warned.

"Yes, all those big ships you talked about. Let me give you a piece of advice. You make one move against League or Hidden World planets, and *my* big ships are going to rain down hell on yours. You see, I moved O-Trell and Hidden World military assets into positions at every one of our planets ready to engage with any Cara'ot ship that arrived in system."

Another look was exchanged. "We've been monitoring all your vessels," Rohan began. "They are nowhere near—"

Donnel shook his head, and a grudging smile touched his lips as he interrupted. "We really shouldn't have let him get cashiered." He cocked an eyebrow at Tracy, "You fucked with the transponders, didn't you?"

"I did indeed. Who knew smuggling would be so educational? We also hacked your cameras and put them on a loop." Tracy folded his arms across his chest, the ribbon and jeweled cluster that designated his rank as First Star Lord pricked his arm even through the sleeve of his jacket and shirt. "Look, we can start another fucking war, rack up thousands if not millions of casualties on both sides. Or we can figure out how to all live together."

"What makes you think the other alien races wouldn't side with us?" Rohan asked.

Tracy gave a one shoulder shrug and jerked his thumb toward Jahan. "Why don't you ask her?"

Jahan smiled at the two Cara'ot and pulled open the door from which she had emerged. "I brought some friends."

A group of aliens stepped into the hall. Tracy hadn't known what to expect. He was pretty sure Jax, Kallapus, and Jahan's brother Dulac would be there, but he was surprised to see Dalea whom he'd written off as a lost cause since she had worked for the Cara'ot, but there she was.

There was a Sidone that Tracy didn't know, but she was wearing a sash embroidered with threads of gold and silver that indicated she was high up in the spiders' governing council.

There was also a woman with cat-like ears, and a twitching tail, a woman Tracy had never met, but knew by reputation, the woman who had seduced the real Rohan, and assisted in replacing him with the Cara'ot who had stolen his life. A woman who was in fact a Cara'ot. The fact she was turning against her own people's murderous plan had to carry some weight, didn't it? Tracy thought, recovering from his surprise.

At her side was a younger woman with piquant human face, but a cat's slit eyes, and tufted ears thrusting through a riot of red, black, and gold curls. A distant memory stirred of a tiny half-breed child clinging to Tracy's leg as he fought to defend those Cara'ot/human children from human troops that had been sent to kill them.

The young woman stepped forward. "You remember," she said softly.

"Yes," he breathed. "But how could you? You couldn't have been more than two."

"You don't forget a day like that," she said softly. She

looked from Rohan to Donnel. "Yes, humans can be murderous and evil and violent, but not all. It was humans who saved us that day fighting other humans."

Jahan stepped to Tracy's side. "And it's not like human's have cornered the market on violence. We all have our issues. Evidenced by the fact you clowns had a plan to kill all the humans after they saved your asses. Saved *all* our asses."

Jax took over. "So, no, we are not keen to join hands or fronds or paws, or claws with you. Because if the Cara'ot are willing to toss aside whole species what's to say that one of us won't be next?"

The Cara'ot stepped forward, but before she could speak Rohan said, "Cara are cara, yet Cara betray cara?"

"Cara is unwilling to become what cara resist," she said as Tracy tried to parse the odd phrasing noting there were different intonations on the various <u>caras</u>. Then he realized a species that had no firm form or gender probably wouldn't use appellations like *he, she, you, they* and *I*. "Cara sent cara to live among them for fifty years—"

Donnel jumped in. "Gotta expect a little contamination," he quipped as he rolled an eye toward Rohan. "And you know, they've kinda grown on me too." With that he stepped away from Rohan and stood at Tracy's side. Tracy gaped at him, and Donnel gave an ironic eye roll and a shrug.

Rohan sighed addressed Tracy. "So, what is it you propose?"

"A peace and reconciliation commission. Hammer out details about how the League will be governed going forward. The status of not only aliens, but the Hiddens as well. Thank God that's going to fall to Boho. I'll just keep on wielding my—"

"Big stick?" Rohan suggested.

"Yeah, that." Inwardly Tracy was quivering. Desperate to get away to monitor the chatter from the Fold site. Mercedes had been steadfast in her certainty that this was a one-way trip, but he wasn't willing to accept that. "Now if you'll excuse me, I'll inform the regent that you've agreed to our proposal. You have agreed, right?"

Rohan sighed and held out his hand. "I suppose we have. I should have predicted you'd be this much trouble back at that first ball."

Tracy gave him a mock salute. "Happy to oblige." As Tracy hurried off down the hall, he heard Donnel say to Rohan, "Looks like you don't get to lose the people suit just yet."

A gentle touch to his elbow slowed his pace. It was Jahan. She glanced up at him. "You all right?"

"No. But I'm not giving up. Not until a lot more time had passed."

34

ARE YOU TWO FINISHED?

Pins and needles raced along every nerve in her body. Mercedes gave a gasp as her body jerked. A warm hand rested on her shoulder pressing her back into the soft surface beneath her.

"Easy, *querida*," a voice murmured. It was a voice she knew, and hearing it made her start to cry.

"It's okay, mom," said another voice that she didn't recognize.

She forced her eyes open. Her vision seemed to swim, but she finally managed to focus on Tracy's face. He was gazing down at her, smiling even as tears rolled down his cheeks. She tried to speak, but only a croak emerged.

The teenage boy standing next to Tracy grabbed a cup off a table and held the straw to her lips. Mercedes sucked greedily at the water and gazed into warm amber eyes.

"Cyprian," she whispered. "How…how long?" The final words emerged in a quaver for this was not the nine-year old she had left behind, his lips quivering as he tried to be brave.

"Don't worry about that right now," Tracy said as he stroked his hand across her forehead.

The soothing only made her more agitated. She tried to

lift a hand to push him away but had no strength. "No, no—"

"Hiding it won't make it any easier when she does find out, dad. Just tell her."

Mercedes registered the use of dad, and how Cyprian seemed to loom over her.

"Oh, my heart, it's been almost seven years."

She tried to process that. Failed. Darkness took her down again.

The next time she awoke her head felt clearer and her body didn't hurt so much. Judging by the quiet beeping of equipment and the antiseptic smell she was in a hospital. Shifting her head on the pillow she found Tracy seated next to the hospital bed, chin on his chest dozing, about to drop his TapPad from his slack fingers.

"Tracy," she said softly.

He awoke instantly, jumped up and leaned in to grasp both her hands in his. "How are you feeling? Do you want water? What do you need?"

"Actually, I'm feeling hungry, and maybe juice instead of water?"

"I'll be right back." He darted out of the room and returned a few minutes later with a tray that held a thermal cup and a glass of juice. The smell of the broth emanating from the cup brought tears to Mercedes eyes as raging hunger gripped her.

Tracy raised the head of the bed. He took a small sip of the broth, and then blew on it. "Little too hot. That should be better." He held the cup to her lips, and she took a small sip. What she noticed almost immediately was that the wedding ring was gone from his left hand. The monitors surrounding the bed betrayed the terror that had set her heart to racing. Tracy stared at her in alarm and reached for the call button on the side of the hospital bed. She grabbed his head demanding,

"Carisa isn't…dead, is she? I don't think I could bear that."

"Shh, no, no, she's fine. We divorced. She's remarried."

The information didn't want to process. She shook her head. "I don't understand."

"The empire's been dissolved."

"I'm not an empress any longer?"

"I'm afraid not, dear heart. There was so much unrest after…after…well, everything that happened. Nobody wanted a boy king, and Boho thought it best if we became a democratic republic. It really was the only way to unify the League worlds and the Hidden Worlds, and of course the BEMs. Our alien citizens were demanding autonomy over their home worlds, and why shouldn't they have it?" He gave her an anxious look as Mercedes let her head fall back onto the pillow.

"What a relief. It's not something I ever really wanted. But you and Carisa?"

"Well, with the League gone Carisa and I didn't need to uphold, well, anything. And she'd fallen in love. Really in love. I couldn't ask her to stay in a marriage of convenience."

"So, who did she marry?"

"Luis. I should have seen it coming. If I had I would have let her go a lot sooner. They're very happy. Have a one-year-old. We're all friends. The girls' alternate weeks."

"And Cyprian. Does he alternate weeks?"

"No, he stays with me. Just visits with his half-sisters."

"When?"

"When did I tell him? He was eleven, but he'd pretty much figured it out before." He rubbed a hand self-consciously across his face. "I did sort of stamp him." He brushed a forefinger down her nose. "Except for that nose. That, my darling, was all you."

"I'll have to apologize to him," she said with a faint attempt at a joke.

"I wouldn't change a thing. You are perfect."

"You're besotted."

"Yes." The color began rising in his cheeks. "And in fact." He reached into the pocket of his jacket and pulled out a small black box. He then went down on one knee at the side of the bed and pulled back the lid to reveal a diamond ring.

"Mercedes Adalina Saturnina Inez de Arango, will you marry me?"

The small stone glinted under the harsh hospital lights. It couldn't have been more different than the enormous teardrop diamond that Boho had placed upon her hand all those year ago.

"Well, that sort of depends on my current situation, doesn't it? I'd hate to commit bigamy." She tried to school her features to look worried, but from the way he was smiling at her she was failing.

"I have some terrible news for you. I'm afraid your husband had you declared dead and has remarried."

Tracy looked at her expectantly no doubt anticipating her to ask who. She honestly didn't care, instead she asked, "And what is my ex-husband doing?"

"Getting ready to run for reelection. And no, I don't plan on voting for him. Now are you going to marry me or not, Mercedes? Because this floor is really hard, and my knees aren't what they used to be."

She made an elaborate show of looking away. "Hmmm, Do I want a broken-down man with bad knees?"

"Mercedes!" he warned.

Though it took all of her strength she leaned over and took his face in her hands. "Of course, I'll marry you," and she kissed him.

He surged to his feet never releasing her lips as he perched on the edge of the bed as he deepened the kiss. Mercedes wasn't sure if her giddiness was due to having been in cryo-sleep for years or an overload of joy.

"Are you two finished? Can I come in yet?" Cyprian called from the doorway.

They broke off and held out their hands to their son.

The End

IF YOU LIKED ...

If you liked *The Thucydides Trap*, you might also enjoy:

The Imperials Saga:
The High Ground
In Evil Times
The Hidden World
The Currency of War

ABOUT THE AUTHOR

Melinda M. Snodgrass studied opera at the Conservatory of Vienna, graduated Magna cum Laude from U.N.M. with a degree in history, and went on to Law School. After 3 years as a lawyer she realized she hated lawyers and turned to writing.

In 1988 she accepted a job on Star Trek: The Next Generation and began her Hollywood career where she has worked on staff on numerous shows and has written television pilots and feature films. She currently has two television series in active development.

In the prose world she writes for and co-edits the shared world anthology series Wild Cards with George R. R. Martin.

In addition, she writes her own novels. She is working on a fourth novel in the Carolingian series and a fourth novel for her White Fang Law series.

For fun she rides her dressage horse, plays video games and spends a lot of time in the gym. (Or she did before there was a pandemic).

BOOK CLUB QUESTIONS

1. Do you think the author did a good job foreshadowing events with the Cara'ot in that opening scene where Ernesto and Mercedes had their private meeting?

2. Was Jahan right to try and keep Tracy from seeing Cyprian? Or was she only delaying the inevitable.

3. Did you realize that Tracy taking a warship into the Freehold solar system violated the treaty with Mercedes?

4. Would it have been better if Mercedes had confessed the truth to Boho rather than sending him off to Nephilm without telling him?

5. Is it ethical for Anselmo to act just a propagandist for the crown when he was trained as a journalist?

6. Cyprian witnessed a terrible act of violence. How does a parent best deal with that?

7. Was it fair for Mercedes to ask Tracy to marry her sister to preserve the monarchy?

8. Should Tracy have said no to marrying Carisa?

9. How did you feel about Mercedes asking Carisa to make this sacrifice? Did it change your view of her or was she just acting in the best interest of the government?

10. Tracy's father, Alexander revered the nobility. Did it ring true that Alexander would have become very suspicious of the FFH and the nobility?

11. Did Carisa's transition from frightened child to powerful, centered, and effective woman work for you?

12. Would you have liked to see Tracy get a noble title or did Anselmo playing up the princess and the pauper make more sense?

13. Did it feel like a betrayal when Tracy and Carisa consummated the marriage, or was he just being fair to his new bride?

14. Were you surprised when Rohan was revealed as an alien, or did you remember Tracy's encounter with the drunk on Wasua back in book 2?

15. Was it nice or creepy that Donnel had been there with Tracy even during the 14 years he spent aboard the Selkie?

16. Was it believable that Tracy would protect Boho from assassination?

17. Did it work for Christina to be the little girl torn from her mothers back in book 2? Do you enjoy those kinds of call backs when you are reading a series?

18. Did it make sense that the Cara'ot wanted to use humans to fight their war, but then remove them from the galaxy? Are humans too violent and afraid to ever coexist with other races?

19. Did it feel right that Mercedes chose to fly the final mission herself rather than lay that burden on another person?

20. It took nearly a lifetime, but were you happy Tracy and Mercedes finally ended up together?

21. And finally, who do you think Boho married?

OTHER TITLES BY MELINDA M. SNODGRASS

Circuit series:
Circuit
Circuit Breaker
Final Circuit
Queen's Gambit Declined

The Edge series:
The Edge of Reason
The Edge of Ruin
The Edge of Dawn

The Imperials Saga:
The High Ground
In Evil Times
The Hidden World
The Currency of War
The Thucydides Trap

White Fang Law:
This Case is Gonna Kill Me, Book 1
Box Office Poison, Book 2
Publish and Perish, Book 3